APPOINTMENT WITH YESTERDAY

Celia Fremlin was educated at Berkhamsted School for Girls and Somerville College, Oxford. During the war she worked for the Mass Observation archives. She began her writing career in the Fifties and her first novel, *The Hours Before Dawn*, was awarded an Edgar by the Mystery Writers of America. Celia Fremlin's most recent thriller is *Dangerous Thoughts*, which is published to coincide with the first paperback publication of *Appointment with Yesterday* and *The Spider-Orchid*.

Also by Celia Fremlin in Gollancz Crime
THE SPIDER-ORCHID

APPOINTMENT WITH YESTERDAY

by

Celia Fremlin

GOLLANCZ CRIME

Gollancz Crime is an imprint of Victor Gollancz Ltd
14 Henrietta Street, London WC2E 8QJ

First published in Great Britain 1972
by Victor Gollancz Ltd

First Gollancz Crime edition 1991

A CIP catalogue record for this book
is available from the British Library

ISBN 0-575-05088 8

Printed and bound in Great Britain
by Cox & Wyman Ltd, Reading

CHAPTER I

MILLY, SHE FELT, would be a good name. Quiet, undistinguished, and as different from her real name as it was possible to be.

Real? Who needed to be real, travelling on the Inner Circle at four o'clock on a Monday afternoon? Staring past the blank, middle-aged faces opposite, she caught sight of her own blank, middle-aged face reflected in the scurrying blackness of the window beyond. She almost laughed at the likeness between the whole lot of them, and at the feeling of safety it gave her. It's because of London Passenger Transport, she mused, dreamy and almost light-headed by now from lack of food and sleep: we're just the Passenger part of London Passenger Transport. How marvellous to be just a swaying statistic, gently nodding, staring into space! Statistical space. Nobody, she reflected, ever brings their real selves with them on to a tube train. None of us have. We have all left our identities behind in some vast spiritual Left Luggage office: and no one could guess—no one, possibly, could ever guess, just by looking—that there is one among all these glazed faces that has left its identity behind not just for the duration of the tube journey, but for ever.

The train was slowing down now, the cold, underground light of Euston Square platform was wiping her reflection off the window opposite: and the fear—familiar now, and as regular as labour pains, coming at three minute intervals throughout the day—nagged at her once again as the train sighed to a halt, and the doors slipped open. Suppose someone should get on who knew her! Suppose one or other of the station men were beginning to recognise her, as she travelled round and round the same circuit of stations, ever since seven o'clock this morning!

Oh, she varied herself for them, as best she could! Sometimes she took her hat off, and sat with wispy hair dangling: sometimes she put it on again: and sometimes she clutched it in her lap, and tied round her head a red silk square. Lucky, really, that this red silk square had happened to be in the bag that she snatched up as she fled out of the house before dawn this morning. Lucky, too, that there had been some money in the bag: a couple of pounds, anyway, and some odd silver: for she had thought of nothing—not of money nor anything else—as she tore up the basement stairs, her breath grating in her lungs with terror at what she had done. How she had wrenched and wrestled at the warped, obstinate front door, with its peeling paint and ancient, rusty bolts! Beyond that door was freedom—she seemed still to be tasting that first rush of icy air into her throat as the door lurched open. After that, all she could remember was the running. Running, running, running, the winter air searing into her lungs like gulps of fire, and her startled heart clamouring for mercy as it fought to keep pace with her terror, her instinctive, primitive certainty of being hunted down.

But she wasn't being hunted down, of course. Who goes hunting along the South London streets at six o'clock on a January morning? And especially along a street like this, with not a light glimmering anywhere, in all those serried rows of windows. For this was not a street of bright, brisk, busy people, the sort who might get up at six to light the fire, to start the kids' breakfast, to get to the factory in time for the early shift. No, this was a street where people lie in bed till noon: till two, or three, or four in the afternoon: where milk bottles stand unwashed and uncollected on steps and landings, and where the names printed under the tiers of bells are yellow with age, and evoke no glimmer of recognition in the red-rimmed eyes of whichever current incumbent might drag himself to the door when you ring. Un-names. Just like hers. How appropriate, then, that she, an inhabitant of that street, should be finishing her life on the Inner Circle, going round,

6

and round, and round, the one place in all the world where you will never need a name again.

She roused herself with a start. Now, Milly, she admonished herself—for it was imperative that *she* should get used to the name, herself, before she had to try it out on other people—now, Milly, pull yourself together! You mustn't keep dozing off like this, or people really *will* start noticing you! Some kind gentleman will come along and say, "Now, Lady, where d'you want to get off . . .?" and then you'll have to say the name of some station, and actually get *off* there! You can't say to him, can you, that you're not going to get off *anywhere*, that you've come here to live, you've moved in, and you're going round and round the Inner Circle, on a ten pence ticket, for *ever*?

So come, now, Milly, what *are* you going to do? You have spent ten pence of the two pounds thirty-five that you had in your bag. You have the clothes you stand up in, including, luckily, your outdoor coat. You are forty-two years old. You have no skills, qualifications, references. Until these last terrible months, you led a life so protected, so narrow, so luxurious, that you are soft as pulp, through and through. You probably can't work at *anything*. You have no friends to turn to, no relatives, because you are Milly now, and nobody, nobody in all the wide world—must ever have the faintest inkling that you have any connection with that woman who ran all but screaming into a London street in the early hours of Monday, January the tenth.

It couldn't be in the papers yet. Not possibly. All the same, Milly felt her heart thumping horribly every time a new passenger got on the train, sat down opposite her, and unfolded before her eyes yet another copy of the back page of the evening paper.

Not that it would be on the back page. It would be on the front page, certainly, once it got into the papers at all; and so each time Milly waited, in growing trepidation, while the owner of the paper turned it this way and that, folding and refolding it as he read, until at last, with any luck, the front headline would swoop into view, often upside down.

Yes, it was still all right. PETROL PRICE SHOCK still occupied the place of honour. No one, yet, would be surreptitiously studying her features round the edge of their paper. So far, so good.

But what would be the headlines tomorrow morning . . .? and now, at last, into her slow mind, still numbed with shock, there seeped the idea that there was need for haste. What had she been thinking of, wasting the precious daylight hours crouched in a corner of the tube train like an abandoned kitten? She should have been hastening to find herself a job, lodgings, an employment card . . . a whole new identity. She should have done all this instantly, today, before her blurred picture began staring up at every strap-hanging commuter in London: before every employer, every landlady was on the alert, peering under the brim of her hat, wondering who it was she reminded them of . . .?

In stumbling haste, she sprang from her seat as the train slowed down, and hobbled on stiff legs towards the sliding doors. Which station it was, she neither knew nor cared: she only knew that she must get out—get moving—*do* something! The long day's paralysis of will was succeeded now by an obsession for hurry. Hurry to anywhere, to do anything— it didn't matter, for the obsession was just as irrational as the paralysis had been, just another symptom of shock, not a real decision at all.

The Outside struck her full in the face, like a breaking wave. The cold, the speed, the people, and above all the bedlam of sounds, pounding against ears that had registered nothing all the live-long day except the endless soothing rumble of the Underground. She, Milly, new-born and newly christened, had been thrust forth from the safe womb of the Inner Circle, and must start living her new life.

8

Here. Now. In the Edgware Road. In the middle of the rush-hour, with darkness falling, and with two pounds twenty-five remaining in her bag.

Gradually, as she stood there, she realised that there wasn't anything she dared do. Not anything at all. Even if she had had the money for a hotel, she knew that she would never dare to push open any swing-door or walk up to any receptionist's desk. Imagine standing there, mouth open, while a polished, glittering girl insolently took it all in, from wispy, uncombed hair to lack of suitcase in grimy, un-gloved hand!

And a job—even worse! Imagine an interview right now ... "Yes, Miss—er?" (Goodness, she hadn't even decided what her surname was to be yet, and whether she was to be Mrs or Miss!) "Yes, Miss K, and what was your last employment? What are your typing speeds? ... Are you familiar with the use of a Something-ator? ... Have you had experience on the sales side ...?"

As she ambled, almost in a trance, amid the pushing, scurrying crowds, Milly suddenly caught sight in a shop window of someone walking just as slowly as she was herself: an old woman with hair sticking out like straws from under her battered hat. For almost a second she didn't recognise her: and when she did, she stopped, her heart pounding. So *that* is what you looked like, after a single day on the run ...! She must buy a comb ... a lipstick ...! Wildly she looked round for a Woolworths—a chemist—a supermarket.

But everywhere the shops were closing. London's day was over: night, and lights, and swarming people swept over the city as over a battlefield when the carnage is finished: and, more desolate than all, Milly knew that by now she not only didn't dare go into a hotel or apply for a job: she didn't even dare to go into a shop and ask for a comb.

A bus labelled VICTORIA was drawing up beside her, and

9

instinctively, without any thought at all, Milly scrambled on to it. As a deer runs for cover to the undergrowth, or a mouse to dark holes in the wainscotting, so did the new-born Milly dart automatically into places packed tight with tired people. Anonymous, bored, preoccupied people, laden with parcels, fumbling for money, pushing and shoving, blank as zombies. Such places were her home from now on: and when the bus reached Victoria, she recognised another of them. The evening crowds, the queues, hundreds of feet long, for tickets, for taxis, for trains ... Milly didn't mind which queue she stood in, provided it was very, very long: and when at last she neared the head of one, she just wandered off and joined in at the tail again.

What must her hair look like by now! And her haggard, sleepless face, devoid of make-up! She pulled her hat tight down over her forehead, and hung her head, so that presently all she could see was legs. Vistas of legs, like columns in a cathedral. No, like trees, like neat pollarded trees, rooted into the stone ... and yet creeping ... yes, the trees were creeping ... flowing, growing, going, across the barren surface, wherefore....

Wherefore what? Was it some quotation from the Bible drifting into her mind? ... "wherefore they shall creep upon the face of the earth" ... something like that ...?

"*Where for?*" yelled the man in the ticket office, for the third time. "Where d'you want to go, lady?"

"Well—I—" In her horror at finding that she had inadvertently allowed herself to reach the head of the queue, Milly's mind had become a blank. "Well—I—Well, where do the trains go to?" she asked idiotically.

"Seacliffe and South Coast, this office," the man snapped tiredly. "Suburban line, opposite Platform Six. Now, come on, lady. Take your time! There's only a coupla thousand people waiting behind you!"

His weary sarcasm stung Milly to panic.

"Oh! Oh dear! Yes!—Seacliffe, please!" she gabbled, seizing like a drowning man on the name that the booking clerk had tossed her. "I want to go to Seacliffe!"

"Single or return?"

"Oh! Oh, single! Yes, single, please!"

Single. What a lovely word. It meant *no return*! No return at all, ever! Fancy being able to buy that, just for money, at a Southern Railway ticket office! With a strange, singing joy, Milly saw her last two pound notes in the world disappearing, to be replaced by a small handful of change, and a small oblong of cardboard. But *what* cardboard! Passport, visa, birth certificate all in one! "Single fare, £1.40" is what it said, but Milly worked out the translation fast enough. It meant that the new-minted Milly was now a citizen of Seacliffe, now and for ever. There, in that unknown town, she was to work, and live, and die, and no one she had known in all her former life would ever find her.

CHAPTER II

IT WAS NOT quite ten when Milly stepped out of the train on to the dark, gusty platform of Seacliffe Station. Already it seemed late at night, as it could never have done in London, and the straggling remnant of passengers who had got off the train with her were scurrying head-down towards the ticket-barrier, as if they feared that the last buses, the last taxis, were already leaving.

Milly followed more slowly. Of what concern to her were last buses and last taxis—she who had no destination, nothing to be late for or in time for? If you are going nowhere, it cannot possibly be too far to walk; and so Milly strolled through the ticket-barrier like a queen, insulated from all the haste and anxiety by a despair so complete as to be indistinguishable from peace.

But once outside, she was compelled to rouse herself. The night wind howled in from the sea with a force which set her gasping for breath and clutching at her hat, her hair, her wildly billowing coat. Around her loomed a width of unknown road, dark and completely deserted, with here and there a street lamp glimmering greenly in the fury of the wind.

Milly set off, exactly as if she was going somewhere. Not with any idea of averting suspicion—whose suspicion was there to avert in this storm-swept emptiness? Rather, it was because there was nothing else that she knew how to do. All one's life, one has been doing things with some sort of small purpose; the mechanisms are built-in, and they cannot cease just because all purpose has suddenly disappeared.

So she plodded on, and though her legs ached with a dull weariness, it did not occur to her to stop; and presently she knew, from the dampness whipping against her face, that she was getting very near the sea.

Ah, here it was! In what a glory of desolation it shouldered its black vastness against the ramparts of the parade—again . . . again . . . again, with all its ancient strength! The spray stung against her face, the wet wind screamed round her icy, aching ears, and tugged and wrestled with the wild, damp strands of her hair. Heavens, what must she be looking like by now! Anyone passing by would think she was a mad-woman, dawdling along like this in the wind and storm, with her hair flying out like seaweed!

Well, and why *not* be mad? The newspapers could put *that* in the headlines, too! Let them! Why not? Why not dance, and laugh, and scream with the screaming wind? Why not hurl herself like spray into the darkness, until her laughter and her screams became one and the same, one with the thunder of the black waves against the stonework, and the long, grating suck of the shingle as the water drew back, pausing for slow, incredible seconds while it gathered up fresh fury from its secret, inexhaustible store?

Oh, but the cold was wicked! Milly pulled up the collar of her coat round her aching ears, and set off walking again. But already the collar itself was soaked with spray, and the wind whistled through her earache as if laughing at this fatuous attempt at protection. She could no longer see any glory in the black waves rolling in; they looked icy and horrible, and she crossed the road to the side where she couldn't see them; where the blank fronts of hotels and shut-up amusement arcades gave at least an illusion of shelter.

As she walked, Milly presently became aware of a strange sense of nostalgia. Some memory, as of a dream, long, long ago, was all about her: and as she came abreast of a little lighted fish-and-chip shop, still open and busy, she realised what the memory was. It was the memory of food. How long was it since she had eaten? Yesterday? The day before? She couldn't remember: and even now she wasn't feeling hungry. She felt no temptation to spend any of her few remaining coins in that bright little bar. But all the same, the momentary smell of food as she passed had been comforting, like a stranger's smile: a reminder that for some people, somewhere, life was still going on.

It must have been after midnight when she finally came to rest, aimless as a blown leaf, in a shelter on the sea-front, a little way outside the town. It was a glass and iron-work affair, three-sided, and by creeping into the furthermost corner, Milly found a little protection from the spray, and from the black, terrible wind screaming in off the sea.

Oh, but the cold! It seemed almost worse in here than outside. Gusts of icy air whirled round her knees, and pierced the soaked fabric of her coat as if it was paper: and presently it began to dawn on her that if she went on sitting here throughout the bitter January night, she was quite likely to die.

Die. She tried to make the word mean something, and became aware, for the first time, of how much she had deteriorated since this morning. Then, she had been shocked, terrified, but biologically intact. She had been reacting to fear as a healthy mammal should—by flight, and by an overwhelming determination to survive. It seemed incredible now, that determination to survive, and all the trouble she had been prepared to take for it! She remembered, wonderingly, how it had made her run, gasping, panting, for the nearest Underground, like a mouse running for its hole. Like the mouse, too, she had been upheld and guided by sturdy and marvellous instincts, handed to her intact and perfect across millions of years of evolution. These instincts, basic to every living thing, had still been strong and vital in her even while she had sat paralysed— defence by immobility—going round and round the Inner Circle: as she had scanned, tirelessly, the relays of insurgent passengers, with every muscle tensed ready for further flight if she should catch sight of an acquaintance, however remote. How anxiously, and with what zestful sanity, she had counted and re-counted the money in her bag, trying to make it come to more than two pounds twenty-five just as if it actually mattered! And as she trundled round and round on the tube, hour after hour, how she had schemed, and daydreamed, and worried about how to establish a new identity, how to get a job, how to find a room. . . . It seemed like a dream, now, that fantastic will to live, and all the effort she had been prepared to make for it! Now, it seemed too much trouble even to pull the draggled edges of her coat together over her frozen knees: and as for the idea of getting up and walking again, of stirring the circulation in her numbed limbs—such purposeful effort seemed incredible now; it was beyond anything she could imagine. . . .

She became aware, presently, of an ominous lethargy, creeping up from her frozen limbs, and beginning to probe, tentatively, into the very centre of her being. These were the fingers of death. She knew it. Strange how she had seemed to recognise them immediately, as though she had known, all her life, exactly what death would be like when it came.

She had stopped shivering, too, in the last few minutes, and that was the most sinister sign of all. One by one, the marvellous mechanisms for preserving body-heat were breaking down. Soon, her temperature itself would begin to drop, and the blood-supply to her brain would fall to a point where anoxia set in. How easily and naturally the old, familiar medical phrases still slid into her mind, even after all this time! A legacy from her first marriage, this: and from the time even longer ago when she had been trying to train as a nurse. Dropping things: mishandling sterilised instruments: so clumsy and nervous over injections that the patients would plead, with real fear in their eyes, for "the little nurse to do it!" Or "the tall nurse", or "the blonde nurse"—any nurse at all, so long as it wasn't Milly!

Only she hadn't been Milly then, of course, she had been Nurse Harris: soon—if only she had guessed it—to become Mrs Waggett, wife of Julian Waggett, the promising young house-surgeon.

No one in the hospital could understand why he had picked on *her*. With his dark, arrogant good looks, his charm, his air of absolute assurance, he could have had any girl in the hospital—or outside it, for that matter. All the young student nurses were more or less in love with him; some, like Milly, with a day-dreaming adolescent passion that declared itself solely by tongue-tied paralysis whenever he appeared on the ward: others, bolder and more experienced, were seriously out to get him. These were the girls who knew how to flash provocation from their cool downcast eyes as they stood by a bedside receiving instructions about a saline drip: who knew how to wear their sober uniform as if it was part of a strip-tease. Some of these sorceresses even managed to date the great man, now and again, and subsequently dined out (or perhaps cocoa'd out would be more accurate) for weeks afterwards on tales of wine and orchids and whispered words of passion.

Not that Julian Waggett had been rich—not in those days. He was only a house-surgeon, two years qualified, and earning such a salary as protest marches are based on. But it made no difference. Although he was only twenty-six, and among the lowest-ranking doctors at the hospital, the indefinable bloom of success was already upon him. Already one felt that the deep-pile carpets of Harley Street were unrolling under his feet as he trod the wards; and when he glanced off-handedly at the bed-end chart, or threw out a casual syllable that would light up a pain-racked face, you knew, you knew without any doubt at all, that those unhurried steps were taking him into his future swifter than the speed of sound.

And the woman who was to step into the future with him? Not for her would be the harried existence of an overworked GP's wife—tied to the telephone, meals drying in the oven, never a night's unbroken sleep. No, whoever finally succeeded in capturing Julian was in for a life of pampered luxury and ease. Service-flats. A town house and a country house. Luxury holidays in the Bahamas. Did he know, Milly (Nurse Harris, that is to say) sometimes wondered, how many thousands of rollers were rolled into how many acres of hair at the Nurses' Home each night, just for him? How many little pots of eye-liner, eye-shiner, skin freshener, pore-cream and all the rest were lined up in sacrificial array on his hundreds of unknown altars in little cell-like bedrooms? And could he ever have believed that those fluffy little heads, which seemed to find it so impossible to understand the blood-plasma tables, were nevertheless capable of compiling timetables far more complicated than anything dealt with at head office, when it came to engineering "chance" meetings with him on corridors or in doorways? And did he know—did it perhaps even amuse him to know—that several young lives had been drastically reshaped—for good or ill—simply by the fact that it was rumoured that he didn't like virgins?

And after all the sound and fury, what happened? He married *Milly*—Nurse Harris, that is to say! Nurse Harris of the gingery hair, and the freckles. Nurse Harris of the thick waist, and the stubby fingers, who couldn't wear eye-make-up because it brought her out in styes. And a virgin to boot. It was no wonder that when the engagement was announced, the whole, vast humming hospital seemed to stop in its tracks for a moment, from the top consultant to the lowest-paid washer-up, all of them asking the same question. Why? *Why?*

All their guesses were wrong. Nurse Harris wasn't pregnant. She hadn't inherited half a million pounds from a deceased uncle. Nor was Julian trying to call the bluff of some disdainful glamour-puss by making her jealous. He really *did* want to marry Nurse Harris. He *did* marry her. There were flowers, champagne, congratulations, and after that, of course, all that the mystified well-wishers could do was to sit back and wait for the marriage to crack up. Six months, most of them gave it.

But it didn't break up. Not in six months, nor even in a year. Two years passed—three—even five; and during this time Julian went from strength to strength. House-Surgeon, Registrar, Senior Registrar. . . . Before he was thirty-five he was a consultant, and with a private practice on the side that was rapidly becoming fashionable. His name, now and then, began to appear in the papers, in connection with some tricky operation on a minor celebrity. By now the prophets of doom were having to eat their words: they had to admit that a man isn't likely to achieve success like this if he is all the time wresting with an unhappy marriage. In some inexplicable way, drab little Nurse Harris must have been right for him. But why?

Milly, of course, knew why. She had known all along, but had had no intention of allowing the knowledge to mar her joy and excitement over her extraordinary good fortune. She had known right from the start that what Julian wanted—nay, *needed*— was a wife who would serve as a foil for his own brilliance. A woman so retiring, so inconspicuous, that in contrast to her dullness his own wit, his own charm, would shine out with redoubled radiance. A woman who never, ever, in any circumstances, would draw attention away from him and on to herself.

And for a while—indeed for a number of years—the lopsided bargain seemed to work very well. Milly was not an ambitious woman, she had no desire for the limelight for herself. Besides, she loved Julian, and rejoiced genuinely to see him where she knew he so loved to be—in the centre of an admiring crowd. She was proud of his success, proud to know that this dazzling, sought-after figure was *her* husband: and she felt, too, a deep and not unjustified pride in the thought that it was she, herself, who in all sorts of dull little inconspicuous ways had provided the background against which his wit and charm could sparkle their brightest, and his talents be displayed to best advantage.

Right from the beginning, Julian had loved to give important little dinner-parties. Even in the early years, when they could ill afford it, he had always insisted that there should be wine, and flowers, and at least four courses of excellent food for their guests. Luckily, Milly was a good cook, though slow, so by dint of anxious planning and long hours at the stove, she always managed to produce a meal that was inexpensive and yet came up to Julian's exacting standards: and if, by the time they sat down to table, the hostess was too flustered and exhausted to join much in the conversation what matter? It was Julian who was the star of the evening, Julian who led the conversation, filled up the glasses, radiated hospitality and charm. Sometimes he would chide her, afterwards, for being "such a little mouse!" but she knew that he liked it really, and she exerted such womanly guile as she possessed to see that her inadequacies remained a joke between them, and never became a serious issue.

But they did become a serious issue, of course, in the end. As the years went by, and success followed success for Julian, the dinner parties became larger, and grander. Little lions from the social and artistic worlds were invited to them, and then bigger lions. Until, at last, secure in his own unassailable reputation, Julian began to feel the need of a wife who would be a credit to him. Not one who would outshine him, of course—as if such a thing were possible!—Oh no! But he needed someone elegant, sophisticated; a fitting hostess for a man in his position. And one night, he looked at his existing wife, nervously sipping her sweet sherry, boring the Finnish Ambassador, and allowing her anxieties about the chestnut soufflé to show on her round shiny face. He contemplated her faded ginger perm, her freckles, and her thickening figure bulging under her black velvet dinner dress; and that had been the beginning of the end.

Milly had seen it coming, of course. She had known, long before he did, that she wasn't going to be able to "keep up with him". It often happened, of course, in their sort of circle. She had seen it with her own eyes, over and over again, among their acquaintances: the brilliant, ambitious husband rocketing his way to the top and discarding his dowdy, middle-aged wife en route, like a snake shedding its outworn skin in springtime. She'd met the wives, too, after the amputation was over: drab, dejected creatures, moaning on and on about the meagreness of their alimony, and about "his" ingratitude after all they had done and all they had sacrificed for him during the early years of struggle.

Had they no pride? It was all true, of course—but even so, surely a woman could keep her lips closed and her head held high? And as for alimony, Milly had thought—and sometimes, to selected cronies, had actually said—that if *her* husband ever deserted her, she would starve in the gutter before she would take a single penny from him!

But she took it, of course, when the time came, just like all the others. When it came to the point, there didn't seem to be anything else she could do. There she was, in the Kensington flat, and with bills pouring in for services and commitments that she hadn't even known existed; and even while she drifted about looking for somewhere cheaper to live, with landladies laughing in her face when she mentioned the sort of rental she had in mind—even in that short time, the second round of bills had begun to arrive. Demands, Final Demands, threats of legal action—what could she do but accept the hundred and fifty pounds a month offered by her former husband, so generously and with such calculated spite? It was, in fact, a larger sum than had been awarded by the Courts, and he

19

explained this gratuitous munificence in a letter written to Milly just after his much-publicised marriage to Cora Grey, the up-and-coming young movie star who had divorced her nonentity of a husband specially for Julian. The two of them had made the front page of the evening papers at the time, and since then their bronzed faces, full of improbably glittering teeth, had leered up against a background of sea and sky in at least two of the colour supplements. No doubt it had all gone to Julian's head a bit: and this explained—or Milly supposed it did—the schoolboy spite, the easy, throwaway cruelty, of the letter he chose to write to her, from his honeymoon paradise, at the very height of his triumph:

"I'm sorry, my dear," he wrote, "that things had to end this way; but there it is. I suppose it's just one of those things, and for my part I'm happier than I've ever been in my life before. Cora is a marvellous girl, we are made for each other. To show you what a marvellous girl she is, let me tell you that it was *her* idea that I should allow you fifty pounds a month more than I am legally obliged to do. Wasn't that terrific of her?—she is the most generous-minded person I have ever known, and just doesn't know how to bear grudges.

"Needless to say, I agreed with her that you should have the money. As she says, a woman in her forties has little chance of starting a new life, and so she really *needs* money: whereas a man in his forties is still in his prime, with a whole marvellous life ahead of him, I'm sorry, my dear: it seems unfair of Nature to have arranged things like that, but that's the way it is: and as you see from this cheque, Cora and I are trying to do what we can to make up to you for the fact that hope and happiness are all on our side.

"Well, that's all for now. We're dining with Lord and Lady Erle tonight, on their new yacht, so must hurry and get into our glad rags. Cora joins me in sending greetings, and she asks me to tell you that she hopes that your remaining years will bring you some sort of contentment. She tells me that she once had a great-aunt who, when her life's work was over, derived a

20

lot of pleasure from growing mustard and cress in the shapes of letters of the alphabet. It was very interesting, she says, waiting for it to come up.

> Yours, with all good wishes
> Julian."

"*I'll show* him!" Milly had thought, as she tore the letter into tiny shreds.

And show him she did. Which was how, all these months later, she came to be crouching here, in this freezing seaside shelter, battered by wind and spray, with no food, no home, and, very likely, only a few more hours to live.

What would Julian say, she wondered, when he read the whole story in the papers tomorrow, or perhaps the next day? Would he just say, with that familiar curl of the lip, "God, how sordid!" Or would he, perhaps, murmur, with a tiny glint of unwilling admiration in those self-satisfied eyes: "Good Lord! I'd never have thought she had it in her!"

CHAPTER III

MILLY STIRRED INFINITESIMALLY on the hard bench, and found that by now even her hips were numb. What was the time? Two o'clock? Or even three? Could it be that she had evaded in sleep some appreciable fraction of her nightlong sentence? There was no knowing. No way of measuring the dreaming and the not-dreaming that wove in and out of her head from the darkness and the storm. When she dreamed of cold, of a cold sharper than human flesh could bear, it was only to wake and find that it was not a dream at all. Her limbs were still there, jutting out of her in four places, and enduring in reality what could not be endured in dreams. It was *their* suffering now, rather than her own, that troubled her; for she, herself, had become very, very tiny, and was moving inexorably, and at an accelerating rate, out of range of their sufferings. She was deserting them, leaving them to fight their losing battle as best they might ... and then, from she knew not where, there would come upon her a fit of shivering so violent that her soul would be jerked back into its proper place again, in charge again, suffering again, sharing to its excruciating limit the agonies of every far-flung cell.

Strange lethargies intervened, and strange awakenings where there had been no sleep; until at last the darkness seemed to break like a dropped cup, and she felt in her dream that some mighty change, some unimaginable glory, was coming over the earth: and when she woke she found that it was so. For when she opened her numbed eyelids there was a faint yellow light spreading over the tumbled waters; the wind had dropped; and it was day.

The light grew, and Milly was aware of something akin to worship as she contemplated her own body. This was the body that had brought her alive through the incredible winter night by the application of first one marvellous mechanism and then another. She remembered how it had first withdrawn blood from the extremities, the hands and feet, in order to feed the vital machinery in the centre: and then, without her even noticing it, it had curled itself up into this bundle in which she now found herself, mathematically arranged so as to expose the absolute minimum of surface area to the searing cold. And after that, when her limbs were numb and all her willpower gone, it had kept her blood circulating and her heart minimally beating by means of bouts of shivering alternating with bouts of drowsing apathy. By these magical, unbelievable mechanisms it had kept death at bay all through the livelong night, and without any sort of help or co-operation from *her*—as far as *she* was concerned, she had been leaving herself to die. And with all this, it had launched at her no reproaches for

22

having landed it in this desperate situation: it did not ask her *why* it had to be kept out like this all through the coldest night of the year, in wet clothes, and with no food inside it. Like a true and loving friend, it had accepted her decision without reproach, and then had put all its energies, all its varied and wonderful skills, into sustaining her through the consequences. I've never had a friend like it! — thought Milly, staring down at her bedraggled person in the growing light; and with this thought there came to her a blazing determination to survive. *She* die of exposure? Not on your life! Why, she hadn't even got a sore throat! Slowly, painfully, she set herself to restore the power of movement to this numbed, miraculous body of hers. As soon as she could move, she would buy it some hot coffee, a roll and butter . . . she felt almost dizzy at the thought of such wonders, and at the realisation that they were still within her reach. She still had *some* money, after all; eighty or ninety pence at least.

At the thought of this sum, the strangest thought imaginable came to her. There was something to spend it on even more important than food. She must have her hair set!

Wasn't this the least she could do? How could she allow her body, her faithful, miraculous body, which had protected and steered her through the deathly perils of the night, to go about looking like a scarecrow?

And it was only much later, as she sat staring at her transformed appearance in the hairdresser's mirror, that she realised that this way of spending her last shillings had also been downright sensible. Now she would be able to look for a job, bargain with landladies, invent stories about lost insurance cards. She was equipped now, to face the brand-new world.

CHAPTER IV

"Yes, well, can you start tomorrow?"

Choking back the rest of her imaginary life-story, Milly stared at her prospective employer incredulously. The woman wasn't even listening! When Milly had first seen the advertisement for a Daily Help, on a board outside a newsagent's, it had seemed obvious to her that the first thing to do was to think out some plausible sort of past for herself: and so for more than an hour she had loitered in an arcade of deserted slot-machines, concocting this wonderful tale which so cleverly explained just how it was that she happened to have no address, no references, and no employment card. And now here was this woman interrupting her in mid-sentence to offer her the job, just like that! For a moment, Milly felt affronted rather than relieved. All those carefully-plotted details about the invalid father, the requisitioning of the family home, the loss of all her personal papers in the move: and then the death-duties, and the mysterious Family Debts—all, all were wasted! Mrs Graham (for such it seemed was the name of this anxious, thirty-five-ish person who kept glancing at the clock and fidgeting with paper-clips)—Mrs Graham didn't want to know one thing about any of it! She didn't want to know Milly's age, her capabilities, or why she had suddenly dropped into Seacliffe like a visitor from Mars. All she wanted, it seemed, was to clinch the deal before (to judge by her agitated glances) Milly should disappear into thin air with a rattle of ghostly chains, or re-embark in her flying saucer, or whatever. Were Daily Helps really as rare as that? Milly could only suppose that they must be, and her spirits rose a little. It was a long time since she had felt rare.

"Can you start tomorrow?" Mrs Graham repeated, torturing the inoffensive paper-clip with nervous fingers. "You see, my other woman let me down rather badly . . . not a question of money, it wasn't that at all. I'm willing to pay thirty-five pence an hour, and lunch as well, she always had a good lunch. And it's light work, Mrs—er—; nothing heavy, you'll find it's a thoroughly labour-saving kitchen, all the equipment and everything, brand new. And a Hoover! With fitments! And there's the Dustette, you can use it for the shelves and everything, you won't need to get your hands dirty...."

By this time, Milly had realised who it was who was interviewing whom, and she adjusted her posture accordingly, leaning back a little in the chair on whose extreme edge she had so far been timorously perching. Now, in her newly-relaxed position, she set herself to listening graciously while her victim reeled off, with anxious haste, the variegated delights in store for Milly if she accepted the job. Up-to-date waste-disposal. Non-rub polishes. No scrubbing.... There seemed no point in interrupting, though in fact Milly had already quite decided to take the job. Or, rather, it never occurred to her not to. From the first moment when she began scanning the newsagents' advertising boards this morning, she had taken it for granted that she would take the very first job that she was offered—if, indeed, she was offered anything at all. Never, in her wildest dreams, had she supposed it would be as easy as this! She, an unknown woman, past forty, with no skills, no qualifications, no references, and wearing a coat still damp from sitting out in it all night! Why, for all this Mrs Graham knew, she might be a murderess....!

"You *will* turn up tomorrow, won't you?" Mrs Graham was saying anxiously. "So many of the women I've seen, they've said they'll come, and then they just don't turn up! You won't let me down, will you, Mrs—er— Oh dear, what *is* your name? I ought to have asked you before."

Milly was just opening her mouth to answer, when she realised that "Milly", alone, wasn't going to be enough. A surname! Quick, quick! She racked her brains to think of something ... anything ... Oh dear, Mrs Graham must already have noticed her hesitation in answering... !

And indeed, Mrs Graham had: but, as is so common with

people in a state of anxiety, she had immediately integrated this new phenomenon into her own special network of worries, and imagined that Milly's hesitation meant that she was wavering over her decision to take the job.

"You *will* come tomorrow, won't you?" she urged, for the second time. "I'm counting on you! I get so tired of people who promise to come and then just disappear! Promise me you won't do that!"

Gleefully, Milly promised. Disappear!—when by this time tomorrow she could expect to have one pound forty in her pocket and a free lunch inside her? Not likely! Besides, Milly had already done enough disappearing, in the last thirty-six hours, to last her a lifetime.

She spent the afternoon in the station cafeteria, where it was warm. She had gone there to steal food, but had found, rather to her surprise, that she couldn't bring herself to do it. Absurd, really, that a woman capable of the deed she had set her hand to yesterday, should today find herself unable to reach out that same hand just to purloin a two pence bread roll!

If she hadn't been so hungry, she would have laughed.

Oh, well. So she wouldn't be able to eat. But there were other bodily pleasures to be enjoyed—pleasures which were now for the first time being fully revealed to her in all their glory: and one of them was sitting down. The sight of a vacant seat in a corner by the radiator filled her with such a passion of longing that she almost fainted with the fear that someone else might get there first! Through trays and trolleys, and all the detritus of Consumer-Man, she battled her way towards the haven of her desires.

At last! Here she was, her head resting against the dark-green décor, and her legs, throbbing with sheer comfort, stretched out in front of her under the table. She felt her eyes closing, but it didn't matter, no one was going to notice. This was a *station,* wasn't it, an outpost of the wonderful, anonymous world she had inhabited yesterday? The world of commuters, where hurrying takes the place of existing—"I hurry, therefore I am!" If you aren't hurrying, then you aren't existing, and that makes it quite all right to sit with your eyes closed, your damp coat steaming—you can even snore—for a whole afternoon, and never a glazed eye will swivel in your direction, nor a single, screwed-up consciousness detach itself from its inner speedometer for long enough to wonder who you are and why you are so tired.

People came, they sat down opposite her, they ate their buns, looked at their watches, and went: and still Milly slept on, secure in the knowledge that she didn't exist. A black cat in the dark: white square on white: what an aeroplane looks like out of sight: you can't get much safer than that.

For two hours Milly slept like the dead, or like the not-yet born; and when she woke, there was an object in front of her so marvellous that for a second she thought she must have died and gone to Heaven. The object was white, and delicately carved; the edges formed a frieze of fantastic beauty and complexity—no, not a frieze exactly; more like petals, petals of a flower, opening out before her, offering itself, in total, smiling friendship.

Milly blinked. Her vision cleared (for one moment she would have said rather that it dulled), and she found herself gazing hungrily at a broken roll, partially buttered, that someone had left to go to waste on a crumb-strewn plate, only a foot away from her.

Milly was amazed. How could things be so easy? No one could call *this* stealing! She twitched the plate furtively towards her, and as she bit deep into the broken crust, and felt the soft, feather-whiteness of the bread against her teeth, she murmured a soundless prayer, she knew not to what or whom. Already the sense of revelation was fading: induced by starvation, and lowered blood-sugar, the vision was being systematically blotted out, gleam by evanescent gleam, with every delicious mouthful.

A shame, really, after all this, that she couldn't manage to finish the roll! After only a few bites, all her ravenous hunger

27

was gone, and she felt quite bloated. She was just about to slip the remainder of the roll into her handbag, to eat later on—for tomorrow's breakfast, perhaps—when a tray lurched into her field of vision. It swayed for a few seconds in front of her eyes, and then came to rest on the table. The owner of the tray, a middle-aged man with greying hair, settled himself comfortably in the seat opposite Milly, reached first for salt and then for vinegar, and then, having besprinkled his sausage and chips liberally with both, he proceeded to unfold an evening paper, prop it against the vinegar bottle, and thereafter seemed to bury himself in it, ladling forkfuls of chips into his mouth like an automaton.

At first, all that the little scene meant to Milly was that she could now, perhaps, slip the rest of the roll into her handbag unobserved. Surreptitiously, she pulled the handbag into her lap, and opened it in readiness behind the screen of the table: then, just before snatching at the roll, she gave a quick final glance across the table to make sure that her companion was still thoroughly engrossed in his paper.

He was. Why, then, did Milly not seize her chance, grab the piece of roll, and snap her handbag shut on it? Instead, she just sat, staring.

... FOUND IN FLAT was all she could see of the headline, but it was enough: enough to freeze her hovering hand; to drive all thought of food from her shocked consciousness. Vainly she screwed herself this way and that, trying to see the hidden portion of the page: vainly she tried to assure herself that it was too early ... too soon ... they couldn't have discovered anything yet.

They could, though. It wasn't too early at all. This was a London paper. Of course the news could be in it—this was just exactly the length of time you would expect the thing to take, allowing for the snail-like reactions of the inhabitants of that haunted street. Or was it? How long would Mrs Roach, on the floor above, have sat listening inertly to the strange sounds in the basement? How long would it be before her dulled senses became aware that something was amiss? And even after she was aware, how long would it have been before she dragged her bulk out of the ancient fusty chair in which she spent her days, and took herself, slip-slop in her downtrodden slippers, curlers twisted this way and that in her sparse hair, out of the front door and down the gusty street to the telephone box at the corner? For there was no telephone in the house—a deficiency which Gilbert had actually boasted of to Milly, in his gentle old voice, as if it was some rare and expensive luxury. "It's the only way to get any peace, these days," he'd said, that day when he took her to his home for the first time: and it was only afterwards, and gradually, that Milly had become aware of what it was that Gilbert meant by "peace".

How long had it taken her to understand? How long was it before she began to guess what it was that she had let herself in for by marrying Gilbert?

Marrying him had seemed, at the time, the answer to all her problems: and so, in a way, it was, for at that time all her problems had been simply the variegated facets of the same problem: the problem of how to "*show*" Julian! Show him that "a woman in her forties" is *not* finished and done for: show him that she, the discarded wife, could still attract, still find herself another man. Show him that what he had thrown away like an outworn glove was a treasure for which other men came begging. Show him, in fact, that she didn't care *that* for him and Cora, and for the divorce, and for all the humiliating publicity! Show him that she could still bounce up again, unquenched and unquenchable, ready to start life all over again. And to show him, above all, just what he could do with his alimony!

"I am returning your cheque," she had written—and the composing of this letter had given her, perhaps, the most exquisite ten minutes of her whole life. It seemed, looking back, that it was just for this ten minutes that she had undertaken the whole thing: had bartered, knowingly, the whole of her future life, with no doubt at all that a lifetime of frustration and boredom was a small price to pay for ten minutes of triumph so perfect and so complete. "I am returning your cheque," she wrote, "as I no longer have any need of—or indeed any right to—further support from you. You will be pleased to hear that I am getting married next week, and am happier than I have ever been in my life. Gilbert is a widower, just sixty, tall and most distinguished-looking, and has a pleasant home of his own in South London. . . ."

She hadn't known, of course, at the time of writing, how much of all this was lies: though she had known that some of it was, and she hadn't cared. She knew, for example, that Gilbert wasn't sixty, but a good many years older: his stiff gait, his feathering of snow-white hair, and above all his hands, tortoise-slow and spotted with old age—all this had made it quite clear, from the very beginning, that he was deceiving her about his age. But so what? All she had felt at the time was a mild gratitude towards him for taking upon himself the burden of telling the lies, instead of leaving it to her. For, if he had not done it for her, she would, of course, have subtracted the decade herself in boasting about her suitor to Julian.

What she *hadn't* known, at that time, was what the "pleasant house in South London" was actually like. But even if she *had* known—even if she could have seen with her own eyes the boarded-up windows, the peeling, ancient paint, and could have heard the slip-slop of Mrs Roach's slippers on the stairs—even then, it probably wouldn't have made any difference. Because at that time she simply didn't *mind* what the rest of her life was going to be like, any more than she minded what Gilbert was like. All that mattered was that Julian should *think* she had made a catch and was living happily ever after. Real life seemed a trivial thing compared with impressing Julian.

And anyway, what the hell? How could life with this harmless old man possibly be worse than hanging on in the awful, well-appointed Kensington flat, pitied by the neighbours, avoided by her and Julian's former friends? Gilbert at least seemed to value her, in his mumbling, fumbling way. He was courteous and deferential to the point of incomprehensibility, and sometimes paid her stiff, complicated compliments, which she couldn't but find pleasing, starved as she had been of any words of approval during recent years.

Besides, she supposed, vaguely, that she would grow fond of him as time went on. He seemed to have led a miserable life—nagged by his first wife into a nervous breakdown, swindled out of his proper pension by the now defunct Indian Civil Service: and Milly rather fancied herself in the rôle of little ray of sunshine to brighten his declining years. And if, in the process of brightening someone's declining years, you can also administer a well-deserved kick in the backside to your ex-husband's inflated ego—well, what normal woman would hesitate?

Milly wouldn't, anyway. She promptly married Gilbert at a Brixton registry office, with two deaf old men captured from a nearby bowls club as witnesses: and she straightaway sent Julian a beautifully touched-up photograph of the wedding, with herself smiling a radiant smile that was quite unfeigned (and how should Julian guess that the joy irradiating her features was inspired not by love's young dream, but by the thought of his and Cora's faces as they received the news?)

Gilbert hadn't come out quite so well: he had a vulpine look which she hadn't noticed in real life, and his smile was glassy, and riddled with false teeth. Still, it wasn't too bad: at least the lines on his face were blurred and softened, so that he looked, in the picture, as if he really could be only sixty. And he was standing well, too, tall and spare, almost military. You couldn't say he looked handsome, exactly—and it was a pity that the fluffy whiteness of his hair was so in evidence—but at least he looked distinguished, in a bony, ghosty sort of a way.

The man opposite Milly suddenly lowered his newspaper, and it seemed, for one awful moment, that his glance rested on her face for just a little too long. Was her picture already in the paper, then?—that very same wedding photograph, perhaps, with the fixed, bridal smiles, now so eerily inappropriate. Just the sort of ghoulish touch that newspapermen love. . . .

The man's glance had left Milly's face now; he looked merely irritable as he twitched over one page after another, folding and re-folding the paper as he searched for some small haven of print on which his flickering interest might rest awhile.

. . . FOUND IN FLAT . . . FOUND IN FLAT—twice more the tantalising letters flashed in front of Milly's eyes, until at last her luck was in, and the front page lay spread out before her in its totality:

STOLEN JEWELS FOUND IN FLAT, she read; and her whole body sagged in an ecstasy of relief.

Nothing to do with her at all! She was reprieved!

Because, whatever they were going to find in that basement flat in South London, it most certainly wasn't going to be jewels.

CHAPTER V

"WELL, ACTUALLY, I was wondering if I could pay by cheque?"

A cheque, signed with her new false name, naturally wouldn't be worth the paper it was written on, but Milly was calculating that, before it bounced back, she would have been able to pay the whole week's rent in full, in cash. She had never dealt in dud cheques before, and she wasn't sure how easy they were to laugh off—not to mention getting the landlady to laugh with you. But of one thing she was quite certain: a trendy little anecdote about the idiocies of the bank's newly-installed computer would sound a lot funnier to a landlady's ears if Milly was already holding out three real, actual pound notes when she laughingly embarked on it.

"Is that all right, then?—who shall I make it out to?" Milly drew the futile, obsolete cheque-book from her bag with quite a flourish, and flicked it open with all the solid assurance of one who really *will* have one pound forty tomorrow, and another one pound forty the next day, and therefore isn't telling lies at all, not really. She was aware, though, as she stood, biro poised, and with an ingratiating smile on her lips, that the little woman who had advertised the vacant room upstairs was now watching her, sharp as a sparrow, from under her grey fringe: assessing her, totting her up: and wasting no time in coming up with the answer.

"I'm sorry. No, I don't take cheques. I'm sorry."

So she didn't take cheques. Just like some people don't take whisky. The tiny interlude of hope was over. Milly found herself being edged expertly back along the narrow entrance hall, past the bicycle, and the gum-boots, and the umbrella-stand, to where the front door still stood open, as if it had known, ever since Milly arrived, that she was one of the ones who would not be staying.

But on the threshold, Milly paused. When she had arrived here (attracted not only by the Rooms to Let sign, but also by the dirty curtains, which suggested that it might be cheap), it had still been afternoon, with faint gleams of sunlight on the tips of the slated roofs. Now, the air was full of dusk. The landlady shivered as she held the door open for Milly's departure: you could see she was impatient, longing to get the door closed again. As for Milly, her mind was empty of further plans. It all seemed too difficult.

"Well, goodbye, then," she said, vaguely, backing out of the little lighted hall. As she moved out of the shelter of the doorway, the icy chill of the coming night flicked at her: the first blades of the cold that was to come touched at her knees and at her throat: and straightaway her body remembered. Before any thought of hers could direct it, it

33

was back through the already-closing door, back into the warm hallway, and fighting for its life.

She *quite* understood, she gabbled, that a person letting rooms has to be careful: she'd be just the same herself . . . the words rattled from Milly's lips like ticker-tape, racing to get it all said before righteous fury took the place of stupefaction in the startled face in front of her. So how would it be, Milly babbled on—and here she smiled into the still-dazed blue eyes with a frank, phoney charm worthy of Julian himself—how would it be if she gave references? She had a job locally . . . her employer . . . a Mrs Graham . . . ?

What on earth would happen if this suggestion was actually taken up, she had no time to consider. But at least Mrs Graham would have heard of her, and would have to say so: wasn't it quite something to have been heard of by someone, in this big empty world?

As it happened, the matter was never put to test. At the word "references", the indignant little body in front of her nearly exploded.

"References!" she spat. "What's the good of references? Anyone can fake a reference! D'you think I was born yesterday?" She didn't, of course, expect an answer to this question, least of all the answer "No, but I was!" which was what almost sprang to Milly's lips, and had to be hastily suppressed.

"Some of the worst tenants I've ever had have come to me with a whole bag-load of posh references," the woman continued. "I wouldn't give tuppence for a reference from the Queen of England herself! And anyway," she finished truculently, "Where's your luggage? I never take anyone who arrives with no luggage!"

At this additional indictment, Milly's hopes suddenly revived. As soon as someone gives *two* reasons for not doing what you want, instead of one, he has as good as lost the game already: unwittingly, he has put himself within range of argument on two fronts.

"My luggage? It's at the station," Milly said, with a

dignity borne of having almost forgotten that everything she was saying was lies. "Naturally, I didn't want to drag it around with me before I was settled, and so. . . ."

A small burst of derisory clapping from up above made both women whirl round and peer up into the half-darkness of the stairs. There, just at the bend of the banisters, two grinning faces had appeared, gleaming indistinctly out of a shadowy framework of beards and hair.

"Attagirl! You're winning!" called one cheery young voice: and the other: "Oh, come on, Mrs Mums, give her a chance! Remember the lies *we* had to tell before you'd let us in!"

The little woman thus addressed rushed like a small charging bull to the foot of the stairs.

"Off with you!" she yelled up into the darkness. "Both of you, off to your room! And I'll thank you to call me *Mrs Mumford*, if you please! Whatever's the lady going to think, hearing you go on like that? She'll think we keep a madhouse here! So off! *Off!*"

A shuffle of laughter, a thumping of heavy feet, and then the banging of a door. Mrs Mumford now turned to Milly almost apologetically, just exactly as if Milly had a right to be standing there in the hallway and passing judgement on the establishment.

"My students," she explained deprecatingly. "They'll be the death of me, I swear they will! Never a minute's peace. . . ."

But Milly did not fail to notice the touch of pride in the sharp voice. "My students . . ." whatever she might say, you could tell already that Mrs Mumford loved having them there.

"I've been taking in students for twelve years come September," Mrs. Mumford informed Milly, temporarily suspending hostilities for the sake (presumably) of a few minutes' chat. "It's the University, you see, it's not more than twelve miles down the coast, they can get there in twenty minutes on the train. The money's not much, though, not when you consider the Sunday dinners as well. I've always done the Sunday dinners for my students, but when you consider the price of meat these days. . . . And the way they eat, you wouldn't believe it, Mrs . . . Mrs . . . Excuse me, what *did* you say your name was?"

"Barnes," said Milly, who hadn't said anything of the kind, and had indeed only just this moment decided on it. "Milly Barnes."

"Ah. Yes, well, Mrs Barnes, like I was telling you, it's a big problem, running a house like this, especially for a woman on her own. Like when I started, you see, my Leslie—that's my son, you know—my Leslie was at home then, he wasn't married. . . . Have *you* a son, Mrs Barnes?"

What a nice idea! Milly toyed with the thought of having a son—or even two sons. After all, they'd be past the troublesome stage by now, and out earning their own living. And what about a married daughter . . . ?

Milly sighed.

"No," she said. It was a pity, but the complications would be too great. These three young people would be expected to come and see her now and again . . . unless of course they all had jobs abroad, in which case this little woman would be on the watch for airmail letters which never came. It was going to be difficult enough to explain why no letters came anyway, without that.

"No—" she enlarged on it cautiously. "I never had any children. Your son must be a great satisfaction to you," she went on, giving the sort of deft about-turn to the conversation which was going to have to become second-nature to her from now on.

"Well." Mrs Mumford paused heavily, pursing up her small mouth in thought. "Well. He's married into a funny family, you see. That's the trouble. It's not that I didn't warn him. I mean, it's not that I want to interfere, or anything like that, I'm not the interfering kind. . . ."

At what point in the conversation had it become no

longer possible to throw Milly into the street? These things are impossible to gauge in retrospect; but certain it is that the realisation that the critical moment was already past came to them both, suddenly. Mrs Mumford's voice abruptly trailed into silence, and she stared helplessly at Milly, almost as if appealing to her for advice. How, she seemed to be asking, are we to start quarrelling again *now*? By what route can we make our way back to the point when I was saying "No, I'm sorry," and holding the front door open for you to disappear into the night? It was a problem in etiquette to which Mrs Mumford's limited repertoire simply didn't extend.

"Well." She said at last: and then, when nothing came of the remark, she tried again: "Well, I suppose."

"Yes," said Milly.

It still wasn't clear who had won: but all the same, they couldn't go on standing here in the hallway for ever: so after a bit, Mrs Mumford led the way upstairs, explaining, from long habit, that no one was allowed to run a bath after eleven p.m. because of the cistern. Only after she had completed this little admonition did she realise that every word of it had been insiduously strengthening Milly's hitherto tenuous claim on the tenancy.

"And of course, no late visitors!" she snapped, hitting out at random now, as she felt the initiative slipping from her grasp: and "No, of course not," said Milly heartily. "I say, what a gorgeous room!"

Nothing in her twelve years of landladyhood had prepared Mrs Mumford for this sort of reaction to her First Floor Back, Business Lady or Gentleman Only: and for a moment she stopped dead in the open doorway, staring first at Milly and then at the room, as if wondering who it was who was going mad. She couldn't, of course, guess that the dingy little carpetless room was irradiated with the primeval, almost-forgotten glory of having four walls, and a roof strong enough to keep out the rain and the savage winter wind: nor that the narrow lumpy bed with its old-fashioned white counterpane was holding out the promise of that most voluptuous of all human joys: lying down in safety, with blankets.

"Oh, I'm going to be so *happy* here!" cried Milly, feasting her eyes on the four solid walls holding up so marvellously against the sleet, and snow, and the bitter wind from the sea. The heartfelt sincerity in her voice seemed to bewilder her prospective landlady. After all these years in the business, Mrs Mumford knew well enough when she was being "got round". She could have taken her PhD any time, in identifying "soft soap" and "flannel", and all the other rent-postponing tricks that the wit of tenants could devise. But this sincere and unqualified admiration for one of her ugliest and most over-priced rooms was something that she could not place.

If you can't place it, it's dangerous. She watched Milly's incomprehensible enthusiasm through narrowed eyes. It was unnatural. And suspicious. And heart-warming.

"Yes, it's a nice little room, isn't it?" she found herself saying, proudly. "And if you look at those curtains, Mrs Barnes, you'll find they're lined. Properly lined. I had them done professionally, I don't believe in stinting, not where my tenants' comfort is concerned...."

Was it those lined curtains that decided the issue in the end? Neither Milly nor Mrs Mumford could have put their finger on it, but by the time Milly had obediently examined the said linings, stroked them with her forefinger, and agreed about the superior quality of the material, not like the rubbish they sell you *these* days—by this time, the whole argument was plainly over. Milly was here to stay. Both of them knew it. Milly had won.

Aggrieved, and not a little bewildered at this turn of events, Mrs Mumford looked uneasily around for some small way of punishing Milly for whatever it was she had done to thus worm her way into the establishment. She expected co-operation from her tenants, she told Milly sharply: and she hoped Milly hadn't brought a radio? They caused a lot of trouble radios did, and she, Mrs Mumford, had always been one for avoiding trouble. Did Milly quite understand?

Having thus re-established her ascendancy, Mrs Mumford took her leave, and Milly was left in undisputed possession of the small cold room, with its bare electric-light bulb and the pale damp winding its slow tides among the brown criss-cross pattern of the wall-paper.

Victory! At last! The sense of victory was like a fever, and Milly was aware neither of cold nor of hunger as she pulled off her blouse and skirt and slid between the icy sheets. And as she lay there, in the darkness, she felt as an athlete must feel as he stumbles, exhausted, past the tape, with the cheering from a million throats ringing in his ears. Only for Milly there was no cheering, only the distant, changeless roaring of the winter sea, and the rattle of her ill-fitting windows as the wind battered against them out of the night.

Oh, but the triumph of it! The glory of lying here, safe, and dry, and victorious, her whole soul glowing, expanding with the consciousness of having faced almost impossible odds, and of having overcome them! What wonders she had performed in the past thirty-six hours! Had she not succeeded in disappearing, without trace, from the heart of a great civilisation which checks and counter-checks, which lists and dockets and supervises its citizens as no civilisation has ever done before? And had she not survived, and survived in perfect health, thirty-six hours of exposure and starvation such as might have brought a trained soldier to his knees? She, a flabby middle-aged woman, with no training, no money, and in a state of total shock, had succeeded not only in surviving, but in finding herself a job, a home, and a new way of life, and all without rousing a moment's suspicion in any of the people involved!

If only Julian could know! "Not fit to be out alone!" he used to say, with such withering scorn, when she happened to have left her gloves somewhere, or to have forgotten the special Polish olives, or whatever, for one of his important parties. "Out alone," indeed! Just let him look at her now!

The dim, unfamiliar shapes of the strange furniture in the

strange room began to melt and swim before Milly's eyes as the deep drowsiness of prolonged fasting stole over her. How clever I am! she congratulated herself sleepily: and as she lay there, basking in the contemplation of her own cleverness, it never dawned on her that, for a person planning to vanish without trace, she had already made two glaring and awful mistakes: one of them so foolish that, really, even a child might have thought of it, and taken more care.

CHAPTER VI

MILLY WOKE FROM a long, dreamless sleep with a vague sense that something was going on. For a while she lay, inert and tranquil, too sleepy to care. Then, slowly, recollection of yesterday's events came flooding back, and with it a realisation of where she was and how she had got here. Slowly, and with a degree of awakening curiosity, she opened her eyes.

At first, the sickening terror almost made her faint, right there as she lay. And the most ghastly thing of all was that the terror was so familiar: familiar like a madman's nightmare, that has to be lived through over and over again, for ever, and from which there is no escape. The shuffling, slippered footsteps: the striped pyjamas sagging from bony shoulders as the tall, stooping figure fumbled its way across the curtained room. . . . The long hands groping, softly reaching into drawers and cupboards . . . searching, fumbling. . . . The terror was so great that at first Milly could neither move nor cry out.

Had her escape all been a dream, then? Had these last two days never happened at all? All that cleverness, all those stratagems and strokes of luck by which she had launched herself so miraculously into a new life—had it really all been too good to be true, as it had at moments seemed?

A dream? A mere fevered, wishful fantasy, bred of the sick, stagnant air of that South London basement—an air thick with obsession, with strange miasmas of the mind, soaked up over the years into the very walls ...?

So it was all to do again? Her decision—her escape? Had she still to face it all in reality, having gone through it once in dreams ...? Milly forced herself to look again into the almost-darkness: and now, with the first shock beginning to subside in her limbs and in her knotted stomach, she was able to observe that the figure was not quite as she remembered. Where was the crest of white hair, gleaming moth-like through the darkness no matter how black the night or how closely-fastened the ancient, creaking shutters? And where was the low, barely audible mumbling, on and on without end or outcome, that always used to accompany these nightly prowlings ...?

Nightly? Why, it wasn't even night! At that very moment the pyjama'd figure had reached the windows ... was drawing back the curtains, knocking over something as he did so, letting in the first white glitter of a winter day. In the cold, sharp light, the figure was revealed to be young, and lanky: tousled, fairish hair flopped this way and that around his ears, and in his right hand he swung a large, battered aluminium kettle. With unspeakable relief, Milly recognised him as one of the young men who had been peering over the banisters last night while she and Mrs Mumford fought out their life-and-death battle of wits.

"Oh!" said the young man, apparently noticing Milly's head on the pillow for the first time: and then "I say!"

He paused, as if for an answer, and then resumed his own train of thought: "I mean. That is. I say, I'm sorry! I didn't think there was anybody here."

Milly still couldn't think of anything to say. She was limp and speechless from relaxation, the aftermath of fear, so she just lay there, contentedly enough, waiting for some sense to emerge from the encounter. He looked quite a nice young man; bearded, and with amiable greenish eyes under shaggy beige eyebrows. Just now his mouth was open.

"It's the hotplate, you see," he volunteered at last,

hitching up his pyjama trousers as he spoke. "I suppose you don't know what's happened to the hotplate?"

"I'm afraid—well, you see, I only came last night," essayed Milly, still dazed: and then she watched, quite unsurprised, while the intruder, with a muttered exclamation, flung open the door of a huge yellow-varnished wardrobe, and began rummaging in its depths. Clanking sounds . . . muffled thuds . . . and then he emerged, wild-eyed, and pushing the tumble of hair back from his face. For a second he glanced despairingly round the room, then he turned, and strode without a word to the door.

"Kev!" he yelled. "I say, Kev! The silly old cow's gone off with the hotplate! *Now* what are we going to do?"

Which hotplate? What silly old cow? Before any guesses could begin to form themselves in Milly's mind, there were suddenly *two* young men filling her doorway. The second one (Kev, presumably) was darker, and distinctly better groomed than his companion. His beard was trimmed, and his pyjamas firmly corded.

"I say, I'm sorry about this," said the newcomer to Milly. "Jacko had no idea there was anyone here, you see."

He paused, and looked thoughtfully round the room. "I say, do you mind if *I* come and have a look?—It must be somewhere." He paused politely for just long enough for Milly to have said "Yes, that's quite all right", if she had so wished: and then he set himself to flinging open drawers and cupboards, delving among hair-curlers, outworn gloves, and long-ago relics of somebody's gracious living—lace-edged table-mats, embroidered nightdress-cases—the sort of things that are too good to throw away and too bothersome to use, and so just right for lodgers.

"You *see*?" said the first boy, Jacko, with a sort of melancholy triumph, when it became clear that his friend's search was destined to be as fruitless as his own: and, "I *told* you you should have helped her pack!" retorted Kevin, "Then she'd never have. . . ."

At this point, both seemed to recall simultaneously the

existence of Milly, who was by now sitting up in bed with her winter coat clutched round her. They looked at her consideringly.

"Miss Childe," observed the one called Kevin, with just the faintest touch of reproach in his voice, "always used to let us make our tea in here. On the hotplate."

"Yes. On the hotplate."

Milly was beginning to hate the hotplate, whatever it was. She met the two pairs of mildly reproachful eyes boldly.

"I don't know anything about it," she declared. "I don't know what you're talking about. *What* hotplate?"

"For our morning tea," explained Kevin patiently. "We always made our morning tea on it. In here," he added explanatorily, and still with that more-in-sorrow-than-in-anger note to his voice. "*Now*, I don't know how we're to make our tea at all! That's the point."

"Yes. That's the point," agreed Jacko.

Both were now looking at her with a sort of guarded appeal, like puppies who know that they aren't *really* allowed to be fed at table. Jacko was clutching the big, useless kettle to his breast, just where his middle pyjama button was missing.

But what could Milly do?

"What about the gas-ring?" she suggested, her eyes lighting upon this appliance as she spoke. "I don't mind you using my gas-ring, if you like."

"You mean there's some *money* in it? In the meter?"

They both spoke together, and with such eager hope that Milly hated to have to disappoint them.

"No," she said regretfully, "I'm afraid not— That's to say, *I* didn't put any in, and I'm afraid, just at the moment, I haven't..."

"No. Oh, well..." Jacko shrugged, sadly, but no longer with any reproach in his manner. During the last minute or two she had imperceptibly become one of them, all in the same boat.

The three of them regarded each other sadly.

43

"Ah, but it was a great little gadget, that hotplate!" sighed Kev, nostalgically, like an old man reminiscing about the vanished joys of his youth. "You could plug it into the lights, you see, and it would hot up a treat, and never cost anybody a penny! I can't imagine what the old cow was thinking of, going off with it like that! I mean, whatever would make her do such a thing?"

"Perhaps it was hers?" suggested Milly mildly: and both boys stared at her as if she had taken leave of her senses. Clearly, the concept of private property simply wasn't applicable to something they wanted as much as this.

"But we've got nothing to make our tea on!" Jacko cried indignantly; while Kevin, with the inventiveness born of necessity, suddenly cried out: "The bed! Like she might have shoved it under the bed, with all the junk. . . ."

By now, both of Milly's visitors were full-length on the floor, grovelling under her bed, throwing up debris like terriers in a rabbit-hole. Shoes. Laddered tights. More shoes. A copy of Nova. Half a candle. . . .

"Hey!" came Kevin's voice, muffled by dust and blankets, "Hey! Look! Ricicles! Anybody like Ricicles?" He squirmed out and up into a sitting position, holding up his find in triumph.

How old they were, there was of course no way of guessing: but the packet was nearly full, and Milly, who till this moment had felt no sensations of hunger at all, was suddenly faint with longing.

"Yes!" she answered. "Oh yes . . . !" and when one of the boys recalled the existence somewhere among his belongings of half a tin of condensed milk, left from the time Janette was here, she felt that happiness could go no further.

Five minutes later she was sitting on Jacko's unmade bed in the cluttered barrack of a room that the two boys shared, and listening to the story of their lives while she shovelled spoonful after spoonful of ageing Ricicles into her starving frame.

The two life stories, it seemed to Milly, were both unusual

44

and surprisingly similar. Both lads, it seemed, came of prosperous families: both had always wanted to be artists, but had unfortunately ended up like this, studying economics at a provincial university. So far, the story seemed a familiar one to Milly. In her young days, too, budding geniuses had been forced by soulless and insensitive parents into training for something dull and practical. But apparently, with these two, it wasn't quite like that. Far from being soulless and insensitive, both sets of parents had eagerly begged to be allowed to finance their budding young geniuses through art school for as many years as they wanted. Paris ... Rome ... Anywhere they liked ... money should be no object.

"But of course," explained Kevin, "that would have been just art-school stuff. Not my scene at all."

"No," agreed Jacko. "That was the thing. It's a matter of integrity, you see. Personal integrity."

Integrity, it seemed, had stopped them doing a lot of things, such as getting a vacation job, or studying hard for their exams. As far as Milly could make out from the narrative, it was integrity, plus their abhorrence of material possessions, that had stood in the way of success at every turn.

"You see, Mrs Barnes, we just don't *want* success," Jacko explained, waving his spoon about to emphasise the point. "Success is a form of death. You know—material possessions, and all that jazz. It's just not our scene."

But wasn't a hotplate a material possession? Milly asked, rather ill-advisedly—and there was a moment of pained silence, as if she had enquired after some unmentionable relative. Then Jacko pointed out, rather stiffly, that it was *their* Ricicles she was eating: they, Kev and himself, believed in sharing, and non-violence, and in respecting the beingness of every human person.

Milly, defeated by all this logic, humbly apologised.

They were very nice about it: and soon she felt that the three of them had been friends for years. She told them the fictional story of her life (the very same concoction that had been so insultingly brushed aside by Mrs Graham yesterday), and their rapt credulity went far to soothe the frustrated creative artist in her: so much so that the selling-up of the family heirlooms almost brought tears to her own eyes: and the thought of the non-existent haunts of her childhood being trampled now by the equally non-existent feet of strangers was wonderfully bitter.

Her good-natured hearers seemed to believe every word of it, and to have all the time in the world to listen: and when she came to the only truthful bit, about how hungry she was, their concern was quite touching. They rummaged around among their hi-fi equipment and their unironed shirts, and found her two starch-reduced rolls and some peanut butter. These, on top of the Ricicles, made her feel wonderful.

After this, they told her about sex, and how they were *through* with that sort of thing: kids' stuff. Yes, homosexuality too, and the perversions, and all that drag—they'd tried the lot: nothing to it. Integrity, that was the thing. Kevin, it seemed, was through with drugs as well: and when Milly asked if that was kids' stuff too, he said no, it wasn't quite that, but he'd been turned right off by going home one vacation and finding his grandmother smoking pot and saying she thought the younger generation was marvellous. It had turned him right off, it really had: and anyway, he informed Milly kindly, integrity, and the discovery of the true self, were possible *without* the aid of drugs. He knew, because he'd tried.

By this time there was not a crumb nor a scraping of anything eatable left, and Milly realised with sharp dismay that she had no idea what the time was! Why, she might already be hours late for her wonderful new job! Ten o'clock, Mrs Graham had said.

"What's the time?" she cried, rudely interrupting an account of Jacko's true self versus the Admissions Board: and for a moment her two companions seemed rather taken aback. They found her anxiety about being in time for work puzzling, and a little shocking: and though they were too kind actually to say it, it was plain enough to Milly that integrity was not really compatible with punctuality. However, they were broad-minded lads, and when they realised that Milly really *was* worried, they took counsel, and Jacko clattered amiably down the stairs to consult the household clocks. He came back with the reassuring news that since the kitchen clock said twenty to eleven, and the chiming clock in the dining room had just struck seven, it couldn't possibly be later than half past nine. Earlier, very likely. Milly would soon get the hang of it, he assured her, after she'd lived here a while.

"Off to work, Mrs Barnes?"

Whether by chance or cunning, Mrs Mumford had mater-ialised in the hallway just as Milly was letting herself out of the front door: and Milly seized eagerly on the opportunity (such opportunities having become increasingly rare of late) of speaking the truth.

"Yes," she said happily, meeting the landlady's watchful eyes with a smile. "I have to be there by ten...." and so saying she stepped triumphantly forth into the frosty, silver-yellow morning.

"Off to work!" How safe, and solid, and successful the phrase sounded! Milly fairly danced along the icy, unfamiliar street, the sea-wind whipping at her scarlet head-scarf, and her ungloved hands pushed deep into the pockets of her winter coat. Off to work! Off to work! What price mustard-and-cress *now*, eh, Julian?

CHAPTER VII

"AH, GOOD MORNING, Mrs—er—! Do you think you could start in the kitchen? There's not much to do really, just one or two things that don't go in the dishwasher; and then if you could just go over the floor with the Squeejee? That's all it needs, it's specially surfaced, you see. I don't believe in hard scrubbing, do you, Mrs Er—all that down-on-hands-and-knees business? I believe in labour-saving, my kitchen is modern throughout, all the latest equipment. I don't believe in *making* work...."

By the time Mrs Graham had reached this point in her credo, the two of them had reached the kitchen doorway, and Milly came into full view of the one or two things that wouldn't go in the dishwasher. Grease-caked saucepans, burnt baking-tins and frying pans... and on every surface in sight lay mountainous, half-dismantled mechanisms, each trailing a greasy length of electric flex, and most of them plastered with ancient remnants of food, each in accordance with its function.

"Yes... yes, of course," agreed Milly faintly, trying to conceal her dismay as she contemplated all these rejects from the labour-saving paradise about which Mrs Graham was still prattling so blithely:

"... can take up to four loads in a morning!" she was saying proudly, patting the dishwasher as if it was a favourite pony: and Milly now turned her awed gaze towards the subject of this eulogy. It dominated the scene like a queen termite, its huge white bulk throned on what had once been a roomy draining-board, but whose effective area had now been reduced to a strip two or three inches wide, on which (Milly could see already) it would be impossible to balance anything much bigger than a teacup.

"The washing-up is *nothing* now!" Mrs Graham was explaining happily. "Just a few cooking things which can be left till it's convenient" (like now, I suppose, thought Milly) "and all the rest goes straight into the dishwasher! All the cups, saucers, spoons, plates—unless they're *very* greasy, of course..."

It seemed to Milly that the thing liked washing up exactly the same things as everyone else likes washing up, and it avoided anything at all difficult or unpleasant: the only difference being that *it* got away with it. Mrs Graham was right now beaming on it with loving pride, as if it had just passed its O-levels. . . .

"It cost me £200!" she informed Milly in hushed tones, "and it's been worth every penny! It's *time*, you see, Mrs Er, that I'm short of: for a person like me, time *is* money!"

It was for Milly, too, of course: in her case, an hour equalled seven shillings, as Mrs Graham of all people, should have known. But Mrs Graham seemed to feel that the predicament was so specially *hers* that Milly hadn't the heart to point out its universality. Instead, she listened with respectful attention while her employer continued:

"You see, I happen to have a degree in Sociology, and if a woman has had any sort of higher education I feel she has an obligation to *use* it, even after she's married, don't you agree, Mrs Er? It's difficult, though, working at home: people seem to think that just because you're at home, they can interrupt you just as much as ever they like. They think they can come in and out bothering you about every tiny thing! My other woman was like that."

Her voice trailed off into a deprecatory little laugh, and she shot an anxious glance at Milly. Clearly, she wanted to make sure that the point had got across, but was fearful lest it might have offended her new Mrs Er in the process. Milly suppressed a tiny smile and was agreeably aware of the first stirrings of a sense of power. Mrs Er's were few and far between.

But after Mrs Graham had gone, and she found herself alone in the messy, alien kitchen, the brief feeling of confidence left her, and she felt something approaching panic. Where should she start? Where was everything supposed to go? Where was the Vim . . . the washing-up liquid . . . ? In the weeks to come, she was to learn that this attack of panic when confronted by a strange kitchen was one of the occupational hazards of being a Daily: and she was to learn, too, how quickly it passed: how, if one set oneself quietly to doing just one thing, however trivial, the other tasks would mysteriously sort themselves out and

49

become manageable while one wasn't looking. But this morning, in her very first job, she didn't know any of this: she thought it was herself, her own inadequacy, that was to blame.

I can't! she thought, I can't! Her hands were trembling, and her mouth was dry, exactly like someone about to make a public speech for the first time: yet even while she panicked, she began, whether by good luck or instinct, to do the right thing. That is, to do *something*. She began blindly pulling the pans out of the sink and stacking them on the floor beside her.

And suddenly, wonderfully, she found that a miracle had happened! She had done one thing! She had cleared the sink! Now all things were possible.

Humming a little tune in sheer relief, she turned on the hot tap to its fullest extent, and as it surged clean and steaming against the stainless steel, she began with real enthusiasm to select an assortment of objects to begin on: she was now positively enjoying the enormity of the mess confronting her. She had joined battle with it, and she was going to win!

But here came the next setback. No dishcloth. Not just that she couldn't *find* a dishcloth: there simply wasn't one. Not anywhere. Nor a floorcloth either, nor any rag of any kind. How on earth was she to wash up all this stuff without one—not to mention the wiping of all these stream-lined labour-saving surfaces, now revealed as a mass of grease, old tea-leaves, and smears of gravy? Milly's fingers itched to get at it all with a lovely, hot, well-wrung-out cloth: and for a moment she stood motionless, surveying the smears and spills, weighing them up against Mrs Graham's degree in Sociology.

Then, her decision made, she marched boldly out of the kitchen and knocked firmly on the sitting-room door.

"No dishcloth?" Mrs Graham was blinking, vaguely, as she looked up from her typewriter, like a kitten just roused from sleep. "No *dishcloth*? But of course there isn't a dish cloth. We have a dishwasher—I showed you, Mrs Er—and so we don't *need* a dishcloth. It's an *automatic* machine, don't you see? The washing up is done *automatically*."

She spoke wearily, as if it was the twentieth time she had had to repeat this same elementary fact. You could see her visibly resigning herself to the idea that Mrs Er was going to prove just as stupid as My Other Woman.

"It's an *automatic* dishwasher," she repeated, stealing an impatient glance down at her typewriter: but Milly stood her ground.

"It's all those saucepans," she pointed out. "The things that won't go in the dishwasher. The baking-tins. And the mincer. And the burnt chip-pan. And all that white, sticky stuff in the Mouli-Mixer—"

"Oh dear. Well." You could see that Mrs Graham was interrupting the recital because she knew it by heart. She must have gone through it many a time with My Other Woman and her predecessors, and she had learned, the hard way, that stupidity has to be humoured.

"You want a rag, I suppose?" she diagnosed wearily. "I'll see what I can find." And with a huge sigh she got up from her typewriter and began rummaging in the bottom drawer of a big mahogany desk. Embroidery silks—hemstitched tray-cloths—postcards—cotton wool—they boiled up like soapsuds round her elbows as she stirred and prodded: and at last, in weary triumph, she produced a torn nylon slip and the half-unravelled sleeve of a knitted sweater.

"*Here* you are," she said: and such was her air of having secured these objects against unimaginable odds that Milly hadn't the heart to point out that they were almost useless for the job in hand, and that what she needed was something absorbent, like an old towel or piece of sheeting.

So she simply thanked her employer meekly, and went back to the kitchen. It took much longer than it would have done, if only she'd had a proper rag, and the final result was not all that she could have wished: but it was certainly greatly improved, and Milly fairly glowed with pride when her employer came in, an hour later, and surveyed the clean and shining surfaces with real approval.

"They're marvellous, aren't they, these dishwashers?" she observed, looking blandly round at the results of Milly's labours. "See how clean and tidy they keep the kitchen! You've no idea the mess we used to be in, before we had one! I'm going to make a cup of coffee now, Mrs Er, could you put the kettle on? I drink a lot of coffee when I'm working. I expect you'd rather have tea, Mrs Er, wouldn't you?"

Milly thought quickly. Did this mean simply that My Other Woman had preferred tea? Or was it a veiled command— coffee in short supply, or more expensive, or something?

Well, and suppose it *was* a veiled command? Who was it, anyway, who had to be careful not to annoy whom? At this invigorating thought, Milly's courage returned.

"No—actually I prefer coffee," she declared boldly: and registering only the faintest flicker of surprise, Mrs Graham took the Nescafé from the shelf, and proceeded to make coffee for the two of them.

"I'm on a special diet, I don't take sugar," she observed, stirring two heaped teaspoonfuls into Milly's cup as she spoke; and Milly accepted the sickly-sweet concoction without protest. In the first place, she could quite see how the specialness of Mrs Graham's diet would be spoiled by other people not taking sugar either: and in the second, she could feel in her body an unwonted craving for sweetness. Even after all those Ricicles, she still felt half-starved, and she watched, almost dizzy with greed, as Mrs Graham reached for a tin of biscuits, opened it, and peered inside.

"All sweet ones!" she said disgustedly. "Arnold—Professor Graham, that is to say—he *will* buy the sweet ones! I've told him a million times...! For two pins I'd do the shopping myself, but it's so convenient for him, the supermarket's right on his way back from the University...."

Milly watched, sick with disappointment, as Mrs Graham began replacing the lid—but just at that moment, something seemed to arrest Mrs Graham's attention. She cocked her head on one side, and set the biscuit tin absently on the table: and Milly, pretending to think it had been passed to her, snatched greedily into the tin.

Had this behaviour looked very odd? Mrs Graham was staring at Milly unbelievingly, and Milly, covered with shame and confusion, was just about to apologise, when Mrs Graham herself began to speak.

"I can't understand it!" she was saying, "I can't understand it at all! Alison *always* sleeps till lunch time! *Now* what am I going to do?"

By now Milly could hear the sounds too—the unmistakeable protests of a baby who considers that her morning sleep is over. Mrs Graham pressed her hand against her white forehead despairingly.

"And Arnold will be back at one, wanting his lunch, and I've still got my correlations to finish! Look, Mrs Er, would you mind seeing to her for me? Do you know anything about babies? If you could just get her up, and change her nappy? And then keep her with you while you do the dining-room? She's no trouble: you just have to see that she doesn't pull down the ornaments, or open the sideboard, or put anything in her mouth, or interfere with the papers on the couch, or get at the china in the cabinet, or play with the lamp flex, or pull the books out of the bottom shelf, or pinch her fingers in the door—Oh, and watch out for the vases, won't you, Mrs Er? She's mad about flowers. And the clock too: now that she can climb up to the clock I just don't know *what* we are going to do. And whatever you do, don't let her cry, because I *must* get on with my correlations, I just *can't* be interrupted any more this morning."

With which instructions, she whisked up her cup of coffee and fairly fled into the sitting-room, shutting the door behind her with a finality that was almost a slam. Milly was left to locate the baby as best she could.

Not that it was difficult. The screams were reaching a crescendo now, and Milly opened the door behind which they resounded with a good deal of trepidation. She was no automatic baby-lover: she only liked them if they were nice, and there was so far no evidence at all that this one was going to fall into any such category.

At the sight of the furious, red-faced little creature, standing up clutching the bars of its cot and jigging up and down in its rage, all Milly's most non-maternal feelings surged into her breast.

"There, there! Now, come along, then!" she forced herself to squeak ingratiatingly across the uproar: and at the sound of her voice Alison at once stopped screaming, presumably from sheer shock. For a moment the two glowered at each other in mutual dismay. Traumatic, that's what it must be, thought Milly glumly, to have a complete stranger walk in like this and yank you out of your cot and start changing your nappy. Surely, even a mother *without* a degree in Sociology might have thought twice about it?

Still, everything has its bright side: it seemed, mercifully, that the effect of traumatic experiences on Alison was to stop her screaming for minutes on end: long enough for Milly to change her nappy, get her leggings on, carry her into the dining-room, and set her down on a rug, where she sat, sucking the plug of the Hoover with ferocious intensity, and following Milly's every movement with unblinking concentration. She remained in this felicitous state of shock for long enough to allow Milly to dust all the furniture, and even to wipe the window-sills and mantelpiece with a damp cloth. After that, inevitably, recovery set in, and Alison began to feel well enough to screw up her face ready for a new bout of crying. At this unwelcome sign of returning vitality, Milly hastily gave the child a pair of nutcrackers out of the sideboard drawer, together with a small brass tray to bash them against: and while Alison was thus employed, she herself got on with the hoovering. By now, she was feeling really pleased with herself. She was managing the job splendidly. Mrs Graham had been really pleased with the kitchen, and surely she would be pleased with this room, too: it was beginning to look very nice, with all the furniture polished and shining, and the last of the crumbs disappearing off the floor like a dream . . . and it was just then, just as she switched the Hoover off, that the telephone began to ring.

It was ridiculous, of course: why on earth *shouldn't* Mrs Graham's phone ring now and again? Why in all the world should it be anything to do with Milly? And yet, as she stood there, behind the closed door of the dining-room, Milly felt her pulse quicken. Her palms began sweating . . . soon her heart was leaping in her throat with great, panicky thuds, and her legs trembled so that she could hardly go on standing. She heard Mrs Graham cross the room, lift the receiver. . . .

"Seacliffe 49901," Milly heard her say briskly, and held her breath as she listened. In a moment now it would be all right. She would hear Mrs Graham saying something like: "Oh hu*ll*o, Christine . . .!" or "Thank you *so* much, Tuesday will do splendidly . . .!" something of that sort, something to show conclusively that it was nothing whatsoever to do with Milly. Well, of course it wasn't. How could it be? No one in all the world knew she was here . . . how ridiculous to panic like this about nothing!

"Ye-es," she heard Mrs Graham saying, in a guarded sort of voice: and then, more decisively: "Yes, she's been here since ten o'clock. . . ." And after that came a pause, which to Milly's ringing ears seemed to last a lifetime. Then Mrs Graham's voice again: "Well, I can't help that, can I? But who told you about her? How did you know?"

By this time, if only her legs would have carried her so far, Milly would have been out of the dining-room window and sliding down whatever drainpipe there might or might not be to the ground three storeys below: but so paralysed was she with the sheer, incredible horror of it, that she could only stand there. Who had traced her . . .? How . . .? Or had it all been a plot, a police trap carefully laid for her? What a fool she had been . . .! Why hadn't her suspicions been aroused by the incredible ease with which she had walked into this job . . .? Why hadn't she realised that it was a trap, that Mrs

Graham must be in league with the police ...? Even as these speculations rang and rattled through her whirling brain, she realised that the telephone conversation had broken off: Mrs Graham was crossing the hall ... opening the dining-room door ... and now she was standing there, in the doorway, fixing Milly with a hard, suspicious stare: and behind the suspicion, there was the faint, unmistakeable flicker of fear. ...

"A phone call, Mrs Er," she said accusingly, "from a neighbour of mine. She's heard I've got a new woman, someone seems to have seen you coming in this morning, and she wants to know if you've got any time left to work for *her*? She wants to talk to you about it. Now, you will remember, won't you, Mrs Er, that you undertook to do mornings for *me*. You won't let me down, will you? From what Mrs Day tells me, I think she may be going to offer you forty-pence an hour, but you *will* remember, won't you, Mrs Er, that you get your *lunches* here. A really good lunch, every day...."

Luckily, Mrs Graham was so thoroughly wrapped up in these anxieties that she did not notice the way Milly almost danced across the hall to the telephone: nor did she hear the breathless relief in Milly's voice as she settled for three afternoons a week with this Mrs Day. It was her *own* sense of relief, not Milly's, that was engaging Mrs Graham's whole attention: the colour was visibly returning to her cheeks as it slowly became clear from Milly's side of the conversation that there was to be no real betrayal. It was only *afternoons* Mrs Er was engaging herself for with the perfidious Mrs Day!

But the suspense, while it lasted, had made Mrs Graham irritable.

"It's incredible, isn't it?" she grumbled, as Milly put the phone down. "The way you can't keep anything to yourself in a place like this! *I* never told anyone I'd got a woman ... I don't know how these things get about! I mean, you've hardly been in the place two hours, and she has to phone up ...! Oh, well. ..."—Mrs Graham made a visible effort to recover her poise. "It's not that I *mind* Mrs Day having you in the afternoons, Mrs Er, not a bit, I'm only too glad, if that's what suits you both. It's only that I do wish people wouldn't go round *telling* everybody.... You *won't* let me down, Mrs Er, will you?"

And Milly, graciously, as became the great lady she had so recently become, promised that she would not.

CHAPTER VIII

MILLY HAD RARELY in her life felt happier than she did that afternoon, as she walked home along the sea-front with one pound forty in her pocket, and with a lunch of lamb chops, mashed potatoes and sprouts still warming her through and through, like remembered joy. The wind had dropped, and through the gathering mist of the winter afternoon Milly could hear the invisible small waves slapping and sighing along the shingle, and she felt herself alive, and tingling with hope, in a way that she had not known since her teens. Oh, she had experienced hope all right, in adult life: wild, desperate, frenzied hopes, sometimes to be fulfilled for a while, more often to be disappointed, to be shattered and destroyed under her very eyes. But this was something different. Adult hopes are hopes *of* something ... that this or that will happen or not happen. What Milly was experiencing now was the sort of hope that belongs normally only to the very young: not hope *of* anything in particular, but just Hope, its very essence, huge, unfocused, as undefined and as ungraspable as Eternity itself.

It was because she *was* young, of course: younger than she could ever remember, only three days old. Propelled by disaster grown too big to grasp, she had finally been hurled like a thunderbolt out of all her worries, all her fears, out of all the burden of her mistakes and crimes, and had crashed down into peace: into the still, golden winter mist, by the side of the quiet sea. It was like dying and going to

57

heaven ... it was like dying as a peculiarly intense form of life ... it was new, new! And in all this new heaven or new earth, whichever it might be, Milly was the newest thing of all!

What a success she had made of her new life, so far! Last night's euphoria was still with her, quite undiminished by that brief panic over the telephone call this morning. Rather, that moment of overwhelming terror and guilt seemed to have done something to her which had wiped out guilt and terror for ever. Because her fears at that particular moment had proved unfounded, she now felt immunised against fear.

It was like being vaccinated—something like that. She was inoculated, now, against trouble, in some way that the doctors don't know of. The sea-mist gleaming all around her was like the lifting of the anaesthetic after an operation ... there was that same dazed, exalted feeling that the pain is all over ... when in fact it may sometimes be only just beginning.

But not all the gains were illusory: Milly was sure of that. She *had* done well as a Daily Help: astonishingly, unprecedentedly well, considering how few things she had succeeded in doing well in her former life. She had cleaned Mrs Graham's kitchen and dining-room really thoroughly: she had kept Alison quiet: she had helped cook lunch; and (she was sure of it) provided real moral support to her employer when, at twelve-fifty or thereabouts, disaster struck, in the form of Professor Graham coming home to lunch a full ten minutes earlier than expected.

"Oh, God!" his wife had greeted him, glancing up from her typewriter with a hunted look. "What's happened, Arnold? You said one o'clock! You said you wouldn't be back for lunch till one!"

Milly, peering through the kitchen door, saw a tall, scholarly-looking man with greying hair settling his umbrella carefully in the umbrella stand. Then he straightened up and walked towards the sitting-room door. At the door he paused, took off his horn-rimmed glasses, all steamed-up from the sudden change from outdoors to the central-heated flat, and set himself to polishing them assiduously with his handkerchief. His mild brown eyes blinked owlishly without them, creating a barrier of gentle non-seeing-ness between himself and his aggrieved wife. Only after he had settled the glasses on his face again and returned the handkerchief to his pocket, did he seem constrained to answer her.

"I got a lift," he explained. "Carstairs has to go to the Library Committee lunch, and so he offered to drop me on the way. But don't worry, dear, finish what you're doing, I'm in no hurry."

"Finish what I'm doing!" His wife, with a huge sigh, pushed her papers aside and ostentatiously fitted the lid back on to the typewriter. "I sometimes think I'll *never* finish *anything* I'm doing! First Alison woke up early from her morning sleep—and now *you're* home! You don't know how lucky you are, Arnold, being allowed to *work* when you're working! How I envy you that room of yours at the University . . . all your things to hand. . . . No one bothering you . . .!"

"They *do* bother me, you know, dear, sometimes," he pointed out mildly. "The telephone goes a lot in my room, you'd be surprised. Committees. Visiting lecturers. Trouble in the typing pool. All sorts of things. I can't always get on with my work as I'd like to."

"But you don't have Alison screaming her head off!" countered Mrs Graham. "And lunch to see to . . . and then I've got this new woman this morning, I've had to settle *her* in. It's amazing how many questions they seem to have to ask . . . *Mrs Er!*"—here she raised her voice to a ringing shout to reach Milly in the kitchen—though in fact Milly could already hear every word of her clear, carrying, complaining voice.—"Mrs Er! Could you hurry the potatoes a bit? Professor Graham is back earlier than he planned. . . ."

How one hurried potatoes, Milly wasn't quite sure. They boiled at the speed they did boil, no matter who went down on their knees to them. But she judged (rightly) that the shouted instruction was meant more as a reproof to Professor Graham than as a command to Milly: and so she simply went on with her preparations for the meal as quickly as she could, and radiated respectful sympathy—on, off, on, off—as Mrs Graham flapped in and out of the kitchen bemoaning her unfinished correlations.

Thanks to Milly, lunch was on the table, and Alison strapped in her high-chair, on the dot of one, and so Professor Graham had nothing to complain of, as his wife assured him, three or four times in succession. He'd *said* one o'clock, hadn't he?

And indeed he wasn't complaining. He sat consuming his lamb chops, mashed potatoes and sprouts with obvious enjoyment, a copy of *Scientific American* propped against the bottle of ketchup in front of him, and on his face the look of a man at peace with the world: a look off which his wife's barbed attempts at conversation bounced harmlessly.

So after a bit she turned her attention to Milly, and began explaining to her about Alison's diet, and how important it was that she should have plenty of salad now that she was eleven months old and on mixed feeding. She pointed out to Milly, with modest maternal pride, that a tomato and a shredded lettuce leaf had been added to Alison's share of the meal: and Milly murmured suitable words of approval, meanwhile watching with fascinated admiration, Alison's skill in extracting from the mush in front of her every scrap of tomato and lettuce leaf and throwing it on the floor. Like most babies in this diet-conscious age, she had a passion for all non-protein, non-vitamin foods, and it seemed to Milly that she and her mother had evolved a very good working arrangement: Mrs Graham talked fluently and enthusiastically to all comers about how much salad she gave Alison and how many vitamins it contained, and what a good effect they had on the child's teeth and complexion (which were indeed perfectly all right), while Alison stuffed herself contentedly on mashed potato flavoured with ketchup. This way, they were both happy. The only loser was Milly, whose task it proved to be to sweep, wipe and scrub

Alison's vitamins from the floor after the meal was over.

Still, one pound forty! Not to mention Mrs Graham's heartfelt "Well, thank you, Mrs Er! You *will* be back tomorrow, won't you? Ten o'clock, as usual?"

Rich, and successful, and sought-after, Milly had sailed down in the lift to the ground floor, and swept like royalty out of the central-heated building and into the sudden, exhilarating cold of a January afternoon, with the white, glittering fog rolling in from the sea.

By the time she had re-lived this triumphant morning in every detail, as she strolled along, Milly had reached the point where she must leave the sea front and turn inland. Actually, this was by no means the quickest way from Mrs Graham's to Milly's lodgings, but somehow she had wanted, in her happiness, to walk along by the side of the sea; to let the sea share it with her, its soft waves rippling in through the mist, just as it had shared with her, thirty-six hours ago, the long night of storm, and darkness, and despair.

CHAPTER IX

WHEN MILLY ARRIVED home—for this was how she already felt about No. 32 Leinster Terrace—she was greeted by a wonderful smell of freshly-baked cakes. Very tentatively—because she didn't yet know what, apart from not having baths after eleven, lodgers were allowed to do or where they were allowed to go—she peered in through the half-open kitchen door. Mrs Mumford, in a torn but colourful print overall, was at that moment up-ending a large round cake-tin over a rack on the scrubbed wooden table. Delicious steam, like incense, rose all around the tin and on either side, intent as acolytes at some holy rite, sat Jacko and Kevin, sniffing the sacred fumes and watching the mystic procedures with reverent adoration.

"I tell you, I'm not touching it till Sunday!" Mrs Mumford was scolding. "It's for Sunday, this cake, d'you think I'm going to be shamed in front of them all by serving a cake for Sunday tea that's been cut into? What d'you think I am? And it's not a scrap of good the two of you looking at me like that, you can keep sitting there till they come and take you away in your coffins, I'm not giving you a single crumb . . .!"

All the while this tirade had been pouring from her lips, Mrs Mumford had been scrabbling about in the table drawer. Now she brought out a long, sharp knife, and, still scolding, she proceeded to cut two generous slices from the big golden-brown cake. Steam surged up from the incisions, and as Mrs Mumford plonked the slices in front of her two devotees, Milly could see the lightness of the texture and the thick scattering of raisins.

"Ah, that's the stuff!"

"Good old Mums!"

Both boys spoke with their grateful mouths already crammed; and Mrs Mumford pursed up her lips in an attempt to hide the smile of pleasure and culinary pride that was threatening to undermine her authority.

"Not a scrap more, not one scrap!" she was beginning threateningly when Jacko at that moment caught sight of Milly hovering outside the door.

"Barney!" he managed to choke out hospitably through his mouthful of cake. "Hi! Barney!" Then, turning back to Mrs Mumford, he cleared a space in his mouth to enunciate more intelligibly: "Hi, Mums, Mrs Barnes is back! Let's have her in to the tea party! Come on in, Barney!"

At this, Milly could hardly do less than put her face round the door and apologise (for what, she was not quite sure, as she had done nothing at all, but it was obvious that an apology was called for). Mrs Mumford meantime contemplated this new arrival with an air of both irritation and relief. "There goes another slice of my cake!" she seemed to be thinking sourly: and also "Thank goodness, another woman, *she'll* understand how put-upon I am!" Accordingly, she set a large slice of cake before Milly, put on the kettle for tea, meanwhile enlarging on the trials and tribulations of being landlady to a pair of idle layabouts who thought that cakes grew on trees, and that three pounds fifty a week entitled them to pester the life out of her all day long, and to eat her out of house and home into the bargain. "See what I mean?" she finished, planting two further slices of cake on to the boys' plates. "Now I'm going to have to make another cake for my son and that minx on Sunday! I can say goodbye to this one, that's for sure!" She gazed with ill-concealed satisfaction at the remnant of her much-appreciated creation, poured Milly a cup of strong, hot tea, and then settled down to telling her visitor about the price of raisins, and how her daughter-in-law had never even written to thank her for the Christmas pudding she'd taken over last year. "Full of best brandy, too!" she grumbled. "It's the last time I'm making the Christmas pudding for *that* lot, and that's a promise . . .!"

Milly, beginning to suspect that this was a promise that had been made, and broken, ever since the son's marriage, answered non-committally, but with all due sympathy. She was beginning to like this snappy little woman and her warm, untidy kitchen: and as for Jacko and Kevin, she felt that she had known them all her life. This was her home. This was where she belonged.

So it was all the more of a shock, when she went up to her room half an hour later, to find a strange suitcase standing just inside her door. It was large, and shabby, tightly strapped, and covered with foreign labels . . . Geneva . . . Beirut . . . Delhi . . . Milly stared at the exotic names in a sort of trance of dismay, while her mind slowly came to grips with the idea that someone else must be moving into her room! Some horrible person with real money instead of a dud cheque-book . . . with real luggage instead of an implausible story about the left-luggage office! The sense of betrayal rose in Milly's throat like sickness. Why had Mrs Mumford said nothing?—Why had she welcomed

Milly into the kitchen to cake and tea, like an old friend, and never a word about this plot to throw her out into the street? Out into the street, right back to the beginning, all her efforts, all her achievements, fallen about her like a house of cards! Had Mrs Mumford heard some rumour about her new lodger—had she guessed something? There had been nothing in the papers this morning, of that Milly had made sure: but what about the evening papers? The evening papers from London? Had there been a photograph? Had Mrs Mumford, seeing the likeness, decided that Better Safe than Sorry, that When in Doubt, Don't— any one of those countless depressing maxims which make life so difficult for anyone trying to get away with anything, and so boring for everyone else? But in that case, why the cake and tea, and the friendly conversation? ... Least Said, Soonest Mended, no doubt ... Milly felt fury boil up inside her, only to curdle slowly into despair. To roam once again homeless through the winter night. ... To fight death off yet again, for what, for what ...? And at this moment a clatter of feet on the stairs announced the arrival of Kevin and Jacko from the kitchen. Were *they* in the plot, too? After all their friendliness this morning, after all that exchange of inmost thoughts, of life-stories true and false, not to mention the Ricicles ... had they, too, connived at her betrayal? She came out on to the landing to confront them: she tried to speak, but something as big as a billiard-ball in her throat seemed to choke her.

"What ho, Barney!" Jacko greeted her gaily: and Kevin, close behind, added: "Have you looked in your room, Mrs Barnes? There's a surprise for you!"

"A surprise ...!" Milly almost gagged on the word ... but now the two young men were upon her, almost dragging her into her room.

"See?" Jacko was swinging the alien suitcase above his head like a trophy: and Kevin added, more soberly: "It was my idea, Mrs Barnes. I got it from a chap I know in

Medical School. Old Mums fell for it like a monkey falling off a log. . . ."

"Yes," interrupted Jacko, "she'd been going on half the morning, you see, about how funny it was that this Mrs Barnes hadn't fetched her luggage yet: and when the Mums starts saying something's funny, then you know it's serious. So we thought it over, Kev and I, and we came up with this idea—"

"*I* came up with it," Kevin interposed. "*You* only—"

"Yes. Well. Anyway." Jacko looked momentarily aggrieved at this interruption to the flow of his narrative: then his native ebullience took over again. "Anyway, like I said, we got this idea of borrowing some luggage for you. Something real classy, to stop the Mums in her tracks! And it so happens that Kev has this classy friend in Medic., so—"

"He's not a friend, I just happen to know him," interrupted Kevin defensively: and Milly understood at once that to admit to upper-class friends would be damaging to his status in the student community. Lads like Kevin and Jacko, busy trying to live-down their glaringly non-working-class backgrounds, had to be careful about this sort of thing.

"He's not a bad guy, though, in some ways." Kevin resumed. "He said it was OK about the suitcase, so long as he could have it back for the summer, and so—"

"We lugged it in as if it weighed a ton."—Jacko took up the story again, swinging the empty suitcase this way and that to emphasise the cleverness of the trick. "We made sure that the Mums heard us coming in, and when she stuck her nose out to see what was going on, we told her we'd fetched your case from the station for you. It was too heavy for you to fetch yourself, we said! Oh, you should have seen us, Barney, humping it up the stairs, gasping and straining at nothing—Look, like this!"

Swinging the empty case to the floor, Jacko reproduced the pantomime for Milly's benefit, bending to the imaginary weight, and panting for breath. "Good, isn't it?"

"As a comic turn, yes," observed Kevin drily. "But as a

serious attempt to kid Mrs Mums that it was a respectable item of luggage belonging to a respectable lady—well, I don't know why you didn't dress up as a clown and sling custard-pies around as well, just to make sure! I was scared every minute she was going to ask us what was in it to make it so heavy—That's all we needed, to have the Mums searching it for bombs, when the whole idea was to lull her suspicions!"

"Oh, gee, it was the best bit of acting outside of the West End for years! It had the Mums eating out of our hands! And was she impressed! Look, Barney! See the labels we've given you!"

Looking closer, Milly saw now that on each of the flamboyant foreign labels, some unknown name had been carefully erased, and "Milly Barnes" had been substituted, in small, neat capitals.

Her two knights-errant seemed so pleased with themselves, and were so obviously waiting for little cries of admiration and gratitude from her, that she hadn't the heart to reveal her qualms about the whole business, or to point out to them that the fictitious story of her life—hard enough to make watertight anyway—was henceforth going to be further complicated by the necessity for fitting into it spells of globe-trotting on this daunting scale. How was a life of devotion to her invalid father in the depths of the country to be reconciled with a giddy round of visits to half the capitals in Europe? Lisbon—Copenhagen—Athens—Madrid ... her eyes scanned the array warily, and she tried to remember how much of the invalid-father stuff she had given Mrs Mumford. ... Or was that the story for Mrs Graham ...? Had she told Mrs Mumford merely that she was a widow ...? From now on, she would keep notes—if necessary in columns, on squared paper—so that she could see at a glance whom she had told what to. System and orderliness were clearly as necessary to a career of deception as to any other calling.

Meanwhile, the two eager young faces were beaming on her expectantly, awaiting suitably fulsome expressions of gratitude and of admiration for their cleverness: and she preferred both, wholeheartedly. The genuine friendship and concern for her that had gone into the prank were heartwarming: as to its wisdom, she kept her doubts to herself. She could only hope that the shrewd-eyed Mrs Mumford was as easily deceived as these two lads seemed to imagine.

After they had gone, all puffed-up and glowing with their good deed for the day, Milly kicked off her shoes, and settled herself on her bed to think. It was cold, but not unbearably so. With the eiderdown over her knees, and her coat clutched about her shoulders, she was comfortable enough, except for her feet, which were aching and tired. She had not noticed her tiredness while she was bustling about at Mrs Graham's, with one eye on Alison and the other on the clock: but she realised now how unaccustomed her body was to hard work. The months that lay behind her had seemed, in the living, to be months of almost intolerable strain; but in point of fact they had been months of rotting; of slow, insidious decay, a slackening of all the fibres, of mind as well as body, under the encroaching shadow of fear.

Shadows . . . shadows . . . a blotting out of daylight, a barricade, thicker than death itself, between herself and the sun . . . this had been Milly's first impression of the basement flat in Lady Street, when she and Gilbert Soames had returned to it after the strained, registry-office wedding, and the nearly silent wedding lunch which had followed for the two of them in the dark, expensive restaurant, both of them sunk in thoughts unmentionable to the other, and scarcely able to eat. Gilbert had paid the huge, futile bill for the uneaten food without the faintest quiver of dismay on his aristocratic face, and had then summoned a taxi and handed Milly into it as though she was a queen. In silence, they had driven back through the tired August streets, heavy with the fag-end of summer, and with the faint, South London haze blurring, ever so slightly, the heat of the afternoon. Milly (already she was thinking of herself, in retrospect, as Milly: her old name had become as remote as a dream)—Milly remembered how she had sat in the corner of the taxi feeling very tidy and compact, and vaguely surprised to find that she was feeling nothing else of any kind. She wasn't even feeling too hot, in spite of her new cream-coloured crimplene suit with its high neck and elbow-length sleeves. So she sat, staring out at the shopping crowds of the Brixton High Road, and at the heavy, muted sunshine, and waited to feel something. For she had not, as yet, given a name to the small, nagging sensation that had awakened somewhere inside her at the moment when she was saying "I will!" She had not recognised it as dismay, still less as horror: and she had, indeed, found it easy to forget about it, after those first few moments. What with the necessity for looking her best and happiest in that photograph that was to go to Julian; and then the difficulty of persuading the photographer to have the prints ready before the weekend—all this gave little time for speculation on such trivial matters as whether her marriage would be a success, and whether the rest of her life, and Gilbert's, was going to be worth living. If only the prints could be ready on Friday, before noon, then there was every chance that Julian would get his copy on Monday. The air-mails were pretty good, usually: letters often crossed the Atlantic faster than they crossed London, that's what everyone said. With luck, the photograph, proof of the wedding, would reach Boston (where Julian—the brightest star in all the glittering brain-drain of that year—had recently landed some kind of high-powered research job)—it would reach Boston first thing on Monday morning. That would be good. Monday morning, going off to work with the shock of it still raw in him, and with no time to go over it all with Cora, the two of them consoling themselves by thinking up catty remarks, and looking for secret strains in the brightness of the pictured smiles.

Yes, Monday morning would be the time. Milly leaned forward in the taxi, bracing herself, using all her willpower, as if that would somehow speed the photographer in his task, and get that thin blue letter airborne, winging its way to Julian almost at the speed of sound.

The taxi drew up half way down the grey length of Lady Street, and Milly felt her husband's—(No! No! how her mind had choked on the word, even in her thoughts!) No, she felt *Gilbert's* bony arm under her elbow, helping her ceremoniously to the pavement. She stood watching while he paid the driver, selected the correct tip, and handed it to the man with that air of authority, of unquestioned rightness, which had first attracted—Well, no, attracted was too strong a word—let us say which had first made Milly feel that it probably wouldn't be too bad being married to him. She liked men to be good with taxis. As she stood there, a sudden memory of Julian being good with taxis hit her like a blow out of the sullen August heat. For a moment she could hardly stand, and so she was glad enough of the steely old arm gliding along under her elbow, helping her across the pavement: helping her past a high iron railing . . . and now it was propelling her down the steep, shadowy area steps. Down, down. . . . She was aware of a chill striking upwards as she left the sultry August heat behind . . . and as she went, the damp, shadowy stone seemed to march gravely upwards, on every side, until at last, here she was, at the bottom of a dank, narrow canyon, out of sight of the sunlight and of the passers-by. The tap-tapping of their unseen feet above her seemed suddenly far off, part of a vanished world.

And now Gilbert, at her side, was fingering through a bunch of heavy great keys. . . . Selecting first the one for the mortice lock. . . . Then for the yale lock . . . then for the special burglar-proof catch . . . until at last the basement door creaked open, and a smell of trapped mildew surged out towards her like water when the lock gates are opened.

Gilbert Soames did not lift his bride across the threshold. He held the peeling old door open for her, courteously, and waited for her to creep through ahead of him into the darkness.

It wasn't quite dark, of course, once your eyes got used to it. Gilbert's flat (Milly's flat too, of course, now, but as yet she wasn't facing that sort of thing) was well below ground-level, but on a bright day such as this a muted grey light managed to seep down and to find its way through the heavy iron bars that protected every window in the flat from burglars. That was Gilbert's explanation, anyway, and at first Milly had thought it plausible enough. In an area like this, he'd said, people living in basements or on the ground floor had to protect themselves as best they could.

But now, looking at the bars from inside, Milly became aware of that strange tremor again, right in the pit of her stomach. Just for one second, she experienced the first, faint quiver of realisation of just what it was that she had done in marrying Gilbert Soames. The knowledge that this place was now actually her home flicked at her mind for a moment, and was gone. Quickly, she thought about Julian, and the way he would off-handedly slit that envelope open on Monday morning, never guessing what was inside.

She became aware that Gilbert had come back into the room. Since their arrival a few minutes ago, he had been padding softly around the flat, almost sniffing at everything, like a cat that wants to make sure that all its familiar corners have been undisturbed. Now he was back in this front room, with its massive ancient, mahogany furniture, and he was looking at her with a curious bright intensity: and it came to her, with a sudden, overwhelming sense of revulsion, that he expected to kiss her.

The intensity of her revulsion took her totally by surprise. Because Gilbert had often kissed her, naturally, in the course of their decorous courtship, and she hadn't minded at all. But that had been different. A kiss, then, had usually been a goodbye kiss, heralding the fact that one more leaden-footed outing was safely over, and that she could now skip upstairs to her solitary flat and think about Julian, and about his and Cora's faces when they heard that she had hooked herself another husband. *Those* kisses had had the same sort of satisfying finality as putting a stamp on a letter—*there*, that's done!—and they hadn't bothered her at all. But now. . . .

"I'll make some tea!" she proposed quickly, and without

waiting for an answer she darted off into the damp, windowless cavern which Gilbert (she had already learned) insisted on calling "the scullery". It served as the kitchen, though, and must have done for years, since it was here that an ancient, grease-caked gas-cooker kept its quiet vigil, undisturbed by the faint, ceaseless footsteps above, tap-tapping their way, unnoticed, out of the nineteenth century and far into the twentieth.

Tea. Afternoon tea. As she searched about for matches, kettle, teapot, Milly turned the phrase around in her mind and found it good. She was here for afternoon tea. For afternoon tea, you arrive at four (just as she was doing), and at half past five you begin to look at your watch and say you think you ought to be going. That's how it would be: she'd been invited to tea by this strange old man, and in a couple of hours she'd be home again, in the peace and solitude of the Kensington flat: maybe ringing up one of her friends to tell her, just for laughs, how she'd been to tea with this weird old man in such a strange, depressing flat, like something out of Dickens, my dear, it really was!

Milly knew quite well, in one part of her mind, that she was playing a game with herself, one of the most dangerous games in the world. She knew, too, that sooner or later the make-believe would come to an end, and the reality of what she had done would come crashing in: and yet, for the moment, she couldn't in any way worry about it.

Detached, even tranquil, in a strange way, Milly part-filled the great iron kettle at the cold tap above the ancient stone sink, and set it on the wavering small flame of the gas-cooker: and as she sat, patiently waiting for it to boil, she suddenly had the oddest feeling, that all this was really, actually happening. To *her*!

For one moment, she was seized by such panic as she had never dreamed or imagined; but instantly she fought it down. She fixed her mind on Julian, and on what he would be thinking next Monday, and on what Cora would be thinking; and very soon reality had shrunk back to its proper size. The size, that is, that would conveniently fit into the small compartment of her mind which was all she had had to spare for it of late.

Now, she looked around at the peeling plaster walls of the windowless kitchen, and at the strange shadows cast by the dim, fifteen-watt bulb, and wondered, for a moment, what it would feel like to realise that she would never cook by daylight again.

To her relief, she found she couldn't realise it. Well, of course she couldn't! All this wasn't happening to *her*. Not *herself*. It couldn't be.

CHAPTER X

H OW LONG HAD she succeeded in thus keeping reality at bay? Stirring restlessly on her narrow bed in Mrs Mumford's First Floor Back, Milly tried to recall the precise moment she had realised exactly what she had let herself in for by marrying Gilbert Soames: the moment when she had first faced, fairly and squarely, the fact that she had tied herself irrevocably to a dreary, ill-tempered old man whom she did not even like, and for whom she felt nothing but a powerful and disconcerting physical revulsion.

There had been no such moment, of course: such cataclysmic moments of self-revelation are rare. What happened to Milly was what happens to most people when they are confronted by mistakes or disasters too big to be borne: they let in the reality of it inch by inch, as it were, a little bit at a time, avoiding at all costs the full, total shock of it. And meanwhile, unnoticed and unallowed for, something in the inmost core of such a person's being is all the time quietly getting used to it. It starts in the body, the very bones and muscles imperceptibly accustoming themselves to the new patterns of movement through the day, the new doorways, the new steps up and down, the new weights and obstacles. Thus, long before she had in any degree resigned herself to her new state, or properly comprehended it, Milly found her hand giving just the right twist to the scullery tap to make it stop dripping: found her feet pausing, without any direction from her, when they came to the broken seventh tread of the dark, evil-smelling stairway down from Mrs Roach's part of the house: found her eyes shutting, of their own accord, just in time to escape the sight of Gilbert sucking the skin from his hot milk, greedily, spinning-out the pleasure of it with smacking lips. By the time full realisation had broken upon her of what she had done to her own life, it all seemed to have been going on for quite a long time.

The evenings had been the worst, in those early days. Strange how those first evenings of her marriage to Gilbert seemed, in retrospect, to have bunched themselves together like frightened sheep, so that they seemed like just one evening, with no beginning and no ending.

Certain episodes stuck out, though, sharp as flints, the horror of them catching at her breath even now, just as it had done at the time: but she could not place them chronologically or set them in any ordered sequence of day succeeding day. Was it the first evening, for instance—or the second?—or maybe later still?—that she had first noticed the earliness of the hour at which Gilbert was accustomed to lock up for the night? She remembered listening to the pad-pad of his ancient gym shoes as he roamed from room to room, locking the doors, drawing the hinged wooden shutters across the windows, fastening the great bolts: and only after he had finished, and had settled down in his big leather chair, with the green-shaded reading-lamp casting a strange cat-glitter into the gloom of the great room—only then did it dawn on Milly, with a sickening stab of sheer horror, that outside the sun was still shining; that toddlers with bare legs and sunsuits clutched their mothers' hands as they wove their way homewards, with prams and shopping, through the heat of the late afternoon.

That was one memory. Was it that same evening, or a later one, when she had found herself in the scullery, rinsing the two teacups meticulously under the cold tap, and setting them upside down on the old wooden draining-board, spongy with the wetness of years? And then the two saucers . . . the two plates . . . And then just standing there, wondering how on earth to make the task take longer, so that she would not have to go back, just yet, to the room where Gilbert was waiting for her in the greenish lamplight, leaning back in his great leather chair, stroking the tips of his long mottled fingers together gently while he waited.

Waited for what? It was many weeks before Milly began to guess at the answer—or, indeed, to realise that there was any particular need to pose the question. These first even-ings, all she was clearly aware of was an intense need to procrastinate: to put off, by any means, the moment when she must join him: when she must push open the heavy door and make her way across the big, shadowy room, aware of his eyes on her continuously as she edged her way between the vast mahogany side-board and the dusty great mahogany table, piled high with bundles of yellowing news-papers, each carefully tied round with string.

"Finished in the scullery, my dear?" he would say politely, as she settled herself in the sagging cretonne-covered armchair that stood across the empty hearth from his leather one. "Yes," would reply Milly, or perhaps "Yes, it's all done": and this, somehow, signalled the end of the little tableau. Gilbert would at last take his eyes off her, and almost with an air of relief would pick up his newspaper and disappear behind it, sometimes for two hours or more.

He didn't like Milly to read, though. If he should look up from his paper and notice that she had a book or a magazine in her lap, he would frown, and mutter, and finally make a great show of folding up his own paper; and then he would sit there, silently, waiting for her to say something.

Had conversation always been as difficult as this? Sitting there tongue-tied in the sombre great room that Gilbert called the dining-room, Milly had racked her brains trying to remember what they used to talk about before they were married? Those Tuesdays and Fridays when they had gone off to a tea shop together after the Industrial Archaeology class—what on earth had they found to say to each other? She could remember that the afternoons had been dullish, and that she had usually been relieved rather than sorry when it was time to go home—but it hadn't been as bad as *this*. Surely not—it couldn't have been. Had they talked about the class, then, and their fellow-students, and the snippets of homework they were sometimes set? Now and again, she remembered, the conversation had become quite interesting, and Gilbert had revealed little bits about his past life: about the house he had been forced to sell at a loss when he went abroad: about the brother he hadn't spoken to for forty years because of some sort of quarrel about their father's estate. Nothing very exciting, but still, it had made conversation of a sort. But now, when Milly tried, in desperation, to revive these topics, throwing bright little questions into the oppressive silence of the great room, something killed them even as they left her lips. They fell, heavy as stones, into the gloom, and the silence surged back, sometimes with a strange hostility in it, as if she had interrupted something.

Around nine o'clock—or sometimes even earlier—Gilbert would lower his paper slowly and rub his eyes with his bony knuckles, prolonging the gesture until Milly's own eyes felt bruised and she had to look away. Then he would unfold his stiff length from the old chair and stand upright.

"I think I'll be turning in now," he would say, and they would exchange a dutiful goodnight kiss, and he would go padding off, around and around the flat, in and out of the rooms, until at last his bedroom door clicked shut with an air of finality, and Milly would let her breath go in a long, shuddering sigh.

As the days went by, her dread lest more than the goodnight kiss would sooner or later be required of her, begun gradually to lessen. He was an old man, after all. But, disconcertingly, her distaste for even the kiss seemed to grow greater, not less, as time went by. The curious feeling of his moustache against her cheek, like a damp nailbrush: the touch of his flabby skin ... sometimes it was all she could do not to jerk her head away, or raise her hands in front of her face, as if warding off a blow.

And then, nearly a week after the wedding, there had come an evening which Milly would never forget or forgive—though who was the one to be forgiven, she would never know.

It was an evening just like the ones that had gone before, with Milly sitting in her now familiar chair at the side of the fireless grate, watching the faint twitchings of Gilbert's outspread newspaper, and listening to his heavy breathing behind it. She had not dared to pick up her own book, for fear of provoking him to lay down his newspaper and wait for her to embark on one of those awful attempts at conversation; and as she sat thus, totally without occupation, it slowly dawned on her that this was Monday. It was the evening of the day when Julian and Cora should have received the wedding photograph: and she had forgotten it!

Forgotten it! The moment of supreme triumph, for which she had casually bartered her life, her happiness, and her self-respect, was over. It had come, and it had gone, and it was finished; and she hadn't even noticed it! All that remained now of that flamboyant gesture of defiance was the price of it: the life-long price which she had contracted, so off-handedly, to pay.

CHAPTER XI

"BARNEY! I SAY, Barney— Oh, I'm sorry! Are you asleep, or something?"

Jacko had switched the light on: now, in deference to Milly's supposed state of slumber, he disconcertingly snapped it off again.

"There's a visitor for you!" he whispered considerately through the darkness. "Shall I say you're asleep?"

By now, Jacko's highly idiosyncratic technique for not waking people had brought Milly bolt upright on the bed, her heart pounding. Like anyone roused suddenly in unfamiliar surroundings, she was taking a few moments to collect her wits and remember where she was: but in her case, there was the additional problem of having to remember *who* she was, as well.

Milly Barnes! That's who! The relief that flooded through her was succeeded by puzzlement. What was the time? Had she been sleeping, or merely deep in reverie? The winter afternoon had still been bright through the window when she had settled on to the bed: now, it was quite dark.

"Put the light on, Jacko, do!" she urged; and then, as he obeyed, she focused her mind on what he had been saying. "A visitor? What sort of a visitor?"

"I say! You look as if the police were after you!" Jacko remarked sympathetically, as the sharp yellow light revealed Milly sitting poised on the very edge of the bed, her outdoor coat clutched round her as if in readiness for flight. Her eyes were still blinking from the alternations of light and dark: under Jacko's scrutiny, she tried to shake the dazed look from her face, and pushed her hair into place as best she could.

"What sort of a visitor?" she repeated, uneasiness stirring in her as full consciousness returned. "A man or a woman?"

Why it mattered so much, she could not think. Either way, it could mean that she had been tracked down by someone out of her past. But the fact remains that as soon as she heard that the visitor was female, she felt the fear draining out of her limbs, leaving them firm and springy, ready for anything.

"I'll come down," she said; and full of curiosity, now, rather than alarm, she set off down the stairs.

The visitor, a rather untidy-looking woman of about forty, in raincoat and trousers, had been left standing in the hall while Jacko came in search of Milly. When she saw Milly coming down the stairs towards her, she looked quite frightened.

"Yes?" said Milly: and then, when the woman still didn't speak, she went on: "Did you want to see me? I'm Mrs Barnes. Milly Barnes."

At this, the stranger looked more frightened still, and for one awful moment Milly wondered if she had made some awful mistake . . . had said the wrong name? had revealed, in some inexplicable way, her true identity? For the first time it dawned on her (in her urgent concern for her own safety, this aspect of her situation had hitherto escaped her) that if people knew who she really was, they would be *frightened*.

"You wanted to see me?" she repeated, warily; and now at last the woman spoke, her face twitching with sheer nerves.

"Yes, that's right. Mrs Barnes. It *is* Mrs Barnes, isn't it? Yes. You see. That is. I hope you don't mind my coming round like this?"

Milly hoped so too, fervently. It depended so much on who the woman was, why she had come.

"No, not at all," she said guardedly: and then listened, with growing puzzlement, while her visitor circled round and round the reason for her presence, never quite daring to pounce.

"I'd like you to be quite, quite honest with me," she was saying. "I shall quite understand. I mean, I wouldn't like. That is, I do realise what a very great deal . . . And how it is nowadays, I mean for everyone, isn't it?" Here she looked wildly round the little hall as if for moral support. "I hate to ask you, really," she plunged on: "And of course I know you haven't. . . . That is, your time must be. . . . Well, we all are,

78

aren't we? And of course. I mean, I do realise that it's very short notice. It's not giving you a lot of time, and I'd never have suggested it, only. But I shall quite understand, Mrs Barnes. I should never have asked you, really. But you see, my other woman...."

At the mention of this familiar character, all Milly's bewilderment cleared.

"When do you want me to come?" she asked; and straightaway all became plain. It seemed that Mrs Lane (for such was the trousered woman's name) belonged on the same grapevine as the Mrs Day who was a friend of whoever it was who had spied Milly going to work at Mrs Graham's this morning: she had, Mrs Lane said, heard from "everybody" that Milly was a wonderful worker, reliable, and very quick: and after a little more flattery it became clear that Mrs Lane was wondering—she was just *wondering*—if all that speed, reliability, and wonderfulness could be hers for forty pence an hour?

How many hours? Why, as many as Milly could condescend to spare....

So that was another two afternoons a week, starting tomorrow! Milly went upstairs her mind awhirl with multiples of forty pence and thoughts of what they would buy after the three pounds rent had been subtracted. Why, by the end of tomorrow afternoon, with Mrs Graham's one pound forty as well, she would be able to pay the week's rent *and* put a shilling in the gas-meter! *And* buy fish and chips ...!

"Kevin!" she called, as she reached the top of the stairs. "Jacko! Guess what's happened!"

They were as delighted for her as she had known they would be; and after a brief and jubilant consultation, it was decided that if she would contribute a shilling for the gas fire, and find some matches somewhere, then they, Jacko and Kevin, would go out and buy pork pies and a tin of Nescafé to celebrate. In Milly's room, because it was smaller than theirs, and so a shilling's-worth of heat would go further.

It was the nicest celebration Milly had attended for years; and ended with her helping Jacko and Kevin to write their long-overdue essays on Agrarian Reform in the second half of the Nineteenth Century. She didn't know anything about Agrarian Reform, but then Kevin and Jacko didn't either, and of the three of them, she proved to be the most adept at re-wording passages from the textbook so that they wouldn't show up as bare-faced copying. Also, she could spell.

She thought idly about taking an economics degree herself; but would it bring in thirty-five pence an hour as *reliably* as her present avocation? And would a single half-day's work at it make you famous overnight, as *her* morning's work seemed to have done? Would people come round begging you, almost with tears in their eyes, to accept lectureships, the way they came begging for *her*?

No. On second thoughts, Milly decided against it; and instead, she studied Kevin's street-map to find the quickest way from Mrs Graham's flat to Mrs Lane's home on Castle Hill. It seemed that if she left Mrs Graham's promptly at two, and took the short cut through the arcade, and then down under the railway arch into the Old Town. . . ."Fifteen minutes," predicted Kevin, "No, I've done it in seven," boasted Jacko, "all the way from the bus depot to the top of the Old High Street. . . ." While they bickered, and the last of the shilling's-worth of gas gulped and died in the hearth, Milly worked out the mileage for herself. Twenty minutes, allowing for getting slightly lost on the way.

Actually, she got more than slightly lost: and as she had not managed to leave Mrs Graham's till ten past two, she was nearly fifteen minutes late, and very out of breath, by the time she lifted the blackened brass door-knocker of The Cedars, Castle Hill. The Old High Street had been steep and winding, and Castle Hill came off it nearly at the top—much further up than it had looked on the map. Milly was very conscious of her flushed face and untidy hair, as well as of her lateness; and she prepared to launch into abject apologies the moment the door should open.

"Call me Phyllis!" was Mrs Lane's immediate greeting; and before Milly could get out a word, she had added fervently *"Please* do!" She was wearing the same trousers as yesterday, topped now by a heavy knitted jersey with a much-stretched polo-neck, and almost worn through at the elbows. Brushing aside Milly's flow of apologies with deprecating little chirrups, she led the way through a cold, lofty hall into a back room which felt even colder, in spite of a small, guttering paraffin heater in the corner.

"Just till we get the coal fires going," Mrs Lane apologised vaguely, gesturing towards this appliance: and then, looking around her with an air of defeat, she continued: "I don't know where to ask you to start, Mrs Barnes. I really don't. It's got out of hand, it really has. Oh dear!"

Milly tried to think of some way of disagreeing, for politeness' sake, but the words dried on her lips. The room looked as if nothing had been cleared away or dusted for months. Books and papers loomed top-heavy on every visible surface, and, interlaced among them, stood mugs of congealed tea, lengths of balsa wood, a dismantled tape-recorder, and empty bottles of gin. Over all lay a sort of top-dressing of crumpled garments: shirts, torn vests, ancient corduroy trousers—all waiting to be washed? Ironed? Mended? By Milly?

"This is my husband's study," said Phyllis. "His den," she amended hopefully, as if that might make some sort of difference. "You know what men are!" she added, with a sidelong glance to see how Milly was taking it. "Do you think?" she proceeded; "I mean, the thing is. Well, it's Eric, you see. My husband. What I want is, Mrs Barnes, if you could try and clean it up a bit? You know—just get it all nice and tidy, but you'll be careful not to touch anything, won't you? Eric just goes mad if anything gets touched."

These instructions made Milly a little thoughtful. Still, forty pence an hour! Besides, this poor woman, with threads of wool dangling from her jersey, seemed so distraught, and was already gazing yearningly at Milly as if she was grateful to her for even *looking* at the room.

"You couldn't start straight away, could you?" Phyllis was saying. "Or would you rather have some coffee?"

The alternatives were a little disconcerting, thus presented: but after her long walk up the hill, as well as the four hours' work that had preceded it, Milly found the courage to settle for the coffee. Besides, she wanted time to think out the task ahead of her, and to learn more about her employer. Already she had sized-up Mrs Lane (or Phyllis, as she must remember to call her) as one of those employers who have at the back of their minds an imaginary dream-home: one which has no relation to the one they are actually living in, but which they believe—and continue to believe—will one day suddenly materialise if they only go on faithfully paying someone forty pence an hour. like sacrificing enough sheep at the temple of Athene. With an employer of this type, a Daily Help's first task is to get as clear a picture of this imaginary dream-home as she possibly can, so that she can then make all her efforts tend in this direction, or at least appear to do so.

So over coffee, Milly reconnoitred the situation. She discovered that Phyllis Lane saw herself as the presiding genius of a warm, welcoming home, where the atmosphere was easy-going and casual. A home where husband and teenage sons were positively encouraged in their messy hobbies, and were never nagged. In her mind's eye, Phyllis saw a blazing log fire in that icy hall; she saw an ever-open front door, and a larder bursting with food, so that friends could drop in and find a welcome at any hour of the day or night. All this, it seemed, had been on the verge of realisation for the last eighteen years: and if only Phyllis could manage not to run out of sugar, and to be in when the coal-man called; and if only it wasn't so difficult parking the car, so that she could shop in bulk. . . . And if only Eric would understand how difficult it all was. . . .

Her faith that all this would change now that Milly was here, was terrifying: and when, in something like panic, Milly pressed for details of her duties, all she could extract from her new employer was that she, Phyllis, felt that a house should be a home, and so would Milly make sure, when she did the boys' rooms, not to shift the spare parts of the bicycle Martin had taken to pieces last summer? He had them carefully arranged on the carpet, and so would Milly hoover in between them, being careful of nuts as she went? And if she *wouldn't* mind putting clean sheets on Michael's bed?—they should have been done ages ago, really, but she, Phyllis, hadn't been able to do it herself, because Michael kept his collection of Bright-O packet-tops on his bed, they were all arranged in sequence, and when he had a hundred of them he was going to send off for an airgun: so would Milly be specially careful not to disarrange them? And the Origami cut-outs they'd had such a craze for over Christmas, they were on the bed too. Oh, and above all, when Milly vacuumed, would she be very careful about the electric train set that was laid out all over the floor? Michael hadn't played with it since he was eleven, but he was still very particular about people not interfering with it. Milly *did* understand, didn't she? Apparently My Other Woman hadn't grasped the point at all.

"It'll be nice having the boys' rooms looking really nice again!" Phyllis concluded wistfully. "It gets beyond me, sometimes, it really does. Boys are so.... After they've stopped being children, I mean."

She smiled, and sighed, and closed her tired eyes for a moment. Behind those drooping lids lay visions of colourful teenage rooms in the Sunday colour-supplements, with Scandinavian wood window-seats, and bright cushions, and one or two brand-new pop records lying carefully-casual on the plain white wood table. My Other Woman had failed to effect the transformation, it was true; but surely this Mrs Barnes would bring it off? After all, she was getting five pence an hour more than My Other Woman.

With a good many qualms, Milly set to work. But first there was the usual problem about dusters, and cleaning rags. Like ninety-nine per cent of other employers, Phyllis Lane proffered, with pathetic eagerness to please, bits of torn nylon, and lumps of abandoned knitting. She listened sadly, like a dispirited child, to Milly's explanation of why they would not do.

"But I've got *drawers* full of them: can't you use them for *anything*?" she pleaded, when Milly turned down the third remnant of tattered quick-knit cardigan, with the buttons still on: and at last, in sorrow and bewilderment, she succumbed to Milly's by now ruthless demand for something like a piece of old towel. Under further pressure, she unearthed a plastic bucket without a handle, and a cannister of spray-on polish that wouldn't spray. Silently, Milly promised herself that she would use her very first bit of surplus earnings to buy herself dusters, rags, and proper tins of polish: she would go round equipped with the tools of her trade, like a piano-tuner, or any other specialist.

Mrs Lane had asked her to start in Mr Lane's study, the room she had first been shown: and for a minute Milly stood looking at it, and felt the panic growing in her. But she defied it. Out of her experience, she whispered to herself: "Do *something*. Do just one thing. Then your heart will stop beating like this, and you will see your way."

While she was still standing like this, waiting for the courage to put her own excellent advice into practice, Phyllis put her untidy head round the door.

"Oh, that's *much* better. Oh you *are* getting on!" she lied desperately: and seeing her employer's panic, Milly almost forgot about her own.

"I'm just getting down to it," replied Milly, soothingly: and even as she spoke, she felt welling up in her the strength to start. Already she had caught sight of the One Thing that could be done.

The dirty mugs and cups. Let them be her salvation. Dregs of tea. Dregs of coffee. Some fresh, some almost mildewed. Milly collected them all up and carried them out to the kitchen—and by the time she came back, she knew that her faith in the One Thing had once again been vindicated. She could see, now, exactly how to tackle the room.

First, the scattered garments. Nothing like clothes for making a room look sordid. She had not forgotten that the absent Mr Lane was due to go mad if she touched anything, but she was using her own discretion as to what a man—particularly a husband—would think of as a *thing*. Certainly not clothes in need of ironing. Nor a hunk of beige knitting in a paper bag. Nor half a wizened grapefruit in a pie-dish. Milly also surmised that the unknown Mr Lane might be prepared to overlook the disappearance of the glum little collection of objects awaiting his manly attention: the broken electric iron: the Teasmaid that didn't make tea any more: the dust-caked Do-It-Yourself china-mending outfit, complete with several cardboard boxes containing all the crockery that had been broken in the Lane household during the last eleven years. She set herself, bit by bit, to remove all the things which, in her experience, a man is happier without. Soon, some surfaces appeared, which could be wiped or dusted. She only wished that her employer wouldn't keep popping her head round the door and telling her how marvellous it looked. It didn't, yet, and by the time it did there would be nothing left to say.

By half past three, Milly was facing a new problem—one that, foolishly, she hadn't foreseen. She was tired. Not pleasantly, satisfyingly tired, as one might be after a long walk, but tired with an aching, urgent intensity that was like nothing she had ever experienced before. Of course, she should have realised that her middle-aged, out-of-condition body would at some point rebel: that aching in her legs last night, after just Mrs Graham's, should have been a warning. What a fool she had been! Gaily, and without a thought for anything but the extra money, she had taken on afternoon jobs for every day of the week, and had never for one moment pondered on whether she would be physically able to do them!

Typical!—she scolded herself. Typical! This is how I've been all my life: this has been at the root of every trouble I've ever had. Why don't I ever learn?

Learn what? That she must be careful in future to take account of her own limitations? Or that anyone can do anything if they once put themselves into a situation where they've *got* to? There is never only one lesson.

And so it came about that, since Milly had *got* to go on working for another two hours, she *did* go on working. She finished the study, and even started on the boys' rooms. She found that her legs would carry her here and there whether they thought they could or not; that her back would bend, and bend again, long after she thought it had reached the limit of its endurance.

And after about an hour, a strange thing began to happen. At half past four, or thereabouts, she became aware, with a dawning, incredulous wonder, that she was becoming unmistakably *less* tired, not more, as she went on working! Psychosomatic? Second wind? Some sort of physiological adaptation to stress? For the second time in her new-born existence, Milly whispered a prayer of gratitude to her own body, with its extraordinary, untapped powers. Once more it had been put to the test, and it had not failed: she and it, in partnership, had beaten tiredness at its own game, and they need never fear it again. For the next half hour Milly worked on, as painlessly as in a dream, her limbs moving in some rhythm which seemed to come from quite outside herself. Only a faint buzzing in her ears, and a certain slowness of thought, still reminded her how near she had been to collapse from exhaustion.

"Would you like some tea?" came Phyllis' voice from downstairs. "Or would you rather finish the boys' rooms first?"

Milly was finding these double-barrelled invitations a little disconcerting: but since the tea was already made, and the two cups and saucers set ready on the kitchen table, she could only suppose that she was meant to accept.

"Tea? Oh, yes, please, I'd love it," she said: and straightaway Phyllis went into paroxysms of apology.

No lump sugar, only granulated. Oh dear. Did Milly mind?

And, Oh dear, there was no cake in the tin. No cake at all, things had been a bit. . . . But there was plenty of Wonderloaf. And jam. And peanut butter. And marmalade. And smoked salmon. . . . While Phyllis scrabbled thus haphazardly in her store-cupboard, throwing suggestions over her shoulder with the abandon of someone trying to lighten a sinking balloon, Milly listened greedily. She would like them all, actually. Except the peanut butter. . . . And the jam turned out to have mould on top. Still, marmalade, and smoked salmon, and four slices of Wonderloaf, were not at all bad for a high tea. Milly felt her strength returning, and would readily have resumed her task in the boys' rooms, but Phyllis wouldn't let her.

"It's half past five—well, just on," Phyllis insisted, though in fact it was not yet twenty past. "I don't want you to overstay your time, Mrs Barnes, you've worked very hard. Yes. You'll come again on Monday, won't you . . . ?"

All the while she was speaking, Phyllis was steering Milly out of the kitchen . . . urging her into her coat . . . pressing money into her hand. "Thank you" she kept saying, over and over again, "Thank you so much. . . ." It was as if it was she, and not Milly, who was on the run from something. . . . Why, you'd think, from her frantic glances at the clock as she hurried Milly towards the front door, that the police were expected at any moment. . . . And just then, as if on cue, there came a knock on the front door.

Phyllis had gone quite white. She looked wildly round, as if for a way of escape. Then, pulling herself together, she stepped forward and opened the door.

No policemen. Just a harmless-looking woman in a fur coat and stylish boots. A flurry of greetings, in the course of which Milly found herself being hastily introduced as "A friend of mine, Milly Barnes, I'm afraid she's just going. . . ." And so, to avert deeper confusion and embarrassment all round, Milly snatched up her bag and went.

At the time, Milly found the episode puzzling, even slightly alarming—did Phyllis feel there was something suspicious about her new daily, which should be hidden from her friends? It was only when she came to know the Lanes better, and had learned just how rich they were, that she understood Phyllis' embarrassment. Like so many rich people these days, Phyllis Lane hated to admit that she could afford anything, least of all a daily help. She liked to think of herself as one of those joyous, infinitely capable mother-figures, who bake bread, whitewash ceilings, and collect driftwood for the fires, as well as running the home single-handed, with happy-go-lucky efficiency.

Not that any of this ever happened—she couldn't even get the coalman to call, and the supermarket only ever sold Wonderloaf. But one day—quite soon, if only this, that and the other wouldn't keep going wrong—one day, her vision was going to come true: and meantime, naturally, she didn't want to be caught red-handed paying the daily help. And caught, too, by one of the most penniless of all her New Poor acquaintances (witness the fur coat and the fashionable boots). If, in that moment of confusion and embarrassment, she had had any time for philosophising, she might have reflected, as she contemplated her fashionably-dressed visitor, that Poverty, these days, is every bit as difficult to ape as Riches used to be.

CHAPTER XII

B Y T H E E N D of the second week, Milly's life had fallen into a pattern which she already felt had been going on for ever. The day started with Kevin's and Jacko's arrival in her room for their morning tea; and always, as part of the ritual, there was the fuss about the gas. The boys seemed to take a pride in never having a shilling for the gas—it made them feel like genuine poor students, and subtly removed the stigma of wealth from the Hi Fi set, and the piles of LP's, and the cine-camera that Jacko's father had given him for Christmas.

And since the non-possession of a shilling seemed to mean so much to them, Milly went along with it, and listened obligingly each morning to the small fuss about it, followed by the small injustice of her always being the one to produce the shilling. Thirty-five pence a week—only an hour's work, when all was said and done. Rarely has so comfortable a friendship been bought so cheaply.

Then, at nine thirty, under the attentive gaze of Mrs Mumford (who always managed to be flicking a duster around the hall at just this hour) she set off for work.

"Well, goodbye, Mrs Mumford," she would say, as she unbolted the front door: and, "Ta ta," Mrs Mumford would reply if she was in a good mood, and, "*Good*bye, Mrs Barnes," if she was not. Either way, she always added, "Back at the usual time, then?"

How lovely, already to have a usual time to be back at!

"*Yes!*"—Milly would cry jubilantly: and then, off into the icy winter morning.

She loved this morning walk to Mrs Graham's: she loved the cold, salty air on her face, and the sensation in her limbs of not being tired yet. This was now a positive, joyous sensation such as she had never before experienced: but then she had never experienced, either, the leaden, desperate tiredness that regularly assailed her in the middle of her working afternoons. Since taking up manual work, she seemed to be living in a new dimension of physical awareness: every muscle in her body seemed to have come alive, to be alert to the stresses and joys of movement; and she was conscious, as never before, of *herself* in charge. It was she, and she alone, who could give the order—"Move! " to an exhausted limb—and it would move.

But at this time, in the bright morning time, nothing of this sort was necessary. Her rested body would swing along through the low mist, or maybe the gleams of struggling sunshine, like the body of a dancer. That's how it felt, anyway; and if it looked more like the body of a middle-aged woman in a head-scarf plodding off to work, what cared Milly? The more unremarkable she looked, the better she was pleased. Then no one would bother to notice the way she always stopped for a few moments at the newsagent on the corner, glancing along the headlines, turning a page here, giving a quick look at the back of a copy there, as if trying to decide which of them all to buy ... and then moving on, with a new bounce in her step, a new assurance in the set of her shoulders, without having bought any of them at all.

And as the days passed, and the headline Milly was dreading never appeared, the morning ritual became gradually more and more perfunctory until, by the fourth week, her assurance had become so great that she hardly bothered to look at the papers at all. Now, she pranced past the newsagent with only the most cursory glance. Yes, they were still on about the London bus strike—as if anyone cared—where *was* London, anyway? She felt remote from it all, and marvellous, and at last totally secure. Nearly a month now, and still nothing about her at all! She must have got away with it—though how, she could not imagine.

And it was then that the first signs began to appear that all was not quite as she hoped.

The day had started just like any other day. She set off for Mrs Graham's in as carefree a mood as ever, with no weightier problem on her mind than the question whether Mrs Graham would, or would not, be going to the library this morning. It was Mrs Graham's habit, once or twice a week, to spend a morning at the University library looking up the current sociological journals, leaving Alison in Milly's care. On these occasions, she evinced so much maternal anxiety, and gave Milly so many instructions, that anyone would have thought that Milly didn't always look after Alison anyway. Because by now it was part of the routine of Milly's mornings that at eleven-fifteen, just as Milly and Mrs Graham were settling down with their coffee, Alison would start crying: and Mrs Graham would frown, and set her cup down, and stare at Milly in a dazed sort of way.

"But she *never* wakes up till lunch time!" she would exclaim, incredulously. "She *always* sleeps through! Look, Mrs

Er, would you mind, just this once . . .?"—and Milly, just as on all the other mornings, would reluctantly gulp down the rest of her coffee, go and get Alison out of her cot, change her, and thereafter endure her unrelieved company for the rest of the morning, while trying to get the work done.

The only difference about the library mornings was that the drama began earlier. At half past ten, or thereabouts, Mrs Graham would start scuttling softly about the flat, glancing at the clock, stuffing papers secretively into her briefcase, speaking to Milly in whispers . . . for all the world as if she was plotting an escape from the Tower. What she was really plotting, of course (as Milly soon realised), was to make her getaway from the flat *before* Alison began crying. She liked to be safely out of the front door and calling over her shoulder. . . . "And Alison will sleep till lunch-time. . . ." *before* the first wails rent the air.

All the same, Milly preferred the library mornings, on the whole. For one thing, it meant that she could plan her coffee-break to suit herself—if necessary leaving Alison to scream for five minutes while she reclined in luxury, sipping coffee that she had made exactly as she wanted it, with exactly the right amount of sugar. For another—and this was the big thing—it meant that she didn't have to use any of the labour-saving equipment in the kitchen at all, and could get on with the work as fast as she liked. On the mornings that Mrs Graham was at home there was always the risk that she would grow bored with the correlations, and come wandering in to say: "But Mrs Er, why aren't you using the . . .?"—dragging from its hiding-place yet another bulky, grease-caked contraption for making a simple task complicated. And by the time that had happened, there was never any going back. In general, and for most of the time, Mrs Graham was as vague and abstracted an employer as one could hope to find, drifting through her housewifely duties with her degree in Sociology clinging about her like a mist, blurring her awareness of any but the most glaring deficiencies on Milly's part. But once she had a labour-saving appliance in her hands she was like a gangster with a gun, nothing could turn her from her purpose. On such occasions she would quite forget how busy she was, and how nobody ever gave her any peace, and would ungrudgingly devote half a morning to following Milly about making sure that she used the Dust-Rite instead of a duster: and while the dust puffed leisurely this way and that around the rooms, and the correlations languished un-cared-for in the typewriter, Mrs Graham would deliver long lectures to Milly about the principle of suction, and how the furniture wasn't *really* clean unless you'd used the Dust-Rite. Nor really dirty unless you hadn't—this last provoked by Milly's incautious demonstration of how much less dusty the table looked after she had done it with an ordinary duster.

So the game, as Milly saw it, was to get the dusting finished before Mrs Graham got around to noticing what she was doing: to get the potatoes peeled with the nice little sharp knife before Mrs Graham came and unearthed the potato-peeler: to wrap the resultant peelings in newspaper and rush them out to the dustbin before Mrs Graham wandered in and caught her not using the waste-disposal unit. She had caught Milly thus on her second morning: and snatching the newspaper-full of peelings just as Milly was about to put it in the dustbin, she had tossed the whole lot triumphantly into the sink.

"There, Mrs Er!" she had exclaimed. "No need to bother with the dustbin! It all just goes down the sink! See?"—and at the flick of a switch an awful whirring noise filled the room. The potato peelings stirred faintly, as if in their sleep, and then settled down again.

"Sometimes it needs both taps on!" Mrs Graham screamed into Milly's ear, above the racket: and they both leaned over the sink and watched the water cascading down among the potato peelings. They were moving around nicely now, and Mrs Graham and Milly leaned over further still. The suspense was awful.

"Look, look!" Mrs Graham cried excitedly. "See? There's one going down! But you have to work them towards the outlet, Mrs Er, don't you see? . . . Isn't there a stick, or something?"

An old mop handle was pressed into service; and after that a wooden spoon; and gradually, with coaxing and prodding from both women, the mound of potato peelings began to diminish. Presently there were only a very few, very obstinate ones left, and Mrs Graham's exultation knew no bounds.

"See?" she screamed, at the top of her voice, in order to be heard above the uproar: "See that, Mrs Er?"—as she spoke, she switched off the machine, so that the final syllable gouged into the sudden silence like a pneumatic drill—"See? They're almost all gone! No need to bother with dustbins in *my* flat, Mrs Er! *Everything* goes down the waste-disposal!'"

But not dead matches. Or milk-bottle tops. Or paper bags. Or chicken-bones. And so each day, when she arrived, Milly's first duty was to extract these and similar items from the horrible mush that Mrs Graham always had waiting for her in the sink. With the sort of unquestioning faith that an Early Christian might have envied, Mrs Graham hurled everything, including rancid fat, into the precincts of her waste-disposal unit, and then waited, in total trust, for the magic to begin.

Which it did, of course, punctually every morning when Milly arrived. Since there was no way of scooping it out at this stage in the process, Milly usually spent the first twenty minutes of her working day poking and prodding at it with assorted implements, with taps and machinery all on at full blast.

Mrs Graham loved it. Often she would leave her typewriter and come and watch, screeching advice and encouragement like a supporter of Manchester United; and the longer it all went on, the better she was pleased. She seemed to feel that having the thing on for twenty minutes was somehow twenty times as labour-saving as having it on for only one.

And so, what with one thing and another, Milly was distinctly relieved to find on this particular morning, that it was to be a library morning. Mrs Graham was on the tele-phone telling someone all about it when Milly arrived (she had her own key to the flat now, as she had to the homes of all her employers: lucky, really, that her crimes had been what they were, and did not include burglary). As she came into the flat, she heard Mrs Graham's voice, loud and clear, from the sitting-room:

"I shan't be back till one," she was saying. "But my woman will be here. She'll let you in, and then you can pick up the lot. And the yellow wool as well, if you like, I don't ever wear it. No, really: it's only cluttering up the wardrobe. As a matter of fact, I'd thought of giving the whole lot to my woman, but you know what they are these days. I daren't risk offending her!"

How do you make a noise like not being offended? Outside the door, Milly was wringing her hands. A yellow wool dress, and who knew what else besides, all going to waste to someone down a telephone! She thought forlornly about the endless drip-drying of her only garments in front of the coin-devouring monster of a gas-fire: she thought of Mrs Mumford's ever more speculative eyes watching her as she set off to work in the same outfit every morning: any day now, she would be prowling round Milly's room, drawing her own conclusions from the empty drawers, and from the locked, feather-light suitcase with its absurd labels.

But what could Milly do? Rush into the room crying "No offence! No offence!"? Or simply "*I* want them!", like a spoilt toddler? Or how about: "My *other* lady *always* used to give me her old dresses"? When you came to think of it, there was no reason why "My Other Lady" should not be built up into just as powerful a folk-image as "My Other Woman".

But while Milly was still debating her unusual social dilemma, the "ping" of the phone told her that her chance was over: and now here was Mrs Graham out in the hall, and telling Milly all about this Mrs Innes, and how she would arrive at midday, and must be persuaded, somehow, to take the lot.

"She's getting fat, that's the trouble," Mrs Graham

confided. "It's compensatory eating, I keep telling her, but she won't do anything about it, and now she's going to start complaining, saying everything's too small. . . ."

By this time, they had reached the bedroom, and Milly's shoulders under her thin blouse fairly shivered with longing when she saw the pile of woollen garments on the bed. Wool dresses . . . cardigans . . . all near enough the right size!

"Get her to take them *all*, won't you, Mrs Er?" her employer was urging. "Don't let her pick them about . . . she'll have this . . . she won't have that . . . all that sort of nonsense! Oh dear, it's so difficult getting rid of things these days, isn't it, Mrs Er?"

Since this was not really a problem for Milly, now or in the foreseeable future, she made no answer. Besides, her mind was already full of scheming . . . If only this Mrs Innes could have grown as fat as fat, and fussy with it!

"If you *really* can't get rid of them—" she opened the subject cautiously, improvising as she went along. "I mean, if you want just to *give* them away, then I wonder if the Bring-and-Buy sale at our Church—they have one every," (here she did a quick calculation)"—every third Saturday in the month, and I've been asked—"

But Mrs Graham had clinched the deal before Milly could round-off the lie properly. "I wish I'd known!" she exclaimed, with just the faintest edge of reproach in her voice. "Then I'd never have bothered about this Innes woman at all. It only ends in having her stay to lunch, or something: you know what these people with troubles *are*. Look, Mrs Er, this Baptists' Fête of yours, do you think they'd be interested in a few books as well . . .?" Her voice blurred abruptly as she swung open a cupboard door and dived into the dusty interior.

"There's several volumes of the 1910 Children's Encyclopaedia, that might interest them," she called hopefully over her shoulder: "And a complete set of—I can't read the name, the backs are a bit torn, but anyway, a complete set of Somebody's Meditation and Reflections, in twelve volumes. Oh, and my old sewing-machine, I've got one that works now, so perhaps this other one might come in useful to somebody...."

The semicircle of floor around Mrs Graham's crouching form was filling up fast; but she continued her explorations with undiminished zest.

"Do they ski at all?" she continued, plunging deeper into the recesses. "There's Arnold's old skis somewhere at the back, he does hoard things so. Ah, here they are! And his army uniform, too, I'd forgotten about that. And what about the portrait of his mother, in oils? I could never stand having it on the walls, so if they'd like it ...?"

She straightened up, pushing the hair back from her forehead, and surveying the chaos around her with a satisfied air.

"There you are, Mrs Er! you can take all those! Oh, and while you're about it, the old carpet-sweeper—"

At last, Milly interrupted.

"But—but I can't carry all that!" she protested: and at this Mrs Graham looked up, and stared at her in a sort of vague surprise, looking her up and down as if this was the first time she had really got around to counting how many arms Milly had.

"Oh," she said: and thought for a moment, painfully, picking away at the bit of her brain, long-disused, which concerned itself with other people's affairs.

"Yes, well," she said at last, reluctantly. "Well, perhaps you could bring something round to put them in, could you, Mrs Er? I've been trying to get this cupboard clear for ages. Oh, and Mrs Er, are these Mission people at all interested in fossils? Arnold has...."

Mercifully, at this point the first tentative protests began to sound from Alison's room. Straightaway Mrs Graham abandoned her discourse, and went into paroxysms of deafness: racing from room to room, head down, as if in a high wind, shovelling papers pell-mell into her briefcase ... flinging on coat and scarf....

"And Alison will sleep till lunch-time," she shrieked, in the nick of time: and managed to get the front door closed before the first real yell of fury resounded through the flats.

Alison loved the old sewing-machine. She spent the whole of the two hours till lunch time contentedly wrecking it, screw by screw, and Milly was able to get on with her work in unprecedented peace and quiet.

By quarter to one, everything was clean, and the lunch was ready in the oven: and—to crown Milly's satisfaction—the unknown Mrs Innes with her unknown troubles hadn't turned up at all: and so Milly had gleefully parcelled up all those woollies for herself. They were already waiting, neat and inconspicuous, behind the kitchen door.

Now, with Mrs Graham's return imminent, she stuffed the sewing-machine back into the cupboard with the rest of the things, silencing Alison's screeches on the subject by a judicious mixture of savagery and blandishments. Then she washed the child's black and oily face and hands, put her into a clean frock, and forced her (by dint of monstrous subterfuge and sleight of hand) to sit and play with a nice clean toy till Mummy returned.

Disconcertingly, it was Daddy who returned first. He looked for a moment utterly panic-stricken when he realised that his wife wasn't back, and that he was therefore going to have to make conversation with the Daily Help. Then, summoning up all his resources as a gentleman and a scholar, he plunged recklessly into speech.

"Good morning!" he said: and fingered his folded newspaper longingly. Was that enough, he seemed to be wondering, or did one have to say something else before one could decently sit down and read?

"Nice day," he ventured, plunging yet further into the uncharted territory of conversation with Daily Helps. "A bit cold, that is. Looks like snow."

"It does," agreed Milly modestly, wondering whether she ought to call him "sir"? Or was it going to be possible always to frame her sentences in such a way that she never had to call him anything?

"Yes. Hm. Yes, indeed. Look, Mrs—" Professor Graham stopped unhappily, and Milly realised suddenly that her problem about what to call him was as nothing to *his* problem about what to call *her*. Unlike his wife, he seemed to be miserably aware that her name couldn't really be Mrs Er, not possibly.

"Look, Mrs—" he began again, and this time Milly came to his rescue.

"Barnes," she prompted cheerfully. "Milly Barnes."

"Barnes. Ah, of course . . . Mrs Barnes. . . . So stupid, do forgive me. Look, Mrs Barnes, did my wife—did Mrs Graham say when she'd be back?"

One o'clock. You'll be off the hook at one o'clock, Milly almost told him; but changed it, hastily, to "Mrs Graham told me she hoped to be back by one. Would you like to wait, or shall I . . .?"

"Oh no! No thank you! Oh, no, no!"—Professor Graham's horror at the possibility of having to talk to Milly all through his lunch stuck out through his natural mildness like a snapped twig—"No, no! That's all right. Don't put yourself to any trouble. I'll just . . ."—and under cover of such politenesses he succeeded in getting himself into the chair by the window, safely hidden behind the protective expanse of *The Times Business News*.

Silly, really, to let it affect her. There was no real resemblance at all. Just a man's legs, topped by an outspread copy of *The Times*—framed, this time, by an expanse of winter sky, swept white by the sea-wind, and empty of clouds. How could such a sweep of pure, unsullied distance bring back to her, as if it was right here and now, a choking sense of claustrophobia . . . of encroaching darkness . . .?

The back page of the paper quivered, just as Gilbert used to make it quiver, in the moment before he softly lowered it, and peered over the top to see, with those strange, silvery eyes of his, what his wife was doing. And now the paper lurched, as it used to lurch in the greenish lamplight . . . it swung to the left . . . to the right . . . it swooped downwards, and once again eyes, questioning eyes, were fastened upon her. . . .

"Did you want something, Mrs Barnes?"

Professor Graham's pleasant, puzzled voice jerked Milly into an awareness of how oddly she was behaving . . . standing here staring, like a hypnotised rabbit, with no snake anywhere.

"No—no, it's quite all right," she stammered, and fled into the kitchen. Once there, she leaned against the sink for a minute, trying to steady her racing heart, to control her gasping breath. One of these days, she scolded herself, I shall be giving myself away! How many times, in these last weeks, have I let myself get into a panic over nothing? First that man in the café, and the headline in his paper about . . . FOUND IN FLAT. And then that first morning at Mrs Mumford's, with Jacko—as it turned out to be—bumbling around her room in the dark. And after that the telephone call at Mrs Graham's. . . . Oh, the occasions were too many to count: and each time, it had been sheer luck that no one had happened to notice her state of shock and inexplicable terror. One day, if she didn't control these reactions, she would find she had given herself away, utterly and irrevocably. When would her body learn not to flood her system with adrenalin at every tiny surprise? When would her brain learn that these trivial little incidents, these chance reminders, were fortuitous, not aimed at her at all?

Aimed at her! How ironic that it should be *she*, now, who should find herself constantly interpreting the bright, preoccupied world in terms of her own fears! Would there not be a strange, twisted justice about it if, in the end, it should be just such an attack of irrational, deluded panic that brought her to her own doom? How Gilbert would have laughed, that strange, silent laugh of his, like a small clockwork motor jerking away somewhere inside him.

It was just as if he was still there, waiting for her, in the black, bottomless past; waiting, in the quiet certainty that, in the end, she would lose her footing in the bright, precarious present, and come slithering back: back into the darkness, into Gilbert's own special darkness, which at first had seemed to be merely the darkness of a gloomy London basement, and had only later been revealed as the black, irreversible darkness of his own disintegrating mind.

For many weeks after her marriage, Milly had refused to recognise the special quality of the darkness: she had tried to fight it off with new fabrics, and higher-watt bulbs. By the time she had nerved herself to go to the doctor about her husband, it was too late.

Perhaps it had always been too late. After waiting all that dark November morning in the overcrowded surgery, among the humped, coughing people, Milly had in the end seen the exhausted young doctor, eyes red-rimmed from lack of sleep, for barely two minutes. He hadn't said much, he was too weary and dispirited: and what he did say wasn't really a lot of use. For by the time she had got around to consulting him, Milly already knew as much about delusional paranoia as any doctor. She knew more or less everything there was to know about it, except how to face it: and that no doctor could tell her.

CHAPTER XIII

HE HADN'T BEEN as bad as that at the beginning. Well, of course he hadn't, or Milly would never have married him. And yet, even then, even in the days of the decorous, best-behaviour outings to tea-shops, there had been signs—tiny, warning flashes—which might have put a more astute woman on her guard. No, not a more astute one, necessarily; simply one who was more *interested* in Gilbert, as a person: one who was contemplating marrying him for himself, and not merely as a stick with which to prod her former husband into some sort of reaction.

Yes, the warnings had been there, all right; and Milly, in the throes of her plans for impressing Julian, had not given a thought to any of them. There was Gilbert's life-story, for a start: swindled out of his inheritance, estranged from his only brother, bullied by his wife, deprived of his rightful pension—what sort of a man is it who has *all* these things happen to him, unrelieved by any spark of generosity from *anyone*? And then there was the matter of his friends—his lack of them, that is to say. It was this, actually—this strange, dignified solitariness—that had attracted Milly's attention to him in the first place. Long before she knew who he was, or anything at all about him, she had noticed the way he always arrived at the Industrial Archaeology class alone: tall and silent, looking neither to left nor right, he would make his way to the furthermost desk of the back row; and throughout the session he would focus an almost disconcerting intensity of attention on the teacher: fixing his light grey eyes—so light as to be almost silvery, Milly had already noticed, before she knew so much as his name—fixing them on the teacher with unblinking concentration, broken only by the occasional need to copy a diagram off the blackboard, or the correct spelling of some little-known technical term. Since Milly herself was bored to death by the classes (her motive in enrolling had been the despairing one advocated in so many advice columns—"to meet people") she thus found herself with plenty of time, in between doodling and daydreaming, to watch this mysterious, white-haired man, and idly to wonder about him. He seemed so alert, and attentive, and purposeful: and yet he never spoke—neither at question-time in the class, nor afterwards, when the rest of the students were gathering in twos and threes, chatting, comparing unfinished homework, waiting for one another to come out for a cup of tea, or to catch the same bus home. Instead of joining in any of this, the inscrutable Mr Soames (this much Milly had learned by now, from the class register) would silently gather up his notes and edge his way out of the classroom, without a word to anyone.

Milly had been intrigued: and, since she had come to the class with the sole purpose of meeting unattached men, she determined (since nothing better offered) to cultivate the acquaintance of this one; and so, for three classes in succession, she made a point of greeting him boldly, with a smile, as he came into the room. He had seemed startled—almost affronted—the first time: the second, he acknowledged her greeting with a politely embarrassed murmur: and on the third, he had actually paused to say "Good afternoon", before retreating to the far corner of the room.

So far, so good. Slow-ish: but then, if the whole of the rest of your life is to spare, then where is the advantage of speed?

It was not until the next Class Outing that she really got a chance to speak to him. Twice a term, or thereabouts, on freezing winter Saturday afternoons, the whole group would go off in a coach to look at some blackish bit of brickwork at the edge of a canal, or something; and Milly would stand, bored to death and freezing cold, with her hands in her coat pockets, and sustained only by the thought that she was *out*. She was *doing* something: no sharp-eyed mutual friend would now have the chance of reporting-back to Julian that his poor ex-wife spent all her weekends moping about the flat, alone. It was as she stood thus, one February afternoon, that the silent Mr Soames had approached her, and, after some minutes' hesitation, had asked her, in a voice stiff with unease but still smooth and cultivated, if she wouldn't like a cup of tea? And she, filled with a mixture of triumph at the success of her campaign, and boredom at the prospect of carrying it any further, had followed him into a waterside café. They had sat opposite one another at the slopped, plastic-topped table, and sipped the strong, tepid tea; and he had let out for her—hesitantly, as through a rusty gate—little bits of information about his troubles.

Troubles, even the dullest, are always mildly interesting at the first hearing; and Milly had been mildly interested. He wasn't too bad, he was better than nothing; and so, from then on, she had allowed the tepid relationship to take its course without any special effort on her part, either to foster it or to bring it to an end. Until, suddenly—it would have been about the middle of June—she realised that under cover of her inattention, the thing had been surreptitiously growing: she realised, with a little shock, that if she chose she could now give Gilbert that last little push that would get him asking her to be Mrs Soames!

Mrs Soames...! Dear Julian, I am now Mrs Soames.... From then on, it had all been as irreversible as falling down a precipice.

Including the bump at the bottom. The utter, stunning shock ... followed by the slow awakening ... the painful flexing of limbs to see what has been broken, what merely bruised and sprained; and finally the dazed survey of the strange, utterly new landscape ... the rocks, the boulders, with here and there the possibility of a path, to somewhere or nowhere, as the case might be.

It must have been two or three weeks after her marriage to Gilbert that Milly began thus to pick herself up after the shock, and to take stock of her situation. She began by facing the enormity of her own folly in marrying him at all: and then, when that quickly proved futile, she began looking for ways to escape.

There were none. None, that is, which would not involve Julian and Cora learning, with gleeful pity, of the failure of her new marriage.

"Poor thing, isn't it pathetic?" Cora would say, tasting the words on her palate, like rare wine: and "The unwanted wife syndrome," Julian would comment, with a shrug. He loved to put things in categories.

No. Escape was out of the question. What was left, then, was endurance. What she had brought upon herself, she must live with. Live, and make something of it.

Make something of it? Milly remembered how she had looked around the underground dungeon that Gilbert called the dining-room: she looked at the mountainous mahogany furniture looming out of the grey light that she must henceforth think of as daylight; and for a moment she had covered her eyes. Make something of it? She must be mad!

Yet Milly was not without a certain dogged courage even then—even in those days, when she had not been Milly at all, and her body had not yet undergone the experience of being tested to the uttermost limit, and not found wanting. Yes, even in those days she had had inside her something almost as useful as courage—a defiant uncrushable pride. The sort of pride that can be used—as a mallet can be used if you haven't got a hammer—as a useful substitute for courage.

And so Milly had uncovered her eyes, and looked again into the lowering shadows which, down here, was all you had of noonday.

"*I'll show you!*" she said out loud, into the gloomy great room, her voice sounding reedy and thin in the oppressive silence. "I'll show you! You won't defeat *me*! Just you wait . . . !"

And straightaway there came into her head a scheme of such boldness, of such devil-may-care bravado, that she caught her breath.

Cushions! For this black cavern of a room she would make bright cushions, scarlet, flame, and emerald! She would scatter them here and there on the black horsehair sofa, and in the shabby great chairs! And flowers, too—dahlias, asters—all the reds and golds and purples of late summer, massed in the centre of that gloomy great table! She would defy the great deathly room, she would hurl colour into its shadows, fling glory into the very face of its darkness: with her own hands, dripping brilliance, she would bring it to its knees!

For a moment, her spirit wavered. Surely there must be some ordinary, practical reason why she couldn't do anything of the kind?

But there wasn't. Gilbert was out today, on one of his mysterious errands "to see a man" about something (the days were as yet far off when Gilbert would no longer go out anywhere, but would stay at home, behind closed shutters, watching her) and he had left her plenty of money for the household shopping. He wasn't mean—one must allow him that, at any rate—and as she stuffed the wad of pound notes into her bag and bustled about getting ready to go shopping for the cushion material and the flowers, Milly found herself indulging in the pious exercise which she had been practising ever more frequently of late—that of listing Gilbert's good qualities to herself in the faint hope that, if only she could make the list long enough, it might somehow add up to *liking* him.

Liberal with money. Undemanding. Unfailingly courteous, even when she had angered him. Affectionate—yes, she must allow him that—it was not *his* fault, after all, if her flesh shrank back at the merest brush of his hand in passing. Helpful about the house, too—sometimes taking over the entire cooking of an evening meal, closeting himself in the scullery for long, mysterious hours, at the end of which he would bring out strange, sour-smelling curries in covered dishes or bitter, spicy vegetable stews. And afterwards, all through the meal, he would watch her face, alert for some tiny grimace, some small, involuntary twist of her mouth, to belie her over-enthusiastic words of praise.

He was helpful, too, about the washing-up—if only she had appreciated that kind of help. It was her fault, not his, if irritation rose into her throat like heartburn as he padded softly about behind her, in and out of the scullery, putting things away, muttering to himself, sometimes, as he did so. Not much, as yet: the muttering seemed, in these early stages, like a mere mannerism, albeit an irritating one.

What else? As she made her way up the area steps, shopping basket in hand, into the unbelievable sunshine, Milly tried to add to the list.

Kind? Well, not *un*kind, anyway. He had awkward moods sometimes; occasional fits of explosive irritability about nothing; and strange, unpredictable spells of sulking—but in general he was quite nice to Milly, in his stiff, inhibited way. Considerate, too; opening doors for her, carrying trays, inquiring after her comfort. And as to sex, his demands were absolutely nil—whether by his own choice or because he had sensed her distaste, Milly did not know, and the last thing she wanted was to find out. Mercifully, he belonged to a generation which does not expect to talk about these things, and Milly could only feel grateful for the repression—neurosis—whatever it was—which made it possible for them to go to their separate rooms each night without ever having to engage in one single word of discussion about it.

As she hurried through the golden September sunshine towards the main road, Milly added up these qualities for the twentieth time, struggling to make the answer come out different for once. She made herself visualise Gilbert's pleasure and surprise when he saw the new cushions . . . and then—who knew?—the sight of his pleasure might make *her* feel pleased? For a few moments, they would be pleased in unison . . . and perhaps this would be the beginning of some vague sort of friendliness between them? Or something?

The new cushions gleamed out of the darkness like jewels in the deep earth; crimson, scarlet, gold and peacock blue: and the flowers on the great mahogany table seemed to be reflected in a deep pool of colour. She had polished the table as it hadn't been polished in years, stacking the old bundles of newspaper all up at one end as she worked: and now the old wood shone darkly beneath the blaze of reds and purples, picking up the colours, and throwing them back with a strange, coppery sheen, as though they were on fire.

Gilbert stood in the doorway, not speaking, staring in what seemed to be a sort of trance. He stood there so long, and with such a complete absence of reaction, that Milly began to feel quite scared. In the quietness, she began to hear her own heart beating. Was he struck dumb with surprise? Shocked, in some way, by the sudden loss of familiar ugliness? Or was he pleased—so pleased as to be at a loss for words? He seemed to be looking with particular intensity at the table, in its unaccustomed glory.

At last he spoke.

"Why have you been disturbing my papers!" he barked out, in a voice Milly had never heard him use before. "What were you looking for?"

For a moment, Milly was so taken aback that she couldn't speak. Then: "I wasn't looking for anything, Gilbert! Truly I wasn't!" (Why so defensive, though, like a schoolgirl accused of cheating?) "All I was doing. . . . That is . . ." (Again this idiotic inflexion of guilt.) "All I was doing was clearing the table. . . . To make it look nice, Gilbert, for the flowers! I've polished it, don't you see? Don't you think it looks nice, Gilbert? Now it's polished? With the flowers . . .?"

Not even for one second did his glance flicker towards the flowers, to see if they looked nice. The light, shining, silvery eyes remained fixed on Milly. They were so bright, one might have imagined they were lit up by mercury lighting from within.

"You didn't find anything, then? You didn't untie any of the bundles?"—his voice was still high and strange— "Remember, my dear, it will be best if you tell me the truth!"

"But—but Gilbert, there isn't anything to tell! *Of course* I didn't untie the bundles—why should I?—They're only old newspapers . . . !"

Her voice stumbled into silence. Under the strange intensity of his gaze she found herself fidgeting, hanging her head. "I—I'm sorry, Gilbert!" she finished, absurdly humble.

Whether it was because of this humbleness, or whether he had somehow satisfied himself that she was speaking the truth, Gilbert began to relax.

"Very well, my dear," he said stiffly. "I shall have to accept your assurances. But please remember, for the future, that I don't like *anyone* to interfere with my papers. Not anyone at all. Do you understand?"

For the next hour or so, he occupied himself in sorting the bundles, and restoring them to their original places on the table.

He would not let Milly help him, and so she sat, idle and

ill-at-ease, while he groaned and fumbled through his self-imposed task, peering closely at each dog-eared package, and muttering: sometimes testing the string, to see if it had become rotten over the years: arranging and rearranging, and sighing heavily to himself, until at last he seemed satisfied. He straightened up, and turned to look at Milly.

"There," he said. "Everything is back in its proper place now, and so that is the end of the matter. We will say no more about it."

He paused, and as Milly watched, a curious look of cunning came over his face, narrowing and sharpening his features until she was reminded of a weasel.

"I've arranged them in a very special way," he said, watching her closely, "so that I'll know immediately if you touch them again."

"But—But of course I wouldn't dream . . . !" Milly was beginning indignantly; but Gilbert raised his hand in a small gesture which somehow reduced her to instant silence.

"I said, we will say no more about it," he repeated, with a strange edge to his voice: and the argument was at an end.

It seemed a long time till bedtime. Gilbert made no further reference to the disturbing of his papers, and as to the flowers and the new cushions, he said absolutely nothing at all. The cushion that was in his arm chair—a brilliant scarlet one—he lifted out carefully, and without comment, and set it on the floor, as if it was a cat that had usurped the best seat; and then he settled down, as usual, behind the newspaper.

Milly, sitting opposite, seethed silently with anger and bewilderment; but since she dared not speak, much less argue, her feelings had nothing to feed on, and so gradually, as the evening ticked by, they withered to a small knot of resentment and incomprehension.

Oh, well. Gilbert was in one of his funny moods. He often got crabby and unreasonable in the evening. Evenings were his worst time.

Or that's what she thought at the time, anyway. She did not know yet, of course, what the nights were going to be like, a little later on.

CHAPTER XIV

WITH AN EFFORT, Milly roused herself. It was quarter past one now, and Mrs Graham still wasn't back. Milly was going to be late for her next job. By the time Mrs Graham had come in, and by the time she had finished reproaching Professor Graham for whatever it was he was doing wrong there behind the newspaper. . . .

"*Arnold!*"

Mrs Graham's voice and the slam of the flat door came almost simultaneously:

"Arnold! Why on earth haven't you started lunch? Whatever are you waiting for?"

A swirl of briskness and frosty air flicked for a moment at Milly's domain in the kitchen, and then moved on. Mrs Graham might be reckless in some ways, but not so reckless that she would risk annoying the Daily Help when there was a perfectly good husband available.

"It's such a waste of *time!*" she rounded on him again. "There's no need to wait for me, I've told you a million times! You could practically have finished your lunch by now, and given yourself a bit of time to relax before you have to rush back!"

"I *am* relaxing," the professor pointed out, placidly. "At least, I was till you came in, my love. And I never have to rush back, as you know very well, dearest. I always leave myself plenty of time."

He had lowered his newspaper as he spoke, and was blinking at his wife over the top of it with a sort of innocent wonder. Or was he annoying her on purpose?

It was hard to tell, for by now Mrs Graham was launched

on a saga of grievance so fluent that nothing he could say, annoying or otherwise, could deflect it even for a moment from its (obviously) well-worn channels:

"If we had a *car*—" she was saying—and from her tone of voice Milly knew that she must have been saying it for years—"If you'd only get a car, Arnold, we wouldn't *have* all this trouble! It would cut your travelling time by an hour a day, at least...."

"But I *like* my hour's travelling time," the professor explained, maddeningly. "It gives me time to collect my thoughts. It's peaceful."

"*Peaceful!*" The word seemed to have touched the very core of Mrs Graham's annoyance. She flung her coat and scarf on to a peg and came right into the room. "Peaceful! And how peaceful do you think *I* find it, slogging about in all weathers? Do you realise that I had to wait *forty minutes* for the bus this morning? Forty minutes, on that icy corner by the library gardens?"

"You must have just missed the twelve twenty-five, then," observed her husband, consulting his watch interestedly. "If you miss the twelve twenty-five there's nothing till after one. I find that myself, when I'm coming from the library."

Whoever it was who first suggested turning swords into ploughshares must have had a shrewd idea of how devastating, in skilled hands, the weapons of sweetness and light can be.

"Oh—you!" cried Mrs Graham, fast losing control of the situation. "I've never known anyone so ...! Ah, thank you, Mrs Er, we're just ready ...!"

The complete change in her voice and manner, from fishwife to lady of the house, almost made Milly drop the joint, from sheer admiration. What acting! And what made it even more of a tour-de-force was that Mrs Graham surely knew—and knew that Milly knew that she knew—that Milly had heard every word of the dispute across the four feet of space dividing the kitchen from the dining-room.

Pure atavism, of course: a race-memory of the days when servants weren't quite real, and so it didn't matter what they heard. And more appropriate—had Mrs Graham but known it—than anyone could have guessed, because Milly, of course, *wasn't* quite real. Not her name, nor her way of life, not anything about her. She was a construct: a figment of her own imagination: a splinter off the final, shattering explosion of her former self, shot out into space, and now somehow taken root, like a dragon's tooth, in Mrs Graham's kitchen. . . .

". . . And did you chop up Alison's lettuce and mix it in as I showed you, Mrs Er?"

Mrs Graham's rather school-mistressy tone, and the exaggerated concern with which she peered into her daughter's plate, annoyed Milly for a moment. Had she not been chopping Alison's lettuce for a long time now, and never a word of complaint from either the carpet or the plastic seat of the high chair? For a moment, intoxicated by that consciousness of power which is part and parcel of being a Daily Help, she toyed with the idea of Taking Offence: of watching them grovel and squirm, pumping out flattery and blandishments on an absurd scale, in a desperate effort to placate her.

But, *noblesse oblige*. Like other ruling classes before them, the Daily Helps of today must learn to wield their power decorously, and to resist its heady corruptions.

Besides, by now Milly realised that the fuss about the lettuce wasn't really about the lettuce at all, nor was it really addressed to her. Mrs Graham was simply trying to re-establish her own image of herself after the quarrel. Outmatched by her husband, she was going to show herself in control at least of a lettuce leaf.

Lunch was necessarily a rather subdued affair after all this. Mrs Graham took over the carving, as she always did when she wanted to show her husband how late it was, and how there was no time to have *him* fumbling about at the job; and while the knife flashed this message across the table in a morse-code of lightning strokes, and slices fell from the leg of lamb like grass before the blades of a mower, conversation would have seemed discourteous: a boorish interruption of this fine flow of communication. Even Alison messed her dinner about more quietly than usual, refraining from saying "Da!", with crafts-man's satisfaction, as each handful landed on the floor. And as to Professor Graham, he showed no signs of being aware of anything at all. With the loose-leaf notebook of his afternoon's lecture propped in front of him, he accepted with apparent contentment whatever food was set before him, and ate it with good appetite. The only sign he made of being aware that anyone else existed was in the way he clutched absently at his plate and glass every time Milly passed behind his chair on her errands to and from the kitchen: a legacy, this, of years of eating in university canteens, where zealous clearing-up women, like seagulls on the Embankment, snatch food from under the very knife and fork of the unwary. Milly wondered if he would ever learn that she, at least, was not as zealous as all that? Or were the long-term effects of Higher Education irreversible?

It was nearly three o'clock by the time Milly got to Mrs Day's that afternoon: but it didn't really matter, because Mrs Day was never in. Milly had, in fact, never met her, and apart from that initial telephone call, and later on a message about where to find the key, she had never spoken to her. Thus she didn't know her at all—or rather, the only Mrs Day she knew was the one she had gradually constructed, clue by clue, from the trail of evidence left around the flat.

A typewriter, with always the same dusty page jutting from the roller:

This may seem, on the face of it, a rather extreme position to adopt, or at least to savour of the disingenuous; but it must be borne in mind that congruence rather than equi-valence should be our aim.

Yes, indeed! Good, safe stuff, congruence! Milly used to wonder about it sometimes, when, at her lowest ebb of afternoon tiredness, she reached this point in the dusting: and to wonder, too, if it wouldn't be rather fun to go on with it—say to half way down the page—and see if her employer noticed? Why, the poor woman might even be grateful; it was obviously something waiting to be finished.

What, though? A highbrow novel—with a publisher's deadline being missed while the crucial pages sat thus immobilised in the typewriter? Or an article for some specialist journal on almost any subject whatsoever with the Editor ringing up, more and more irate, as press day drew near? Or could it even be a love-letter—there *were* couples, Milly knew, who in the heat of passion wrote this sort of thing to each other endlessly, in the interests of analysing their relationship to shreds. She imagined the poor man sitting alone in his attic/boarding-house/loveless mansion, rushing for the post each morning, his soul afire with longing for polysyllables that never came.

When she was at her very tiredest, Milly would toy idly with ways of continuing the passage that would fit all of these three possibilities. As she slumped over the dusting, taking the weight off her feet as best she could, appropriate sentences seemed to flow through her exhausted brain with extraordinary fluency:

But of course, as far as this is concerned, there are two ways of looking at the matter, neither of them entirely atypical, and neither (at least from the point of view of the onlooker) either more or less convincing than any other possible approach. For it must not be forgotten that the factors previously cited may well be only marginally relevant to the particular point at issue. In saying this, one is, of course, discounting the more obvious considerations: it is a matter, really, of the concepts applied, and the level of coherence aimed at . . .

Why, one could go on like this for ever! Milly was amazed that the clever Mrs Day should be finding any difficulty with it. She must be either a very busy sort of woman, or a very muddled one. Muddled, probably: a truly busy woman either finishes this sort of thing, or she refrains from starting.

Or perhaps the incomplete masterpiece wasn't hers at all? Perhaps she had a highbrow lover who had brought his typewriter to his assignations just once too often, and had thus found himself out on his ear, minus the end of his paragraph?

Yes, this seemed the most likely. It was more in keeping, too, with the Mrs Day revealed by the rest of the flat.

Her bedroom, for instance, strewn with fringed ponchos and psychedelic cat-suits. Four kinds of eye-shadow and a blonde hair-piece belied the learned pretensions of the typewriter: while flimsy shoes, kicked here and there as though the wearer had shed them triumphantly the moment she entered the flat, suggested that her feet were killing her more often than not—sure sign of an exciting social life. No one has ever been able to get far in the glamour stakes unless her feet are hurting.

What did *Mr* Day think of it all? So far, Milly had found no conclusive evidence of his existence, unless you counted the cigarette ash all over the place, and the permanent presence of a man's overcoat on a peg in the hall. Though this, of course, could just as easily have been left behind by the congruence man, when he leapt up from his typing and fled before the onslaught of Mrs Day's scarlet, inch-long nails.

If there *was* a Mr Day, then he must be a very tidy man, Milly decided, as day by day she tidied the all-feminine clutter from Mrs Day's bedroom floor. The bed, too, though a double one, had a decidedly feminine look, with its pink nylon sheets and matching frilled pillow cases; not to mention the pink panda night-dress case, with its simpering Walt Disney eyelashes and the zip coyly camouflaged along the length of its stomach. No doubt such a creature passed muster with the occasional lover—occasional lovers put up with almost anything, knowing that tomorrow they will be safe back in their own beds with their indigestion tablets to hand. No doubt such a one would easily bring himself to smile benignly on the awful panda, and to agree that it was cute. "You must *pander* to it, darling!" Mrs Day perhaps giggled, each time, as she shimmered out of her cat-suit . . . and each new lover in turn would be enchanted by such wit. But a *husband*? To have this sort of thing year in and year out ... it would be an odd sort of man who would put up with it.

Well, and perhaps Mrs Day's husband *was* an odd sort of man? Perhaps it was he who had fixed up that great mirror opposite the foot of the bed, in which you could see yourself as you lay propped against the pillows (Milly had tried, and so she knew). The Days could sit and watch themselves drinking morning tea, if they liked. They could see not only their partner's ugly, contorted face during a quarrel, but their own as well. Lovely.

Sometimes, as she enlivened her solitary afternoons with this sort of thing, Milly felt it was rather sad that poor Mrs Day couldn't do that same sort of thing about *her*. But there were no clues that way round: no data on which to work. Just a clean flat in place of a dirty one, and, on Fridays, the removal of the envelope with two pounds forty it. Even the most fanciful employer couldn't build much of a picture of her Daily Help out of that.

Just as well, actually. Every now and then Milly went quite hot and cold wondering what would happen if her unknown employer *did* walk in suddenly, and see what she was doing.

Not that she was doing any harm: nor, in the long run, was she skimping her work at all. She always did the two hours' work for which she was paid. It was the way she set about it—the way one *does* set about things when entirely alone and unobserved—that would have caused the raised eyebrows.

For the first thing Milly did, when she arrived tired, straight from Mrs Graham's, was to choose the most inviting of Mrs Day's new library books, and settle herself on the sofa with it. Mrs Day must belong to a very good library: the latest shiny best-sellers always seemed to be lying on her window-ledge almost as soon as they were published. Sex, cancer, the end of life on earth—all the most popular topics were laid out for Milly's delectation week by week: and having made her choice, Milly would lie and read greedily, for twenty minutes or more, gobbling the pages with the uncritical gusto that comes from book-starvation. Access to books had been difficult for her of late.

And so there she lay, often till past three o'clock, in Byzantine luxury: central heating, absolute peace and quiet, and—if she cared to look out at it—a wonderful view through the picture window, right across the tiled roofs of the old town, to vistas of wintry sky and grey, tumbled sea. It was a lovely bit of the day, and Milly looked forward to it all morning. And later, as she bustled about the flat, she would often find herself stopping . . . to read a picture postcard that had arrived . . . to try on a pair of Mrs Day's gold sandals . . . to examine the framed photograph of a handsome young man who might be Mr Day and then again he might not . . . or to sit on the edge of the unmade bed reading an article in the *New Statesman*. . . . This is what is called self-discipline, greatly lauded nowadays in contrast to discipline of the more old-fashioned kind. Its only disadvantage, for Milly, was that it made her two hours' work at Mrs Day's take at least four hours, which was very tiring, and got her home too late to put her feet up before going out for fish and chips with Jacko and Kevin.

The first thing Milly noticed, when she arrived on this particular Thursday, was that *Education for Death* was still there. She recognised it from right across the room, sleek and successful-looking, with its shiny red lettering and the crude silhouette, in vivid black, of a child with round white eyes, and round white buttons all down his front, and his hair sticking up all over his head—presumably with horror at the education he was receiving.

Milly noted its presence with relief (Mrs Day had a maddening habit of returning her books to the library just as Milly was getting properly into them), but before she settled down to it, she took a quick look round the flat to assess the nature of her afternoon's tasks. It was different every time. Sometimes the bedroom was a shambles, and the sitting-room virtually unused: sometimes the other way round. Sometimes the kitchen was so cluttered with dirty crockery that you could hardly move, at others the washing up had been done, but there were beer bottles all over the bathroom. You never knew. And what made it more complicated was that Mrs Day sometimes made hasty, last-minute efforts to make the place look a bit better—shoving dirty glasses behind the window-curtains, kicking crumpled paper handkerchiefs under the bed, or tossing a clean newspaper lightly over the place where the cat had been sick.

None of this helped at all, of course, but Milly presumed that her employer meant well. Anyway, it wasn't too bad this time. A saucepan had been burnt and not left to soak: and whichever character it was who threw his cigarette-ends into the electric fire as if it had been an open grate, had been visiting again: but otherwise everything was much as usual. There was one of Mrs Day's scribbled notes, though, propped up for Milly's attention against the flour-bin:

If Mr Plzpwrdge rings up, it read. *Please tell him to skrr the dgllrwn and not to rwrwll prrrn beivoose until I let him know.*

Thank you. A. L. Day

Milly sighed. Mrs Day was always leaving notes like this, and Milly often wondered what happened about them.

Please wash the strt grr thoroughly had been the first one, followed, the very next Tuesday, by *Please be careful not to rdvool the qumqmvruin gra pllooll without removing the plug.*

Milly had done her best. She had washed thoroughly everything that looked in the least like a *strt grr*; and as to the *qumqmvruin gra pllooll,* she had played for safety, and avoided anything that had a plug on it at all, for fear of *rdvooling* it.

So far, the method seemed to have worked all right. Anyway, she had not as yet found any fierce notes pointing out that the *strt grr* was still *filthy.* Thus it was with a fairly tranquil mind that she tossed this latest specimen into the waste-paper basket (if and when this Mr *Plzpwrdge did* phone, he would presumably know himself what he was talking about), and settled herself happily on the sofa to read.

CHAPTER XV

BOTHER MR *Plzpwrdge*! The telephone was already shrilling through the flat before Milly had read so much as a page of her chosen volume. Why couldn't the wretched man have rung later on, when she'd only have been working? Dragging herself from her comfortable couch, she got herself reluctantly across the room, and picked up the receiver.

"I'm sorry, Mrs Day's not in," she said. "Can I give her a message?" She did not make her voice very encouraging. He had not even said he *was* Mr *Plzpwrdge* yet; with any luck she could avoid learning his name altogether, and then none of it could possibly be her fault. "She'll be back about half past six," she added, cautiously, and waited for the pleasant middle-aged voice to say very well, it would call again later.

But it didn't go like that at all.

"Who's that speaking?" the voice asked—and it seemed to Milly that a slight sharpness had come into it. "Who is it, please?"

"I—Oh, I'm just visiting here, I'm just—well—just a friend . . ." gabbled Milly, some instinct—or was it by now just habit?—preventing her telling the simple, innocuous truth about her rôle here.

"Oh. Oh, I see. Well, look, I'm sorry to bother you, but perhaps you can help us. Do you happen to know of a Mrs Barnes who works for Mrs Day? A Mrs Milly Barnes? We've been given to understand that she comes two or three afternoons a week and . . ."

"She doesn't! She isn't! There must be some mistake! Mrs Day doesn't know anyone called Barnes . . . !"

Only after she had got the receiver back on the hook did Milly realise what a complete fool she had made of herself. This man, whoever he was, might have been ringing up about something perfectly harmless—an offer of another job, perhaps, or to ask some market-research questions about detergent. *Now* what was he going to think? Frantically, she tried to recall the exact wording of her wild, muddled assertions, and to work out what an outsider would deduce therefrom. That she was lying, obviously: or else that she was half-witted. How could she—or anyone—know for certain that Mrs Day didn't know anyone called Barnes? You can know of your friends that they *do* know a Mrs Barnes, but how can you possibly know that they don't?

Oh, she had been a fool! A fool! And after her resolutions of only a couple of hours ago, too! Milly sat with her head in her hands, staring down at a crumb of ginger biscuit on the carpet, trying to understand what it was that had driven her to behaviour so insane.

Fear, of course. Some people might prefer to call it guilt. The ever-present knowledge that she was wanted for murder.

Murder. This was the first time that Milly had allowed the word to come into her mind uncensored. Murder. She waited for guilt, long repressed, to burst from her subconscious and wash over her in an intolerable tide.

Nothing happened. She said the word again, aloud, this time into the empty flat. Murder. I have committed murder.

Still nothing. Nothing that could be identified as guilt, anyway. Fear, yes; and a lively determination not to be caught. These were familiar feelings by now, almost old friends, but they could not possibly be described as guilt.

This was ridiculous! Summoning up all the honesty she possessed, all the power of self-scrutiny, Milly probed deep into her inmost heart, searching for the black core of guilt that must lie there.

No good. The most profound and earnest piece of soul-searching that she had ever undertaken revealed absolutely nothing except a vague, generalised resentment about the whole business. "It's not *fair*," something inside her was childishly complaining, "why should *I* be a murderer when other people aren't? It's not *fair*!"

She tried again. "I have killed. I have committed the ultimate crime. I have taken a human life."

Still nothing. Human lives are being taken all the time, some by disease, some by cars, some by over-eating. To have contributed to one of these commonplace events seemed— well, not exactly trivial, but lacking in some essential element of evil. Somehow there was nothing there for guilt to feed on—it was like one of those imitation foods with no nourishment in them, that are designed to make you slim.

What was wrong? Why did she have no proper feelings? Was it that Gilbert's life had, in the end, been so divorced from reality that it was not a life at all? And did it follow from this that his death could not be a real death?

Was *this* the immortality that men have dreaded in their hearts since the beginning of time—the immortality conferred upon Tithonus as the ultimate vengeance of the gods?

Had Gilbert brought this ultimate vengeance upon himself as he sat in the thickening darkness behind the closed shutters in Lady Street? Towards the end, darkness was the only thing he trusted: he screamed at Milly, sometimes, if she so much as switched on the light in the scullery so that he could see it shining under the crack of the door. After such a denial of life, how could Death get him when the time came? On what could Death's skeleton hand get a sure grip in such a case? When bony hand encountered bony hand in the darkness, who would have been the one to flee in terror . . . ?

She should never have let her husband get into such a state: that's what the overworked young doctor had said, reprovingly, a month or two before Gilbert died. She should have brought him round to the surgery: and no, of course he couldn't prescribe anything without actually seeing the patient, how could he, it would be most unethical. . . . And then, when the old man never turned up, and the wretched, jittery wife stopped pestering at the surgery, he must thankfully have written-off the whole business. What could he have done, anyway? One more marriage foundering in the familiar welter of recriminations and mutual accusations of paranoia. What did people think doctors *were*?

And perhaps, if Milly had recognised the nature of her problem a little earlier, while Gilbert was still willing to walk in the light of the sun, she might perhaps have persuaded him, on some pretext, to go along to the surgery with her. Or even to allow the doctor to visit him at the flat, which had not yet become a fortress, barricaded against all comers. And perhaps, at that stage, medical treatment might have been able to achieve something. But while Gilbert was no worse than this, Milly was still viewing her disastrous marriage as just this—a disastrous marriage, which she must learn to live with and to alleviate as best she could. And unfortunately it so happened that the very ways she devised to improve her husband's spirits might just as well have been so many carefully graded provocations, each one a little more traumatic than the last— so little did she comprehend, at the beginning, the nature of the shadows she could feel gathering about her.

First, the matter of friends. According to her not very penetrating observation, it seemed obvious beyond all question that Gilbert was suffering from too dull and solitary an existence. Pottering about in this dreary flat all day . . . never seeing anyone but each other, no wonder it was driving them both up the wall!

Cheerful, varied company, then: that was the first necessity. A lively to-ing and fro-ing of visitors to brighten the poor chap up, take him out of himself.

Milly was not so blind, even in those days, as to suppose that she could let loose a chattering horde of her own former acquaintances on a man like Gilbert, with any hope of success: and so she tried, tactfully, to find out who *his* friends were, preparatory to bombarding them with invitations.

There were none. Absolutely none at all. When this fact was finally borne in upon Milly, she could not think what to do.

Naturally, she hadn't supposed that Gilbert could boast any very scintillating circle of acquaintances, but she *had* imagined that there would be at least an old colonel or two, bumbling on about polo in the nineteen-twenties, and perhaps offering Gilbert an occasional game of chess, lasting for hours and hours under the green lamplight. She had expected to be bored by Gilbert's friends, but not as bored as she was by Gilbert on his own; and she was therefore quite ready to put a good face on it and make them warmly welcome.

But now it seemed that no sort of face, good or bad, was to be required of her: and when she pressed him, saying that there must be *someone* he'd like to have round, he gave her a strange, considering look, and did not answer. By evening he was in one of his sulks. He did not speak to her all through supper, and straight afterwards he retired to his armchair with the newspaper. He opened it and held it outspread before his face, as usual, but Milly knew that this time he wasn't reading it. Nor was he dozing, or letting his mind wander: rather he seemed to be more than usually alert and awake, as if he was waiting for something.

By the next morning he was his usual self again: and perhaps if Milly had taken the hint, and forthwith laid aside her plans for livening up his social life, things might have turned out differently. But unfortunately her enthusiasm for changing his way of life was only whetted by this setback, and she set her ingenuity to work to overcome it. *Her* friends were out, obviously: *his* didn't exist: so what remained but to take matters into her own hands and invite, without consulting him, a pleasant, middle-aged couple who had been at the Industrial Archaeology class last term? Whether they were still there this term Milly didn't know, because she and Gilbert no longer went. Why they didn't she wasn't quite sure, and something warned her that if she asked him about it he would go into one of his moods. As yet, she was far from understanding what lay at the root of these "moods", but she was beginning to be just a little bit scared of them, and to have a vague sort of instinct about the things that would be likely to trigger them off.

Thus she said nothing to Gilbert of what was in her mind: instead she quietly wrote a letter to the Davidsons, c/o the Institute, and when Mrs Davidson's reply came, saying that she and her husband would be delighted to come to tea on Saturday, she made sure that she took it from the postman herself, without Gilbert seeing it. It would be better, she calculated, to spring it on him at the last minute, then he would not have time to work up a lot of silly objections.

Rarely can wifely miscalculation have had such disastrous consequences. That Saturday afternoon tea-party proved to be one of the most shocking experiences of Milly's whole life. Even now, months later, the thought of it still made her face grow hot. The scene was still as vivid in her memory as if it had only just happened . . . the scalding tea streaming in a brown tide across the clean white tablecloth and on to the floor . . . the two visitors, stiff as waxworks with shock . . . and herself, first stunned, and then rousing herself to a flurry of apologies . . . and then the mopping-up, as if it had been an ordinary accident, with the unfortunate Davidsons doing their appalled best to pretend that nothing much had happened. . . .

It had been unfortunate, perhaps, that Gilbert had happened to be out when the visitors arrived. If he had been there when they came through the door, all smiles and hand-shaking, he might have reacted differently. As it was, even the brief forewarning that Milly had planned was denied him, and he walked into his wife's tea-party utterly unprepared.

For a moment, he just stood there, staring; just as he had stared when Milly had brightened his flat with flowers and cushions a week or two before. There was nothing actually very remarkable about his demeanour, and only Milly noticed the curious brightness that was coming into his eyes, a luminous look, as if a light had been switched on from within. The Davidsons, already giving little chirrups of appropriate greeting, noticed nothing: and so, as he padded swiftly towards the

table, it was only Milly who was so paralysed with fear that she could not move. The Davidsons, naturally enough, assumed that their host was approaching to shake hands, and Mr Davidson had in fact already half-risen to his feet, and was saying something like "Ah, Soames, good to see you again—"
—when Gilbert picked up the large earthenware teapot and smashed it down into the middle of the table: and then, without a word, turned on his heel and walked with the same soft, swift steps out of the room.

Of the flurry, and panic, and embarrassment which ensued, Milly could not remember much detail: the next thing that was clear in her mind was Gilbert's coming back into the room—was it ten minutes?—half an hour?—later, and mumbling some sort of apology, explaining, confusedly, that he "had had a lot of worries lately". She remembered the desperate eagerness with which everyone had seized on this, and had pretended frenziedly that it was an adequate explanation: and then, shortly afterwards, the Davidsons had left, in a whirl of gabbled politenesses and glassy smiles. She remembered how she had longed for them to go, and never to see them again: and at the same time had dreaded, with a growing, sickening terror, the moment when she should be left alone with her husband.

But strangely, when they were at last on their own, Gilbert had not turned on her in fury as she had expected. On the contrary, he treated her for the rest of the evening with even more consideration than usual, jumping up to open doors for her, to carry trays; and all of it done with a sort of pitying affection which Milly could not understand at all, and which filled her with unease. Only just before bedtime did he refer to what had happened, and when he did it was in terms so extraordinary that Milly was awake the rest of the night puzzling about it.

"I don't want you to think, my dear, that your friends are not welcome under my roof," he began, seeming not to notice the way Milly's mouth fell open at this understatement of all time. "But I would just ask you to be a little bit more careful. Those two today—I know you didn't realise it, my dear, and I'm not blaming you—but those two have been on my tracks for a long time."

"*On your tracks?* What on earth do you mean, Gilbert?" The words were out before Milly had had time to weigh them, and a flicker of irritation crossed Gilbert's face.

"Now, don't pretend to me, my dear," he warned her gravely. "That is something I don't like, particularly from my wife. You know—you *must* know—that many people would like to get at my memoirs. Many, many people!" The last words were spoken with a strange mixture of regret and a sort of unholy triumph: and Milly could only stare.

"Your—your memoirs?" she got out at last.

"Yes, yes—" he gestured impatiently at the piles of newspapers that still lay in yellowing heaps on the table, untouched since the day he had forbidden Milly to move them. "It's all in there—all the material for my life's work. As soon as the material is complete, I shall start on the writing. Till then, I want *no one*—I repeat, *no one*, not even you, my dear—to look at a single word of what is in those papers. Do you realise," (and here the strange brilliance was coming back into his light eyes, and his arms gestured in a wide arc), "do you realise that in every one of those papers there are articles about *me*? Did you realise that? No? Well, now you see why they mustn't get hold of any of them. They mustn't see one single line. They could use it against me, you see. . . ."

Milly refrained from asking "Who could?" She was beginning to see, as in a glass darkly, what sort of a thing it was that she was up against, but she would not, as yet, give a name to it. What nonsense!—was all she allowed herself to think. He's talking nonsense! How *could* there be articles about *him* in all those thousands of papers! And with this thought, the worm began to wriggle in the bottom of her mind, the Bluebeard worm, and she knew she would not rest until she knew what *was* in those old papers, so carefully saved, and parcelled up, and arranged. . . .

It was on the Monday, over a week later, that she got her chance. Gilbert was going out, as he still did at times, "to see a man"; and as soon as the shadow of his progress up the area steps had ceased to swing in sweeps of darkness and grey light against the dining-room window, she siezed on the nearest and most accessible of the packages, and began tugging delicately at the string. It must all be done to perfection. She had already noted the exact position of this package among the rest, and now she must so undo the knot that she would be able to do it up again *exactly* the same. . . .

The Times, of June 15th, 1935. Milly pored over the faded pages with a kind of tense, shapeless expectancy, with no faintest idea of what it was she was expecting. Her eyes scanned news of wars, and of wars to come; of fashions; of political speeches, and of cricket; but nothing, anywhere, about Gilbert Soames, in any shape or form. Here and there a passage was marked by a light pencilled line down the side: but never was it anything that (as far as Milly could see) could possibly have been connected with her husband, at any stage in his career. The marked passages weren't even interesting in themselves—just a few lines of a parliamentary speech here, or an announcement about the sales of pet food there. . . . Milly shook her head baffled, and moved on to June 16th. Only the same sort of thing again. . . . Likewise June 17th . . . and 18th. . . .

It was when she was halfway through July 12th that she became aware that the print was harder to read than it had been at first. The grey light had become greyer while she wasn't noticing . . . and only now did she look up to see why.

Gilbert's face, flattened and expressionless against the glass, was watching her through the area window.

CHAPTER XVI

STRANGELY, THE EXPLOSION of rage that Milly was waiting for never came. Gilbert simply set to work to parcel the papers up again, applying himself to the task with the same meticulous care that he had shown before, putting on his gold-rimmed glasses now and then to examine a passage more closely, or to check on the number of a page. He did not seem to be listening to Milly's muddled lies—how the string had broken... the bundle had fallen off the table ... she had only been trying to get them back in the right order.... As the implausible excuses tumbled from her lips, he neither silenced her nor made any comment on what she was saying, but simply went on with his task, peering and muttering, as if he was alone. And when it was finished, and the bundle re-tied to his satisfaction and replaced among the others, he settled himself in his big chair as usual, with his green lamp at his elbow, and the pages of *The Financial Times* hiding his face.

Sitting opposite him in the green shadows, not daring to read or to pick up any sewing, Milly kept waiting for the expected explosion, but still it did not come. It seemed that, for some inscrutable reason, she had got away with it: and it was only gradually, as the days went by, that she realised that this was not the case at all.

The first thing she noticed was that her morning trip down to the shops in the High Road was no longer the free-and-easy affair it had been hitherto. Up till now, Gilbert had given her a generous weekly allowance for housekeeping, and had left her to spend it when and as she liked. But now all this was changed. Now, he wanted to know exactly which shops she was going to ... what she was going to buy ... when she would be back ... and at the end of a fortnight she discovered, with a strange cold feeling in her stomach, that he had been keeping a record of it all ... the exact time she had left the house each day, and the exact time she had returned....

But by then there were already other changes that had forced themselves upon her awareness. Each day he had been closing the shutters and fastening the doors a little earlier, at first imperceptibly, and then at an increasing rate, as if he was trying to win some mysterious race against the golden October days, and reach the dark ahead of them. Soon, it was barely two o'clock when the flat was plunged in lamplight, and evening was upon them.

Evenings had always been the worst part of the day, and this gratuitous extension of them was terrible. Milly did not know how she was going to endure the hours till bedtime, with Gilbert silent behind his newspaper, and herself sitting in tense and bitter idleness in the chair opposite. Sometimes she would let her eyes wander along the worn leather backs of the books on the shelves at her side, and lay plans for slithering this or that volume out without a sound in the hope of reading for a little without Gilbert noticing. But rarely did she manage it. At the faintest sound of movement—or sometimes even before that, when the whole thing was still only a plan churning in her mind—he would lower his paper, or rouse himself from his doze, and look across at her.

"Are you bored, my dear?" he would ask politely. "Then let us talk," and laying down his paper he would sit waiting for her to say something. She tried: sometimes she tried quite hard, racking her brains for something that might amuse him, but it grew harder and harder. Their life was narrowing daily: they were cut off more and more from anything that might have provided conversation. Milly could almost hear the creaking as the walls closed in on them.

"Let's have a cup of tea," she sometimes said, as an excuse for darting into the kitchen: but lately he had taken to coming out after her, ostensibly to help her carry the tray, but in fact, Milly knew, it was to check up on her. Because several times lately, when she had made the tea by herself, he had questioned her when she came back to the dining-room. What had she been doing? Why had she been so long? How could it take—here he would consult his old-fashioned gold watch—twelve and a half minutes to make a cup of tea? She was filling the kettle too full on purpose, he accused, so as to spend extra minutes away from him.

This was so exactly the truth—and yet it sounded so mad when put into words—that Milly denied it hotly, with a sense of genuine indignation: and at last he seemed mollified. But it was only a few days after this that she found, under his pillow, with the record of her shopping expeditions, another, newer record: a list of all the times that she had spent alone in the kitchen each day, worked out to the nearest half minute. Some of the items were mysteriously underlined in red, and marked with a small cross in Gilbert's neat, cramped hand.

It was on the morning when she made this discovery that Milly made up her mind that she had had enough. This was it. Packing only her night things and a spare cardigan, Milly set off for the shops at her usual time that morning, promising to be back by twelve at the latest. She walked, briskly as always, until she was out of sight, and then she began to run: to race, as fast as bus and tube would carry her, to Felicity's.

Felicity was one of her old acquaintances from happier days: an old acquaintance of Julian's, too, of course, but that couldn't be helped. As she hurried through the watery November sunshine towards Felicity's flat, Milly toyed longingly with the idea of making a clean breast of everything: of pouring into Felicity's sympathetic but over-enthusiastic ears all the pent-up follies and miseries of the past months.

But it wouldn't do. Felicity would no doubt be all kindness and concern, and quite uncensorious (well, after her own three divorces, she could hardly be otherwise) but the trouble with kind, uncensorious people is that they are incapable of keeping anything to themselves. Their kindness makes them want to share the delights of gossip with all and sundry, while their uncensoriousness makes them blissfully unaware that the spicy news they are spreading is particularly discreditable to the victim. Within days—hours, very likely—of Felicity's learning that Milly had left her new husband, a dozen versions of the story would be winging their way across the Atlantic, each one more scurrilous than the last. How Julian and Cora would enjoy taking their gleeful pick from the rich and varied menu thus set before them free of charge!

Felicity was naturally surprised to see Julian's ex-wife after so many months of non-communication, but she seemed quite pleased, and agreed amiably enough to Milly's plea to be allowed to stay for a few days: and if, out of her long and varied experience of matrimony, she took with a pinch of salt Milly's story about Gilbert being away for a few days "on business", and about being nervous of sleeping alone in the flat—well, there had been times when Felicity herself had been driven to dishing out this sort of rigmarole on her own account, and the last thing she would do would be to call another woman's bluff. She did not know yet what this Gilbert character had been up to, but she knew very well from her own personal experience that when women told lies it was always the man's fault, he drove them to it, the sod, and so the least they could do was to back each other up. Besides, that way you got the whole story, drama-side up. So she urged her visitor most cordially to stick around for a while. It would be quite a convenience, actually, to have someone here, as she, Felicity, had to be out such a lot, and her current boy-friend (an absolute *sweetie*, you *must* meet him) had recently given her a Siamese cat: and it so happened that Felicity absolutely *adored* everything about Siamese cats except looking after them, and so, if Milly didn't mind . . .?

The matter having been thus arranged to the satisfaction of both, the two women settled down to a pleasant afternoon of gossiping, answering the telephone to Felicity's friends, and watching television. It was about eight o'clock, and they were idly discussing the question of whether to go out to dinner, and, if so, which of Felicity's admirers should be invited along to pay the bill, when there was a knock on the door: and when Felicity went to open it, Gilbert walked in.

Milly did not even feel surprised. It was as if she had known this was going to happen. She could not even bring herself to wonder how her husband had traced her—whether he had followed her, or had simply gone to the phone box at the far end of Lady Street, and kept phoning all the numbers in her address book until he hit on someone who knew she was here. It wouldn't have taken long. Felicity had been chattering to friends on the telephone all the afternoon, by now half London probably knew of Julian's ex-wife's escapade.

But in any case, there seemed to be no need of a natural explanation. Standing there in the doorway, so straight and still, his hair gleaming like the wings of a white bird, Gilbert radiated a strange power, and it was easy to imagine that he had been guided by some sense not quite of this world; even that he had been magically transported by the powers of darkness through the November night.

What had happened next? All Milly could remember afterwards was that from the moment she saw her husband standing there, so quiet and tall, his eyes glittering like cats' eyes, she had known she would be going back with him. Not for one moment had there seemed to be any choice. She supposed she must have said goodbye to Felicity; must have apologised, and made up some face-saving story to explain Gilbert's sudden appearance when he was supposed to be away "on business". Anyway, the next thing she could clearly remember was sitting in the corner of a taxi, in the dark, with Gilbert sitting very straight and still beside her, and not speaking a single word. She remembered the bright lights of the West End reeling away behind them, to be replaced by the dim sodium lights across the river, fewer and further between as the taxi wove its relentless way towards their home.

She did not know what her punishment would be: but she knew enough, by now, to guess that whatever it was, it would not fall immediately. Rather it would come upon her piecemeal, over the next days and weeks, almost while she wasn't noticing. She would not know when it began, nor when, or by what route, it would reach its unimaginable end.

Even after they were home, Gilbert still did not speak: nor did Milly defend herself, or make excuses. It had gone beyond that. Only after Gilbert had gone all round the flat, bolting and securing the doors and windows, did he finally bring himself to make an observation. Wandering casually towards the book-shelves, and searching along the rows of old leather-bound books, he came upon the volume he wanted. He turned the pages thoughtfully: then paused for a minute. As he read, he began to laugh, that strange, silent laugh of his, setting his gaunt body jolting soundlessly, as if there was a time-bomb ticking away somewhere deep inside him:

"You know what the ancient Scythians did with their runaway slaves?" he said to Milly from across the room, and without raising his eyes from the book. "They used to blind them!" He laughed again, gently, as his eye travelled down the page. "They made just as good slaves, you see, like that, as they only had very simple tasks to perform. It didn't matter at all."

The chiming of Mrs Day's ornamental gilt clock roused Milly from her daydream. Three o'clock already, and nothing done!—not to mention the precious reading time frittered away to no purpose! Jumping up from the telephone corner where she had been sitting, immobilised by memories, ever since that disturbing telephone call for "Mrs Barnes", Milly determined to think no more about any of it. Collecting her dusters and brushes, she set off for Mrs Day's bedroom—usually the storm-centre of operations—to tackle the by now familiar medley of cigarette ends, underwear, coffee cups and evening dresses, with a cross Persian cat asleep in the middle of it.

But the memories were not so easily dispelled. All the while she was squeezing flimsy, glittering garments into the packed wardrobe, trying to find hangers for them all, Milly felt the past lingering all about her, like a taste in the mouth. It would not leave her alone, with its if's, and if only's, and supposing's.

Supposing she had refused to go back with Gilbert that evening? Supposing she had said, boldly: "No, Gilbert, I'm sorry, but I'm not coming. Felicity has invited me to stay, and I'm staying!" What would have happened then? What would have been the course of her life thereafter?

Even as she posed the question, she knew that it was futile. What happened had happened. It had had to happen. The sense of inevitability was as strongly with her now as it had been then, when, unresisting as a puppet on a string, she had followed Gilbert down all those stairs and into the waiting taxi. There was nothing else she could have done. That was how it had seemed then: that was how it still seemed now, when she looked back. It had been fated: she seemed to have had no option: she had been a pawn in the grip of forces outside her control.

This, of course, is the way people usually do feel when they have come to grief through taking on grave and extensive responsibilities for fun. When the full weight of their casually-undertaken commitment finally comes to rest on their shoulders, and there is no longer any way out, then it is that they experience this sense of helplessness, this feeling of being a pawn in the hands of fate, a plaything of the gods: and they rarely remember, by then, that it was they, first, who treated the gods as playthings.

It is amazing how much your hands can accomplish without, apparently, any assistance from the mind at all. By the end of the afternoon, Milly had completed all her usual tasks in Mrs Day's flat, and had set off for home, with only the briefest spells of conscious attention to what she was doing:—one when the cat brought half a lobster into the bathroom for her inspection, and she had to decide what to do with it: and the next when the swing doors of the block of flats thrust her forth out of the lush central heating into the gusty winter night, with a wet wind lolloping in from the sea, stinging her into momentary consciousness as it caught at her face, and at her ears, and at her gloveless hands.

CHAPTER XVII

AFTER THAT EVENING, Gilbert's deterioration was swift and terrible. It seemed to Milly that there was something almost purposeful about the way he forged onward towards the abyss, as though nothing and no one should stop him. He seemed, at times, to be seeking the Dark Night of the soul with an intensity and passion that other men have devoted to the search for gold.

She knew by now, of course, that he was ill; and when her belated resort to the local doctor produced nothing helpful, she tried to calm her growing panic by telling herself that it was an illness, like any other illness.

But it wasn't like any other illness; that was the trouble. And then there was always the feeling—inescapable for the trapped onlooker—that the patient has somehow *chosen* to be ill in just that way rather than in any other: that if he had been a nice kind person to start with, he would have gone mad in some nice kind way. . . .

Maybe there is some grain of truth in this: Milly had no means of knowing, as she had been acquainted with her husband for less than a year, and had anyway devoted precious little of her time so far to trying to understand him. Now, when it was too late, she did try to make some sort of contact with his disintegrating mind, if only for her own safety: but by now such efforts were futile.

It was the day after her abortive attempt at escape that Gilbert nailed up the area door; and that same evening he fixed bolts on the dining-room door, inside and outside. Now, when Milly wanted to go shopping, she had to go up the dark basement stairs to the ground floor, and wrestle with the bolts and chains and double locks on the ancient, peeling front door. Often, as she struggled, Mrs Roach, who inhabited that floor, would hear the groaning and the grinding of the rusty metal, and would shuffle in her slippers out of her fusty bed-sitting-room, and stand watching, almost like Gilbert himself. Milly knew that Mrs Roach disapproved of her—she would hardly even exchange a "good morning" on most days—and this made her nervous and clumsy: it was sometimes five minutes before she finally got the creaking old door open on to the blessed light of day.

But soon even these brief excursions came to an end. Gilbert had taken recently to coming up the basement stairs with her, and taking his stand in the doorway to watch her as she set off down the street. When she came back she would often find him still standing there, watch in hand, and if she had been longer than half an hour or so he would sometimes be actually trembling, with a terrible, silent rage.

Half an hour. Then twenty minutes was all he would stand for: and then ten; and presently there came the time when he forbade her to go shopping at all. He had arranged for Mrs Roach to do it, he informed her, coldly, since she, his wife, was not to be trusted. Thereafter their diet was restricted mainly to things that could be bought at the poky little corner shop— sliced bread and tins of things mostly—since Mrs Roach was reluctant to drag her bloated body further than this, even for generous pay. Soon the milk was tinned too, for Gilbert would no longer allow the milkman to call, insisting that Milly left messages for him hidden among the empty bottles.

And now the time came when Gilbert would no longer open the window shutters at all, for fear "They" would look in. The era of the long night had arrived: and now that it was here, Milly realised that she had been waiting for it for a very long time. She seemed to have known, all along, that this was how it would all end.

End? It was only December even now: and the strange thing was that no sooner had Gilbert achieved the timeless, unbroken night towards which he had been so quietly and purposefully moving all these weeks, than he became passionately, obsessionally preoccupied with the passing of time. A hundred times a day he would ask Milly what the time was, drawing out his watch to check on her answer: comparing his watch with the clock in the kitchen: checking and counter-checking.

Sometimes he would scream at Milly that she was deceiving

him, telling him the wrong time on purpose. She would be bringing the lunch in, say, at one o'clock, and he would suddenly heave himself round in his great chair to scold and storm, confronting her with his heavy gold watch with its hands pointing to three, or four or even five. . . . No matter how closely she tried to watch, Milly never seemed to catch him tinkering with it; and so presently, in the weird, darkening world that was closing in on her, she began to feel that the watch itself might have become malignantly alive, in league with its master to put her in the wrong.

And now his time sense began to swing like a great pendulum in the dark, gathering momentum. Sometimes he would call for his supper thinking that night had fallen when in fact the bright, frosty day beyond the shutters was only just beginning. At other times—and these were the most terrible of all—he would think that night was day, and would come creeping into his wife's room at dead of night to find out why she was asleep. She would wake, then, from strange uneasy dreams, to find him shuffling around her room, softly opening drawers, peering into boxes, fumbling about among her clothes and other possessions with his old fingers.

The first time this happened, she had called out to him, in spontaneous terror:

"Gilbert! What is it? What are you doing?"—but she had never done so again. So strange had been the look in his shining eyes as he strode swiftly to the bed and leaned over her: and so strange had been the things he'd said:

"Why, my dear, I just wondered if you were ill?" he began, softly. "It seems so strange of you to be lying here, at past midday! It's nearly time for lunch! Aren't you going to cook me any lunch?"

This first time, Milly had argued, and shown him her watch in some indignation: and at last, in reckless determination to prove herself right, she had wrenched open the window shutter and shown him the moonlight filtering down, grey and silent, from the deserted street above.

At first, she thought it was a tom-cat setting up his caterwauling, very suddenly, from the silent area steps. Then she realised that it was Gilbert screaming. He wrenched the shutter from her hand, and slammed it shut, shooting the bolt home, and slotting in the great metal catch.

"So *this* is how they get in!" he jabbered, his voice cracked and shrill with fury. "*This* is how I am being betrayed! In my own house . . . ! By my own wife . . . !"

Less than five minutes later, Milly was only too willing to agree humbly that it was lunch time. That she had overslept. That she was sorry. Anything. . . . Anything at all. And thus it came about that, in the small hours of that December night, she had cooked him one of his beloved curries, rice and all, and had served it with a trembling smile, carefully referring to it, in a small, shaking voice, as "lunch".

After this, she had pretended to be asleep, always, when she heard the nightly roamings beginning. Sometimes she would watch, through barely opened lids, as he peered and poked among her belongings, his white hair gleaming and bobbing in the faint light through the open door. At others, she kept her eyes tight closed, listening, willing the soft rustlings to cease, that she might know he had gone away.

And sometimes he had: and then that would be the end of the night's terror: but more often than not he would end by rousing her, and insisting that it was lunch-time. After that first night, Milly never argued again. She got up and cooked his curry, or whatever he might fancy, immediately.

There was something strangely inert, she sometimes felt, about the way she allowed herself to be thus carried along with his insane delusions, and sometimes she was puzzled by it. Fear of him did not seem to be quite the whole explanation, for even her fear, now, was beginning to have a strange passive quality about it, as if she was no longer a real, autonomous being with a real life to be lost or saved. Wherever it was that Gilbert was going, she knew now that he was beginning to drag her with him: already she could feel the tug and pull of it. Before long, as the black storms rose higher in his disintegrating mind, she, too, was going to lose her footing and be sucked along, irrelevant as a spinning twig, towards the darkness where his spirit boiled and churned. . . .

It was towards the end of December when Gilbert began to imagine that Milly was trying to poison him: and at first Milly did not take in the significance of the new symptoms. She noticed a slight tightening-up of his surveillance of her activities in the kitchen, she was never alone there at all now, for even a minute. But this was a difference in degree, not in kind, and anyway she was beginning to be used to it now. As she bustled from cooker to sink, she took it for granted now that out of the corner of her eye she would be aware of the tall, waiting figure in the doorway, just as she would be aware of the roller towel hanging white and motionless in its usual place. In some ways, it was less disturbing than it used to be, because he did not pad around helping any more. Instead, he just watched—or sometimes, as it seemed to her, listened. This puzzled her at first: and then one day, she stopped and listened too. She became aware, as he had been aware all along, of the faint, endless tap-tapping of footsteps on the pavement far above. Tap-tap-*tap*, they went: or tappity-*tap*-tap-tap . . . and suddenly she knew, in sick terror, that she must never stop and listen like this again. For she had heard the sounds, just for one telepathic second, through Gilbert's ears, and—just fancy!—they were in code, tapping out messages! So that was why he never took his eyes off her—he was watching for the moment when she would begin to understand, and to tap messages back! How terrifyingly easy it would be!—three cups placed in quick succession on the draining-board—*tap*-tap-tap . . . or the wooden spoon knocking too rhythmically against the side of the pan—trr—trr—trr—as she stirred! After this, she carefully blurred and muddled the sounds she couldn't help making, and hummed noisily as she worked.

Perhaps it was not surprising if, after all this, she should have taken little note of the fact that Gilbert was gradually becoming more and more fussy over his food. Such a trifle it seemed, in comparison with all the other problems. It was an odd kind of fussiness, though, and seemed to have little to do with the quality of Milly's cooking—she had, in fact, long since learned how to please her husband (in this department at least) by producing highly spiced, highly flavoured dishes, hot with pimentoes, and peppers, and green chiles. He didn't seem to mind much about the basic ingredients, and thus had noticed no deterioration in the menu since Milly had been limited to the tins and packets of stuff that were all Mrs Roach could be bothered to buy. No, he still liked his food, and ate it with appetite: but he had developed an annoying habit— that's all it seemed to Milly at first—of changing plates with his wife just as the meal was about to begin. Just as she had it all served out, and was already picking up her own knife and fork, he would lean across and slide her plate away from under her very hand, and deftly substitute his own. Usually he would murmur, deprecatingly, some sort of explanation—"You must have the bigger one, dear, I'm not very hungry today": or "Do you mind—I'd rather have the one without so much rice." Sometimes one or both of them might already have started when the long, gnarled fingers slid across the table and closed upon her plate. She never protested, even though she often found it impossible to eat the food thus exchanged. The thought of his fork having touched it, straight from those old lips, turned her stomach. And so there she would sit, pushing the food around her plate, and trying to look as if she was eating. And when she glanced up now and then, and noticed him watching her, his features narrowed with cunning, she did not understand the significance of what she saw.

She had been noticing a peculiar unpleasant smell in the dining-room for some days now: and one evening, early in the New Year, she siezed her chance to investigate. Gilbert was for once out of the room for a few minutes, as Mrs Roach had just come down with the week's shopping, and he was busy in the scullery examining the purchases and putting them away. This was a task he would no longer trust to his wife: and

Milly calculated that it would be some minutes before he returned. She knew his slow movements, and the punctilious thoroughness with which he would examine every package: she could hear the low mumbling of his voice even from this distance, as he checked and re-checked each item against the list. Swiftly, she pushed the heavy dining-room door almost shut, and made for the corner of the room from which she was sure the smell emanated. The corner behind Gilbert's great leather chair. . . . Somewhere among those ancient leather-bound books. . . . Behind them, perhaps, right at the back of the shelves. . . .

What she had expected to find, she did not know. When she pulled out the first matchbox, full of old boiled rice, she simply felt that there had been some sort of a mistake. It just didn't mean anything. But when she found the next one, with dried remains of scrambled egg in it . . . and then the one full of mince that had gone green . . . and the one oozing with decaying stew . . . then, indeed, she knew that she had crossed the border into madland, and that there might be no return . . . and now here was the king of madland himself, come back into his own . . . leaning over her, blotting out the last of the light. Darkness blazed from him as from a black sun, and she prostrated herself before it in gibbering, slavish terror. The time of the blackness was come, the black dawn was breaking and there would be no more day. The shrieks and howls from the bottomless pit were already loud in her ears, they came from Gilbert's lips . . . and now she began to feel her sanity itself twisting from her grasp. He was upon her . . . his bony fingers danced like lace . . . he was screaming like a madman—because, of course, he *was* a madman: and at this thought, strangely, her mind snapped back, like good quality elastic, and she was sane again.

He had not killed her, nor even injured her in any way. She could feel no pain anywhere. He must, at some point, have hauled her to her feet from behind the chair, because here she was, standing, with his hands gripping her shoulders, while he howled and shrieked with fear, right into her face.

Fear. This was the first time she had ever observed that fear was what racked and tore him, a degree of fear beyond the comprehension of the sane. And even now, the fact hardly registered. So great was her own terror that she could not even understand his words, let alone the nature of the passion that lay behind them.

Presently, it all seemed to have been going on for hours, her standing there, and his voice streaming into her face. She found she was taking in the gist of it: how she had been putting poison in his food for a long time now; but he had foiled her—ha ha, *how* he had foiled her!—by changing round the plates each time! Did she think he hadn't noticed the way she always refused to eat her helping after they had been changed?

Milly listened almost with interest. And sometimes, Gilbert himself seemed quite to forget that his listener was also the arch-villain of his fantasy, and spoke as if she was a sympathetic outsider, to whom he was confiding his wrongs. He explained how he had been collecting these samples from his wife's uneaten platefuls to send off for analysis: and how the analysis would prove that she had been stealing his sleeping-pills and crushing them up into his food. He had noticed, he confided, that his hidden store of sleeping pills, which he had had by him for years, was diminishing, and he knew his wife had been stealing them, but he could not find where she hid them. He had searched her drawers and cupboards over and over again.... She was very cunning... that was why they had chosen her for the job, because she was so cunning....

Barely an hour later, Gilbert was in his usual chair, with the newspaper held in front of his face, as if nothing had happened. Everything was as usual again, except for one small detail: he would not have the light on any more. In the darkness, Milly could hear the twitchings of the paper, and the familiar rustlings, as he turned the pages, and folded them this way and that as if to make them more convenient to read.

He never mentioned the poisoning again. Indeed, there were not many more days, now, for him to mention anything. Already it was the fifth of January.

He seemed to have forgotten his suspicions. He ate the meals Milly gave him, and dozed, and seemed disturbed by nothing, except the light. He hated to have any lights on now. Even his own green lamp he would only switch on now and then, for meals, or to check on the time: and when it was borne in upon him that without a light Milly simply could not cook his meals, he fumbled among his belongings and found her a torch. And thereafter, groping and fumbling, to all appearances as mad as he, Milly produced her meals by torchlight, humbly thankful for this insane concession which spared her total darkness. She knew, and somehow did not mind, that her behaviour had gone beyond humouring him, and that she had become a madman's puppet, battered by terror into a subservience that was close to idiocy.

That way, a ghastly, twilight peace was brought into being: and by giving in to all his mad whims, by following at heel, like an obedient dog, down the twisting path that led to the black caverns of the insane, she managed to maintain this peace, precariously, for four whole days.

And then, on the fifth day, it all began again. For the first time in several successive nights, Gilbert once again roused his wife in the small hours, and demanded lunch. As he flashed the torch into her dazed eyes, and shook her by the shoulder, he seemed strangely eager and alert, like a child bursting with some wonderful surprise that he has been forbidden to tell. Milly had only once before seen his eyes as bright as this, and their strange, silvery brilliance sent a chill through her, like the touch of the finger of death.

Worn out with terror and despair, Milly staggered from her bed at his bidding, threw on some clothes, and stumbled across to the kitchen. And as she stood at the cooker, numb with hopelessness, stirring curry powder and turmeric into the mess of tinned mince and dehydrated vegetables, it came to her, quite suddenly, and with a strange, quiet certainty, that she would never be doing this again.

The feeling faded as quickly as it came, but it left her with a curious sense of power, of being in control of what was going to happen, whatever it might be. And so when she saw that Gilbert was back at his old tricks again—changing the plates round when he thought her back was turned—she almost laughed. She felt that it would be fun—yes, *fun!*—to jerk him out of his idiotic suspicions. By placidly eating the helping he had allotted to her, she would make him see, once and for all, that he was mistaken, and it *couldn't* have been poisoned.

It was horrible. It made her feel sick and awful at this hour in the morning, but she was determined to go through with it. But she had barely had a couple of mouthfuls, when Gilbert's gnarled hand, green in the lamplight, flashed like a snake across the white tablecloth.

"You've changed them back!" he hissed between his teeth. "You've changed the plates back while I wasn't looking!"— and before she had time to protest, the plates were once more changed round, and she now had in front of her the plate from which Gilbert had already begun eating.

So. She had made him see his mistake, all right, but the mistake he saw was one which fitted nicely with *his* picture of the situation, not with hers. Within his system of thought, a wife who could double-cross him by magically re-changing plates under his very eyes, was far more credible than one who merely wasn't trying to poison him at all.

Triumphant, full of sly glee at the thought of having outwitted her, Gilbert fell to, smacking his lips, and plying his fork greedily. Milly did not try to protest, or to point out that she *couldn't* have changed the plates back, even if she had wanted to, since he had been watching all the time. She didn't even try to make any further show of eating what he had so gleefully placed before her. It wouldn't do any good. His delusion was complete now, perfected by months of skilful toil. It was unassailable now by the assaults of reality in any form.

So she just sat, quietly, her hands in her lap, waiting for what she knew was coming.

"Not feeling well, my dear?"

Gilbert's voice, gentle and solicitous as always on these occasions, came to her across the dimly illumined table. "Don't you like this delicious curry, that you made yourself?"

She could not see the sly sarcasm in his eyes, for they were downcast to his plate, from which he was still eating hungrily. But she saw the vulpine look come into his face, and the champing jaws. She watched the familiar narrowing of his features, as suspicion worked inside him like yeast.

Familiar? Well, of course it was, after all these months. But what was not so familiar was the way his face not only narrowed, but then swelled out like a balloon . . . and then narrowed again . . . out, in . . . out, in . . . for all the world as if his skull was breathing, instead of his lungs! For a moment— so accustomed was she by now to helplessly confronting new and terrifying symptoms—she found herself accepting it, raking among her half-forgotten nursing expertise for the significance of a breathing skull. It meant that the brain was breathing too, of course. Breathing-brain, or cerebropulmonosis, was one of the early symptoms of . . . and at this point she noticed, dimly, that her thoughts had become nonsense. She was half-dreaming, on the edge of sleep, right there as she sat. And now—what do you know?—*her* skull was breathing too, in, out, in, out, just like his, swelling as if it would explode. And it was then that she knew, without any doubt at all, that she was drugged.

The curry. Gilbert, in his madness, had imagined that it was poisoned, and it was! He had fancied, in his deluded state, that sleeping pills were crushed into the plateful she had given him, and they were! And in heavy dosage too, for she had only had a couple of mouthfuls before he had changed the plates round all over again. Everything had been done in exact accordance with his mad fantasy—but by whom?

Strangely, with her brain pulsating like a dynamo, and already awash with sleep, she was able to understand it all more clearly than she was ever to do again. It was Gilbert who had done it, naturally. In this moment of drugged dizziness, she could follow his train of thought with perfect ease. What is the most certain way of proving that your wife is trying to poison you? Why, by actually discovering poison in the food she serves to you, of course! And what is the most certain way of actually discovering poison in the food she serves you? Why, by putting it there, of course! The simple, unassailable logic of it struck her as forcibly as it must, a little earlier, have struck him.

Too clever by half, though: that was *his* trouble! It was going to be funny when he found out how he had double-crossed himself, changing the plates round a second time, as soon as he saw her beginning to eat her share! He'd landed up with the poisoned one himself! She giggled weakly, wondering how soon he would find out, and what he would say.

Wait, though. He wouldn't say anything, because by the time he found out he would be dead. That took the edge off the joke, rather. Still, it would be quite funny, all the same. She watched, fascinated, while a bit of rice dribbled down his chin and on to his tie, as it sometimes did when he was over-eager about his food. This time, she wasn't even disgusted. It was almost interesting, to watch it happening for the very last time.

He had laid down his fork. He was staring, first at her plate, and then at his own, as though trying to work out what had happened. Milly watched his puzzlement in a detached sort of way, as if he was already dead, as if it was already no concern of hers. She watched his face grow pinched and grey as some new and monstrous suspicion began to work inside him like a digestive juice, breaking down data from the outside world and re-constituting it into the special kind of nourishment needed by his fantasy. She watched his eyes narrow, and knew herself to be watching, as if it was a physical process, the building of the new suspicion into the old. She could see him joining, dove-tailing, filling in the cracks, until the job was perfect: and then, and only then, did he speak:

"You're lying!" he said to her, very softly, and leaning towards her across the table, intimate as a lover in the dim light. "You've lied to me all the time! You've pretended to put poison in my food to frighten me! You thought it would frighten me into letting that precious doctor come! You knew he was after me. You knew he was in league with them, he's been trying for years to worm his way into my house, only I've been too clever for him! And now you, my own wife, thought you'd trick me into letting him in by telling me I'd been poisoned! Didn't you? Now, don't lie to me, my dear, it is no use at all, I can see into your mind. I've seen into it all the time! Do you think I haven't seen you slinking off to his surgery, when you'd sworn to me you were only going shopping? Do you think I haven't watched, and waited, and timed you, and found out just how long you spent in there plotting against me? I have a record of it, I've kept a record . . . and of the phone calls, too. Did you think I didn't know what you were up to, sneaking off to the phone box, and betraying my whereabouts to him . . . promising to let him in when he came to get me. . . . You, my wife, betraying me. . . ."

Gilbert's slow rising from his chair was like a snake uncoiling. Never taking his eyes from his wife's face, he worked his way round the table towards her, holding on to the edge of it with one hand, and feeling for his keys in the depths of his trouser pocket with the other.

Was the drug beginning to take effect at last? He must have had ten—twenty—times the dose that she'd had. When he spoke, his voice was still firm, but strangely monotonous:

"You thought you'd tricked me, didn't you? You thought I was fool enough to believe that you really *had* given me poison! What sort of a fool do you take me for? Do you think I couldn't see right into your evil, treacherous mind, right from the very beginning? *I* knew what you were up to—of course I did!" Here the strange and terrible laughter began:

it rocked him, silently, from deep within, until he had to clutch at the back of her chair for support. As he stood thus, half leaning over her, his next words seemed to hiss down into her ears like wind.

"That is the last trick you will ever play, my dear. What I am going to do to you now will make it quite, quite certain that you will never be able to play any more tricks, ever again. But first, we must fix the door. We must fix it so that no one will go in or out any more. There will be no need. After this, there will be no need. . . ."

Snatching the keys from his hand was surprisingly easy. So was the push she gave him, which sent him staggering backwards, right across the room, and before she could know where or how he had fallen, she was gone. Outside the door . . . locking and double-locking it, and shooting home the great bolts that Gilbert had fixed there only a few weeks ago. From inside, she could hear a floundering, thumping sound, but by the time she dashed past the door again, with coat and handbag, it had ceased. She fancied she could hear another sound now, fainter and much more sinister: a scratching noise, a small scrape of metal, as if he was fiddling, somehow, with the lock . . .

The next thing Milly knew, she was in the street, running, running, through the icy January dark: and although she knew it could not be true—for had she not locked the door, fixed the great bolts, and hurled the keys, the only set of keys, far away into the night?—even though she knew all this, every nerve in her body, every cell of her racing blood, told her that Gilbert was already on her track. Why wasn't he dead? Or in a drugged coma at least? What was the strange strength of his madness, that could fight off the onslaughts of such a dose? Let him die! —let him die *quickly* she prayed, as she raced along. Let him die before he can get the door undone . . . before he can somehow break down the bolts . . . master the lock . . . ! The sound of her own footsteps echoing in the empty streets seemed to have multiplied, until now it seemed that there were footsteps everywhere, racing as she was racing through the winter blackness that was not yet morning. A race, a race to the finish, between her, and Gilbert, and Death. The three of them, strung out along the dark streets, with her (so far) in the lead; then Gilbert, gaining on her relentlessly with his long, stiff stride, the lamp posts spinning away behind him; and lastly Death, pounding along in the rear, the icy air of the January dawn whistling through the sockets of his eyes.

It was only after she had been travelling round on the tube for quite a while that Milly's heart began to slow down, and she gradually took in that she was safe. Gilbert must be dead by now, or so deep in coma that nothing would ever rouse him. And it was not until later still that the implications of this began, gradually, to force themselves upon her slowly clearing consciousness. When they found him—when the police came to investigate—they would find the door locked and bolted on the outside: they would learn the cause of death, and that the dead man's wife had suddenly and mysteriously disappeared. In the face of all this evidence, how could she ever convince them that she hadn't murdered him?

She had, of course. That was the trouble.

By sitting watching while he ate the drugged meal: by locking him in the room so that he could not go for help: by taking no steps herself to inform doctor or police: by all these omissions and commissions, she had killed her husband as surely as if she had done it with her bare hands.

CHAPTER XVIII

MILLY REACHED UP and touched her hair. It was damp with the sea-wind, and her face was stinging from the blown spray. From these things, and from her icy hands, she knew that she must have been walking home from Mrs Day's

along the sea front: but she remembered nothing of it, so totally
had she been reliving the awful weeks that had brought her
former life to an end. Looking about her now, she saw that she
was nearly home. Already it must be quite late, for the little
lighted shops on the corner of Leinster Terrace were just
beginning to close, and at the sight of these familiar landmarks,
the black memories fell away, like an illness when recovery has
set in.

She was here! She was safe in the present! These were the
lights of Seacliffe, and this salty wind that whipped at her scarf
and through her hair was the wind of now! The past was gone,
she had escaped from it for ever: and that night, her dreams,
for the first time, were all of Seacliffe. Strangely, they were not
very happy dreams, a thread of stress and anxiety ran through
them all. She dreamed that she had lent Kevin Mrs Graham's
typewriter, and somehow could not return it in time, she was
hurrying with it towards a bus stop, and the driver would not
wait, though she shouted at him, and waved the typewriter as
she ran, trying to explain to him about Mrs Graham's degree in
Sociology, and how angry she would be. Next she dreamed that
she had lost a parcel of clothes, and Mrs Mumford would not let
her leave the house till she had found them. "But I never even
groped them!" she seemed to be protesting, with the mean-
ingless intensity of dreams—and woke to the sound of torren-
tial rain beating against her window, and the grey, half-light of
the winter morning warning her that it must already be nearly
nine.

It was bad enough getting to Mrs Graham's in weather like
this, but walking from there to Mrs Lane's was worse still. She
had no mackintosh, or umbrella, the way was almost all uphill,
and by the time she arrived her scarf clung like a bit of limp
washing round her soaked hair. As she slopped through the
puddles at the side of the house, and pushed open the side door,
she prayed that there would be some heating on somewhere.
She had had enough of all those bright open fires that would be
glowing in every room once Phyllis had "got things organised".

A housewife who is still trying to get things organised after eighteen years is unlikely to spring many dramatic improvements on you between Monday and Wednesday; and so Milly was unsurprised to find the heating arrangements unchanged—small, bronchial oil-heaters muttering and scolding in odd corners of the high, draughty rooms. The kitchen was a nice surprise, though: all the burners of the gas cooker had been turned full on, including the oven, and the dry, airless heat wrapped itself round Milly's chilled body like a warmed blanket the moment she stepped into the room.

Lovely! As she stood right up against the open oven door, the heat puffing gloriously against her soaked skirt, Milly hastily forgave Mrs Lane—Phyllis, that is—for all that imaginary driftwood, and for the undelivered loads of coal.

But where *was* Phyllis—Milly was training herself to think of her employer by her Christian name, as requested, but it was difficult, particularly since Phyllis still persisted in addressing her, Milly, as "Mrs Barnes". It was the sort of inverted snobbery you had to expect, Milly supposed, from people rich enough to own a draughty great house like this, with cobwebs all over its ornate, inaccessible ceilings, and an acre of neglected garden. Such indifference to the opinions of the neighbours argued money on quite a big scale . . . and it was at this point in her musings that Milly heard the unmistakeable sound of a row going on. Voices, suddenly raised, came from somewhere across the hall—from Mr Lane's study, it must be. . . . Squelching cautiously across the kitchen in her still-soaked shoes, Milly pushed open the door into the hall and listened, agog with curiosity.

Alas: the proverb about eavesdroppers is usually all too true: rarely indeed do they hear any good of themselves.

"I said the *filter*!" Mr Lane (it could only be him) was yelling. "What the hell's happened to the filter? Can't you tell that bloody woman to leave my things alone?"

Milly stiffened, and raked her conscience. What filter? What did it look like? Was it made of tin? Or paper? Or plastic? Could she have thrown it away as rubbish? Or added it to Michael's electric train set? Or put it away in the knife-drawer with all those apple-coring gadgets and the cake-icing outfit? None of these suggestions were quite the right kind of oil to pour on the troubled waters behind that study door, so she just kept very quiet, glad to be where she was. When a man is carrying on like this, it is good to be the one who is not married to him.

She could hear a soft pitter-patter of words from Phyllis now, evidently meant to be conciliatory: and then Mr Lane's voice bellowed forth again:

"Well, get rid of her, then! Why can't you ever get a decent, capable cleaner who understands her job? *Other* women don't have all this trouble with their servants!"

It might have been Julian himself speaking! *Other* women can do this. . . . other women can do that . . . other women seem to manage. . . . Milly, lurking out in the hall, shivered with sheer thankfulness that, on this occasion, she was merely the erring domestic, and not the hapless wife. Some one else, this time, had to smooth it all down, calm the raging husband, and get the matter put right without offending the char, or the cook, or whoever. Look, Mary/Doris/Maureen, I wonder if you could possibly . . . if you wouldn't awfully mind . . . you see my husband is rather particular about his . . . and so if you *could* possibly do it this way and not that way. . . . Placating, groveling, abasing herself before them, and all the while aware of Julian in the background, despising her, maddened by her devious timidity ("Why don't you *tell* them what you want done? Are you mistress in your own house, or aren't you?").

"Are you mistress in your own house or aren't you . . .?" Mr Lane was shouting, and Milly's heart twisted with pity for poor Phyllis, knowing exactly what she was going through. She longed to burst into the study crying: "It's all right, it's all right! I shan't be offended if he shouts at me, I shan't give notice! I daresay it *is* my fault about the filter, just tell me what the wretched thing *is*, and then I might remember what I did with it . . . and anyway, it'll probably turn out that he lost it himself, and then that'll be your fault, too . . . !"

". . . how the hell you can expect me to remember what I put in which drawer!" Mr Lane was blustering defensively: and

151

from the way the drawer slammed shut, Milly knew that the filter had turned up in it, exactly where he had put it himself. "It's impossible ever to find anything in this bloody house! The whole place is like a pigsty! What does that damned woman do with herself all those hours you pay her for?"

"Hush, Eric! She'll hear you!" Phyllis was trying to speak in an undertone, but her voice was squeaky with dismay. "I think I heard her come in ... !"

"You 'think you heard her come in'! Well, that's just great, isn't it? Is *this* what she calls half past two? You let her come swanning along at ten minutes to three, and—"

"*Quarter* to, dear," Phyllis interposed nervily: and Milly could almost have shouted at her. It would only make him angrier; and it wasn't as if a matter of five minutes this way or that affected the principle of the thing.

"... tell her you're not standing for it! Tell her that if it happens again, she can bloody well look for another job!"—and if Milly had only realised that this was the parting shot, she would have been able to leap out of sight in time. But as it was, she miscalculated the timing entirely. She had assumed that still to come was the bit about being ashamed to bring his friends home, and about his shirts never having any buttons on ... and so when he burst from the study like a charging bull, he was only just able to skid to a halt in time to avoid colliding with her.

He was not a big man. The red, engorged face and the small bloodshot eyes were barely on a level with her own, and the first thought that flashed through her mind was: He's not like Julian after all! Not a bit like Julian!

"Ah! Er! G-good afternoon, Mrs Barnes," he stammered: and giving one hunted glance into the study behind him he turned and fled up the stairs as fast as—or perhaps even faster than—his dignity as master of the house would allow.

Milly shrugged. The husbands were all like this—terrified to a man. At the beginning of her career in domestic service, she had sometimes indulged vague, Jane Eyre-ish daydreams, in which the unhappily married husband of one of her employers found himself watching her as she worked . . . felt himself soothed by her quiet efficiency . . . and increasingly aware of the wordless sympathy in her modestly downcast eyes. But she knew by now that you could keep your eyes modestly downcast for ever, and radiate enough wordless sympathy to power the whole of the Marriage Guidance Council, and not one of these husbands would notice a thing. How could they, when at the first tremor of Daily-Helping in any part of the house, they would be off like mountain deer, dodging from ledge to ledge until the danger was over? Milly amused herself for the first part of the afternoon by studying Mr Lane's itinerary as he slunk from room to room, alerted by Milly's dread footfalls approaching, or by the menacing hum of the vacuum cleaner, moving in for the kill.

Milly wondered how Phyllis was going to tackle this business of her lateness. "Tell her she can bloody well look for another job," had been Mr Lane's suggestion, from the safe distance at which he had been at pains to put himself: but Milly knew very well that whatever else Phyllis said, it wouldn't be *that*. The charge of unpunctuality was not unjustified, Milly well knew. It was impossible, sometimes, to get away from Mrs Graham's on time, what with lunch so often being delayed, either because Professor Graham was late, thus keeping them all waiting, or else because he wasn't, thus interrupting his wife's train of thought just as she was about to type her final sentence. Milly couldn't go until she had cleared up lunch, and naturally she couldn't clear up lunch until it had been eaten. And then there were Alison's vitamins, often trodden deep into the carpet, and needing ten minutes' hard scrubbing to remove them. They again couldn't be cleaned off the floor until Alison had finished throwing them there. So, one way and another, Milly rarely got to the Cedars before twenty or quarter to three, and so far there had been no fuss about it at all. Now, of course, there would have to be one.

"Er! Mrs Barnes!" Phyllis gave a bright little laugh and edged further round the kitchen door, clutching the doorknob with hands that Milly knew were sweating. The poor woman looked as if she were going to her own execution.

"*What* a wet day!" she gasped out, with a ghastly, fixed smile on her face, and not looking at Milly. "Oh, dear, yes! *What* a stinker! The rain, I mean. Doesn't it? Oh, Mrs Barnes, how *clever* of you! Doing all those! Oh, you *are* making them look nice!"

It was true, actually: and if only Phyllis hadn't always said this about everything, Milly would have glowed with pride. All this blackened Edwardian silver had been quite a find, really. In her afternoon jobs, Milly was always on the look-out for tasks which would get her off her feet for half an hour or so, and so when she came across this lot on a top shelf of the icy great room called the library, she had pounced on them and borne them off in triumph to the nice warm kitchen. And so now, half an hour later, here she was, sitting happily at the kitchen table, rubbing the beauty back into one blackened teapot or sauce-boat after another, while lovely warmth puffed against her back from the oven, and her aching legs rested surreptitiously on the bars of a chair under the table.

"Oh, it *will* be nice to have them done!" Phyllis jabbered nervously. "Oh, Eric *will* be pleased! He's always saying. . . ."

I bet he is, thought Milly: and wondered at the same time if this was the lead-in? If so, how was it going to go? How was the unfortunate Phyllis going to work round from Mr Lane's alleged delight in the polished silver to Milly's shortcomings in the matter of punctuality?

"Eric *does* so like to see things looking . . ." Phyllis went on, her words gathering speed as the crunch drew nearer. "Well, a man does, doesn't he, when he's fond of? I mean, so much of it has been in his family since. He was only saying today how nice the house looks since you've been coming, Mrs Barnes."

Having overheard the actual tenor of the conversation to which Phyllis was presumably referring, Milly found it hard to suppress a slight start: but Phyllis seemed to notice nothing, and continued: "And so we were wondering. It's only a suggestion, Mrs Barnes. I mean, it's not as if. We. I. Eric thinks. From *our* point of view, I mean, if you were here as long as possible? So we thought, I thought, if you *could*, by *any* chance, get here by quarter past two instead of half past . . .?"

Then, when the wretched woman is a quarter of an hour late, it'll still only be half past, and Eric won't know a thing about it: Milly could have finished the unspoken part of the sentence for her. It was a shame—it really was—that all this conglomeration of lies was to achieve nothing.

"I'm terribly sorry," began Milly—and she meant it—"But it's my other job, you see. I can't leave there until after two, and so. . . ."

"Yes, yes! Of course, of course! I quite understand! Don't worry about it for one moment . . . !"

Poor Phyllis! This panic-stricken servility—Milly saw it clearly now—was largely forced on her by the fact of being rich. Moralists have been saying for thousands of years that riches are a burden: and now, in the twentieth century, it has suddenly become true, in a perfectly straightforward and practical sense. In the old days, Milly mused, anyone who could afford to own all this real silver would also have been able to afford someone to stop it getting tarnished like this. Anyone rich enough to live in a large house like this, with its vast fireplaces and high, ornate ceilings, would also have been rich enough to employ a team of living-in servants. Sturdy young girls in aprons and print dresses would have lit the fires, polished the grates, and brushed the cobwebs off the ceilings. The coal-man would have come of his own accord, and there would have been someone working full time in the garden. Service on that sort of scale was what money used to buy: now it can only buy things. And so the rich *do* buy things— what else can they do?—and as their possessions pile up, and there are still no extra hands to polish them, or send them to the cleaners, or get them repaired, or even to put them away—so, inevitably, does a special kind of plushy squalor begin to invade the homes of the great—a squalor that grows, like mould, on cheques and dividends, and multiplies, at an accelerating rate, with every increment of income. No wonder wealthy husbands become so irascible—the more money they bring home, the more messy and disorganised their homes become and the more distracted their wives ("I can't understand her, she's got *everything*!"—never realising that just as *something* inevitably takes up *some* of your time, so *everything* is liable to take up all of it). No wonder that the less efficient of the wives (like Phyllis) were tending more and more to turn their backs on the whole thing, and to pretend to be poor. This way, they hoped, gracious living would no longer be demanded of them, nor an elegant appearance; and while this did not eliminate the problem entirely, it certainly lightened it. A problem tackled in a torn jersey is a problem halved.

Milly finished the last of the ornate Victorian cakestands, pushing her cloth in and out of the now-shining scrolls and curlicues, and realised, with a shock, that it was already nearly five. No time for the bathrooms now: even the hall and stairs would have to be skimped. Oh, well; that's what came of possessing two bathrooms *and* a lot of valuable silver: you couldn't expect to have all of them clean at once. She'd give the bathrooms a real good do, Milly promised herself, next time she came.

Next time? When she got home that night, she found Jacko sitting on the stairs, waiting for her.

"Thank God!" he greeted her dramatically. "We thought you were never coming!"

A man, it seemed, had called to see her that afternoon. No, he hadn't said what it was about—just that he wanted to make some enquiries. Sort of po-faced he'd been, like he might be from the Town Hall: Jacko hadn't liked the look of him at all.

CHAPTER XIX

THE POLICE! IN that instant of certainty, it was not fear that engulfed Milly's consciousness, but fury—speechless, impotent, fury.

After all this time! Just when I've really put it all behind me! Just when I've discovered that I don't even feel guilty! Just when it's all properly over, and my new life has really got going! It's not fair! It's not fair!

". . . but it's all right," Jacko was saying—and his voice, which had seemed infinitely far away, suddenly snapped near again, and hope twanged back. "It's all right, Barney! I told him you didn't live here! I told him we'd never heard of you!"

He looked so pleased with himself: Milly felt the shock subsiding. Surely, if it had been the police, they wouldn't just have accepted the word of a long-haired student, and gone meekly away? Come to that, how had Jacko guessed . . . ?

"Jacko, that was sweet of you: but how could you know that I didn't want to see him?" she asked, warily. She tried to remember which of her life-stories it was that she had told to Jacko and Kevin: not one that included being on the run from the police, that was certain.

"Well—'enquiries', of course," explained Jacko knowledgeably. "It's just another word for 'trouble', everyone knows that. I mean, they aren't going to be enquiring whether you want five thousand pounds, gift-wrapped, for your birthday, are they? Besides, it wasn't just you, Barney: it was the Mums I was worrying about. She can't bear tenants who attract officials to the house, it's like if they brought in lice, or leprosy. And you can't blame her, really . . ." here he lowered his voice, and his eyes took on a nostalgic, faraway look, as of battles long ago: "Like the time Miss Childe got a man in to look at why her food cupboard wouldn't shut properly, and it all ended in a van-load of inspectors swarming in to measure whether there was sixteen cubic feet of space in the downstairs loo . . . the Mums never got over it. So you see, Barney, we must keep him away from the house at all costs—or else pretend that he's your long-lost

brother, and even that not after 11 pm. But not to worry—"
here Jacko got to his feet, and squared his rumpled shoulders
proudly—"I'll look after you, Barney. If that creep comes back,
I'll see that he gets what's coming to him!—I say—" the
knight-errantry faltered a bit as they set off up the stairs
towards Milly's room, "You don't mind do you? I thought I'd
better stay in your room for the evening in case anything
happens, so I've moved some of my things in."

He had, too. The hi-fi set—the tape-recorder—a pair of
shiny boots—half a dozen books on economics lying open on
the chairs and on the bed. Milly looked around doubtfully,
wondering if she wanted protection on quite this scale.

"No, I suppose I don't mind," she said. "It'll save gas,
anyway." This was magnanimous, because it was most
decidedly not *her* gas that was being saved: a fug like this
could not possibly have been built up by less than three of her
precious shillings from the saucer on the mantelpiece. "Is
Kevin coming in too?" she added, mentally dividing her bread,
milk, and tin of Scotch broth into three, and adding a third of
a banana each.

"No, well. That's the thing, actually." Seeing him now
clearly, under the glare of the bare electric light bulb, Milly
noticed for the first time that he looked pale and tense: the
jaunty manner sat uneasily on him, as though Jacko was
finding the part of Jacko suddenly rather a strain.

"What's happened?" she asked: and suddenly it all came
out. Nothing to do with the Town Hall man at all—he had
evidently been a mere incident in Jacko's harrowing afternoon,
no more than a convenient excuse for button-holing Milly the
moment she came in. No, his real preoccupation was quite
other than this, and centred (so Milly at last gathered from his
circumlocutory narrative) on the presence—yes, she was still
there—of a certain Janette in Kevin's and Jacko's joint bedroom. She had, it seemed, been closeted there with Kevin for
"hours and hours", while Jacko had had to camp out like a
refugee in Milly's room, with nothing to do but write his essay
on Statistical Method (which anyway didn't have to be in till

next week, and so it was a cock-eyed waste of time working on it now), and to brood on what was going on behind the forbidden door. It was lucky, he conceded in a choked voice, that there happened to be all those spare shillings in the saucer or he would have frozen to death, on top of everything else.

Milly had heard of this Janette before. She was the shadowy, amorphous girl-friend who always seemed to have come yesterday, or to be coming tomorrow, but was never here today. When Jacko or Kevin mentioned her, which was not often, they spoke of her with a sort of off-hand resignation as if she was a neighbour's cat for which they felt a vague responsibility: and now here was Kevin triumphantly locked in the bedroom with her, and Jacko, white and near to tears, locked outside it.

"There hasn't been a sound since teatime," he gulped. "They must be. . . . They're. . . ."

Kid's stuff, Milly remembered: and now here was the jaded veteran of a thousand sexual encounters not even daring to pronounce the correct words.

She consoled him as best she could. Yes, she had to agree, they probably *were*, but so what? This Janette, she wasn't specially *Jacko's* girl-friend, was she? No, no, of *course* she wasn't! Nor Kevin's either! That was the whole *point*, didn't Milly see? It wasn't *serious*, they'd *agreed* it wasn't serious, and now . . . and now . . . !

It wasn't that it was boring: far from it: but Milly was getting hungrier and hungrier, and flattered though she was by being chosen as Jacko's confidante, she found herself watching, with increasing fervour, for some gap in the jeremiad into which it wouldn't be too heartless to insert a suggestion about opening the tin of soup. In the end she got her way by roundabout means: by first getting Jacko to put some sad music on the record-player, then something a bit less sad, and by the time a loud pop song was drumming through the room, and Mrs Mumford had yelled up to them to turn that noise down, the mention of food no longer seemed blasphemous. It was just then, as it happened, that Kevin and Janette reappeared,

very cheerful and friendly, with a bottle of cider and a
packet of frozen kippers. With these substantial supplements
to Milly's tin of soup, there was plenty for everyone, and even
Jacko began to cheer up. Soon, Mrs Mumford was yelling up
the stairs a second time. She expected *some* consideration, she
shrieked, and did they know what the time was? The third
time, she didn't yell, but stamped up with a tray of tea and
freshly-baked mince-pies, and demanded that a waltz be put
on the record-player. If they were determined to shake the
house to pieces with their great elephant feet, she scolded, they
might at least do it dancing something that *was* a dance. What,
they didn't know *how* to waltz?—she'd show them, if it was
the last thing she did! And though it *wasn't* the last thing she
did, not by a very long way, she *did* show them; and they
showed her how to gyrate to *their* rhythms, and by the end of
the evening Milly was finding it incredible that anyone could
ever want to make Enquiries about anything. Life is so simple, if
only you don't make Enquiries about it, and if the Town Hall
man had turned up then and there, Milly would have told him.

He didn't, though: nor was there a summons for her in the
post next morning, nor a policeman waiting outside Mrs
Graham's flat to arrest her as she went in. And though Mrs
Graham's phone went several times during the morning, it was
never for Milly. Through the wall, she could hear Mrs
Graham's voice, bored and irritable, exactly as if it was her
husband each time, but of course it couldn't have been.

Only when she arrived at Mrs Day's that afternoon did
something happen which forced Milly to think again about her
unknown visitor of last night. As usual, there was a note
waiting for her, in Mrs Day's wild writing, but this time it
wasn't about the *strrt grr*, nor about rinsing the *hwrf grool* in
three lots of cold water: it was a telephone message. A Mr
Loops, it seemed, had *phouled* asking for Mrs Baines, he
wanted to get in touch with her *ooplardy*, and would *phoul*
again this *umpternoon*.

He wouldn't, though. Milly made sure of *that* by taking the
receiver off. Then she set about her work with unusual speed

and concentration. No reading today; no lounging about on sofas, or speculating on why there should be a scarlet dog-harness on top of the deep-freeze, and no dog. Mrs Day's new flower-patterned tights, slit neatly open all down one leg, left her incurious. She just wanted to get finished, to get out of the place. Even though the telephone was effectively silenced, she still felt uncomfortable every time she caught sight of it. She pictured Mr *Loops* (or was it *Soap*, or *Reeves*?) fiddling about right now, at the other end of the wire, dialling and re-dialling, calling the operator . . . It seemed to bring him horribly near.

She finished her work much earlier than usual, while it was still just light, and as she hurried home through the damp, gusty twilight, her nerves were all on edge, as if she knew, already, the news that she was going to hear.

Yes, the man had been here again; and this time he had not been so easily put off. He had attempted to start an argument about Milly's non-existence, and Jacko had only managed to get rid of him by pretending that he, Jacko, was in a fearful hurry, already late for a lecture. At this, the man had given up—but not before looking at Jacko in a very funny way, and saying he would be calling back later on.

"Well—thanks, Jacko," said Milly dazedly. She was still in her outdoor things, she had not yet closed the front door, and now there was no need. Turning around, she walked out into the night.

At first, she could not decide where she was walking, or why; but gradually, as her dazed wits cleared, she realised that she was after all doing quite a sensible thing. She only had to stay out until Mrs Mumford's locking-up time, and her persecutor would be foiled, at least for tonight. After the magic hour of eleven, Mrs Mumford would admit nobody, on any pretext, and Milly would be able to sleep in peace. Briefly, she thanked heaven for the pockets of narrow-mindedness that still linger on, especially in small towns like this. With a permissive London landlady, she would have been doomed.

Doomed? What a drama she was making of it all! Why was

161

she allowing a second visit from this same man so to throw her?—it was no more, and no less, sinister than the first one. He was no more likely to be a policeman or a detective today than he was yesterday—less, if anything, because surely police working on a murder case move faster than this? Having alerted their victim by a first visit, surely they wouldn't just leave her to her own devices for another twenty-four hours? Not that it wasn't prudent to make herself scarce for the evening, all the same. "Like he might be from the Town Hall," Jacko had said: and if she was going to have to make up a whole new batch of lies about her insurance stamps, or her tax-assessment, or something, then she didn't want it to happen at home, with Mrs Mumford hovering attentively in the background, checking the new lies against the old.

Milly felt that she had walked a very long way, but it couldn't actually have been more than a mile or two, because she was only now coming into the straight, wide road that led to the station. It couldn't be very late, either—not more than half past six or seven—because the brightly-lit little booking-hall was alive with commuters just off the London train. They were pouring out from the lighted entrance, pulling up their collars, re-tying their scarves as the wind caught them: and Milly was suddenly and disconcertingly reminded of her own arrival here, nearly four weeks ago. For a moment, as she watched the hurrying, anonymous people fanning out into the dark, she had the strangest feeling of going backwards in time. Just as she had arrived here on a night of damp, gusty cold, the station lights flickering weakly in the wind, so, now, she seemed to be returning, on just such a night, by the way she had come ... back into the train ... back to Victoria Station, joining once again the creeping queues, head down, scarf once again pulled across her mouth to avoid recognition ... back, back, into the Underground, circling round and round, back-wards, backwards, spiralling back and back until she was thrust out into the icy streets of the January dawn, her heels once again clattering in the emptiness as she ran. Ran, and ran, but the other way, this time, towards and not away from that basement in Lady Street, where Gilbert was still waiting, watch in hand, checking on how long she had been away.

Milly rubbed her eyes. She shook herself, and stamped her cold feet. It was all right: that old crone silhouetted against the lighted tobacconists was not Mrs Roach, she couldn't be, this was Seacliffe, not Lady Street. As she blinked, and stared around, trying to get her bearings once again, she had a swift impression of a crest of white hair, glimpsed above the heads of the hurrying crowd; but in a moment it was gone, and the nightmare was gone too. She was here! She was now! The awful power of the past was receding, slipping back into the dark as suddenly as it had come, and she could scarcely even feel, now, the places where its icy fingers had momentarily touched her soul.

Idly, to fill in some of the time till eleven o'clock, she wandered into the station cafeteria, buying a newspaper as she went. As before, she found herself a table by the radiator; but this time, she had a cup of coffee and a roll and butter of her own, properly paid for. Her own newspaper to read, too. No need, this time, to peer and twist this way and that to catch a glimpse of other people's. Her feelings, too, were changed, and although she scanned carefully every column, every paragraph, for something about the Lady Street Murder, there was a curious lack of urgency about it. It was as if she knew, already, that this was not the direction from which the blow would come.

CHAPTER XX

"Ah, *there* you are, Mrs Er! I wonder if *you* can help me? People keep ringing up and asking for a Mrs Barnes! All yesterday, and now they've started again today. I can't get on with *anything*! *You* don't know anything about a Mrs Barnes, do you, Mrs Er? It's not someone *you* know?"

163

Mrs Graham was sitting with her hand resting irritably on the telephone, looking harassed and aggrieved. She always reacted to having her time unexpectedly taken up as another woman might to having her handbag stolen, and she was looking at Milly, who had just arrived, with a mixture of appeal and accusation.

"No," said Milly. It was not so much a lie as an automatic reaction, like blinking the eyes in response to sudden movement. The turmoil of shock and alarm which had flooded over her at Mrs Graham's words had rendered her quite incapable, for the moment, of deciding whether to lie or not to lie. The weighing-up of the question whether it was more dangerous to deny her identity than to admit it, was simply beyond her. So, "No," she said, and watched the room spin round her, with Mrs Graham's face revolving in the foreground, like a white ping-pong ball on the end of a string. Gradually, the whirling furniture slowed down, came to a standstill. Mrs Graham's face came to rest too, came into focus, and Milly began to hear the words formed by her moving lips.

"It couldn't be more inconvenient!" she was grumbling. "I'm just starting to summarise the Class C2 responses, and I seem to be twenty interviews short! Twenty! It will invalidate the whole survey! And all that fool of a Miss Bracken can say is that she thinks they were all sent in! *Thinks!*—I ask you! And then she has the cheek to suggest that I should simply extrapolate from the interviews I *have* got! *Extrapolate! Me!* I may not be the most punctilious researcher in the world, Mrs Er, but that's one thing I'll never do. I'll never extrapolate!"

One felt there should have been a roar of applause at this heroic declaration: but all Milly could find to say was "No". "No, I should think not, indeed!" she amended hastily, as Mrs Graham's raised eyebrows warned her that her response had been altogether too tepid. To find herself accused of condoning the evils of extrapolation as well as of murdering her husband was *too* much, and for a moment she just stood there, while her problems swayed like shadowy swing-boats in front of her, huge and ungraspable, and steadily gathering momentum.

They were closing in on her. They were moving in for the kill. No use, any longer, pretending that someone wanted to offer her a job, sell her an encyclopaedia, or ask her opinion about a new washing-up liquid. Indeed, it wasn't just "someone" any longer, it was a whole host of them, assembling to hunt her down. "People keep ringing up," Mrs Graham had said: even allowing for exaggeration, the words could hardly refer to fewer than three. They knew where she worked now, as well as where she lived. And that Mr Loops yesterday . . . he was in the plot with the rest of them, of course he was: which meant they had tracked her down to Mrs Day's as well . . .

"In the plot"—"tracked her down"—"They"—"Them"— Where had she heard these words before? In the urgency of her panic, Milly did not pursue the thought. The important thing, now, was to plan her getaway—either a simple physical one in the form of packing up and getting on a train, or a more subtle one based on lies, and more lies, told with expertise and panache.

Who better qualified than her for such a task? Toughened as she was by a prolonged survival-course in deception, she would be able to out-lie the lot of them; against her impassioned falsehoods they would break themselves as against a rock, and she would be free. . . .

But how much did they already know? The first principle of successful lying is to assemble in front of you all the data already irrevocably in the hands of your opponent, and see how it can be rearranged to your advantage. You can't subtract anything, of course, but you can add bits: and if you are clever you can twist a bit here, alter a sequence there, until the whole tenor of the thing seems to be changed, and they are left staring in blank dismay at the case they thought they had against you, and wondering what has hit them.

But first, you have to find out exactly what their case *is*: what data they have so far succeeded in assembling against you. . . .

"*Data* isn't the problem!" Mrs Graham was proclaiming (how had she got on to this from the extrapolations?). "Any fool can collect the *data*. It's the interpretation that counts, especially with the D-E's. As I keep trying to make Miss Bracken understand, the 'Don't know's' aren't just . . ."

"No, indeed!" said Milly heartily—and Mrs Graham stared at her, startled, but vaguely pleased by support from this unexpected quarter. "I do so agree with you, it's what I've always thought myself," continued Milly recklessly. "But this woman who rang up, this Mrs Barnes, did she say what she wanted?"

Milly had deliberately muddled the issue, got it all wrong, so that Mrs Graham should overlook her odd persistence in the pleasure of putting her right. There are moments when an ounce of confusion is worth pounds of apology and explanation.

"Who?" Mrs Graham looked vague for a moment. "Oh, you mean all those wrong numbers! No, Mrs Er, it wasn't the Barnes woman who was *ringing*, it was . . ." here she paused, studying Milly's IQ as one might study the physique of the man who has come to move the grand piano.

"Oh, well," she concluded, with a sigh that conveyed more clearly than words the boredom she felt at the prospect of trying to make such as Milly understand. "Never mind. It's not important. Though I do wish people would listen to reason, I really do. That man this morning, he just wouldn't take 'no' for an answer, he kept saying he *knew* she was here. Apparently the woman has run away, or something, and he all but accused me of harbouring her! *Me!* As if I've got nothing better to do!"—here she rattled a fresh page into the type-writer, signifying unassailable busy-ness.

"And now, Mrs Er, if you *wouldn't* mind . . .? I'm an hour behind already, it's been just one thing after another the whole morning. . . ."

Milly gave up, and retired, chastened, to get on with her work. Through the ceaseless clackety-clack of the typewriter behind the closed door, she kept listening for the telephone, but it only rang once. From the bored, slightly aggrieved tones of Mrs Graham's voice, it might have been absolutely anything: Professor Graham saying that he was going to be late (or early) for lunch: someone wanting to borrow a book: or perhaps a friend or relative in sudden, desperate trouble, and expecting Mrs Graham to interrupt her typing to listen to it. Mrs Graham's vast and unselective capacity for boredom could have embraced the lot. Milly listened through the door until her ears sang and her very jawbones were tense, but she could pick up no clues. And after a while, soothed by the droning of the Hoover and by all her familiar tasks, Milly gradually gave up thinking about the problem. Anyway, there was nothing she could usefully do. As with any cat-and-mouse game, the mouse stands to gain most by remaining in his usual hole, alert and inconspicuous, relying on his smallness, and on his intimate knowledge of the terrain. It is the cat who must stick his neck out, make the rules, and generally get things going.

CHAPTER XXI

MILLY STOOD FOR a number of minutes after she had arrived at Mrs Day's, staring down at the telephone and wondering if she would feel safer if she took the receiver off or if she didn't. The pale winter sun, higher and higher every day now, was flooding in through the wide window, showing up every finger-mark, every dingy streak, on the elegant white instrument. Milly noticed, wonderingly, that her fingers were fidgeting to get at it with a damp cloth, just as if nothing had happened. They seemed as if they were separate animals altogether, quite unconnected with herself, and with her seething brain, lashing itself into a fever of indecision as to whether to leave the thing alone to do its worst, or to silence it, as could so easily be done. It was like deciding whether to give tranquillisers to a savage guard-dog. To do so, you have to go uncomfortably close, and yet not to do so may result in being torn to pieces later on. There is no way of guessing in advance which will work best: no evidence one way or the other. No one knows, least of all the guard-dog.

Milly picked up the receiver and laid it gently on the polished table, and at once it began muttering at her in feeble protest. Straightaway, like an over-anxious mother with her crying baby, she snatched it up and restored it to its proper place: then wished she had left it off after all. The whimpering would have stopped in the end. Off with it, then—the spoilt thing!—let it whine itself to sleep, with her safely out of hearing! She would shut the door on it, she would run to the other end of the flat and switch the Hoover on till it was all over! Then, at last, her nerves would begin to relax, and she would be able to get on with her work safe in the knowledge that the telephone not only *wouldn't* ring, it couldn't!

Safe? What sort of head-in-the-sand logic was this? By disconnecting the telephone she was cutting herself off from the *awareness* of danger, not from danger itself. The danger was still there. Biting its nails, perhaps, in some nearby telephone box—maybe only a stone's throw away—and getting more and more impatient with the monotonous line-engaged tone. Tactics would be changed . . . and the first she would know of anything amiss would be the sound of the lift moaning to a halt out there across the landing.

By then, it would be too late. Whereas if she left the telephone in working order, she would at least get some sort of advance warning—enough, surely, to enable her to go racing down those six flights of softly carpeted stairs (no lifts, thank you!—she felt trapped enough already!) and out into the wild, wide, windswept world, where surely she would have the same fifty-fifty chance of freedom as a deer, or a fox, or any other hunted thing?

Already she could feel flight mustering in her limbs, speeding-up her heartbeat. Her hand, as she re-connected the telephone yet again, was trembling with a build-up of muscular energy as yet un-needed. From her brain the alert had gone forth, and throughout her body general mobilisation had begun: Milly found it hard, with this turmoil of activity going on within, to slow herself down to the pace of dusting... of handling ornaments... of washing up wine-glasses, putting them away on the high shelf of the cupboard. A slender glass stem snapped, brittle as ice, and tinkled sadly to the floor... Milly felt herself moving among Mrs Day's fragile possessions like a battering ram. Already the sensitivity had gone from her fingertips, the delicacy from her movements: all her finer sensibilities were already in cold-storage, packed away to leave room for the essentials—strength, speed and cunning.

When the telephone finally did ring, it was almost a relief. Milly knew, now, exactly what she was going to say to them: she was inspired, the lies almost told themselves. No, she would tell them, she wasn't Mrs Barnes, Mrs Barnes was no longer working here. Oh, yes, there *had* been a Mrs Barnes, certainly there had, she had worked here until—when was it? Two?—three?—weeks ago. Would that be the Mrs Barnes they were looking for? And no, she was very sorry, she couldn't tell them where Mrs Barnes was working now she had moved— gone after a job in Birmingham, someone had said. There'd been some sort of trouble about her references, or something, and she's had to leave in a hurry....

That would fox them! A big place, Birmingham. They could hunt down Barnes-es there for weeks on end, and as fast as they eliminated one lot, another batch would appear... Barnes after Barnes, rolling in without pause over the smoky Midland horizon.

And meantime, the Seacliffe police would have stopped bothering. Once the search had moved out of their district, they would surely lose interest... they must have plenty else on their minds, with hooligans smashing up deckchairs, and everything. And as for the big men in London—Scotland Yard, or whoever it was—surely their enthusiasm, too, would flag once the trail had grown as cold as this? London ... Seacliffe ... Birmingham ... and already the dockleaves and the nettles beginning to sprout on Gilbert's grave, somewhere or other in the crowded, neglected cemetery you could just see from the top of the bus as you travelled towards Morden.

They didn't solve all their murder cases: how could they? No doubt they did their best, but you can no more trace every murder to its bitter source than you can trace the course of a stream beyond the place where it merges into marshland, spreading out into a formless no-man's-land of bog, and reeds, and treacherous patches where, if you are not careful, you can sink nearly to the waist.

Surely Gilbert's murder stood as good a chance of going unsolved as any? There was nothing newsworthy about it, nothing obviously bizarre to challenge the ingenuity of police or detectives, or to stir the popular imagination. The victim was not a beautiful young girl: the suspect was not a member of high society. If Milly could only put them all off the scent for even a few days, she would be safe. Their other files would begin to pile up ... their in-trays to overflow. ... After all, the police are only human, and in any human transaction, if you can once get muddle and procrastination working on your side, you're home.

"Barnes? Mrs Barnes? No, I'm afraid not. ..." Now that it came to the point, Milly found herself gabbling nervously. The lies, spoken out loud, sounded less convincing than they had in the imagination, and she was hurrying to get to the end of her rehearsed speech before her nerve cracked. "No, I'm afraid there's no one of that name here at the moment. But there was a Mrs Barnes working here not long ago. I wonder if that's the one you mean? She left—let me see—two or three weeks ago, I think it must be. Someone told me she was moving—to Birmingham, I think they said. ..."

"*Barney!* Have you gone nuts, or something? What the hell do you think you're playing at?"

"*Jacko!*" The relief was so great that for a moment it was

indistinguishable from the terror that had preceded it, and Milly just stared at the pink wallpaper in front of her, and waited for her blood to start flowing again, and for her brain to start comprehending the miraculous new turn of affairs. "Jacko! Why didn't you——? Your voice sounded all——! Oh, Jacko, I'm so *thankful*! I thought you were——!"

"Yes. You sounded like that's what you thought," Jacko commented drily, his voice sounding very small and far away. "Look, Barney, what the hell's going on? Have you got the sack, or something? We rang you about sixty thousand times this morning, and the hag kept saying you didn't exist. . . ."

"Jacko! At Mrs Graham's, you mean? So it was *you*, then, all the time! Oh, but how marvellous . . . !" The relief, the sudden lifting of fear, was almost more than Milly could sustain. The pale sunlight seemed to dance in the room, the very air shimmered with freedom, such freedom as she had never thought to breathe again.

Was it three breaths of it she drew, or four? Then Jacko's voice again:

". . . and so we tried to put him off, just like we did the Town Hall wallah yesterday, but it was hopeless. He just wouldn't believe us when we said we'd never heard of you; and you see, Barney, by that time the Mums was poking her nose out of the kitchen, wanting to know what it was all about, so we just couldn't keep it up any longer. Well, I mean. But I wouldn't worry too much, Barney, really I wouldn't. He seems terribly harmless, this one, like he couldn't hurt a fly if you paid him. He must be about a hundred for a start, you should just have seen his mop of snow-white hair. Said his name was Soames."

CHAPTER XXII

AN HOUR HAD passed, and Milly still had not stirred. The room was in shadow now, the brief winter sunlight had faded from the rosy walls and gleaming mirrors. It was already quite hard to read the figures on the dial of the telephone, at which Milly was still staring, vacantly.

She did not know how long she had gone on talking to Jacko, nor how long she had been sitting here since the line had gone dead.

There was no reason to move. It seemed to her, now, that she had known all along that this was how it was going to end. All the time she had been on the run, dodging the police, watching the headlines, concealing her identity ... all this time she had known, somewhere deep inside her, that it was not merely the Law from which she was fleeing, but something much more terrible. Her fear of being arrested for murdering Gilbert had been genuine enough, but it had all the time masked a quite different fear, one too terrible to confront: the fear that she had *not* murdered him. The fear that somehow, somewhere, he had survived, biding his time, perfecting his plans for her punishment. He had waited while the moon waxed and waned once, and now he was on the move.

No, Jacko had assured her: he hadn't told the old boy her address at work; he wasn't *quite* a fool, thank you. Though it was always a bit of a help (he pointed out aggrievedly) if people would tell you what the hell they were up to before they let you in for this sort of thing. And no, he didn't know where the poor old carcase had gone now, he hadn't said. And yes, of course he, Jacko, would phone her if anything cropped up. She could count on him and on Kevin too, even though nobody ever told them anything.

So Gilbert was already on the prowl through the darkening streets: peering into the cafés, the bus shelters, his white hair raked into a cockatoo-crest by the wet wind from the sea.

How long would it be before he found her? That he would do so in the end, she never doubted. Already the feel of him was all about her, she seemed to feel the strange power of his madness guiding him as he roamed the ill-lit streets, staring left and right, through lighted windows and through solid walls, with his shining, visionary eyes.

Ridiculous! was she taking leave of her senses? Madness was a disability, not a rare and valuable gift! It rendered a person *less* able to achieve his purposes, not more! Where a sane person would seek his objective in a strange town by asking the right questions, following up the relevant clues, a madman would be driven hither and thither by a bizarre logic of his own, getting nowhere, banging up against the relevant facts only at random, like a fly in a window. Milly felt her strength returning. The sheer, gibbering terror had passed, and she began to take stock of her situation.

Here, at Mrs Day's, she was comparatively safe, at least for the moment. No one, mad or sane, would be able to trace her to this address in the space of a single afternoon, via such a trail of mis-information as they were certainly going to encounter as they went. Like a mediaeval baron surveying his moats and drawbridges, Milly reviewed the obstacles that such a person would have to surmount. First, Mrs Mumford, tight-lipped, minding her own business if it killed her. Then, Jacko and Kevin, lying tirelessly on her behalf to all comers: and lastly (if they ever got so far) there was Mrs Graham who, in her sublime unconcern with things which only involved other people, didn't even know that Milly had a name, let alone an address, or a continued existence beyond her, Mrs Graham's, front door.

She would stay here, then, here in Mrs Day's flat, for as long as it was possible to stay. Why, perhaps Mrs Day would take her on as a proper housekeeper, living-in! It was just what the flat needed, actually, someone permanently around to clear up after the all-night parties, to iron the crumpled finery, put the orchids in water ... and it was just then that she heard the sound. The soft whine of the lift gliding to a halt . . . the doors sliding open, smooth as cream.

Well, and what of it? There were other flats on this floor, weren't there? It could be anybody . . . absolutely anybody.

It was funny, certainly, that there was no sound of footsteps after the opening of the lift doors, but not so funny that it need set the veins pulsing in your temples like this. Were not the carpets in this building thick and soft, the acoustics carefully planned to deaden footfalls? Absurd, then, to imagine that someone must be lying in wait out there, or advancing soundlessly in ancient white gymshoes. . . .

She seemed to know, though, what the next sound was going to be, and when she heard it, the shock was the shock of recognition rather than of fresh terror.

It had all happened before, that was the thing: happened exactly as it was happening now, only at a different door, opening on a different flat . . . the slow fumbling at the latch . . . the faint scratching of a key inserted by unsteady fingers, and then the door swung silently open. . . .

"Oh!" said the girl: and for a few seconds she and Milly stared at one another in mutual stupefaction, each separately trying to reconcile a turmoil of imaginary expectations to a completely unforeseen reality.

The newcomer was a heavy, thick-set young woman, with a big, freckled face devoid of make-up, and she was wearing a grey jersey and navy blue skirt which (Milly found herself inanely reflecting) the exotic Mrs Day wouldn't have been seen dead in.

Where on earth did so unglamorous a figure fit into Mrs Day's glittering life? Friend? Relative? Or—yes, that was the most likely—she must be a betrayed wife come to have it out with her husband's mistress! That's how she'd come to be in possession of the door key, of course: she had found it in the pocket of his suit when she was sending it to the cleaner's, and then (driven by curiosity and by the chronic insecurity of the plain and dowdy wife of an attractive man) she had searched the rest of his pockets . . . had come across the

174

love-letters, the pressed orchid. . . . No wonder, after all that, that the poor girl had been a bit non-plussed at the sight of Milly! Probably she had never seen the legendary Mrs Day, and was right now trying to fit Milly to the part, twisting her hands agonisedly as she did so, with her doughy jaw dropped open.

"I'm afraid . . . !" began Milly, and "I thought . . . !" interrupted the girl; and then they both gave up simultaneously and stared at one another again.

"I've come for my coaching," the girl volunteered at last—and at the sound of the hesitant small voice, Milly suddenly noticed how very young the visitor was, and how paralysed with shyness—noticed, too, the bulging briefcase she was clutching.

"Mrs Day—that's our headmistress—she said just to let myself in, as she'd be late. I—I'm sorry . . . she didn't tell me there'd be anybody here. . . . It's my A-level physics, you see, I was away all last term. . . ."

A headmistress! How one lives and learns! For the second time in five minutes, Milly found all her presuppositions being turned upside down: and her mind was still spinning from this second effort of readjustment, when the buzzer sounded on the front door.

For some reason, she wasn't frightened at all this time. Somehow, she assumed that it must be Mrs Day herself, and was all agog with curiosity at the prospect of actually *seeing* this many-sided character. "Yes?" she said confidently into the mouthpiece, and heard the caretaker's voice in reply:

"Mrs Barnes? Good, you *are* still there, I thought you might have gone. Your husband's here, Mrs Barnes, he's come to call for you. I'm sending him up now."

CHAPTER XXIII

Running, running, running, all over again, through dingy, ill-lit streets, only this time there was so little sense of escape. She remembered how her lungs had laboured, just as they were labouring now, seared by the freezing night air. Only then there had been a taste of dawn in the January darkness: now, the black night was only just beginning. There had been hope then—though she had scarcely been aware of it—hope of escape, of a new life somewhere on the far side of despair, of new worlds yet untried beyond the horizon of her experience. She had thought then, as she raced through the dark, deserted streets that zig-zagged away and away from the basement in Lady Street—further and further, ever safer, ever more anonymous—she had thought, then, that she was actually escaping: that if she could only run fast enough, and far enough, then she could be out of it all, her very identity left behind like an empty packing case with all the rest of the debris.

Not now, though. From the moment when she had flung herself out of Mrs Day's flat, and out of the life for ever of Mrs Day's astonished pupil, she had known, in her heart, that there was nowhere to run; that this was the end of the road.

Oh, she had run, just the same: had run like a madwoman, down all those flights of richly-carpeted stairs, round and round ... down and down. ... There was a curious moment when Gilbert must have been barely two yards away, as the lift slipped up and past her, gliding upwards in the opposite direction to her headlong flight.

She had not even glanced towards it. On to the bottom she had sped, without pause or backward look. Nor had the startled voice of the caretaker delayed her. The heavy glass door swung back against his exclamation of surprise and protest, slicing it off, and she was out and away, hurling herself from the lights and warmth of the flats as from a high rock, plunging headlong into the dark beyond.

Yes, she had run, all right. She was still running, her breath coming in short, painful gasps and her heart lurching. Already she had reached the outskirts of the town. The houses were smaller, and shabbier, the street lights dimmer and further and further apart, until presently there were no more lights and the darkness was unbroken, except for an occasional orange gleam from a window as a curtain was twitched aside and a face peered out, idly censorious, to see who it could be, running so fast and so noisily through a respectable suburb at such an hour.

Still she ran on: and after a while she felt the road change to something rougher under her feet. She found herself stumbling against cobbles—or was it dry tufts of winter grass?—And now she could just see that the path ahead of her was forking in two directions, one winding up towards the downs, the other curving down to the right ... it must be towards the beach. Already there was a salty tang in the air, and that sense of emptiness and uncluttered distance that is unmistakeable: the sea could not be far away.

It did not matter which of the two paths she chose, for she knew by now that she was running nowhere. The options were at an end. Whichever way she chose now, to left or right, it would still be the way back. Back ... back ... by the same way she had come. ... It had come to pass just as she had foreseen it—was it only yesterday?—as she stood at Seacliffe station watching the London trains come in. The past had got her. It had caught up with her at last. She could feel the weight of it, dragging her backwards and downwards, even while her legs still went through the motions of running. It was like riding to your death on a stationary bicycling machine.

Strange how her legs would not give up, even now! Still they ran: ran, and ran until her heart seemed to be beating some strange tattoo behind her ribs ... tapping out messages ... telling her something. ... She could hear voices, just as Gilbert had once heard voices:

"Milly!" they mocked: "Milly Barnes! *What* a name to choose!" and as she ran faster, trying to outdistance them, she seemed to hear their laughter, rollicking in the dark air that raced away behind her.

They had given themselves away, though! She knew now what they were after. They were after her new self, her new identity.

How could they be so unfair? She had worked so hard on this new self, with such skill and with such determination. Out of the jumbled-up remains of a broken, terror-stricken criminal, she had succeeded in piecing together a perfectly respectable Milly Barnes, a re-conditioned, good-as-new model, capable of earning its own living, even of making friends for itself.

"Milly Barnes! Milly Barnes! *You're* not Milly Barnes, there's no such person!"

She had not outdistanced them after all! They were back ... they were all around her! They were siezing on her ... laying hands on her new self ... confiscating it, as if she had been smuggling it through the customs! "It's mine!" she kept crying, "I've got a right ...!" but all she could hear was their maddening laughter ... and now here were their hands, tweaking at her, pulling her back, weighing her down, until her legs could carry her no longer, and she sank to the ground.

She knew, really, what it was she had done, and why They had been sent to fetch her. She wasn't supposed to be here at all. She was a reincarnated soul without a passport ... somehow, she had slipped illegally between the frontiers of life and death, dodging the regulations, jumping the queue, getting herself re-born before her time.

And now they were pulling her back, dragging her down to the place where she belonged. "You're not getting away with *that*, my girl!" she heard them say, amazingly clear and loud against the noisy thudding of her heart. "Re-birth isn't *that* simple—whatever made you think it was? And so now it's right back to the beginning for you, Milly Barnes, with it all to do again—and *properly,* this time. . . . !"

Milly opened her eyes. She found herself staring ahead into a sky so black and so full of stars that at first she thought she had died, and was floating free of the earth's atmosphere, heading out into space.

But then, after a few seconds, she became aware of a pressure against the back of her skull and against her shoulder-blades. She was lying on the hard ground, flat on her back, staring up into the incredible night sky, completely cloudless, and scoured by the cold into this unimaginable brilliance.

What time was it? How far had she come? Painfully—she must have bruised her shoulder in falling—she raised her head, and far away over the black sea she saw the crescent moon sinking, and knew that it could not be very late—not later then nine, anyway.

How long did that give Gilbert to track her down? Say she had fled from Mrs Day's at about six—what would he have done first, when he found her gone? He would have glided down in the lift again, he would have sought out the caretaker. "She went *that* way," he would have been told. "Towards the Avenue.... No, I'm sorry, sir, there was nothing I could do, she was going like a mad thing. I tried.... I called out to her...."

And then what would Gilbert do? She saw him pacing stiffly across the dark town, the strange, predatory look sharpening his features, until he seemed to be sniffing the night air, to left and right, like a beast of prey. And people would help him, of course they would—a white-haired old man in such a state of anxiety and concern. "Yes, she went in *that* direction," they would say, pointing: and "Yes, we wondered if she was all right, but we didn't like.... Oh, not at all, only too glad to be of help...." and on he would come, on, on, sniffing this way, sniffing that way, until at last all the muddled directions, all the well-meant advice, all his own strange, supra-normal perceptions, would begin to focus in a certain definite direction ... would converge, at last, on this spot where she was lying.

She must move! She must hide! She must *do* something! Milly staggered to her feet, and on limbs stiff and almost numb with exhaustion, she tried to begin running again. But in which direction? She had a mad feeling now that Gilbert was everywhere. Ahead, crouched in the dry winter grass. Behind, padding soft as a shadow through the outskirts of the town. Up in the Downs he would be lurking, too, his white hair like tufts of sheep's wool, just visible through the dry, crackling gorse and winter furze: and down there at the sea's edge also she would find him, looming up behind the breakwater like one more rotting timber, his terrible silvery eyes shining in the light of the moon.

Nowhere to turn. . . . No way to run, and yet run she must, for fear had possession of her limbs and would not let her be.

She came at last to the beach, at the point where the parade petered out into a slippery concrete ramp. She scrambled over the damp stone, and landed, with a scrunch of pebbles, on the shingle beneath.

The noise was terrible. For several minutes Milly crouched, absolutely still, under the shadow of the ramp, waiting to see if she had given herself away.

No sound. Nothing: and at last she ventured from her hiding-place, tiptoeing painfully over the stones, until at last she reached the limits of the shingle belt, and felt her feet sinking into soft, powdery sand.

The tide was far out, and as Milly moved towards the distant line of foam at the water's edge, she had a strange sense that she was no longer moving at random; she was walking towards a rendezvous, to keep an appointment fixed long, long ago. And it was no good turning round and walking the other way, for if she did the rendezvous would be there, as well.

The soft sand had become firm under her feet, then wet, and wetter still, until now, as she approached the curving scallops of foam that defined the limits of the almost waveless water, marking it off from the glistening expanse of sand, she felt her feet sinking in once more, squelching at every step. She could feel the water soaking in above the soles of her shoes.

Far off to the right—a hundred yards or more—she could just make out the breakwater, gaunt and jagged against the starlit water. The treacherous light of the moon seemed to be playing games with the black timbers, they stirred and wavered in front of her tired eyes . . . one of the taller, narrower ones almost seemed to be detaching itself from the main body—lurching with a strange, lollopping gait out across the sand.

The Voices. Was it in moments of great and unendurable fear that they came to you? They were not mocking her this time, they were not even calling her "Milly" any more—"Milly Barnes" was just a bad joke that had come to an end.

"Candida!" she heard them call, faint and far away: and then, nearer and clearer, "Candida! Candida!"

The syllables of her old name, her real name, beat upon her out of the past, their rhythm rang like the hooves of a galloping horse alongside the quiet sea.

She put her hands to her ears, she tried to black out the sound of the past thundering towards her; she stared, with dilated pupils, across the faintly-gleaming stretches of sand which spread away into the darkness as far as she could see.

Was she going mad? The black upright timber *had* moved nearer . . . this was no trick of moonlight . . . ! it had detached itself from the breakwater, it was rocking towards her across the glimmering sand. In a few moments it would be near enough for her to glimpse the white hair, flying wild under the moon.

"Candida!" the voice came again, "Candida? What in heaven's name . . .?"

She did not believe it. Even after she had recognised the voice beyond all possibility of doubt; had recog— d the swing of his shoulders, too, as he ran—she still did not believe it.

All the same, it was necessary to say *something*.

"Hullo," she said, in a small voice. "Hullo, Julian!"

CHAPTER XXIV

GILBERT WAS DEAD. At first, that was all she could take in of Julian's tirade, as he sat beside her on the breakwater in the light of the dying moon, berating her for her folly, just as he always used to do.

Gilbert was dead, had been dead for nearly a month now. This was the third time Julian had repeated the information, and yet still she kept asking the same inane questions, seeking confirmation by repetition. What about the Mr Soames who had called at Mrs Mumford's? Gilbert's brother, naturally. Surely she knew he *had* a brother? The poor devil was nearly out of his mind with the worry and strain of dealing with his late brother's affairs single-handed (he was quite a lot older even than Gilbert had been), and with the complications arising from the fact that he wasn't legally the nearest relative. *She* was—and she had chosen to disappear! To go swanning off on a seaside holiday under a false name, leaving everyone in this mess! Did she, by any chance, realise just exactly how much trouble and expense she had caused? Lawyers—Bank managers—ground landlords—they'd all been going crazy trying to get in touch with her . . . and now, to crown everything, he, Julian, had been compelled to fly over from Boston, at vast inconvenience, to help sort it all out!

Gilbert was dead. The words drummed through her brain, deadening the sound of Julian's scolding. He was dead, and no one, now, would ever know that she had murdered him.

For there had been no inquest—no awkward questions. The harassed, overworked young doctor had scribbled a certificate of Natural Causes (Gilbert was an old man, after all: what more likely than that he should suffer a stroke or a heart-attack?). And as to the door, locked and bolted on the outside, there was no mention of this at all in Julian's story; and so it must be presumed that, somehow, no one had noticed it.

It would be Mrs Roach who had undone the bolts, for it was she (Julian had explained) who had found the body. She must have undone them without comprehension, her slow mind not taking in their significance. No doubt Gilbert's habit of locking and bolting everything was so familiar to her that it no longer made any impact: she must have failed to put two-and-two together and to realise that, on this occasion, it could not have been he, himself, who had fastened the door. And afterwards—naturally enough—the shock of finding him dead in his chair would have put the matter right out of her mind.

Dead in his chair. In his great leather chair, with the green-shaded lamp at his elbow. Strange to think of him sitting there, just as he had always sat, at peace for the very first time.

Far out across the black water the moon was setting. Staring out along the jagged silver track, Candida thought about her responsibility for Gilbert's death, just as she had tried to think about it once before, when she was still Milly.

She had murdered him: that, she had already faced. What she had to face now was the knowledge that she was not going to be punished for it. No one, now, would ever know what she had done. No blame would ever attach to her, no penalty would ever be exacted.

Fixing her eyes on the magical silver track, that led from the infinite right to her very feet, Candida waited, as she had once waited when she was Milly, for the first pangs of the terrible, haunting guilt that would be with her to the end of her days. Guilt that would gnaw secretly at the dark roots of her being, giving her no rest. Guilt on this sort of scale must be waiting somewhere for her, somewhere under the glittering vastness of the sky?

All she could feel was an unutterable thankfulness that Gilbert was dead. Dead like the dinosaurs, and Shakespeare, and the kings of Babylon. Dead as she would one day be, and Julian, and the glistening ribbons of seaweed that today slapped so proudly against the timbers under the winter moon. Are we to ask of each and all of these deaths, Whose fault was it?—However did it happen? Under the shadow of the millennia, such questions dry upon our lips; they become a blasphemy against the benign cycle of birth and death, against the miracle of evolution under the turning circle of the stars. Even the humming of a gnat contains more of truth and wisdom.

She could feel no guilt at Gilbert's death: only a confused sense of participation. But his life—Ah, that was another matter! Whatever small wrong she might have done him by killing him paled into insignificance by the side of the wrong she had done by marrying him.

That was the wickedness. There, if anywhere, lay the lifelong guilt. She had married not merely without love— plenty of women have done *that*—but without the faintest desire for anything he could provide at all. She had not even married him for his money, or for the security he could offer—for even these motives can leave a man with some shred of self-respect, some shred of pride at having provided his woman with at least *something* that she needs.

No, she had left no shred of anything for Gilbert. She had not married him for anything he had, or was. She hadn't married him as a person at all, but as a thing, a handy weapon, a stick with which to beat her former husband.

Well, and did a man like Gilbert deserve anything better? He was a crafty and bitter old man, even before he went mad. All his life he had quarrelled with everybody, distrusted everybody, destroyed every relationship that had ever come his way. What had he ever done, or been, that he could expect anybody to marry him for love?

She had never thought before of how it must have seemed to him. After a bitter, lonely life of enmities and hatred, now here, suddenly, is a woman who mysteriously seems to *like* him! Who actually seeks his company! Nobody has ever sought his company before—and good riddance, damn them!—but here, at last is someone who *does*! A woman, too . . . Not unattractive . . . not much over forty. . . . Can it be—can it possibly be—that something new and magical may yet be going to happen to Gilbert Soames, in this last decade of his life? Can it be that here, at last, is the woman who will break down his frozen inhibitions, soften his bitter, vindictive spirit . . .?

No. Well, naturally not. That sort of thing just doesn't happen. His new wife left his inhibitions exactly where she found them—and was thankful to do so. She shrank from his fumbling touch. Instead of love she gave him fear . . . instead of friendship, defensive withdrawal. Just as everyone had always done. . . . She was one of Them after all . . .!

Candida understood about Them now, as she had never done while Gilbert was alive. For now she, too, had known what it was to hear the faint, menacing whisper of their approaching battalions, had felt, once or twice, the first tentative touch of their icy hands. She had known what it was to hear Them down every harmless telephone . . . to see Them in every careless gesture.

It was because she had been on the run, of course, in fear of her life: for it is fear that brings Them flocking. They can smell it afar off, like vultures hungry for blood.

What fear was it, then, that had brought Them flocking around Gilbert, flapping and screeching, confounding his judgement and finally blotting out his sight? Fear of something he had once done? Some enemy he had once made, long, long ago? Perhaps, if she had been a quite different sort of a wife, he might have confided to her his dark story, or such of it as he still remembered, during the silent, deathly evenings. Now, no one would ever know.

It wasn't her fault! It wasn't *she* who had driven him mad: he was already far gone on the course of which she saw the terrible climax, long before she met him. Once she realised what a state he was in, she had done what she could. She had done her best, in the face of the awful odds.

Naturally, she couldn't have been expected to do for him the things which a woman who actually loved him would have done: to have put her warm arms round his stiff, wary body: to have answered his cold, formal kisses with warm, spontaneous ones: to have said, sometimes, "Don't be such an old silly!" or

185

"You *know* that that's nonsense!" when his bizarre delusions first began peeping through.

Did he, in the beginning, imagine that Candida was going to love him like that? Did he daydream, like a foolish adolescent, of a real flesh-and-blood relationship, utterly beyond the capacity of his warped and frozen soul?

What right had he to dream such an impossible dream? Or to go to pieces when Candida couldn't make it come true? No one could! Probably no one could even have given him ordinary friendship, or even companionship, so hollowed out was he by the long years of bitterness and suspicion.

All right, so they couldn't. Then they shouldn't have married him. To marry someone in the clear knowledge that nothing can be given, nothing received—that was the wickedness: and no wickedness on his side would ever cancel it out, or justify it. On that August day, in the Brixton registry office, she had committed a crime against Gilbert far worse than the crime of murdering him—and yet one for which the Law provides no penalty at all. Strange.

Suddenly, Candida felt herself Milly again: buoyant, carefree: impervious to remorse because she had only just been born. Candida felt in her own bones Milly's toughness, her zest for survival, her hard-won capacity for cutting-off from her former self and living each moment as if nothing had ever happened before.

The Voices had been wrong. They had been talking platitudes, as Voices so commonly do. "You can't run away from yourself" had been the theme of their discourse: but the truth is that you can. She had. She had become Milly, and as Milly she had acquired an entire new repertoire of strengths and skills—not least of which, she now realised, was the recapturing of some of the special qualities of childhood: above all the child's untramelled eagerness to explore the next minute, the next hour, as though it was a voyage round the world. All these new skills and aptitudes, so painfully acquired by Milly, were now at Candida's command, to use exactly as she wished. If she chose, now, to by-pass guilt and remorse, and to concentrate on getting on with the rest of her life, she could easily do so. Milly had provided her with the techniques.

And in fact, when it came to the point, it hardly seemed a matter of techniques at all: it seemed the most natural thing in the world simply to put it all behind her, as Milly would have done.

Cautiously at first, and then with increasing boldness, Candida made herself face the things she had done. Without self-deception or self-justification she contemplated the full extent of her folly and wickedness in marrying Gilbert, and thereafter escorting him blindly to his death.

Still she felt nothing that could be identified as guilt. All she could feel was a vague and not unpleasing sense of her own superiority to the blinkered, self-centred bitch she had once been.

Was this a special sort of detachment peculiar to the twice-born, a privileged kind of opting-out? Or was it simply that it is almost impossible for anyone under fifty nowadays to experience guilt in the true, crippling sense in which our grandparents experienced it? Nowadays we are told constantly that we are all riddled with guilt-feelings, and that it is this over-developed sense of guilt that is at the root of all our ills: but surely, by now, this is more of a folk-memory than a fact? It was true once, no doubt: but can it possibly be true still? We have been told so often and for so long that no one is ever really to blame for anything: that it is all due to what Mother did, or Father, or Society. And what Mother did is itself the result of what *her* mother did, and of the pressures of Society in *those* days ... cause behind cause, rolling in out of the infinite, as far as the eye can see or the mind can reach, leaving nowhere any place where guilt can come to rest, can settle and take root. ...

"And of course that Roach woman wasn't much help!" Julian was saying—and Candida jolted herself out of her reverie to listen—"Apparently the old harridan had been going around telling everyone you weren't married to Soames at all, that you were 'No better than you should be'—I think that was her phrase. And of course everyone believed her—why not, in this day and age?"

Why not indeed. In the darkness, Candida was smiling. How ironic that the old woman, in her would-be malice, should have done her victim such an utterly unlooked-for service! Because, of course, this misconception delayed considerably the moment when anybody began seriously to search for Candida. All the while they were assuming that it was merely Gilbert's mistress who had (so conveniently for all concerned) seen fit to make herself scarce, no one evinced the least interest in her where-abouts. It was the missing brother they were after at that stage, for he was the presumed next-of-kin. It was he who must sign the papers, pay for the funeral, sort out the incredible chaos of Gilbert's accumulated possessions. And it was only after this brother had been found, and had been ineffectually muddling with Gilbert's papers for several days, that it came to light that Candida really *was* Mrs Soames, really *had* been married to Gilbert. Then, of course, the search for her started in earnest.

". . . I hate to say it, my dear Candida, but I've never in my whole life encountered such an incompetent way of disappearing! First you give yourself some daft phoney name, and then what do you do but straightaway sign a cheque with it! So, of course, the first thing Brother Soames finds on the doormat is this letter from the Bank, asking who the hell is Milly Barnes?

"Mind you, *he* seems to have been pretty slow in the up-take, too. Apparently he just shoved the letter in among the rest of the papers, and forgot all about it. It took *me* to point out that it might be an idea to find out who this Milly Barnes was—Not that I hadn't already guessed, of course—who else would be acting so plumb daft? And anyway, I'd already heard from Felicity What's-her-name that somebody'd seen you two or three weeks earlier hanging around Victoria Station, looking as if you'd committed a murder, or something. So, putting two-and-two together. . . ."

Of course. It had been a daft thing to do. By hanging around a main line station all through the rush hour you are exposing yourself to just about as high a statistical chance of being recognised as it would be possible to achieve if you were specially trying. And as for Mrs Mumford's cheque—that had been idiotic, too, but how else could she have got a roof over her head that night?

After that, it had all been easy for Julian. Victoria . . . Seacliffe . . . Leinster Terrace. Candida could visualise the impatient scorn with which Julian would have brushed aside Jacko's implausible lies . . . the effortless charm by which he would have manoeuvred the tight-lipped Mrs Mumford into telling him everything she knew, including the fact that her newest lodger worked for a Mrs Graham—had, in fact, offered this lady's name as a reference, only Mrs Mumford had never taken it up, on account of her low opinion of references in general (how courteously, in the interests of his ulterior motive, would Julian have listened to these opinions, betraying neither boredom nor impatience, charming to the last). And then the phone calls to Mrs Graham, and finally a visit to her in person, and the extracting from her of the information that her Daily Help worked also for a Mrs Day.

From *Mrs Graham*? *Information*? But Mrs Graham had never bothered to learn so much as her name!

Not her name, no. But her other jobs, yes. Because this was something that affected *her*, Mrs Graham. The fear of piracy by her dearest friends had never been far from Mrs Graham's mind since that first morning, when Mrs Day had rung up with that treacherous offer of five pence an hour more.

So, on from Mrs Graham's to Mrs Day's . . . and Candida knew the rest.

Or most of it. Why, though, had he referred to himself as her *husband*, in talking to the caretaker?

She felt Julian give a tiny start.

What a quibble, he protested! Christ, after nearly twenty years of marriage, it was a slip anyone might make!

The moon had set now; and though the filmy rim of the water could no longer be seen, a soft gobbling sound in the shallow water at their feet warned that the tide had begun to turn. In

189

the starlight, Candida could just make out the sulky hunch of Julian's shoulders, and knew that he was discomfited, and in a moment would think up something to blame her for.

"You never answered my letter," he said, aggrievedly; and for a moment Candida stared at him, in total bewilderment.

"What letter . . .?" she was beginning—and then, suddenly, she knew.

Answer it! That letter which she had torn into a thousand pieces . . . the letter which had goaded her through the nights and days, had driven her onward like one possessed, into folly, wickedness, and crime . . . *Answer* it!

"Oh, I was going to," she replied lightly, her eyes on the hurrying swirls of the awakening water, just visible in the starlight. "I was going to, but you see I was waiting for the mustard and cress to come up first. I wanted to see if it spelt R.A.T."

He laughed; and she felt a tremor of surprise go through him. Suddenly she realised that in the old days she had never cheeked him like this in answer to his bullying. This was something new. Something that Milly had bequeathed.

". . . I suppose it was then that I got my first inkling of how impossibly touchy and possessive Cora could be," Julian was saying. "You see, the crazy thing was she'd more or less *written* the damn letter for me—we were both a bit drunk at the time, and I remember how we laughed when she suggested the bit about the aunt! But no sooner had I posted it than she turned on me like a mad thing! Storming at me that I didn't love her, that secretly I still loved *you*, or I could never have sent you a letter so pointlessly, so deliberately cruel! She accused me of trying to sting you into some kind of reaction, by any flamboyant, childish means I could devise, and declared that this proved I still cared! And by God, Candida, I've been thinking about it a lot lately, and I realise she was right! I *did* still care! I still do! Candida, when my divorce comes through, will you marry me?"

The cheek of it! The unutterable, brazen impertinence! Now that Cora had thrown him over: now that he was no longer quite the brilliant success he had once been—*now*, Candida was good enough for him again!

For this was how it must be with him: she could see it clearly now. That Boston research job must have been a step *down*, not a step up ... perhaps he had overestimated the permissiveness of the permissive society, particularly where it impinges on the medical profession: perhaps he had found, to his dismay, that the betrayal of an innocent wife *does* still cause raised eyebrows in some quarters, even nowadays.

Whatever it was, his conceit must have taken a beating, and so now here he was, with ego bruised and bleeding, limping back to Candida. And without so much as a word of apology or remorse!

How often had she dreamed of this very scene, during the long nights in the empty Kensington flat, and during the lonely, drifting days! Julian magically back again ... pleading with her to forgive him ... begging her to marry him all over again ... to give him one more chance!

There had been all sorts of endings. Sometimes, after a wonderful scene of remorse and forgiveness, she had fallen into his arms. Sometimes, proud and aloof, she had spurned him, watching, with icy scorn, as his haughty features crumpled. ...

Out in the dark, a small wind had risen with the turn of the tide. Candida could hear the tiny waves lapping restlessly at the foot of the breakwater, limbering up for their journey up the dark sand. Against the starry blackness, she could see Julian's dark bulk, but not his face. After twenty years, she did not need to see his face: from the set of his shoulders, from the tilt of his half-seen jaw, she knew exactly the expression of self-satisfied expectancy he was wearing; the smug look of a man who has no doubt of victory.

Julian, my boy, you've got another think coming. This isn't the Candida that you remember, all meek and compliant. *This*

Candida has Milly in her, a woman of whom you know nothing!

"Will you marry me?" he repeated, still with that cocksure confidence in his voice and bearing.

The conceit of the man! The insufferable, unbelievable smugness! The monstrous, insupportable arrogance!

"Yes," she said.

Her friends, naturally, were less than whole-hearted in their congratulations. "Some people never learn!" they confided to one another wryly, with a shake of the head.

But Candida *had* learnt, of course. The only thing was that, as is so commonly the case, the lesson she had learned from her experiences was quite other than the one which seemed so obvious to the onlookers.

"*Betrayed* is an exciting escape into a fascinating world of fallen angels and an intense and timeless love story. Jamie Hansen is a fresh new voice in paranormal romance." —Christine Feehan, *New York Times* bestselling author of *Dark Curse*

"Enter a world of magic, chance, and love everlasting!" —Gena Showalter, *New York Times* bestselling author of *The Darkest Kiss*

"Sacrifice, sex, and suspense. Hansen provides them all in this spellbinding tale of love across the ages." —Caridad Piñiero, author of *Blood Calls*

"Deftly written characters and a plot that twists like a maze make *Betrayed* a timeless tale of curses, betrayal, fate, and love. I savored this story and didn't want this one to end." —Vivi Anna, author of *Blood Secrets*

"*Betrayed* is a passionate debut by an author of remarkable talent and maturity of style. Lyrical prose spins a tale that is intelligent and unflinching, enthralling and richly imagined. I loved it! It's a gorgeous, lush, and compelling novel. If you try just one debut this year, make it Jamie Leigh Hansen's. You will be grateful to have 'discovered' her from the first." —Sylvia Day, author of *Ask for It*

"Haunting, hypnotic, and powerful, Jamie Leigh Hansen's *Betrayed* is a welcome breath of fresh air for fans of paranormal romance." —Deidre Knight, author of *Red Fire*

"Jamie Leigh Hansen's *Betrayed* is fresh, original, and compelling, with a to-die-for (literally!) hero, a strong, believable heroine, and a fascinating villain. I can't wait to read more!" —Jenna Black, author of *Hungers of the Heart*

Cursed

Jamie Leigh Hansen

TOR®
paranormal romance

A TOM DOHERTY ASSOCIATES BOOK
NEW YORK

This is a work of fiction. All the characters, organizations, and events portrayed in this novel are either products of the author's imagination or are used fictitiously.

CURSED

A Tor Book
Published by Tom Doherty Associates, LLC
175 Fifth Avenue
New York, NY 10010

www.tor-forge.com

Tor® is a registered trademark of Tom Doherty Associates, LLC.

ISBN-13: 978-0-7653-5721-2
ISBN-10: 0-7653-5721-6

First Edition: December 2008

Printed in the United States of America

0 9 8 7 6 5 4 3 2 1

For Craig

For our girls
Always

Acknowledgments

There are many people I would like to thank for their help and support. Just know if your name is not listed, it's because it's written on my heart, not my brain, and the two don't always communicate well. Any errors are mine to claim.

Jeanne—Friend, computer goddess. What would I do without you?

Jolene—You are an inspiration.

Desireé—For all the readings of all my drafts, thank you.

Dondi and Judy—Thank you both for your patience, encouragement, and enthusiasm. Every artist suffers insecurity at times and you both helped fight away all of mine.

My family and friends—Thank you all for making the launch of my first book such an awesome success!

Christine Feehan, Gena Showalter, Sylvia Day, Jenna Black, Caridad Piñeiro, Vivi Anna—Thank you all so much for reading and loving *Betrayed*.

Lisa Renee Jones—Your advice was amazing. Thank you for all your time.

Natasha—Thank you for everything. My dream never would have come so alive without all you've done for me.

Tor—Heather, Anna, Jozelle, Megan, Theresa, Seth, NaNá, thank you all. Neither *Betrayed* nor *Cursed* could be produced so well without you.

My therapists—For keeping me healthy and taking away my pain so I can live my dream.

Cursed

Prologue

✦

October 8, 2004
The Tunnels of the Forgotten Ones

• EVEN DEEP IN the midst of tangling green vines, trees, and shrubs, the wind reached them, flowing around them both and twisting the black edges of Draven's cloak until it flapped like bat wings. It was dark here, with a cloud-hidden moon and few stars to brighten the sky. The air held a chill that wrapped around a body, at first falsely soothing, then knifing bone deep. Draven shivered, but couldn't tell if it was from the weather or the consequences they were about to face.

At Draven's side, Silas stood as stalwart as ever, his long white wings folded neatly behind him, the ends tucked against his ankles. His innate light was temporarily muted by Draven's innate darkness, hiding them from the brown-cloaked figure that approached on their right, but not from the two Seraphs guarding the sole entrance to the Tunnels of the Forgotten Ones.

Nothing could hide from them.

Each fearsome angel had six wings formed of a blazing fire so bright it only paled in comparison to their eyes. The light of the Divine filled their orbs so they saw with perfect truth and justice. Something Draven had never managed to do.

The Seraphim stood to each side of an entrance that was the darkest, most impenetrable black.

The Tunnel of the Forgotten Ones was a barren mountain prison that held caverns blocked by large boulders. The only beings strong enough to move them were the Seraphim. All their strength, backed by the power of God himself, sealed tight each tomb. Escape was impossible.

It was a cold place, a prison worse than any mortal could imagine: solitary confinement in the most oppressive, deeply disturbing atmosphere. In this place, minds broke, evil manifested, and death never offered a reprieve.

There was only one reason the brown-cloaked Dugan would be here. Deep inside the tunnels laid his mistress, one of the darkest of the original fallen angels, the very catalyst that had begun Draven's alliance with Silas so long ago: Maeve. Maeve of the long, furiously red curls and deep, dark emerald eyes that were pure temptation. Maeve of the mesmerizing face and perfectly alluring body that stirred lust in so many with shocking ease.

Maeve with the lush red lips and vicious jealousy that had cursed her son to relentlessly crave his half-brother's destruction. Those same lips would curse Draven and Silas unto eternity once she discovered their treachery.

Nearly a thousand years ago, Draven and Silas had combined their gifts and skills to break her curse upon the two brothers. But their first attempt had only altered the curse and made the situation worse, damning two more innocents. But now, after nine centuries of suffering, it was done. The curse was broken and the four souls trapped within it were free.

But now so was Maeve. She would be freed from this prison because the curse gone awry had placed her here, not the evil she had done.

One of the Seraphs disappeared into the tunnels with Dugan, leaving the remaining Seraph to stand guard—not that more than one was necessary. What would a thousand years here have done to Maeve? Would she be weak? How long would it take before she came for them? Months? Hours? Seconds?

"We could run," Draven offered, now that they wouldn't be overheard.

"You must be joking," Silas scoffed, disbelief on his face.

Draven shrugged. "I'm just saying, it's an option."

Silas shook his head and returned his gaze to the tunnel entrance. "It isn't worth contemplating. Not only would she find us, but it would negate whatever good we've managed to accomplish."

And doing good was their sole purpose. Doing good meant earning redemption. For humans, it was an easy matter to pray, repent, and have faith that they were forgiven. For Nephilim, children of humans and angels, the issue wasn't quite as clear-cut.

Draven's arms crossed, leather-gloved hands sliding into the wide sleeves of the black cloak. "Then hiding is out, huh?"

Silas emitted an irritated growl.

Draven smiled briefly, then shivered at a sudden burst of cold wind. Breaking the curse after so many years of heartache and disappointing failure had filled them with a heady, giddy confidence for a short time. Sheer hubris had convinced them they could make a difference, but that kind of innocent belief wasn't available now. Reality had set in.

Maeve would come for them, would likely kill them. They wouldn't have ten chances to get it right this time. No reruns, no do-overs. To win on the first try was a long shot, but it was the only one they had.

"If she eliminates us, they will be vulnerable," Silas whispered. "She will unravel all we've accomplished. Dreux and Kalyss will lose the lives they fought so hard and long for. Geoffrey and Alex will be cannon fodder to her and Kai will once again be her pawn."

No. Draven had sacrificed far more than Silas even knew. Nothing would be undone at this late stage. "Not if their allies are strong enough."

"What allies? Even including the two of us, we are nothing against Maeve at full strength," he pointed out.

It was a simple fact, but not one Draven would allow to defeat them. "Then we have work to do, allies to gain, before she *is* at full strength."

Draven went silent as Dugan exited the tunnels, a limp, blanketed form stretched across his arms. Behind him, the Seraph returned to the opposite side of the entrance from his companion. The Seraphs watched as Dugan surged into the trees, very near where Silas and Draven stood.

Draven froze as Maeve passed them. The stench of death clouded the air, vile and pervasive. When the two had passed, Draven's leather-gloved hand grabbed

Silas's bare one. "Come. We need to know where he takes her."

• TIME HELD NO meaning for Maeve as she waited, drifting from shadows to blackness, from confusion to moments of rare clarity before slipping back into the oily onyx of oblivion.

She was getting stronger. It wasn't the first time she'd had that thought, but it was the first time she remembered having it before. Familiar hands caressed her skin and soft lips traced every inch of her flesh. Dugan. He cared for her. Kept her safe from her enemies. He would make her stronger. So she could . . .

Maeve blinked, but there was no difference to the darkness, nothing visual to focus her mind, so she quit trying and relaxed against the satin-covered pillow and mattress. Heat blanketed her side as Dugan's strong body cradled hers, his fingers gliding up her arms to her neck, then ever so slowly down her collarbone to trace the sensitive shallows there.

This was how he fed her, her prized servant. How her mind could open, functioning better with each tense thrill that charged through her. His hot breath brushed her ear, her neck, tightening the tips of her breasts. His passion swirled in the air, sinking inside her pores, nourishing deprived cells and revitalizing deadened nerves. Fucking was her sustenance. Adoration her dessert.

"Yess . . ." she encouraged him. Lust rode him hard and for a brief moment, she could remember when she had ridden him harder.

She hated being fragile. She hated weakness of any kind, but this was worse. Days, weeks, *centuries* of being deprived of her will, her freedom. Her strength, her mind, her power—all out of her control, at the mercy of those too foolish to relish true freedom. They had robbed her of life. Vitality. But they wouldn't rob her of vengeance.

Dugan moved, leaning over her. Wet muscle pressed over the tip of her breast before he blew a hot breath against the peak.

Maeve floated, boneless and sprawled, his touch so light it was barely there. Yet the soft abrasion of his callused fingers down her torso and over her concave stomach stirred embers inside her. Carefully tending them, fanning them until they blazed. Once, she'd been insatiable. Her lusts devouring hundreds. Now, only one man sufficed.

His touch was gentle, careful not to break her. After long, strained moments, she recognized the slightly furred limbs that stroked her thighs. There was more to this man than nature had given him. Maeve raised a hand to his chest, her fingers trembling as they searched over his hard muscled skin, up to his neck. There was something. . . . She needed to remember.

Dugan bent to her neck, finding and licking a particular spot that craved attention. Just returning his touch intensified her passion. Yes. This was what she needed. The inferno inside her built, and her touch lowered to the small black face at the center of his chest. She stroked around it, missing the many eyes, and a high-pitched purr vibrated her hand.

The eight long, furred limbs she'd given him wrapped

around her thighs and pulled them wide. His fingers separated the tender folds of her sex, spreading the moisture to her dehydrated skin. Yes, finally, she could produce her own lubricant.

Maeve arched. She loved being worshipped. She needed it, fed her power with his lust and heat and faith. Her hand rose high. Higher. There. She traced the intricate pattern hammered on the wide metal torque encircling his neck. Another inch to the left and she found it.

Smooth and square, the emerald felt cold to the touch. It should have warmed with the heat of his skin, but the power within it prevented the abatement of the supernatural chill. The power was strong, created when she was at the height of her skills. She could draw from that, use it to enhance what was left of her.

Dugan settled over her, four furry limbs now circling her thighs, four circling and twisting around her arms as his fingers pulled her nipples and his lips and tongue feasted at her neck. Agonizingly slow, he slid into her, stretching her and pulling out before sliding deeper.

Maeve grasped the emerald and inhaled slightly. Just enough. Dugan slid inside all the way. A deeper breath and she released her hold on the emerald. It wouldn't do to take too much, or she'd break it and the curse held within.

No matter her desperation, she couldn't allow that to happen. Dugan would kill her if she set him free. Even a thousand years of the tunnel's damage wouldn't compare to what he would do to her if he learned how long she'd held him.

Chapter 1

Four and a half months later . . .

• THE TUNNEL WAS black, with not even a torch to light it. The atmosphere was so thick it sucked and clawed at her, ripping away any oxygen that could fuel her lungs. Sometimes it seemed the weight of the world rested in this spot, so heavy nothing could alleviate the atmosphere of oppression and doom.

Elizabeth trailed her hands along the rough walls. The tunnel seemed warm, but the sharp, jagged rocks were cold beneath her fingers. Her hands shook but her steps were steady. She knew this path, and journeyed here quite often.

Just up ahead thick steel doors blocked many twisted paths to caverns that lay even deeper in the tunnels of her mind. Her right hand stretched toward a door. She read each dent, each scratch like braille. Behind this door were some of the best memories of her life.

Sometimes it was locked and she stood pounding against the steel, crying and begging it to allow her inside. Those were the nights when her dreams had a power all their own. Helpless against the force of her own mind, she would turn and continue farther, deeper into the tunnels.

This time she didn't want to enter that room, and she passed the door quietly, her nightgown whispering against her ankles. She couldn't see it but she knew it was long and golden and transparent in the candlelight. No, tonight wasn't a night for happy memories from her past. It was a night for something different, something secret.

Ahead and to her left was the door she dreaded. The one she edged past, her back pressed to the opposite wall. Even through the thick steel and heavy locks, she could hear the whispers of what waited for her beyond it. The cries and screams of every painful moment in her life called to her from behind that door. It held a monster who crouched, waiting to drag her in.

Elizabeth held her breath, her right hand reaching farther along the tunnel. Her legs shook now. Her steps weren't as certain. She prayed not to make a single sound that would awaken the monster. She didn't want to enter that room tonight. She never did, but the choice wasn't hers. One misstep and the door would open. The monster would grab her and she would scream—scream until morning.

Elizabeth eased past it, but she couldn't breathe yet. Instead she ran, putting as much distance between her and that door as possible. Down twists and turns, her hair flying behind her, her hands blindly scraping over rock walls and steel doors with leather hinges. These doors weren't locked to her. They were mostly empty, waiting to be filled, though she didn't know what with.

Although she couldn't see where she was going, the atmosphere warmed and she knew she had arrived at the deepest, darkest, most secret caverns of her mind.

The places where no one could reach her and spoil what lay within. These rooms were the closest to her heart.

Elizabeth placed her hands on a door, her fingers tracing the heated lines and cracks. Her chest heaved with the effort to draw breath. She had made it through the darkness, past the door of sorrows, to this door—the door of wishes and secret desires. Sometimes it was empty, mocking her for daring to dream. But she hoped, with her cheek held tight to the smooth steel, with trembling hands pressed to the hot metal. She needed so desperately for the room to not be empty tonight. Keeping her eyes squeezed shut, gripping the latch with her fist, Elizabeth eased the door open just enough to squeeze through.

Dreading the moment when she would find herself alone, she faced the heavy door, and leaned on the steel portal until it slowly closed. She wasn't brave tonight. She was afraid to hope and dream and be wrong.

But gentle hands, large and hot, eased around her and settled on her stomach, pulling her back to a hard chest and the moist, seductive heat of a man's breath on her neck. Elizabeth's breath stuttered out and her heart leaped inside her chest. Her trembling hands cupped his against her stomach, allowing them to warm and steady her.

The shake and tremble of her body melted as she leaned against him, her blood now hot, molten. His breath grazed the sensitive skin at her nape just before his teeth scraped against her ear, sending shivers all down her spine.

"Hi, beautiful."

Elizabeth smiled. She was only beautiful with him.

Tilting her head, she opened her eyes and stared through the candlelight into his caressing, green-and-gold gaze.

"Hi, Alex."

• ALEX WAS DREAMING. Only in his dreams did Beth Ann Raines come to this room of black stone walls where they were trapped together in a tangle of bare skin and burgundy satin sheets. It was these moments he yearned for. These times he wished were real.

"Now, Alex," Beth Ann demanded, her sexy, breathless voice teasing his ears.

This dream happened so rarely that the torture of making it last was the greatest pleasure of all. Clenching his fingers in her golden hair, Alex said, "No. Not yet."

Too soon, they'd find their release, hold each other close and fall asleep. When he awoke, he'd be back in his apartment, the bed beside him empty and undisturbed. Alex withdrew from the kiss, pulling back far enough to stare into her eyes—the most dazzling blue imaginable and they were passionately focused on him. If only that lasted longer than the dream.

His hips continued to move with that quick, shallow friction that stole her breath—and his. Which was good. It kept him from begging her again to stay and face what lay between them and let it grow into the spectacular future he knew was theirs for the taking.

Perhaps it was best she wouldn't stay. The dreams were unique, vivid, and special, but they'd never manifested in the real world. They'd only left him to wake up to an empty, lonely bed. Or worse, a bed that wasn't empty and a face that wasn't hers.

It hadn't taken long to realize it didn't matter how much he cared for a woman or took pleasure in her body, the morning after one of his dreams he felt nothing for her—nothing compared to what he felt for Beth Ann.

Beth Ann's creamy, soft legs cradled him, her fingernails dug into his back as she bit his chest in small, demanding nips. Here, she wanted him. Here, she loved him. And *here* felt better than any waking moment with any other woman.

Unable to hold back the words, Alex gave in. With a guttural growl that barely masked his pleading, Alex said, "For God's sake, Beth Ann, stay with me. Love me." And because his mind warred with his heart in a constant struggle for dominance, he added, "Choose me or let me go."

She gasped as her legs tightened around him and her nails dug deeper into his skin. With an expression full of both pleasure and agony, she whispered, "I can't."

Holding her tight, gripping her hair and trapping her with his body for as long as he could, Alex drove them both to the edge. One final thrust and they both arched, tension bowing them taut in a release so great not even the long gouges made by her nails halted it.

But as soon as the pleasure ebbed, the pain burned. Long streaks of fire stung his back until a blue light shone from behind him, momentarily bright against the darkness. He felt the itch as each wound re-knit itself, leaving his back as smooth and unlined as it had begun.

Alex released her and brushed damp tendrils from her brow. She'd bitten her bottom lip until it split, and a thin line of blood marked her soft flesh. Normally it was hard to see a wound and do nothing about it, but with

Beth Ann, it was impossible to do nothing. Alex touched her lip with his thumb and blue light glowed from his fingertips. Her lip instantly sealed as his split open, bringing the damage into him, then his body healed and both marks were gone.

"You should leave this for *me* to nibble on." Alex lowered his head for one last kiss. "I'm much gentler."

She caressed his cheek, giving him a familiar apologetic smile. "I wish . . ."

"I know." Alex buried his face in the curve of her neck. He couldn't be upset with her. It was only a dream. His dream, at that. And until he could figure out how to stop having it, he just had to deal with the endless disappointment.

• ALEX OPENED HIS eyes, knowing the bed beside him would be empty. But he hadn't expected to wake up in the dream bed, in the dream room. Usually when Beth Ann left him, the dream was over and he was left alone in his apartment, missing her more than ever, wishing she was real. But the burgundy curtains hanging from the corners of the four-poster bed left no doubt he was still dreaming.

The candle had burned lower, proof that time had passed while he slept. Rising from the bed, Alex pulled on his dark green sweats and matching AK Martial Arts T-shirt, staring at the door. It was always locked so he couldn't leave, even when he wanted the dream to be over. He hated that door.

Bringing the candle with him, mixing cinnamon apple pie and sex in the air, Alex reached for the handle. It had never opened before, but he had to try. He'd always wondered what was on the other side. An end to the dream? Or Beth Ann? Was she waiting to share more of herself if he was brave enough to follow?

Alex pulled the door wide and stepped out into a forest so thick, so lush, it was barely lit by a moon over half-full. Cupping his hand protectively around the tiny flame of the candle, Alex continued forward. There was a click behind him. Alex looked back in time to see the door disappear beneath rustling trees and tangling vines.

Alex stiffened as the atmosphere changed, an ominous chill flowing around him. His stance became looser, more fluid, and more deadly. Blowing out the candle, he set it down before continuing. He stepped cautiously, sliding past dark shrubbery and low hanging vines to a break in the tree line. Alex jerked a few steps forward, his surroundings all too achingly familiar. He'd nearly lost everyone he loved here.

Movement brought his eyes to the center of the small clearing and a hellish light brightened around him, trapping him. It was the same kind of barrier that had left him helpless to aid his friends, beating at the light like it was bulletproof glass. The barrier didn't come down unless a heart stopped. And the bitch in the center didn't have a heart to sacrifice.

He'd only seen Maeve once in a vision, but hers wasn't a power to be forgotten. Her hair was the deep, dark red of garnets and her eyes were a bright hard green to match the cursed emerald at her throat. Once broken and beaten, now Maeve stood alive, well, and holding a dagger to Beth Ann's throat.

"Come forward, healer. We have much to discuss."

With his heart in his throat and his hands held carefully at his sides, Alex left the relative safety of the tree line. Beth Ann's eyes were wide in her pale face as she held absolutely still, her chin lifted to accommodate the blade. Her gaze kept shifting to the side, but Alex couldn't surmise her message.

Maeve laughed. "Your hands don't scare me, Alex."

Suddenly, all became silent and though Maeve's mouth still moved, Alex didn't know what she was saying. Straining to listen, he tried to move closer to her, but his body was frozen. Only his eyes could move. Alex searched the darkness, trying to find the unseen menace.

Until a voice as deep as the pits of hell, as resonant as his darkest nightmares, spoke in his ear. "I look into the future and this is what I see."

Like spotlights in the darkness, the trees to the sides of Maeve lit, showing huddled figures at their base. He should have seen them before but they'd been shadowed, hidden from his gaze and only now fully revealed.

As the delicate features of each small face were bared to his gaze, Alex fought harder against the spell that bound him. He didn't know them, had never seen them before, but they were children. That alone strengthened his resolve to save them.

"They are your future, every single one of them. Including *her*." Alex looked at Beth Ann, until the voice moved and he could see a figure at the edge of his vision. Not a man, but something else. Something black with red embers burning within it, like a snuffed fire that still smoldered. "They were once *my* future. Let's hope you aren't as foolish as I."

Alex looked at the children filling the clearing. He

counted ten children of varying ages and his eyes
widened, swinging to Beth Ann. The children weren't
theirs, together, but as he watched her gaze shift to each
of them, bright with tears, full of love and determination to save them, he knew they would be.

His future. Alex swallowed, but couldn't speak.

"You can save them. If your love is great enough."

With a burst of movement, Maeve struck and the clearing ran red. Screams filled Alex's ears—his own among
them.

• "IT STARTED OUT as one of *those* dreams." Alex had
told Geoffrey enough about them before that no more
explanation was needed. He tightened one hand around
the grips on a case of pop and the other hand around his
grocery bags as he headed toward his truck. He always
needed fuel on research nights. "So how can the rest of
it be real?"

"It might not be, but there's nothing about Maeve that
should be taken lightly. The best, the safest thing to do
is treat the dream like a warning."

Setting the groceries in the bed of his truck, Alex
said, "What I don't understand is how she could even
know about Beth Ann. I haven't seen her in years, so unless Maeve can tap into my dreams, Beth Ann shouldn't
even—"

Alex stilled, staring as a heavily laden grocery cart
rolled past his truck, pushed by a slim blonde woman in
khaki shorts that showed off a pair of long legs and a
short-sleeved peach top that made her tanned arms look
soft and entirely biteable.

"Judging by the sound of your tongue hitting the ground, I take it you just saw her."

"How did you know?

"Murphy's Law, destiny, fate—pick one." Geoffrey's tone was as flat as ever, but something gave it a grimness that sent chills along Alex's spine. When a man had lived for close to a thousand years like Geoffrey had, it was prudent to pay attention to his words.

"So you're saying I should treat every part of my dream as real? Believe the voice really knew the future?"

"There are different views about visions, Alex. Some believe they can be changed. Some believe they can't, that whatever is seen will come true. And some fight so hard to prevent it, they *make* it happen. It becomes a self-fulfilling prophecy."

"Just friggin' great." The first time he'd seen Beth Ann in years and he would put her in danger whether he left, stayed, or went over to her. And at some point in the near future, he would watch helplessly as a homicidal bitch took her life because if he tried to stop it, he might *cause* it.

"Not the best of choices, I agree. The question we need to ponder is: if the vision can't be changed and it is destined to happen—"

"—Then how do we fix it *after* it happens?"

"Exactly."

"And I thought it was going to be difficult." Alex snorted and watched Beth Ann lean into the back of her Durango, her bottom wiggling side to side as she re-arranged a mountain of groceries. He licked his lips, but even his tongue was dry. *Excuse me, miss? Can I help you with your groceries before my enemies target, torture, and murder you?*

"Are you going to talk to her?"

"And say what? 'I know we haven't seen each other since you turned me down for prom, but some evil witch-slash-demon visited my dreams last night and threatened you and our future children, so can I stick close?" Alex snorted.

"I have never known you to be speechless, Alex." Geoffrey paused for a moment. "I may have prayed for it, but that request went unanswered."

"Be careful, old man. I might accuse you of having a sense of humor."

"I'm sure I could disabuse you of that notion."

"True." Alex smiled. He'd been a black belt for years, but five months of mixed martial-arts training with Geoffrey had taught him several painful lessons.

"Now armor up and go talk to her," Geoffrey commanded in his I-have-led-knights-in-battle tone.

"Sir. Yes, sir!" Alex snapped out like the smart-ass he was, before he hung up the phone. He'd go talk to her. Surely talking wouldn't lead to the vision? On the other hand, if whatever he did was destined, then did it matter what he chose?

Yes, his choices mattered. Even if only to himself.

A loud splash punctuated the quiet of the relatively empty parking lot and Alex turned to see white liquid pooling around Beth Ann's feet.

• ELIZABETH GRIPPED HER hair at the sides of her head and stared at the river wending its way around her shoes. It was just a gallon of milk—overpriced, surely—but only one plastic container of a liquid that was probably too full of hormones to be truly healthy. But it was so symbolic of all that was wrong in her life that it was all she could do not to cry over it.

Who was she to know if something was necessary to a growing body's health? It wasn't like she'd ever had time to read, prepare, and learn how to be responsible for another person's well-being. She wasn't a mother, a nurse, or a pediatrician with years of knowledge to pull from the moment a situation required action. She was a software programmer, for God's sake!

Elizabeth took a deep breath, pulling it in until both lungs were full and her chest was puffed out. She held it a moment before exhaling. She had to regain control of herself here and now, before it was gone completely. Lord knew there wouldn't be time to do so later. Again she inhaled, clearing her mind of all problems except the most immediate. Step One—remove shoes from milk.

"Can I help?"

Elizabeth looked up into a pair of sparkling hazel eyes that were all too familiar and her breath whooshed out in a loud, embarrassing raspberry.

Alex laughed.

Elizabeth smiled helplessly, quick to step out of the milk. He looked just as she'd imagined. His hair was a touch longer, his arms thicker, and his chest broader than she'd remembered, but otherwise he was still the Alex she'd gone to school with. The Alex she dreamed of, when life was overwhelming and she needed to feel his arms around her even if only in her imagination.

Alex winked, then leaned forward and grasped the handle of the broken jug and turned toward the trash cans at the side of the building. Elizabeth took that as the perfect cue to remember how to breathe. Seriously, a shirt stretched over hard muscles and a tightly rounded butt that perfectly filled his black jeans should not equate to speechless ninny. Elizabeth shook her head and stared down at the milk puddling beneath her car. And around her flat tire.

With a wordless moan, she fell to her knees, mindless of the dirt, and pulled at a piece of glass wedged into the sidewall of her tire.

"Makes you just want to crawl back into bed and start the day over, doesn't it?"

Elizabeth swallowed thickly. Just last night she'd crawled into a bed and the man standing behind her had been waiting in it. "Desperately."

Chapter 2

• "Do you have a spare?" Alex's voice was so close it made her jump.

She paused a moment, thinking. "I think so."

Elizabeth rose to her feet and peered through the bags littering the back of the SUV. Shoving a few bags here and there, she located the multi-use crowbar, ducked under the Durango and loosened the spare tire. When it was free, she rolled it to the ground and they both stared as it sank even lower than the other tire.

Elizabeth's eyes widened. She wouldn't cry in front of him. She didn't cry in front of anyone, ever, if she could help it. She shook her head, her voice a hollow echo inside her skull. "This can't be happening."

Alex knelt beside her, his eyes soft with sympathy. "Got a lot of people waiting for you?"

Elizabeth's shoulders sank and she looked at the tires again. "Yeah. A lot."

Alex shrugged. "Well, we could call your husband and—"

"I don't have a husband," Elizabeth said in a flat voice.

"Oh." His tone was carefully even. "Fiancé?"

Elizabeth shook her head, her dazed eyes still on the two flat tires. "Nope."

"Boyfriend?"

Elizabeth wasn't deaf to the curiosity he tried to hide, or his interest in her unattached status. A month ago, she would have been jumping for joy inside. "Nope. And no father."

"I see." Trying to understand, he hesitantly asked, "No one?"

She swallowed and licked her lips. "Just me."

"What about all the people waiting for you?"

She smiled, or tried to, but her problems seemed insurmountable. She needed her car. Being without it wasn't an option, but over the last few months, her bank account had dwindled to a point that replacing the tire posed a serious problem, especially since tires had to be replaced in sets of two or four. "They can't help."

With a definitive nod, he said, "Well, you've got me."

Alex walked across the parking lot purposefully and Elizabeth stared after the man who'd fueled a thousand fantasies. Her eyes widened with surprise, relief, and, because this was her life, more than a bit of concern. Elizabeth looked at her car, disappointed she'd had to let her AAA coverage lapse, reduced her insurance so it didn't include towing, forgotten to keep her spare in good condition, and had no ready cash that could be wasted on stupid emergencies. Not that there were smart emergencies, but still, small, annoying accidents weren't what needed her attention most.

Money. She'd desperately needed to never again feel this crushing sense of panic. Like she was at the bottom of the ocean and couldn't breathe; the surface was too far to reach, but she could only keep swimming anyway.

Well, she hadn't wanted this sense of despair, but then, there were a mess of things she had now that she hadn't wanted. And the alternative, dropping it all and running far, far away, was completely unacceptable.

A shiny blue truck pulled up behind her. She turned and watched Alex climb out and come around to her side. Just add a cape and he could be her personal Superman. Elizabeth snorted. No man was *that* good. Besides, she didn't need saving. A ride home was just a little temporary help, not a lifetime commitment. Alex started unloading bags from her vehicle into the back of his and she moved to help him.

"I really appreciate this. Thank you." She didn't know quite what else to say so she grabbed a few bags and put them in the back of his truck. On the driver's side of the bed, she could see two plastic bags and a case of pop.

Her shopping used to be that simple. She'd pop in for five minutes, grab whatever she needed for a weekend alone, and leave. So much could change in just a few months.

"Don't worry about it. Not a big deal." He didn't look at her, but embarrassment heated her cheeks anyway. What an impression she must be making. She'd tried so hard to be different, independent and capable, but she was right back where she'd started. Welcome home, Beth Ann.

No. Elizabeth shook the thought away. This wasn't the same and *she* wasn't the same. She just needed a ride home. She'd figure out where to go from there.

Elizabeth grabbed her purse, checked the car, and locked the doors while he put away the cart. Then she pulled herself into the truck, wishing she wasn't quite so short. As if mocking her, he slid smoothly behind the steering wheel and closed his door. "That is so unfair to short people everywhere."

Alex looked at her and gave that heart-stopping grin she'd dreamed about for twelve years. Shifting the truck into gear, he headed to the exit and paused before turning onto the street. "Where to?"

Willing her heart to work at a normal pace again, she gestured. "Take a right, past Hamilton, and turn on—"

"Is it where you lived when you were in high school?"

Elizabeth turned wide eyes to him. "You remember?"

He shrugged and switched gears, the veins in his hands and forearms bunching with each movement. There was something sexy about a man comfortable driving a standard.

Competent, smooth, graceful. Alex was still everything he'd been back in high school. She may have spent most of her time buried in books, working to excel in her classes, but she'd had more than enough time to notice him.

He'd been no slouch either. Often, she'd found the top grade she competed for was held by him. It hadn't seemed fair. Handsome, graceful, athletic, smart. He'd been everything her young heart had wanted. Needed.

He caught her staring and she jerked her gaze away quickly, but not before she saw his lips curve, laugh lines now marking the corners of them. Her face was hot, but inside she shook like a leaf in the wind. Guys who could smile had always been the most attractive to her. A darkly handsome brooder had never been her type, not after seeing Alex's easy laughter and humor. Besides, she brooded enough for anyone. She'd been that way even in high school.

She'd wanted to die back then. She'd cried and thought about it and even planned it, then she'd come up with something better. A blueprint for her life that included graduating, going to college on whatever scholarships she qualified for and getting a job with a hefty paycheck. It was a plan that would take her far from Spokane and everyone in it.

Unfortunately, the plan hadn't included developing a relationship at the tail-end of her senior year. A relationship that could become so important she'd throw away everything she'd worked for. Because she'd known, even then, Alex could've been worth it.

But it didn't matter. It had never been about his worth. It had been about hers.

Alex's voice rescued her from her thoughts. "I thought

you'd be married by now. You know, the two-car garage, three kids bit. What have you been doing?"

Amazingly, he sounded genuinely interested. Elizabeth lifted her chin and a certain amount of pride entered her voice. "Designing and beta-testing software applications for Simogen Software. I was in Seattle."

His eyebrows rose and his lips curved into a light smile. "I can picture you doing that. You must have loved it. What made you come back?"

For the barest moment, she basked in his simple belief in her. No argument, no clichéd jokes about a blonde actually *thinking*, just acceptance. Then, remembering his question, her smile tightened. "I didn't really have a choice. What do you do?"

"Kalyss and I are partners in a martial arts studio."

"Oh." She blinked, her smile pasted so firmly on her face she probably looked like she'd just had a Botox injection. "That's perfect for you. You were always a natural athlete."

Her stomach plummeted. Kalyss. Of course. They'd been so close all through school, it only made sense they'd be partners. Were they partners in life as well? She felt sick at the thought. "Do you two have any kids?"

The light changed and the truck stopped rather abruptly. Elizabeth put her hand on the dash for balance. Alex apologized and carefully put the truck in neutral. "She's pregnant with her first right now, which she's thrilled about. She thought for years that she wouldn't be able to have children."

Elizabeth's conscience ripped at her. How could she feel jealous? She'd turned Alex down and left, never looking back. She'd gotten exactly what she wanted. "That's wonderful. Congratulations."

He chuckled. "I'll pass that on next time I see her. Which might be sooner rather than later, if her husband refuses to let her teach classes."

"Her husband?" She could breathe again. "So, you . . . don't teach classes?"

He glanced over, his sparkling eyes focusing on her. His gaze was warm, almost knowing. Her lungs seized for a painful beat and she stared at him, heat rising in her face.

A slow smile stretched his lips, as if he could read her mind. Then again, it was more likely she was just that transparent. The light changed and Alex shifted into gear. "I do. But I'm on vacation right now."

With his attention focused on the road again, she could breathe. Unbelievable, the way he could still make her feel. Elizabeth clenched her hand at her side. "Oh, that's great. Are you planning any trips?"

"Not at the moment. Just relaxing for a while," he said, sounding strangely grim.

She looked at the hand in her lap, barely noticing his tone. She'd had a vacation just last year, to Cancún. Hot sun, cool water, sandy beaches, and a sexy boyfriend, the trip had been enjoyable, but now it felt like forever ago. "Relaxing. Right."

The truck slid to a smooth stop along the curb in front of her house. Knowing what he'd see and hating it, Elizabeth braced herself.

"Is this it?"

The shock in his voice made her cringe.

* * *

• ALEX SLOWLY SLID from behind the wheel and stared at the house in front of him. It wasn't the cracked and peeling red paint, the dirty white trim, or the gutters hanging partially off the roof that horrified him. Or even the uneven concrete front steps hugged by broken handrails. It wasn't the sagging wooden fence around the front yard, or the gate that hung, listing at an odd angle.

Beth Ann left the cab, shutting the door firmly, her eyes closed and humiliation burning across her face, as though she thought he was judging her. But he wasn't. He was actually completely speechless with a mind-numbing terror that he couldn't even begin to explain to her, though he would have to soon.

The bright blue sky brightened the air around them, the sun shooting yellow rays through dark evergreens to the bare and patchy grass, and a small turtle-shaped sandbox where three little girls with plastic shovels built lopsided castles. In his dream, they'd been tied together, their eyes wide with fat tears.

From the side rails of the porch, a blond boy hung like he was climbing a ladder, his blue eyes sparkling with mischief. In the dream, they'd been slightly darker and his chin had been stubbornly angled, determination gleaming like a promise in his eyes.

Between two large pine trees, swinging gently in a hammock with a book perched on his chest was another blond boy. In Alex's dream, his face had been a study in concentration, matching the look he wore now.

Alex almost expected dark clouds to begin to roll and

pitch over the house, but no. Maeve didn't have them, wasn't here. They were simply a family enjoying the front yard, as kids were wont to do. There was no danger here. Yet.

Bags rustled behind him and he turned to see Beth Ann reaching for her groceries, a tight, closed look on her face. Alex took a few bags himself, swinging them over the side.

A teen version of Beth Ann, from her bouncing ponytail to the frown lines between her eyes, stomped up and declared, "Here, you take her. I can't get her to shut up for the world."

Elizabeth turned in time to wrap her arms around a squirmy baby girl, the bags in her hands banging together before the girl took them. "Is she changed and fed?"

The teen rolled her eyes. "Duh." She swung around and headed toward the house, yelling for the others to help with the groceries.

The baby quieted almost instantly, grabbing Elizabeth's ponytail and stuffing it in her mouth. Then she squirmed, looking around and seeing Alex, and she nearly jumped from Elizabeth's arms toward him. Elizabeth tightened her hold and faced Alex with a hesitant expression on her face.

Alex couldn't breathe. A baby. He didn't want to think about where she'd been in his dream. He only knew a keen sense of disappointment. He'd hoped, somewhere deep in his mind, that the baby's presence had meant two things. One, that she was his and Beth Ann's, a symbol of their love and unity. The second was time. Time to love Beth Ann, conceive and birth a child before Maeve came to him. But this baby was only a bit smaller than the one in his dream, not very noticeably different at all.

Which meant Maeve was coming very soon. If he stayed, they would be at her mercy. If he left, he could kiss any chance between Beth Ann and himself good-bye. But maybe being here and then leaving them led to their capture. Or it was destiny and his choice made no difference.

Alex watched Beth Ann adjust her grip on the baby and reach into the back of the truck. Which risky choice could he live with the best? Alex smiled at the baby, who giggled and pulled Beth Ann's hair again.

Maybe there was still a chance to prevent the tragedy. He'd ask Beth Ann a few questions, get a sense of what was happening to her family and if anything seemed like Maeve's influence. If all was good, he'd leave. Try to spare them. Dredging up a light tone he feared wouldn't ring entirely true, he said, "You've been busy."

• ELIZABETH GLARED AT Alex and pulled up a few more bags. She just wanted to get the groceries and say good-bye, survive the night and hopefully have a better day tomorrow. But his statement irritated her. Maybe she could stand to lose a few pounds, but there was no way in hell her body looked like she'd given birth six months ago, let alone to ten kids over twelve years. "They're not mine."

"Who do they belong to?" His eyes were gently curious, empty of the judgment she'd feared.

Elizabeth hiked the baby up on her hip, deciding to answer him. What was the worst he could think? "Five of them are my older sister Dallas's. Three are my younger sister Felicia's. Two are my brother Bobby's."

Alex's brows raised high. "I see. One hell of a babysitter you've become."

If babysitters never left their charges. She rolled her eyes. "You have no idea."

"So Dallas has five kids? Wow." His tone was amazed, but not quite shocked.

But why would he be? Her sister had always had a reputation. She removed Veronica's tight grip from her breast and resettled her on her hip. "Yeah."

Alex reached for the child's newly freed hand and tugged at her fingers. Veronica grinned at him, then dove for him, taking Elizabeth's hair with her. She yelped, he laughed, and the baby chuckled.

"Which bags are ours?" Elizabeth looked down at the blond, blue-eyed imp smiling at her.

She put a gentle hand on his head and looked at Alex. "This is Tommy."

Tommy shrugged her away and grabbed the bags Alex handed him. "Don't bother confusin' him with all of us. He won't be around long enough to remember."

He turned and walked away, swinging the bags and nearly spilling what was inside. Thank God it was only bread.

Her mouth hung open, shocked at his rudeness. Part of her choked up at the matter-of-fact way he dealt with the appearance and disappearance of various men in his life. The other part reddened in embarrassment.

"He's right, you know." She glanced at Teddy as he adjusted his glasses and reached for more bags from Alex. "If we're all introduced at once, they just leave faster. Grandma had most of us hide in our rooms for the first few visits."

Teddy carefully looped one hand through the handles and wrapped the other around the bags. Turning, he slowly walked up the sidewalk with the eggs. Knowing who to hand what was a skill Elizabeth had been forced to learn the hard way.

Alex's thoughts were closed to her, but he seemed to be trying to decide if he was going to stay for a visit or run screaming. She couldn't blame him. He'd only signed up to get her home. Not for a lifelong career in babysitting. Of course, she hadn't signed up for that either, but she wasn't one to shirk her duties. Especially not for a guy.

Her mom had never lacked for men, and up to four months ago, they'd come and gone with stunning regularity. But having the kids hide in their rooms? Like they were something to be ashamed of? Elizabeth might want to run and hide from all the responsibility, the overwhelming difficulty of it all, but she was not ashamed of these kids.

She firmed her mouth and resettled the baby on her hip. Then she faced Alex, not quite knowing what to say. The last of the bags came out of the truck and he handed them to Teddy and Tommy.

"Aunt Lizzie! The toilet is overflowing again," the older set of twins sung in unison as she turned to see them hanging over the upstairs balcony, balanced on their stomachs with their hands waving wildly.

"Lizzie?" Alex queried.

"Get *off* the edge of the balcony!" she yelled, hating the sound of her strident voice. The demonic duo disappeared into the house, giggling. No doubt they were the ones who'd clogged the toilet. Elizabeth closed her eyes until she caught her breath and stilled her shaking knees, then opened them and answered Alex.

"Everyone likes to think of their own nickname for me, it seems. I've learned to answer to just about anything, but I prefer Elizabeth."

"Good to know." He laughed at the outrageous faces the kids were making as they pushed her to hurry. "I could fix the toilet for you, if you'd like."

"No!" He looked startled and she realized the word had come out a little too emphatic, but she really didn't want him to see inside the house. The outside was bad enough. Elizabeth smiled shakily and tried again. "You wouldn't want to start fixing things. Once you do, it never stops. You'd be trapped."

"Okay." He hesitated, his eyes holding hers for a few moments. He looked at his nearly empty truck—almost reluctantly, though she couldn't imagine why—then back to her. "Well, it was nice seeing you again."

She smiled back politely, forcing away a sudden urge to beg him to stay. "Enjoy your vacation."

"Lizzie! It's filling up the bathroom!" David leaned over the edge of the balcony again, the smile on his face showing his desire to make her scream again.

"I'm coming. Get down from there!" she yelled, suddenly understanding the ugly tone that had so often filled her mother's voice. She grimaced at Alex. "I need to . . ." She nodded toward the house.

"And I need to . . ." He nodded toward his shiny blue truck. "See you around."

"She said she's coming, Shelly. She just needs to flirt a little more."

Her face was officially on fire. "Bye."

The cracking sound of splitting wood rent the air and David screamed.

Breath froze in Elizabeth's lungs. A strip of wood was loose, one end still nailed to the balcony, the other hanging over the edge. David held on to the very end by one hand, his free arm trying to grab hold of something. His legs flailed as he yelled for help. A flash of nausea froze her in place as she watched in wide-eyed, speechless horror.

But Alex wasn't frozen. He vaulted the low front fence and reached the porch just as David's hold on the broken balcony gave way and he fell into Alex's arms. Safe.

Her shaking arms tight around the baby, Elizabeth entered the yard through the gate and walked to the porch. She blinked away tears and cleared her throat, but her thoughts were stuck in an endless loop. David had fallen. He could have died. The guilt would have been hers to bear. This was her watch. The kids were her responsibility. She swallowed, but her mouth was dry.

Alex set David on his feet as the kid stared at him in awe. Obviously, the little terror was none the worse for his stunt, but Elizabeth wanted to huddle in a corner until her panic went away.

She looked up at the broken edge of the balcony. The whole thing hadn't fallen, but it was dangerous. A wild fury filled her mind. Fury with David for not listening.

Fury with her mother for letting the house fall apart. Fury with all three of her siblings for leaving their children's lives in someone else's hands. But most of all, Elizabeth was furious with herself for not doing a better job of making their home safe.

Everyone stood quiet, the children staring at her face as if they could see the anger building within her. Exercising extreme control over her voice, Elizabeth spoke in a tone not to be disobeyed. "All of you, in the living room. Nowhere else, just the living room. Now."

Shelly reached for the baby and Elizabeth handed her over. The kids filed into the house and the door shut behind them. Alex was staring at the balcony when Elizabeth turned to him, the frozen fury slowly giving way to quivering muscles that trembled with relief. "Thank—"

Alex abruptly faced her, his tone grim and his eyes hard. "I'm not leaving."

Chapter 3

• "TELL ME YOU didn't cause his fall," Silas demanded, his face nearly as white as his knuckles.

Draven shrugged. "Luckily, I didn't have to."

"Luckily?" Silas's voice rose in horror. "Draven, he's a kid. Innocent."

With a smoky voice as thick as the black steam that

emanated from the all-encompassing cloak, Draven said, "Need I remind you we've lost Dugan every attempt to follow him to Maeve? Or that, according to the prophecy shown to Alex, this same innocent child, along with all his cousins, will be killed because of our failure? We don't have *time* to pussyfoot around, Silas!"

"Neither will we succeed in any of our endeavors if we become the very thing we're fighting to escape!"

Draven's gloved hands clenched with frustration. "Sometimes being nice and gentle is not the right choice."

Silas shook his head. "The end does not justify the means."

"There are exceptions," Draven insisted.

"I disagree." Silas crossed his arms, his tone and stance saying his position was final.

Draven stayed silent, breathing heavily. After a moment had passed, Draven reasserted, "I did not cause the child's fall."

Silas didn't appear convinced.

• *I'M NOT LEAVING.*

Elizabeth stared at Alex, speechless. He passed her and went through the front door like it was his own home. He was the least of her worries at the moment, though, so she followed him into the house and closed the door quietly behind her.

"Teddy, would you please show Alex upstairs?" Teddy rose from the couch and led Alex away, his steps soft and quiet and Alex's determined, purposeful. Elizabeth faced the remaining children, seeing the little ones playing with their dolls as Danielle sat close to her twin on the love seat, both eight-year-olds knowing they were in trouble. Tommy and Kevin stared at her from the couch.

"I don't suppose any of you know anything about a pickle jar sticking into the side of one of my tires?"

Tommy gulped.

• BETH ANN — ELIZABETH—looked the way Alex felt inside: shaky, nauseous, and afraid. He almost hadn't reached the kid in time. In fact, if he hadn't been on guard, watching for some sign of Maeve, he might have been a second too slow, a breath too late.

Alex followed Teddy up the stairs. As he went, he looked around, trying to distract himself from his fears and calm down. The outside of the house was in desperate need of repair, but the inside was worse. Dark walls and dark furniture minimized any light from nearby lamps. What looked like decades worth of clutter filled every table and shelf, spilled out of the entryway closet and covered the floor. It was a depressing sight.

Everything around him needed a thorough cleaning, yet each child was dressed in good clothes with no holes or rips. Their hair was well groomed, and their shoes in decent shape. The kids weren't exactly clean, but after playing outside, they wouldn't be. A really difficult situation had been dumped on Elizabeth, but it looked like she'd done her best, focusing on what was most important—the children. Alex respected that.

But damn, was this just the worst day of the year for her or what? Spilled milk and a flat tire were nothing. A kid falling off the balcony, though, that had the makings of a disaster. He might have just broken his leg or arm, but he could have easily died. Which meant it was good he'd been here. This time.

Alex followed Teddy to the end of the hallway. As he opened the balcony door and faced Alex, his gaze was piercing, as if to cut through any crap Alex might throw at him. Alex grinned. "Thanks."

"Sure." Teddy stood rigid, watching Alex's every move. "Thanks for looking at it."

Alex nodded and carefully stepped through the door onto the wooden balcony. "We wouldn't want to have one of the little ones fall from here."

"David and Danielle are the only ones stupid enough to go out here like that. We keep the door shut and locked, but they always manage to get through." Teddy was irritated, his lips pursed and his eyes glaring. Yet Alex didn't feel the boy was mad at him.

Watching the floor, Alex eased his feet over each inch, listening for creaking, feeling for soft wood or sagging. Reaching the sides without incident, he shook the low walls, grateful when they didn't budge. "It seems pretty sound, except for this spot where the wood is wet."

Teddy's discerning gaze met his again, and Alex had to wonder how many men were stupid enough to pat him on the head but otherwise ignore him.

"Then we just need to seal the door shut so the twins can't get through."

Alex doubted Teddy's "we" included him in any way, but if not him, then who? There was only one adult with all these kids. All their parents were absent for one reason or another. So absent Elizabeth couldn't even call them for a ride home. He had yet to see her mother, let alone any of her boyfriends. No. Despite his fears, he'd already chosen. For good or ill, he wasn't leaving. They needed him. Elizabeth needed him. She just didn't realize how much.

Teddy shifted, his expression closing down. "I didn't mean you."

Hating that his own hesitance had caused the boy's reaction, Alex reached out and gave his shoulder a light squeeze. "I'm not sure what tools I have that might work. I'll check the bathroom then go look in the truck."

Teddy looked at the door to the side of him. "Can you fix the toilet?"

"Probably not, but I can try." Alex grinned at him, inviting Teddy to share his humor. "I can make it work for tonight, but I think I need to talk to one of my friends. He's much more *experienced* at these sorts of things than I am."

"That's cool." Teddy smiled, but Alex felt his considering gaze follow him into the bathroom.

Alex removed the lid of the toilet tank and inspected the interior. Woodworking, he knew. Porcelain toilets, however, were a new animal. He knew to put the wire on the lever, make sure there was water in the tank, and how to unclog it. That was about it.

Wait a minute. Had Teddy said *one* of them? Did that mean *all* the bathrooms needed to be fixed? Just how many were there, anyway? Alex turned to Teddy. "I'll be right back."

"Okay."

Alex smiled at him and walked down the stairs, seeing the kids sitting around the living room. The little kids were playing dolls, the twins were kicking ass on

Dark Alliance, and one boy sat facing the corner, holding a jar in front of his face. There was no sign of Elizabeth until he reached the bottom of the stairs and saw her in the kitchen, rustling through bags of food.

Her mouth was pursed, her brow furrowed, and the look in her eyes stressed. Would he add to her troubles by bringing Maeve to her door? Had the damage already been done? Elizabeth pulled a few cans out of the sacks and set them on the table, her strong hands gripping them with ease. She appeared delicate but capable at the same time.

But even the most self-sufficient of people needed help once in a while. In the end, would he help or hinder her? Alex opened the front door and stepped out on the porch. There wasn't a clear answer, but he wanted to stay. Hell, he'd always wanted that.

Closing the door behind him, Alex headed toward his truck and his toolbox. Several sets of eyes made his back itch. Keeping his stride and stance casual, Alex reached for his cell phone and said, "Call Geoffrey."

• THE FRONT DOOR opened, drawing Elizabeth's gaze. Alex's back filled the doorway briefly before he shut it behind him. For an instant, she could see that same image through the memories and emotions of her eight-year-old self. Only it wasn't because of Alex that her mother had leaned against the door and slid to the floor, mascara dripping down her cheeks.

Mary Beth had sobbed, broken and helpless in a way that had always torn Elizabeth apart to watch. She had run to her mother and wrapped her arms around her, holding her mother's head against her little chest and offering comfort the way her mom did whenever she fell from her bike. "It's going to be okay, Mommy."

"I thought Earl loved me, Bethy." She'd spoken softly, as if the pain were too great to bear. "Why can't he love me? That's all I want."

"I love you, Mommy. More than anyone."

"I know you do, baby."

"You don't need him, Mommy. You've got us."

But they hadn't been enough. Not Elizabeth, her sisters, or her brother. Her mother had a hole in her heart. A need that none of the men she'd turned to could ever fill. It was that same need that drove her sister Dallas, no matter what she sacrificed, no matter how often she was disappointed.

Elizabeth refused to have that problem. She probably had that same hole and no man, even a good man, would be able to fill it. No man would be so important to her that she collapsed weak, begging, and pitiful when he left.

Alex was the type who would say good-bye first, at the very least. But if just seeing him walk out of the door made her chest feel tight, it was imperative to send him packing as soon as possible.

"Aunt Lizzie!"

She blinked and looked down as Kevin ran toward her, Tommy pulling on his arm.

"I didn't mean to," Tommy snarled.

Kevin shoved him away. "Tommy let Benjamin out!"

Elizabeth's brow wrinkled as she tried to figure out who Benjamin might be. After mentally cycling through

all their names, she still came up blank. Who could forget the name of one of their nephews? What kind of—

"Who's Benjamin?" Shelly asked, saving Elizabeth
from a mental lashing.

"He's my spider," Kevin said.

Elizabeth gasped, just hearing the word making her
want to screech. She swallowed weakly and tried to
speak calmly. "When did you get a spider?"

"See, I told you she'd be mad," Tommy gloated.

"I'm not mad," Elizabeth assured Kevin. "When—"

Still looking worried, but too concerned for his spider
to give in to it, Kevin said, "I found him when you were
outside flirting with that guy."

"I wasn't—"

"Yeah, you were." Shelly rolled her eyes. "I'm surprised you didn't hop in his truck and beg him to take
you away."

Cheeks suddenly hot, Elizabeth scowled. "I wouldn't
do that."

"Bet you want to," Tommy sang sweetly.

From the other room, three shrill screams shot straight
through her ears, nearly laying Elizabeth out cold. Kevin
bolted from the kitchen, shouting, "Benjamin!"

Elizabeth ran after him in time to see the three little
ones, all very much girly-girls, jumping up and down in
helpless tears as a daddy long-legs crawled over one of
their Barbies.

Kevin gently cupped his hands around the spider
and slid it into an old jelly jar while Elizabeth tried to
shush the girls. But they weren't ready to be shushed.
Their cries climbed higher and higher, building into a

shared hysteria. Suddenly, the loud sounds of battle and sword fights crashed over everything, even the girls' screams.

"David! Danielle!"

"We couldn't hear the game," the twins whined in sync.

"Shut the TV off."

"We're almost at the next save point," they wheedled.

"You can fight your way back to this point tomorrow. Turn the game off. Now."

Grumbling, they shut the video game off and threw their controllers on the floor. Elizabeth snapped. She was done with that crap. "You two, pick those up nicely or you're grounded from it for a week."

They whined. She ignored them. "After that you can take the girls up for a bath."

"But we haven't had dinner, yet," Jessie said, her little eyes wide and dry.

"Don't worry, sweetie, I'll feed you." Right before she sent them all to bed very early. "Teddy, find the little girls clean jammies and help the twins." The whole bathroom might end up covered in soapy water, but then she'd have six clean kids instead of three.

"You remember the toilet's still broken, right?" Teddy asked. They all eyed her, still hoping to get out of it.

"Use the master bathroom tonight."

With no more excuses, six pairs of shoulders slumped. Teddy herded them up the stairs. Elizabeth could count on him to watch over them all. "Kevin, put away the spider, then you and Tommy clean up the living room."

"But we didn't make the mess," Tommy argued.

"I don't want to hear it." Already exhausted, Elizabeth headed for the kitchen. She'd begun the day a little earlier than usual. After getting the older kids packed off to school, she'd had the toddlers and the baby with her when she'd gone to the hospital that morning.

They were too small to fully understand that the tubes and monitors meant their grandma was sick. But next week was Spring Break, and she'd be damned if her mom put off seeing the older kids any longer. The good-byes would be rough, she didn't doubt that, but the kids deserved more than silence. They deserved closure.

Seeing Shelly almost had the grocery bags unpacked, Elizabeth offered a very heartfelt, "Thank you."

Elizabeth handed a cracker to the baby and she mashed it into her high chair tray before stuffing bits in her mouth. She smiled at Veronica, loving her uncomplicated happiness. The toddlers' earlier screams still reverberated in her eardrums. What the hell was she going to do about Kevin's spider?

Elizabeth took a deep breath, wet a rag, and started wiping out the refrigerator. "Did anyone call while I was gone?"

Shelly snorted, unpacking the bags on the table. "Stupid phone never quit ringing. Woke Veronica up from her nap."

Elizabeth rose, rinsed the rag, and knelt again. The silence stretched. Shelly did this just to get a rise out of her. She raised her brow and locked her eyes on the teen. "Well?"

Shelly grinned and stacked two more soup cans in the pantry. "You probably want your boss's message first, huh?"

Elizabeth twisted the rag with extra force as she rinsed it out. Her tone perfectly even, she said, "That would be nice."

"He said to call him."

Elizabeth spun around. "That's it? He didn't say anything specific?"

"No, he didn't." Shelly pursed her lips with her typical "adults-are-always-giving-me-a-hard-time" expression.

Elizabeth raised a doubtful brow.

Shelly huffed, then snapped, "Geez, do I look like a friggin' secretary?"

Elizabeth gave her a stern look before flipping on the light to the laundry room. "That attitude is not necessary."

"Sorry." Shelly shrugged, obviously unconcerned, and began pouring bags of cheap cereal into Tupperware containers.

Elizabeth shook her head at her. She wasn't Shelly's mother, or anyone else's for that matter, and they both knew it, which made it difficult to maintain any kind of authority. Elizabeth tossed the rag on the pile of dirty clothes, flinched at how huge it was, and hurriedly flipped the light off. Dinner first. "Who else called?"

"Rehab. Aunt Felicia disappeared."

"What?" She came to a dead stop and stared into Shelly's eyes. They were flat, unsurprised, almost mocking in the face of Elizabeth's shock. Grabbing veggies off the table, Elizabeth took them to the sink, turned on the water, and rinsed them.

Shelly shook her head. "I don't know why you're surprised. I told you it wouldn't work when you first asked."

Elizabeth sighed. "I know you did. I just thought a little help would . . ."

"Some people can't be helped."

Elizabeth wanted to argue, she really did. The kids shouldn't be so cynical. She needed to convince them people could be redeemed, didn't she? But she couldn't. Not and be honest. "Anything else?"

Shelly finished clearing off the table. "Uncle Bobby called."

"Why? The lawyer already said he can't leave prison to go to the funeral. I can't help him."

Shelly sprayed cleaner on the table and wiped it down. "That's what I told him."

"What'd he say?" Grabbing a knife and starting on the vegetables, Elizabeth could only imagine. Her brother was in a place where the only thing he had to think about was himself. Which meant most of his conversation centered on *his* wants, *his* needs, *his* feelings.

And his twin, Felicia. Their bond superseded a lot, something his twin girls, Sarah and Jessie, understood well. As did David and Danielle, Felicia's identical pair. The Raineses had been blessed with three sets of twins, though the toddlers were so close in age and friendship, they could've been triplets.

"He needs more cigarettes." Shelly began to assemble the ingredients to make spaghetti.

Elizabeth shook her head with disbelief and dumped onions and peppers into the sauce pot. "*Sure.* I'll get right on that."

Shelly turned to her and grinned. "That's what I said. Pass me the tomatoes."

Elizabeth tossed her a can of stewed tomatoes. "And what did he say to that?"

"I need to drop the attitude. He may be in jail, but he's still the adult and I'm just a kid. Blah, blah, blah." She opened the can and dumped the tomatoes in the pot.

Elizabeth struggled to keep a straight face.

"It's okay, you can laugh. I won't take it as encouragement. Wouldn't matter anyway, I'd still talk to him like that."

Elizabeth shook her head and started putting together a fresh salad. "I'm sorry. I just can't believe . . ."

"What?" Shelly scoffed. "That your siblings care more for their addictions than for their kids? Don't stress, Aunt Beth, it's not your fault this family is full of losers."

Elizabeth paused, looking at her. "I meant I couldn't believe he still thinks he deserves your respect."

The teen didn't say anything, just met her gaze in stubborn defiance.

"You think I'm a loser, too?"

Shelly held her gaze, then wavered. Finally, she shrugged and stirred the spaghetti sauce. "Doesn't matter what I think, Aunt Beth. Soon as you find a replacement, you're gone."

And that, Elizabeth knew, was what made her a loser in both their books.

• *SOON AS YOU find a replacement, you're gone.*

Alex held still in the doorway to the kitchen. She wanted to leave. He couldn't really blame her. She had a lot to deal with; even more than he'd known. He'd talked to Geoffrey about her bad day, but that had been before he'd learned about her brother and younger sister. And according to the kids upstairs, her mother was in the hospital dying.

At what point did things stop being difficult and become something else? When was it not just bad luck? Alex looked at his hands, then back at Shelly. She'd seen him standing there, though Elizabeth couldn't see him from this angle. The girl had been warning him off, carrying on a double conversation with more skill than most adults could accomplish.

Shelly's blue eyes bored into him again, looking so much like her aunt she could have been Elizabeth's daughter. Her message had been loud and clear. Adults were unreliable, but Elizabeth was all the kids had. He wouldn't be allowed to mess that up. She'd probably expected him to run from all the dirty laundry she'd laid out in front of him, but he wouldn't.

Alex met the teen's gaze head on. He *wanted* Elizabeth, they *needed* Elizabeth, and they would soon need him. Whatever he choose to do, the vision would likely come true. He hated that he would bring danger to them, but he was fooling himself if he thought he could prevent the terrible vision. He didn't know what actions led to the vision, so how could anything he did be a "change"?

He'd suspected that even before approaching her, and Geoffrey's research had convinced him it was true. If there was anyone Alex trusted, it was Geoffrey. And now Elizabeth and her family's safety would depend on that trust.

When Alex didn't duck his head and run for the door,

Shelly's eyes narrowed in consideration. Alex gave her his best reassuring gaze, his chin firm, his eyes steady.

Elizabeth chopped on the cutting board, making neat piles of olives, cucumbers, and tomatoes. Her movements were slow and deliberate. He could practically see her mind churning. Something about the expression on her face stirred his curiosity. He wanted to know what was happening inside her, on a gut level he *needed* to know.

Slender and strong, her spine curved gently to her ass. The soft cotton of her shirt hugged the curve of her breasts as she twisted slightly, accentuating the dip of her waist and flare of her hips. The peach fabric contrasted lushly with the creamy gold of her skin, creating a mix of soft textures begging to be stroked.

He'd already done so a thousand times in his sleep, but his mouth watered at the thought of doing it for real.

But reality never went as smoothly as dreams. If he walked up behind her, she'd stiffen, not melt. If he put his arms around her, she'd struggle. And if he cut himself, then healed instantly, she'd scream.

Alex scowled. He couldn't tell her about the threat of Maeve without proof of the paranormal. He couldn't show her that proof without assurance she wouldn't freak out and make him leave. Hell, Kalyss had already known of her own gift before being confronted with a statue who became a man, and she'd still hesitated to believe. He couldn't just pop the proof in front of Elizabeth and expect her to be calm.

Which left him with only one option.

* * *

• ELIZABETH SHUT THE front door behind her and stepped to the edge of the wide front porch. Pulling her sweater tight against the cold spring night, she wrapped her arms around herself. Alex leaned against his truck, arranging his tools behind the front seat. Today was ending so much better than it had started.

She was going to miss him when he left. She always missed him when she awakened from a dream, feeling chilled without his arms to surround her. She hated that she felt unsafe without his chest bracing her back. Unwanted without his breath brushing past her ear.

But now it would be even worse, because instead of suspecting what she would be missing, she was positive of it. But her course had been set long ago. Men were a weakness to the women in her family. Relationships didn't work. And to begin one at this point in her life, while her mother was in the hospital and ten kids depended on her for everything, wouldn't be just a mistake, it would be the height of irresponsibility.

Life was difficult enough when she ached for a touch she could never truly feel. It would be nearly impossible living with the memory of a smile that curled her toes. Or the mischievous glint in his eyes as he'd teased the kids during dinner. How much *fun* the meal had been with him encouraging everyone to talk and laugh.

She'd never quite learned how to do that. To laugh and play for the sheer joy of doing so. She was typically turned off, closed down, shut out. But tonight she'd felt connected in a way she hadn't in years. Not that she was a sour or depressing person. She was quiet, contemplative, and comfortable in her own head.

She imagined anyone watching her would get bored,

yet, strangely Alex's gaze had been hot, searing, every time she met his eyes.

The truck seat clicked back into place and Alex shut the door. Halfway up the sidewalk, the truck's lights shut off, leaving them with only the moon, the stars, and that faint city haze of light to see by. His long legs ate up the distance between them in only a few steps. Gripping her sweater in tight fists, she forced a smile. It was time to say good-bye. A clean break was best for both of them.

Alex halted at the base of the steps, his hazel eyes smiling at her. Ever-present laugh lines visible at the corners of his mouth. All too easily, Elizabeth could see them in fifty years: him grinning at her, teasing her until she relaxed.

Digging her nails into the sides of her arms, Elizabeth yanked herself back on track. Before he could say anything, she rushed to say, "Thank you for your help tonight."

His eyes widened, then he shrugged and stepped closer. "I'm happy to help a friend."

Did his voice sound deeper? Or was she imagining things because it was night and the stars were soft as candles? "Well, really, I appreciate it."

Alex mounted the first step. "I don't want your gratitude, Beth Ann."

"Elizabeth," she corrected automatically. A knot formed in her stomach. "Then what do you want, Alex?"

"You."

She scowled. "I'm not *that* grateful."

His eyes shone with amusement. "Good. Because I said I don't want gratitude, especially *that* kind."

Relief made her knees weak. Much as she might want him, never would she pay for a few fixed toilets with sex. Elizabeth unclenched her hands and lifted her brows. "Then I'm not sure what you want from me."

Again, he stepped closer. This time, though, he tugged on the trailing ends of her sweater and used them to pull her closer to him. When his eyes met hers, they were completely serious. "Everything."

Chapter 4

• ELIZABETH FROWNED EVEN as her pulse leapt for joy. Where had this come from? Alex had been laughing, playful, and mischievous all night, but now he was intense, focused, and all his attention was on her. Only in their dreams had she seen him like this, and now, as then, it kicked her desire into overdrive. But this wasn't a dream.

"Alex, I—" She shook her head. "I don't have anything to give."

His head cocked to the side as he considered her words. "That, I do not believe."

"What are you looking for?"

"Like I said, I want all of you."

"You can't have me."

"Why?"

She scowled in disbelief. "Are you serious? Do you really need to ask?"

Alex looked at the house behind her, then back. "This is simply a tough situation. Situations get better. I want a real reason."

"What's your reason for wanting me?"

He grinned. "I've always wanted you, Elizabeth. You know that."

She looked away because he was right.

Alex settled his hands on her waist. "The last thing you said to me was, 'Not in this lifetime'." Alex's voice grew harder with each word. "You said that, then you disappeared. You didn't even go to graduation." His face was completely exposed by the porch lights behind her. But his eyes were dark. "I'm not so self-centered I believe it was my fault you left."

"No." She shook her head adamantly. He didn't deserve to think that for a second. "It wasn't."

"It's been twelve years and I haven't forgotten you. After seeing you today, I only want you more. Dreams aren't enough."

Cold sweat burst at her nape, a mix of anger, guilt, and fear. Anger with herself, guilt for what she'd done to him, and fear that he would find out. Shaking from her knees up, Elizabeth jerked away from him and broke all contact. "Then don't dream, Alex. Save yourself and don't dream of me, because there's nothing for you here."

Alex reached for her as if to pull her back. "Elizabeth . . ."

She evaded his grasp and grabbed the door handle. "Go home, Alex. Thank you for today, but that's all there is. All there can be."

"Elizabeth, I don't understand."

She shut the door and locked him out.

• ALEX STARED AT the closed door for a long moment. Her reaction didn't make sense. He slowly backed down the porch and went to his truck. Taking a deep breath to hold his thoughts at bay and his actions under control, he got in, started it up, and pulled gently away from the curb. Whatever his next move was, he was fairly sure a tire-peeling temper tantrum wouldn't help his cause.

It took until he was halfway to the dojo before he could identify his reaction. Fear. But not fear of Maeve or death or danger. No. Once again, he'd made a move and Elizabeth had run away. At this rate, he'd be old, gray, and feeble with nothing but erotic dreams to keep him warm.

Then don't dream, Alex. Save yourself and don't dream of me.

If only it was that fucking easy. Alex narrowed his eyes and slammed the stick shift into third gear. The dojo. He had to hold on 'til he got there, then he could let his anger out. And why shouldn't he be angry? He wasn't blind. He'd seen the glances, the attraction in her blue-eyed gaze. He'd heard the disappointment in her sexy voice when she'd thought Kalyss's baby was also his.

And he'd sure as hell seen how her nipples had tightened to succulent little points he craved to taste whenever he stood close. Her rejection was a lie, and she denied both of them, not just him. And that simply didn't make sense.

Alex didn't even bother with lights as he entered the workout room of the dojo. Street lamps outside shone through the glass, casting a low, ghostly glow over the instruments around him. Toward the corner stood the wooden dummy his father had made for Alex last Christmas, and that's what he went for. The polished dark wood gleamed in the dim light, inviting him to lose himself in mindless motion.

Alex stopped and bent his knees, crossing his hands in front of him, palms flat and down. Three posts were angled toward him, two pointing at him, chest high, and one going down. After a deep breath, he brought his hands up hard, his left hand high, palm slapping the top pole, and his right hand low, the palm hitting the second pole.

It was a two handed X-block—the basis of a Naihanchi Kata. With a swipe of his foot against the dummy's lead leg, he completed the first combination. Then he repeated it, adding a strike to the rhythm. Gradually, he began to flow, striking harder and faster, his bare palms slapping the wood.

His father was good with wood. Always had been. He'd made cabinets and furniture all through Alex's childhood, selling them to different companies around town and building a solid reputation as a talented craftsman.

But more important to Alex was his dad's reputation as a father and a husband. His parents loved each other and that formed the basis of Alex's dreams for the future. He wanted what they had. He wanted to build a marriage and a family and construct a safe, solid home for his children. He wanted to teach them skills, guide them through life while standing beside a woman whose smiles brought him contentment, whose laughter inspired his happiness.

And maybe when the kids were grown, Alex and his wife would sell their house and take off cross-country in an RV, seeing in person everything they'd only read about or seen pictures of the way his parents did, determined to enjoy their dream before their bodies were too old. Or Alex finally gave them grandchildren to spoil.

Alex couldn't take MMA on the road and online the way his dad had with woodworking, but traveling together for even a short vacation with the woman he loved was a possibility for the future, and that's what he wanted most. A future with possibilities.

But the woman he wanted was Elizabeth and she refused to consider any possibilities. Refused to even speak with him. She had the weight of the world on her shoulders and felt no inclination to find *anyone* to help her carry it.

He'd made a mistake, depending on the attraction between them to give him a place in her life. She still wasn't ready for anything personal, but there didn't seem too many other options. He could physically pick her up and carry her along, forcing her wherever he thought it best to go, but that maneuver had gotten Geoffrey killed. At least twice. He couldn't wait patiently for her to come to him. It would really never happen, then.

So, what was his best approach? There had to be one, damn it. She *needed* him. Whatever else they were facing, the threat he'd seen in his dream was the most important.

He needed a way in, a way to stay. Clearly not a romantic one. He'd been useful today, but fixing toilets wouldn't last forever. Of course, there were plenty of other things that needed fixing. Alex pounded the dummy harder, waiting for it to crack against the punishment.

So his choice was to forget his dreams, stay close to what he couldn't have, and work his ass off. He wasn't afraid of hard work, but was it even possible to be that close to his desire and not go for it? If there was anything he could never be, refused to be, to Beth Ann, it was simply a *friend*.

Again, his conscience prompted him to tell her the truth about Maeve, about his gift. He wasn't comfortable keeping such crucial knowledge a secret. And danger could create a closeness she'd find difficult to break, a devilish thought. But no, considering the type and weight of her responsibilities, that would earn him another door in the face. It was too big of a risk.

A bright light suddenly blinded him. Standing as still as possible, he blinked until his eyes adjusted. When he could see, his best friend stood before him. Kalyss stood in perfect battle-ready form, her knees bent, her fists blocking her face, her core straight. She gave Alex a challenging stare. Alex looked around the empty sparring room, then back at the short blonde in front of him. A few months ago, she could've kicked his ass. Partly because he couldn't bear to take that final, finishing shot. Not against Kalyss. A fact she happily took advantage of whenever it suited her.

But after she'd left for her honeymoon, Geoffrey had worked Alex pretty hard. His skills were now up a notch or ten and he couldn't risk it. Especially not while she was pregnant. Whether from science, prayer, or Alex's growing ability to heal, Kalyss's conceiving a child was a miracle not to be chanced, no matter how bored and over-protected she felt. Alex returned her glare with one that was distinctly unimpressed.

Kalyss widened her eyes and pleaded, "Please?"

In his best imitation-Geoffrey tone, Alex said, "I think not."

"Aw, come on!" She scowled at the injustice and Alex looked to the door again, praying help would arrive. And it did.

"Be nice, love." Dreux and Geoffrey walked into the room and Dreux slid his arms around Kalyss, his hands settling on her stomach. "He knows I'd kill him."

Dreux wasn't wrong, and unlike some people, Alex wouldn't survive being dead. Dreux knew more ways to kill than even Geoffrey had died from. Not that he'd have to use them. No, Dreux would probably just turn his finger to stone and tap Alex on the head and that would be all she wrote. Alex gave Kalyss a mocking smile. She growled and he laughed silently, pointing teasingly at her nose to bug her.

Kalyss pointedly ignored him and looked over her shoulder at her husband. "I just wanted to move a little. Nothing dangerous. Besides," she snarled at Alex's annoying finger. "He deserves it!"

She tried to escape Dreux's arms, but he tightened his hold as his arms turned to actual granite from his shoulders to his fingertips. She was completely trapped in an unbreakable hold and, judging from her pouty face, she knew it.

Alex grimaced. "Please never tell me all the things you use that little trick for."

Kalyss lowered her chin, her eyes cold with annoyance. "Keep making cracks like that and I *will* tell you—in detail—starting with his—"

"Ack! La-la-la!" Alex covered his ears and turned away from them. "I can't hear you. La-la-la."

Through his hands he could hear her laughing, which was pretty much his goal. Before he could congratulate himself for distracting her, though, Kalyss asked, "So how did it go?"

Damn. So close. Alex exhaled and reached for a fresh towel from the stack they kept on a shelf. He glanced at Geoffrey, but spoke to Kalyss. "I thought Geoffrey filled you in?"

"Oh, he did." Kalyss watched him with concerned eyes, not a bit deflected. "Maeve's on her way soon. Beth Ann has it rough. I'm not asking about all that stuff."

Three pairs of eyes zeroed in on him. Oh, goody. He rubbed the towel over his face and neck. "She prefers Elizabeth, not Beth Ann."

"And?" Kalyss tilted her head and tugged on Dreux's arms until he released her. Coming closer as she examined Alex's face, she pursed her lips and angrily said, "You've got to be kidding."

"What?" Alex tried to ask innocently.

"She pushed you away again," Kalyss huffed, her hands on her hips now.

"Don't get all protective. It's no big deal." Alex shrugged. Kalyss knew how important this was to him. She'd known him forever. She'd picked up the pieces Beth Ann had left the first time. She'd watched him ruin perfectly good relationships as he backpedaled away from commitment. "And you of all people know how hard it is to convince a strong-willed woman to fall in love."

"We're not talking about me," she snapped.

"You're not, but," Alex looked at Dreux. "I really feel for you, man."

Dreux chuckled. "And I understand your pain."

Kalyss rolled her eyes. "Fine. She's *just* like me. Our situations are totally similar."

Dreux tugged on her ponytail. "No one is like you, love."

Alex watched her irritation melt. "I know you don't like Elizabeth—"

Kalyss shook her head and gestured toward him. "I just don't understand her. You're a great guy. She should give you a chance."

"Well, I need to figure out an excuse to go back—"

"Fix her tire and bring her the vehicle," Geoffrey said, calmly logical.

Alex looked up, stunned by the obvious suggestion. "Good idea. How else would she get it?"

Kalyss snorted. "Don't underestimate strong-willed women."

Alex grinned. "Okay, so that'll get her to open the door. How do I keep it open?"

"Take off your shirt." Kalyss blushed as all the men gaped at her. Looking at Dreux, she muttered, "Well, it helps. There are just certain sights a girl can't forget, no matter how 'uninterested' she may be."

Alex laughed. "I think walking up to her door without

a shirt on when there's still snow on the ground might be just a bit too obvious."

Kalyss gave him a wide-eyed, innocent expression. "It's almost melted."

Geoffrey leaned against a table and crossed his arms. "You said she's a programmer?"

"Software designer, yeah."

"We could use that. If her job is in Seattle and she's here, she's obviously not working. Chances are likely they could use some money."

"True. But what do we need software for? A basic setup covers everything for the dojo. She'd see through that in a heartbeat."

Geoffrey raised a brow. "It would be for me."

Alex pictured the bookshelves full of research Geoffrey had gathered in his nine hundred and some-odd years. "There's a difference between a project and a career."

Geoffrey's eyes met his. "Maeve isn't done with us. She's going after Elizabeth. You want Elizabeth in your life. The kids need her in Spokane. The paranormal world will need to be explained to her, preferably before Maeve holds a dagger to her throat. And I have a need to find information in my files in a more efficient way."

And if anyone had the money to employ a specialist full-time, it was Geoffrey. Alex nodded. "So, we bring her back her vehicle, tire fixed, and you offer her a job."

"Spring break is next week," Kalyss offered. "We're doing day camps at the dojo. We could keep at least a few of the kids busy and safe while she works."

Alex thought through their obstacles and options and

nodded. "Then that just leaves figuring out how to survive when Maeve comes to call."

Geoffrey shrugged. "Make sure that when she shows up, I'm here."

Alex grinned slightly. "I appreciate the offer, but somehow, I don't think the answer will be that easy."

"Why do you say that?"

"Because Maeve's much more powerful than her son. In my dream, she took out everyone at once."

• VAMPIRE MOVIES AND TV shows were lies, all of them. Every single one she'd watched in the past few months was full of shit. A centuries-old demon couldn't regain all of her strength in an instant after sucking the blood from a human. It took longer than that, no matter how powerful the creature.

Maeve held out one unsteady hand, reaching for the vanity in front of her. Candles lit her chamber, casting a soft glow around a room full of the dark, vibrant colors she preferred. Easing to the stool, she faced the mirror.

It had taken an achingly long time for her cells to rehydrate, her flesh to fill out, and her hair to darken to its natural bloodred color. Hours of painstaking effort. Weeks of Dugan reading to her from books and newspapers, stories from both realms so she could catch up on much of what she'd missed. So much time had passed, so many changes had struck the world and she'd missed it all. Nearly one thousand years. The world had left her behind.

After her flesh had filled, her eyes were able to adjust

and she'd begun to read for herself. Not just read, but watch movies and TV and learn the Internet, devouring every bit of information as fast as her starved brain would allow. But no matter what she'd been able to absorb, one crucial piece of information eluded her. *Who had interfered with her curse and trapped her in the tunnels?*

Bitterness and helpless fury twisted her mouth, her thin red lips a mockery of the lush, tempting flesh they'd once been. Dugan, of course, told her how beautiful she was, but she wasn't stupid. She knew how she'd changed.

Maeve reached for the rough, uncut emerald that lay like a hunk of meteor rock on the table before her, channeling her fury and power into it. There wasn't much she could do with the overwhelming bursts of emotion now, but with time, she'd be able to wield them like the most deadly of weapons.

Dugan had informed her that Dreux had broken her curse, awakening her, but he couldn't show her how. Who had helped the bastard? And what had happened to her son? Kai was missing and her most valued emerald, the one she'd poured centuries of power into, had disappeared with him. Dugan had attempted to answer these questions during the months of her weakness, but soon . . . soon she'd do the searching herself.

First find who had interfered and trapped her, see the extent of their resources, and decide how to avenge herself. Then she could search for her emerald. With it, she would be powerful enough to face anyone. Punish *anyone*. From there, she could return to her original plan for her son and his bastard half-brother. Dreux still had a few of his father's sins to pay for, and once he did, she could regain the powerful status she'd had before.

Cloth whispered at the entrance of her chamber and Maeve watched through the mirror as Dugan appeared, the cowl of his cloak pushed back so his handsome face showed. She could tell immediately from his darkened eyes and the slight slump of his shoulders, that once again he had nothing for her. No clues, no leads.

How she hated to be disappointed.

Maeve saw her lips thin in the beginnings of a snarl and forced them into a smile of pleasure instead. His punishment would have to wait a bit longer. She needed him too much right now. She grabbed the emerald from her desk again and held it tight, the rough edges biting into her fingers. A haze of red fury filled her and she had to fight it back, channel it into the rock.

Dugan stilled behind her, noting her brief snarl. "I am sorry, Goddess. The vermin have hidden well."

Slowly, seductively, she turned on the stool and crossed one shapely leg over the other until the royal purple of her satin negligee rose, exposing her thigh. Dugan's eyes followed each movement and his tongue moistened his lips.

Leaning back, she allowed her bountiful breasts to push at the edges of her low, squared bodice. The matching robe, a sheer purple, slid down her shoulders, baring each creamy white slope to his worshipful gaze. "Then today is not the day. But don't worry, the day will come, pet. Soon."

Grasping the rough emerald tightly, she fed every surge of anger into it until the red haze lifted and she could focus on her gorgeous servant. Tall and muscular, only she could see him as he really was. The pride in his stance. The intelligence in his silvery eyes. The health in his long, thick, golden hair. His subservient attitude lulled everyone else into barely noticing him. But she knew the truth.

She'd never settled for anything less than beauty in her men. This was not to say they were perfect. She'd opted out of perfection long ago.

Rising to her feet, she used every ounce of control over her body she'd gained to glide toward him. It was a barely passable imitation of her former seductive walk, but it would do for now. Reaching for the ties that held his cloak closed at his throat, she loosened them and spoke softly in his ear.

"You know how to make it up to me." Fisting her hand in his long hair, Maeve pulled his head lower until his silver-eyed gaze met the hunger in hers.

He smiled gently, lust brightening his eyes. "Anything you wish, Goddess."

She'd once had a temple full of men like him. Men who worshipped her and fed her powers with their lusts until her skin glowed as white as the moon, her eyes as deep as one of her emeralds, and her hair as bright as fire. Of them all, Dugan was the one she'd most craved, then and now.

Opening his cloak further, Maeve could at last see the beaten gold-and-silver torque that surrounded his throat. At the center lay her large, square-cut emerald. Maeve pressed her smiling lips to the gem and inhaled slightly.

Jealous of her kiss, Dugan's left hand gripped the thick curls at the back of her head, forcefully tilted her face up, and kissed her as passionately as she'd wanted all those months ago when she'd been too weak to handle it. Someone definitely needed to pay for that. A goddess of lust should never be too weak for great sex.

Dugan's right hand spread across her back, pressing her against him. On cue, two long, black-furred limbs stretched from beneath his cloak, their sharp tips scraping up her sides, raising her negligee over her chest. Two more surrounded her hips, pressing dimples into the back of her thighs and lifting her from the ground.

Two more held her legs open, wrapping them around his waist, until she was exposed to the seventh limb's sensual glide. The fur brushed against her sensitive skin until tingles shot from her groin to her breasts and she rubbed against him, moaning into his mouth. Another glide, then the spider's eighth appendage guided his cock inside her. Hard and hot, he filled her just the way she wanted. Needed.

Maeve arched her hips, riding him, loving the rush of blood and hot liquid through her body. Strength flowed through her limbs and she moaned again, devouring his lips. With one hand, she opened his cloak further down his chest and stroked the spider's black furred head.

Dugan moaned, a high-pitched purr mixing with the baritone of his voice. Holding her tighter, he used the spider's appendages to angle her just right and pounded one powerful thrust after another deep inside her core, trembling in her arms with the force of his devotion.

Maeve smiled, her lips curving against his. She knew his feelings and thoughts. Knew his mind. And oh, how he would hate her if his mind were ever free to remember all she'd forced him to do and become. Remembering her deception added spice to the moment. Tightening her grip, Maeve rode danger and death until he exploded inside her.

• ELIZABETH WAS JUST finishing the dishes when Shelly found her. The washer chugged and the dryer thumped in the background, insulating her from the various noises of the house settling in for the night. All she could think of was the confused and hurt look on Alex's face when she'd pushed him away and told him to quit dreaming of her. She'd hated what she'd done, but it had been necessary.

Shelly poured herself a glass of milk and leaned against the counter. "So you sent him away?"

Elizabeth paused. Shelly was unpredictable. She could have any opinion imaginable. Unfortunately, she also had a knack for baring hidden truths that were uncomfortable to face. She rinsed out the dishrag and started wiping down the counters in swift, efficient motions. "Yeah."

"Mom would call you an idiot," Shelly stated.

It was true. If there was a pair of broad, male shoulders within a ten-mile radius, Dallas would find a way to lean on them. And the man who owned them would fall all over himself just to make her smile. "No doubt your grandma would, too."

Shelly shrugged. "Yeah, but what do they know?"

Elizabeth smiled, relaxing. Shelly shared her opinions about her mom's and sister's boyfriends. Sending Alex away was a good decision. And it marked one more large difference between Elizabeth and the other women in her family. "Their way just isn't my way. It's possible to do things without leaning on a man. Look at how much Mom's last boyfriend accomplished around here."

Shelly snorted. "Yeah, the TV got a real workout. I understand. You made the right decision."

Elizabeth nodded. "I think I did. It's not a good thing to continually look to someone to save you. You have to learn to depend on yourself in tough situations. Who's to guarantee getting involved with Alex wouldn't have turned out to be the same kind of bad situation Mom and Dallas always land in?"

"I don't know, he was pretty helpful tonight." Shelly swallowed the last of her milk and went to rinse the glass. "Don't you need to learn to accept help when you really need it? 'Don't cut off your nose to spite your face' and all that?"

Elizabeth shook her head and turned to wipe off the table. "It's true up to a point, but if you make accepting help a habit, you never learn your own strength. I think this family has the fortitude of giants. We just don't use it."

Shelly dried and put away the glass, her brows pursed in a thoughtful frown. "What if you're wrong and we're not that strong?"

Moving on to the highchair, Elizabeth shrugged. "You never know unless you try. It's a cliché, also, but one that's always true."

Shelly grabbed the broom and dragged its bristles slowly but thoroughly across the floor, watching as dirt and bits of paper and food formed a pile. "Who decides when you've tried hard enough?"

Elizabeth studied her niece. "Right now, me. I decide."

Shelly nodded. "And you made the right decision for you . . . but is it the right one for us?"

Chapter 5

• BY THE TIME she'd cleaned up, washed more of the never-ending pile of clothes, and staggered upstairs, Elizabeth's eyelids refused to stay open, her muscles ached, and her body dragged with fatigue. She wanted nothing more than to collapse in her own bed. Only her refusal to give in to her exhaustion helped her through brushing her teeth and showering before she yanked on panties and a T-shirt and fell on top of her unmade bed.

Making it had been a standard in the past, but when she had to stumble out of it at six in the morning and was unbelievably busy for the rest of the day, the bed became her least concern. Elizabeth closed her eyes, waiting for sleep to claim her; frustrated that she never seemed to accomplish anything more than existing each day.

But her mind started running, bouncing from one chore to the next. She had to buy a new tire and have it put on her car before she'd have a vehicle again. And the electric bill had arrived. Finally she was up to date and only had to pay one month's worth. She'd emptied a large portion of her savings for that. And the water. And the back taxes.

They were about to lose the phone service. The plumbing needed to be redone. And several of the kids already needed new shoes, the ones she'd bought three months ago now too small. She sighed. Tomorrow was Saturday. She'd have them for nine days. She'd have to get them to help straighten up the house so Child Protective Services wouldn't condemn it as unlivable. She was due for a "surprise" inspection any day now and it would be integral to keeping the kids together in one home, as one family.

Elizabeth punched her pillow into shape and closed her eyes. The look on Alex's face when he'd first seen the house came back to haunt her. She was living a nightmare—one she'd tried to escape twelve years ago. But nightmares were never willing to release their victims. Hers had called her home and trapped her in dark dreams every night since.

Mama, why didn't you tell me how bad it was years ago, so I could've sent the money up then? Come home sooner? But she knew why. Elizabeth had pulled away from her family. She'd gotten away and never looked back.

It was her own fault she was in this position. If she hadn't run away and stayed away, maybe she could have helped Mary Beth sooner. Turned Bobby away from the path that led to prison. Kept Felicia away from drugs. Saved Dallas from men who didn't want her kids.

Maybe . . . no. There was nothing Elizabeth could have done. Her mother had chosen alcohol and cigarettes long ago and nothing Elizabeth said or did changed her mind. As for her siblings, she'd grown up the same way they did, so the only difference between them was that Elizabeth had the determination and drive to reach for something better. But maybe they all had that too. They just couldn't figure out a way to reach for it that didn't involve something illegal, immoral, or both.

Elizabeth sighed and rearranged the blankets around her. She'd never understand her siblings, but she had no choice but to reach out to them. To save them so they could return to the children who needed them. Elizabeth needed to get them home one way or another, give them their kids, and keep close enough to them so that even after she returned to her high-paying job and organized life, things would never disintegrate this far again.

Maybe then she could try again with Alex. Just the thought made tears sting her eyes. Holding her breath, she fought the tide of emotion. No, not even then. There was too much danger, and things she couldn't even begin to explain to him. He'd never understand. He'd never forgive her.

Her mind whirled to ever darker and more devastating thoughts until she finally drifted off to sleep.

• "Aunt Lizzie?" a little voice whispered.

Elizabeth blinked one eye open. The clock had only moved ten minutes from the last time she'd seen it. With a sigh, she asked, "What is it, sweetie?"

"Brenda's having bad dreams 'bout da spider."

Elizabeth didn't have to wonder who Brenda was, since Jessie held a ragged Barbie in front of her. With a husky, I-desperately-need-sleep voice, she whispered, "You know how to get rid of bad dreams?"

Jessie shook her head.

"You pray for God to take them away."

Jessie nodded and her tiny shoulders slumped like she'd been brushed off. "Okay."

Elizabeth pulled the covers back. "Come here, baby. We'll pray together."

Jessie crawled into the bed, snuggled her butt to Elizabeth's stomach and held Brenda tight.

"Aunt Lizzie?" Elizabeth looked up to see Jessie's twin, Sarah, and their cousin Abby. "Can we cuddle with you? We're having bad dreams, too."

Elizabeth smiled gently and held out a hand to help them climb up. She led the girls in the Lord's Prayer, pausing and smiling after every line while they mimicked her.

Elizabeth covered them all, feeling the three little bodies snuggle close against her. Closing her eyes and breathing in the smell of clean babies, Elizabeth smiled. She should have felt uncomfortable, used to sleeping alone as she was, but somehow she didn't. Instead, she felt part of the family. Elizabeth snuggled closer to them and found it easier to idly drift this time.

Her old room had become storage for every stray box and bin. Even with all the kids, it hadn't been cleared out and claimed. But until four or five months ago, only Felicia's three kids had lived here, and they'd fit nicely in the two rooms. Then Bobby had gotten arrested and his girlfriend had disappeared—adding the twin toddlers to Abby's room. When Dallas's last relationship had failed and she'd left her five kids with Mom while she found a new situation to settle into, the rooms had begun to burst at the seams.

Then Mary Beth had gotten sick and Elizabeth was still spinning, trying to make sense of everything. So, for now, her old room lay like a forgotten tomb, dark and musty with the door perpetually closed. It somehow seemed worse this way.

She could change it, though. With just a few bucks, she could paint the walls a shade of pink or lavender or blue or yellow. Then small white shelves, hung here and there, cluttered with as many of the girls' stuffed animals as possible. Their dollhouse could fit in the tiny corner where there was a built-in desk, the drawers holding all the accessories.

Elizabeth sank into sleep, dreaming of the room until she'd decorated it perfectly. The walls were painted and bordered. A rug with matching colors was placed in the center of the room over the hardwood floors. A precious bunk bed she'd seen in a magazine graced one wall, with a slide instead of a stair coming from the top bed. A third loft bed with a playhouse underneath and a princess canopy over the top ran adjacent to the bunk bed, opposite the outside windows where bright yellow sunshine spilled in.

Elizabeth scooted the fourth chair under the small table in the center of the rug. She put a large, fluffy, stuffed gorilla in it and arranged a teacup in his hand. Setting a cup and saucer before each chair, she admired the pretty cream porcelain with pink roses. It was everything she'd wanted as a little girl. She couldn't have it then, but it made her happy to give it to the girls now. In a year, Veronica would replace the gorilla and there would be four tiny girls enjoying the room.

Elizabeth backed toward the door, checking all the small touches that made it paradise. A fairyland they could grow up in, protected from the ugliness of the world for as long as possible. With a smile, Elizabeth opened the door and ushered in three little girls carefully covering their eyes, their identical dresses different shades of pink, blue, and green to match the walls. Each dress had a hem full of ruffled lace and sported a big satin bow at the small of their backs. Matching ribbons wrapped around their ponytails, bows flopping on top with the tails streaming down their backs.

The girls removed their hands from over their eyes and the room was suddenly full of high-pitched gasps and excited shrieks. Abby ran straight for the dollhouse, her blue dress and blond hair flapping behind her. Jessie ran for the bunk beds, quickly climbing on top so she could barrel down the slide, her green dress bouncing up over her knees. Sarah, in pink, sat next to the gorilla and pretended to pour tea for them both.

"I take it you like your new room." Elizabeth laughed.

All three looked up, smiles blinding her with their brilliance. Then she was bowled over with a chorus of "Yes! Yes! Yes!"

"Thank you, Aunt Lizzie!"

"Pretty!"

"Your da bestest aunt, ever!"

After a quick hug from each of them, they abandoned her for the pleasures of their room. The sun hit the crystal sun catcher in the window and rainbows danced all around them. She'd never given a gift that had been so well received. One that made her happy just to watch the pleasure it brought. For someone with so little experience of a child's likes and dislikes, she'd done well.

With a smile, Elizabeth reached for the door, opening it silently so the kids could play without distraction. As she backed out, she twisted the lock on the knob to keep the girls safe inside. They would be fine in the dream room she'd created. There was nothing here that threatened them. Pulling the door shut, Elizabeth was enveloped by a familiar darkness so inky black, no light could penetrate it.

• ELIZABETH HAD NEVER approached the room of wishes and desires in jeans and a T-shirt before. They just weren't as romantic as a softly flowing gown. Perhaps that was a good thing, though. Tonight was different. She was more lucid than normal, her logical mind awakened. Alex shouldn't be there. She just had to make sure.

She'd left the kids safely playing in the room of childish fantasy, far from the room of sorrows. And they couldn't leave, couldn't wander. She'd locked the door, protecting them from the darkness of the tunnel and the terrifying things found there. There was no risk to them. Not like the risk to Alex.

Elizabeth stepped further into the blackness, her hand firmly pressing the rock walls. Her heart didn't pound with fear while rushing past the monster. She'd bypassed him entirely for the first time since coming home. Just knowing that helped her breathe easier.

She'd planned to come and help her mom through a few tests and then return home. She'd never believed Mary Beth would actually be sick. She'd known forever lung cancer and cirrhosis of the liver were risks her mom had taken, but now her body was demanding payment in full for a lifetime of poor choices.

When she'd come home, she'd known her nieces and nephews were here, that she'd finally be able to meet them all. But that they'd all been abandoned by her siblings, well, that had been a surprise. That she would become fully responsible for them had been a shock. That she was still here months later was a staggering blow.

But she wasn't here permanently. Because of that, there were certain decisions pertaining to her life that didn't need to be based on the children. Her relationship with Alex was one of them. She'd find the help they needed another way. Alex didn't deserve to be used when she had no intention of following through with anything else.

She'd told him good-bye at her front door tonight, but if she'd unconsciously drawn him to their chamber she'd give a different sort of good-bye to the man who'd held her through all her roughest patches. One last dream to end all their dreams.

Her hands didn't shake with anticipation. Instead, she hesitated, her stomach tight with a mix of guilt and uncertainty. She'd told him not to dream of her. He'd never know the pain it had caused her just saying the words. The push-pull between them had tormented her for years, but she'd never managed to make a clean break of it.

But she needed to give him up. They couldn't continue a half-relationship. He'd wished for it to be different for a long time, but she'd fooled herself into believing it didn't really affect either of them. She'd been wrong and now it was time to take responsibility for creating their dream world and keeping the contact between them alive and real.

Elizabeth paused outside the door. Which would be worse, to open the door and see him waiting—or to not see him at all? She'd already given him up once in pursuit of her dream. Wasn't that enough of a sacrifice? She grabbed the latch. This was *her* Alex. The secret desire she kept safe and hidden, so no one could spoil it. Elizabeth squeezed her eyes shut and leaned her forehead against the door.

She didn't want to do this. Who would really know if she didn't? She'd be returning to Seattle soon and he'd never know. She could fuzz his memories, alter the room before she left it. Maybe then the dreams wouldn't affect him when he awakened. She wouldn't have to lose him completely.

Elizabeth sniffed and forced back her tears. *She would know*. And if she continued the deception, would she be any better than her family? Would she be a person she could respect? Or even a person she liked?

She had to say good-bye. It was the best for both of them.

"I know you're there. I can feel you, Elizabeth."

She started at the sound of his voice, then the meaning of his words registered. He could feel her through the door? Elizabeth took a deep breath. Straightening her shoulders, she unlatched the door, stepped inside, and allowed it to swing silently shut behind her as her eyes adjusted to the candlelight.

Already, the atmosphere was thick, tense. She'd never

felt so unsure of her welcome in this room. Did he want to be here? Did he want her there?

Alex's back pressed flat against the headboard of their large, four-poster canopy bed. One long leg stretched in front of him and the other bent at the knee, supporting his elbow. With his brows drawn together, he appeared deep in thought. Not angry or hurt, but very, very serious.

His words low, Alex said, "Hey, lover."

Elizabeth flinched. She was wrong. He *was* angry. Probably more so than she'd ever seen him before. "I'm sorry I—"

"Don't."

Hard and clipped, that one word pierced straight through her. Her eyes widened and she stared at him, already anticipating the pain of a fight. Dreams and fantasies weren't supposed to be filled with arguments, but once she entered the room with him, it was all too real.

They'd built a relationship here, one that didn't make sense anywhere else. She knew him and he knew her. This was Alex raw, still a nice guy, but so much more.

"Don't give me more empty apologies, Elizabeth. They're too easy for you."

Alex moved in a sudden burst of speed. Now he stood in front of her, his dark green drawstring pants riding low on his hips. His body fit that of a martial arts instructor, his torso ridged and toned in a way that dried her mouth and twisted her stomach. Alex had always been defined, but he'd grown even more so since working out with his friend. He even seemed taller, though she knew he wasn't. Her forehead had always come to his lips, the perfect height for him to kiss her tenderly when she was upset.

He didn't look ready to kiss her, though. His glittery hazel eyes burned with fury. They intimidated her with their demand for answers. She stayed braced against the door, all words flying from her mind as she stared wordlessly at Alex. His dark hair was long and loose, falling to his shoulders, and so wet it was black. As though he'd just climbed from the shower before he'd fallen asleep.

"My apologies are never empty or easy. We need to be over," she whispered, mournful. He looked so handsome, it was no wonder she'd always wanted him. Now his beautiful eyes narrowed, the humor that usually lit them from deep within was gone.

He shook his head. "No, it doesn't work that way. These are my dreams. You are what I want even when I try not to."

She knew the dreams were real. He didn't. He thought he was dreaming all the things he wanted to say to her. But his words, his feelings, were true and he meant them, so she continued. "It's unfair and it sucks, but you need to find someone outside your dreams."

"Don't you think I've tried? But there's always this feeling that I'm settling for second best. That if I hold out just a little longer, I'll get what I really want." His hands closed around her upper arms, determined to keep her there. Desperation twisted the lines of his mouth. "I always return to you."

Her eyes filled with tears. "You deserve far more than I can ever give."

"You can give. You just *won't*. And you never tell me why." The pain of that filled his eyes and stole her breath. She hated when he was angry, but it killed her when she hurt him. The sad thing was . . . she always hurt him. "Why is the answer no?"

Elizabeth tried to tell him. The words were on the tip of her tongue, ready to spill free, but they weren't right. She couldn't explain adequately without hurting him even more. How could she look him in the eyes and simply say: *I will never choose you because I love you.*

In what world would that even make sense?

She held out her hands in supplication. "I can't risk it. I'm sorry."

Alex released her. "Risk what? Tell me and let's decide together if it's a fair bet or not. Because ending the dreams won't change a damn thing. I'll still love you."

Elizabeth clasped her hands over her heart, holding his declaration inside where it filled her chest like a deep, satisfying breath. More than anything, she wanted to return the words, declare her love as loudly and openly, but those words lodged thick in her throat. "We just can't be, Alex."

"Why?" Alex wasn't a huge man, but when every sinewy muscle, ridge, and vein stood out on his bare arms, he seemed plenty big. He backed farther away and his hands and arms moved in wide expansive gestures. His voice boomed off the walls, filled with his frustration, incomprehension, and anger.

"Because of a houseful of kids? Let's have more! A broken-down house? It's a lifetime project. If you enjoy it, it's never a burden. Because you have a little family drama mixed in with a lot of tragedy? This is life and life is what I want to share with you. Do you really think those things would drive me away?"

Elizabeth closed her eyes and swallowed. If only that was all. "No, Alex. You're probably the only man in the world who would stay."

"Then what's wrong with me?"

Her eyes widened with surprise. "It isn't you. You've done nothing wrong." Then she lowered her lashes, needing at least a semblance of protection from his fierce expression. "But if I did choose you, and you ever wanted to leave, you wouldn't be able to. I would find you. I would *keep* you."

Within the space of a breath, he was there again, looming over her. His hand was beside her head, his mouth inches from hers. His determined gaze bored into her. "Then where do I sign up?"

Elizabeth blinked, unable to look away. "You don't understand."

"I do."

She shook her head. "No, Alex. This is it. This is good-bye."

"No." He shook his head. "This isn't the end of anything. One minute you want to devour me and the next you push me away. You're confused, Elizabeth, but I know what *I* want."

How had this gone so wrong? She pushed at him, but he didn't budge. "There's too much you don't know, Alex."

Alex captured her hands and held them on either side of her head. There was no humor in his face at this moment. Pure male stubbornness sharpened his features. "It doesn't matter anymore. First thing tomorrow morning, I'm coming back."

She opened her mouth to argue more, but he kissed

her. Not a gentle, seductive brush of lips against lips, but full throttle. Like he was a race car driver out to win the Indy 500. Her toes curled in her shoes, then her shoes were gone and her bare feet clenched against the stone floor.

Alex released her hands and she immediately slid them around his shoulders. She still wanted to say good-bye, but it was so much nicer to say it this way. She couldn't deny herself one last pleasure. When he lifted her up, her legs squeezed around him and her jeans and T-shirt disappeared so there was nothing to hinder him. Alex tugged down his sweatpants and pressed the broad head of his cock where she was wettest. Elizabeth clenched her fists in his hair and slid down on Alex until her body held every inch of him.

Still they kissed, passionate and demanding. Her lips felt swollen and chafed. Already, deep inside, she quivered with that high-pitched ache that built with each thrust of his hips, each groan that vibrated from his chest. This was the moment that she could freeze in time. When he was deep and hard inside her and they were the closest they could possibly be. This was what she wanted to remember.

Elizabeth clenched tight and screamed her orgasm into his mouth as Alex rode her each step of the way. Only when she'd finished did he release her lips and bury his face in her neck. Adjusting her hips for maximum depth, he drove in forcefully, fiercely. She was so creamy and prepared, she loved it. Pleaded for it. Urged him to possess her as thoroughly as he ever would.

She almost missed it when his sharp teeth pressed

into her skin, not deep enough to draw blood, but marking her as his all the same.

• ELIZABETH SPRAWLED ON the bed, naked and spent and alone. She'd finally sent Alex away. Why couldn't he accept good-bye? She wasn't confused. She knew exactly what she wanted. She also knew why she couldn't have it. Unfortunately for them both, she had to end it.

Elizabeth rose, dressed, and shook the sheets over the bed until the dark satin drifted down, settling gently into place. Blowing out the candle, she edged over to the door, slipped through to the corridor beyond, and pulled it closed behind her.

A key settled into her closed fist. Running her fingers over the door, she found the lock. Elizabeth inserted the key and firmly turned it. The click that accompanied it was so final, so devastating, she sagged against the steel, trembling from the numbing cold but unable to leave. Not yet.

Time passed as she knelt at the door, her forehead pressed against the cool metal. She couldn't tell how long it took her to notice a presence behind her. Her monster was back.

"Hello, Daddy."

"Hello, Elizabeth," he rumbled in a voice that always made her quake inside. "Is he gone?"

"Yes. He's safe."

"That's probably the best—for now." His large, hard hand came to her shoulder and a squeak of fear escaped her lips. "I have something to show you."

Elizabeth licked her lips and shook her head. Why did he insist on showing her his visions? There was never anything she could do about them. Never a way to prevent them or change them. There was too much pain inside her already for her to accept more. "No, Daddy. Not tonight."

"You must see." His tone was implacable. "This is too important to ignore. You must see it now or it'll be too late."

"Why? Nothing will change. Nothing ever does."

"The visions I show you are necessary to prepare you, Elizabeth. But this one is different."

"No!" Scrambling to her feet, Elizabeth ran.

Chapter 6

❖

• HER MONSTER FOLLOWED, his steps booming strikes of thunder. Her tennis shoes—thank God she'd worn them tonight—whispered against the stone floors, squeaking as she turned corners. The steps behind her never halted. Never slowed.

Angry heat blasted her back, growing hotter with each pursuing step, but she refused to give in. This was what made her father a monster. She could never escape him or the doom he foresaw.

But this was her mind, damn it. Elizabeth veered off

toward an uncharted area. As he followed, she erected doors to block his path. Steel barriers she could shut as she ran past.

They slowed him, but not much. No matter how fast she ran, she couldn't escape him. She couldn't breathe and her body ached from the lack of oxygen. Her steps grew clumsy. It was time to make a stand. She skidded to a halt, nearly running straight into a dead end. Hard stone surrounded her. There were no candles, but a glow brightened the room.

Visualizing ten thick steel doors with no space between them, Elizabeth shut and barred them all, soldering each shut. He'd have to fight through all of it to reach her—which he began to do.

With each pounding strike against the doors, her stomach clenched and she wanted to vomit. Elizabeth pushed her hair out of her face with shaky hands. She could only pray the toddlers remained happily playing in their fantasy room so they wouldn't wake in bed beside her, hearing her nightmarish moans.

Elizabeth leaned back against the walls, her knees shaking. The doors had to hold him, because she had nothing left.

• "STOP, SILAS." DRAVEN grabbed his arm and held him back. "I know you want to save her, but you can't. She knows who stalks her. He is her father."

Silas eyed the fallen Seraph, watching him peel away thick steel doors as if they were nothing more than aluminum foil. "He's going to hurt her."

"Not physically."

Silas glared at Draven. The callous disregard for Elizabeth's plight grated on his nerves. How could he simply watch as a woman ran in terror, dodging behind every bit of protection she could devise in her efforts to escape? How could he watch and do nothing? He'd suffered enough of that with Kalyss. This was a fallen angel—a demon. The no-interference rule didn't apply.

"Mentally is no better. It might as well be physical."

"We must see what he wishes to show her," Draven insisted.

"Look at him, Draven. How can his visions mean anything when they are likely twisted to suit his own purpose?"

"Because his visions are never corrupt. They happen just as he shows them."

Silas turned toward Draven, his gaze narrowed. "He showed Alex the one of Maeve. You're saying that will definitely happen?"

"Yes." His voice held no hint of doubt.

"You're saying we can't save them? I refuse to believe that."

Draven's hand tightened on his arm. "The vision *will* come to pass. That's the trick. They must be saved after it happens, which is nearly impossible."

"But it can be done?"

"What leads to the vision also leads to the decisions made after it. What they do now will save them. Or doom them. Which is why we need to know this vision. The more information, the better."

The fallen Seraph tore the last door from the cavern walls and tossed it to the side. Elizabeth's face was framed by the black rock, her eyes wide, her cheeks pale. Then she disappeared, blocked by the mountain of darkness that was her father.

• THE DOOR BURST open behind her and heat blasted her back. Before she could escape, hard fingers circled her arm and she was pulled around to face her nightmare.

He towered over her, a mountain of brimstone with horns sprouting from his temples. Anger narrowed his vibrant blue eyes, all the more defined by the melted-charcoal ridge of his prominent brow line and the coal-black of his fierce face. Red peeked through the burned rock like embers of a banked fire—the only light in his hard, dark form.

"You can't hide forever, Elizabeth. The truth will become known."

She winced and tried to run through the door behind her. Hard hands closed about her head, the fingers pressing from her temples to the base of her skull. "You will see. This is too important for games."

"I hate this. I can never change it, never fix it. Do you understand what that does to me? Do you even care?"

"This is different. You must pay attention." His voice gentled, but the fingers pressing into her head didn't. It made her dizzy at first, like she'd stepped into a kaleidoscope of ever darkening colors. They moved and swirled, the colors mixing to a dark brown trunk, branching forward. "The future is not a straight line, it is a tree. And each decision you face shoots forth a branch, one for each possible choice you can make. The closest branches are the largest, the most looming decisions you'll make. Look behind you."

She did, only instead of gazing at him, she saw a thin green road twisting through tangled black briar. It was the path she'd traveled so far. Straight at times, curving at others. Thin when traveled with doubt, thick with boldness when not.

"Now, look forward."

Three trunks stretched before her, each wide with strength, with possibility. The one she was turned toward ended abruptly in a sheared-off stump.

"That is the path I've already shown Alex."

She tensed.

"Yes, I know him. I saw him and he saw me." His voice hardened, his disapproval clear. "As I said, you cannot hide. The truth will become known. Now, look to your path, Elizabeth."

She faced forward again. A large mark seared from right to left across all three branches, slicing the right branch through and stopping just before slicing away the other two. The left branch grew thick and green, un-marred by the thin cut at its base. The cut was scarred over, but the branch had continued to grow healthier and stronger than even before the cut.

The middle branch stretched forward, withered and dis-eased, growing longer, but thin and weak, with no leaves or fruit ready to bud. Like a tree after a snow storm, when kindness would cut it down. But this branch knew no kindness. "This is the one I will show you."

Elizabeth cried out, reaching for the healthier, hap-pier path, but her father's grip remained firm, steering her away from it.

"I know you want happiness, but you are not ready to

choose what will lead you to it. You will reject the path I lay before you, believing you know a better way. Trust me, I know the folly of that, daughter. There is a difference between free will and willfulness, and it's a painful lesson to learn. I will show you the path of willfulness, in the hopes you turn from it."

Her view narrowed until only one path lay before her, a bridge covered with an arbor of blackened roses.

• ELIZABETH STOOD IN a graveyard at night. Nearby streetlamps barely saved her from total blindness. A cold wind blew thick layers of multicolored leaves across the ground and around the jean-clad legs of the man standing before a row of granite headstones.

"Alex?"

He looked up, his gaze brutal in its empty coldness. "Hello, Elizabeth."

She stopped abruptly and looked around. It disturbed her to see Alex so cold, despite sending him away earlier. Even his tone was empty of the warmth that he'd always held for her. The change was abrupt and painful in its contrast.

Lines bracketed his mouth in slashes that spoke of pain and grief. Nothing in his expression or stance spoke of welcome.

"Alex, what's happened?"

He unlocked his clenched jaw and rolled his shoulders, seeming to force himself to talk to her. "Something went wrong. I'm not sure exactly where, but a decision was made that was irrevocable."

Before she could round the gravestone to stand at his side, Alex came to hers. His arm out to block her from proceeding. "Not yet. There are a few things you must see, first."

The world spun, blurring together before righting itself. They were in a crowded bar. Loud music pounded around them and through gyrating, dancing bodies. Bodies that never quite touched them as Alex guided her to a darkened corner where two men were talking. Nearly too quick and smooth to be seen, they shook hands. One pocketed cash and the other pocketed something else as he walked away.

Elizabeth didn't recognize him, so her gaze returned to the dealer. His blond hair had streaks and tips of black that perfectly framed his eyes. His blue eyes sparkled dangerously, inviting anyone brave enough to come a little closer. She wanted to cry. "Not Tommy!"

Moving away, Alex said, "Come. There's more to see."

"What the hell is this? I'm not Scrooge. I don't need to see past and present to get the point. I did something wrong. And because of that, the kids suffered and their lives took a wrong turn, right?"

Alex stared at her a moment, his lips tilting up in a cynical smirk. "So tough. So in charge. You think you know what this is about."

She shook her head.

The room spun again. The room they appeared in was completely silent, startling after the volume in the bar. It was her apartment in Seattle. Tastefully decorated, clutter-free, and startling in its emptiness.

Elizabeth watched herself set a Christmas card on the mantel. Against it, she leaned a snapshot of her office staff standing in front of a colorfully decorated tree. The other, older Elizabeth touched the picture, then she walked away. Lines marked her face. They weren't the kind from laughter, but the result of years of squinting at a computer screen and pursing her lips in thought or disapproval.

With a snap, she flipped the switch of the tiny tree on her coffee table. Little white lights lit up the tiny orna-ments. Underneath it sat one present wrapped in cream paper with a metallic gold ribbon. Her boss wrapped them the same every year. Chuck said the cream and gold lent the gift importance, a sense of quality even if the gift inside had only cost a dollar. Not that his gifts were *that* cheap, but it was all about the impression they made.

The older Elizabeth lit a couple of votives and opened her window to the city lights. After creating the perfect Christmas atmosphere, she did what she'd done last year and the year before. And, since this was a vision of the future, what she'd do for a few more years to come. She turned on her computer and began to work.

Only now, standing on the outside, not focused on the technical problems of her latest project, did Elizabeth notice how quiet her apartment was. Only now, after spending three months in the home her grandparents had built, did Elizabeth notice how the lack of clutter made it feel so empty. To see that her one card was from the office, her one gift from her boss, well, that was . . .

"Okay," Elizabeth burst out. "So the kids are broken and I'm pathetic. I'm still not sure where this is leading, Alex. What did I do or not do to make this happen?"

Alex gave her another smirk, but this time his eyes

were sad. "It was nothing big, Elizabeth. It never is. Small choices made each day are like turning one minute degree at a time. You'd be just as lost if you stood in the middle of a forest and spun in circles."

"What does that *mean*?"

"It means you didn't make just one choice. You may have had one goal, but all the small things leading to it added up. Be careful of every choice you make, Elizabeth."

She looked back, around her apartment, at the life she'd built for herself. It wasn't things or money that she'd missed during her time in Spokane. It wasn't even the quiet so much as the calm. The space to deliberate over each choice so when she made it, she was certain it was the right one. She missed the security and sincere belief in herself that had provided the basis for everything she'd accomplished.

Knowing her thoughts and opinions were valued. Knowing they were backed by research and solid facts. Knowing she was in the right place, doing the right thing.

She had none of that anymore.

That was why she'd wanted to go back to the life she'd created for herself, not because she feared change or hated the weight of responsibility, but because she wanted space to think. The chance to keep her life on the best track she could. Now she had to wonder—was it a good enough reason? What direction did she need to choose for that healthy, strong branch of her vision-tree to become real?

"It's time to go, Elizabeth." Alex said the words and her apartment swirled around her, tilting and weaving, the colors blending. They appeared back at the leaf-strewn graveyard. This time, the wind cut through her jacket and she had to wrap her arms around herself to hold in heat.

In front of the row of headstones, beneath a half-empty tree, stood a woman and two men. Alex walked toward them, but they didn't respond to his presence.

"Come on, Shelly. It's freaking freezing out here." An older boy tugged at Shelly's arm, trying to pull her away.

Elizabeth tensed, examining the changes time had wrought on the graceful teen she had spoken to just hours ago. Hugging a threadbare coat around herself, Shelly knelt and brushed a few leaves from a granite marker. Her tear-filled eyes rimmed with deep smudges, the kind made from lack of sleep and too much worry. Grief had carved deep lines on her young face. Elizabeth stepped forward, compelled to comfort her.

"I'm not ready to leave yet, Tommy."

Elizabeth's steps faltered.

"I don't want to be here all night. I've got business to do."

The changes in him, just between the earlier vision and this one, were shocking. Tommy was unnaturally thin, with twitching hands, and sores marking his face. His faded jeans and black T-shirt were tight and worn.

Her hands pressed to her chest, Elizabeth examined the three people. Shelly, Tommy, and Kevin. What had happened? Where was Teddy? The toddlers and the baby? Who lay in the graves?

This couldn't have happened just because she'd returned to Seattle. She would have only left them with someone who would take care of them. Their mothers. If Felicia didn't shape up, the only choice was Dallas. How could that one choice lead to the destruction of the happy, bright children she'd cared for? Forcing her limbs to move, Elizabeth stumbled forward just as Shelly looked up.

"Wow. Never thought she'd show," Tommy said.

"Well she shouldn't have." Shelly rose to her feet, pushing past her brothers. "You should have stayed away, bitch."

Elizabeth's eyes widened and she stopped in her tracks. Shelly's mouth was a hard, twisted line and her eyes held nothing less than hatred. "I don't understand."

"You never did! And it's too late to change now. They're gone, all of them. And it's all your fault!" Shelly charged forward.

Elizabeth watched her approach, unable to halt her, and suddenly, terribly certain she deserved it. Kevin grabbed Shelly, but his eyes were cold, slicing into Elizabeth with pitiless contempt. "Leave her alone, Shelly. She's not worth it."

Shelly struggled against his hold, never turning her gaze from Elizabeth. Her mouth curved in a devious smile before she said, "You really don't get it, even now. I can see it all over you, like a message painted on your face that only I can read. I tried to help you—but you were too stupid. It was a waste of my time."

"Shelly," Kevin warned.

"Let me explain clearly, so even you can get it." Shelly glanced behind her and Elizabeth followed her gaze. Alex sat on a headstone, his back to them. Shelly faced her again. "We survived because he loved us. *He* saved us. But you, our aunt, our blood, failed. You only know how to run. You don't even care what you leave in your wake."

Elizabeth stared at the granite stones. That cowardly part of her that wanted to run flipped and rolled inside her chest and she didn't want to meet Shelly's eyes. Her voice was bruising enough.

"I told you it wouldn't last. We lost them. Sarah, Jessie, Abby." Shelly paused a second. When she spoke again, her voice was choked. "Veronica. All the little ones were adopted out. We don't even know where they are. Kevin finally found us, but too late. Too late to be the family we were."

The little ones *couldn't* be gone. Her body was lying in a bed, cocooned by the heat of their little bodies. She'd locked them safe in a room she'd created for them. But what about . . . "Teddy?"

"He wouldn't abandon us the way you did. Not on purpose."

Elizabeth waited for more, but leaves fluttered through the air, drawing her eyes to the headstones. This time, Elizabeth examined them. She passed Shelly and the boys, barely noticing them disappear. Their purpose in the vision was done. Rounding the headstones, she read the names. Geoffrey and Dreux—strangers. Kalyss—oh, no. But seeing Teddy's name brought her to her knees.

Alex sat on the ground next to her, his back supported by one of the stones. Elizabeth looked into his eyes, studied his grim expression. "All this to tell me to make better decisions? To weigh my options carefully? Is there someone who actually believes I don't do that already?"

He shrugged.

"This is ridiculous. Everything! I weigh *everything*!"

"Then you make your decisions based on what, Elizabeth? Logic? Fear? Practicality? Figure it out before you're led down a path you don't want to go on."

"How can I determine by staying or leaving how others lead their lives? That doesn't make sense."

"That's the wrong question, Elizabeth."

Elizabeth looked at Teddy's tombstone. "How did he die? What led him here?"

"He wouldn't abandon those who needed him."

Elizabeth sensed a hint of movement and looked up. Alex seemed to be fading. "Alex?"

"It's time, Elizabeth." He eyed her from head to toe, seeming to fix her in his mind. At last, a hint of the warmth he felt for her showed faintly as he slowly turned transparent. "Danger is coming. Choose well."

Between one breath and the next, he faded, sinking into the grave beneath him. Behind where he'd been, the words of the headstone became legible.

ALEXANDER MICHAEL FOSTER. HE WAS LOVE.

A strident buzz jerked Elizabeth awake. Her eyes flew open to stare blurrily at the ceiling and she shifted her numb arms from underneath the warm bodies all around her so she could turn off the alarm. It was all she could manage before curving into the soft little bodies of her nieces and allowing the tears to flow.

• WHEN GOD CREATED the world, He'd made three realms. The barrier between each acted as a two-way mirror, so He could watch all of creation, Nephilim could watch themselves, and humans could only see their world reflected back to them. Yet, they all walked the same earth. Thus it was that Silas and Draven stood inside Elizabeth's room watching her cry, and she'd never know they were there.

"How do you know so much about her father?" Silas asked Draven his most pressing question first.

"He was Maeve's lover."

"And you trust him?" Silas looked at Draven, hating that there was nothing for him to see, nothing to base his judgments on. Draven was an enigma in too many ways.

"I trust no one."

Silas didn't doubt that he was included in that statement.

"However," Draven continued. "He betrayed Maeve when he told me of her plans for Dreux and Kai. He'd seen both of us in a vision, working together to stop her. He was the reason I came to you."

"Why would he do that? A house divided will not stand."

"The Angel of Foresight fell when he thought he knew better than God what should happen and what should not. He feels loyal to no one. When the world no longer fits as he believes it should, he seeks change. This is why he was known as the mercurial weather god, Adad, in Babylonia."

"Adad will seek change even at the cost of his lover?"

"Even then."

This meant the fallen Seraph's loyalty could never be trusted. His goal would be ever unfathomable. "But his visions are true?"

"Yes. Always."

"But Geoffrey was dead and he can't die."

"Yes, he can, if his mind believes it."

"The last one he showed Elizabeth held not only the possibility for change, but also a guide."

"She is at a crossroads. We should take comfort that he seems to be fighting for the best outcome for this family. Whatever direction he is ultimately working toward, his efforts coincide with ours for now."

"We need to talk to him."

Draven nodded in agreement. "We'll have to wait until she dreams again."

Chapter 7

◈

• ELIZABETH BLINKED THE sleep from her eyes. Nine o'clock. She couldn't regret it, though. After so many long and involved dreams, she'd really needed the extra two hours of deep, dreamless sleep.

At least she didn't smell fire or hear any screams. What the hell. She'd go ahead and make her bed *and* take a shower before dressing. A half-hour later, she hurried into an old pair of jeans and a T-shirt from her high-school days and put on socks and shoes, having learned the hard way that walking around barefoot in this house could be hazardous to her health.

Pausing at her mother's vanity, she swept her wet hair up into a ponytail. She had too much to do to have it in her face all day. But as she held it up with one hand and wrapped the band with the other, she saw something on her neck. Teeth marks with faint bruises around them. Alex had bitten her.

Elizabeth fumbled for her mother's foundation and smoothed it over the bite until the marks disappeared and the edges of the makeup were smooth.

The second floor was strangely silent as she headed for the stairs. Dare she hope the other kids had slept in, too? Maybe she could have the kitchen ready for breakfast before anyone other than the toddlers woke up. Get a head start on the day. She grinned and tiptoed down to the living room. In the distance, she heard Veronica crying and Shelly trying to soothe her.

"See, told you she was up. We can turn the volume on now."

Elizabeth's shoulders slumped as she took in the twins sitting in front of the TV, manipulating the video game controllers. So close. "What are you two doing?"

"Just playing, Aunt Lizzie."

"Thank you for playing quietly. I'd appreciate if you keep that down while everyone else is in bed."

"Yes, Aunt Lizzie," they chorused sweetly.

She smiled tightly and headed toward the kitchen. At least the kitchen would be clean and breakfast easier to make. She swept in through the doorway, then stopped in shock.

Stupid, stupid, stupid. Tommy supervised the three toddlers making their own bowls of cereal while Teddy poured the milk. Which explained why three boxes of cereal were open and scattered across the table while the milk lay precisely at the halfway mark in each bowl. She forced a smile.

"Thank you, boys, for getting a head start on breakfast." She turned away from the devastation of the table to the sink, already full of dirty dishes. She had washed them all just last night. But the memory of that was all she had to comfort her.

Thinking quickly, or as quickly as her sleep-deprived mind allowed, she ducked into the laundry room and shut the door. It was dark and quiet, making the sounds of the house distant and mellow. She closed her eyes and breathed deeply, fighting off exhaustion. Coffee would definitely be added to the morning's agenda. She didn't always need it, but today she would. Elizabeth took a deep breath and flipped on the light. She stared in disbelief.

The piles of unwashed clothes had grown exponentially. At this rate, she could do laundry all weekend and still have nothing for the kids to wear to school on Monday. She turned and banged her head on the door.

"Aunt Lizzie! Alex and a strange guy are breaking down the front gate!" David yelled from the living room.

Shit. She needed coffee and quiet. Her vision had been all about making wise decisions, but at the moment she couldn't decide something as simple as using cream or milk in her coffee.

She straightened with a sigh and pulled the door open. She wasn't ready to face Alex. And why was he here when it was dream Alex who had said he'd come back? Alex didn't remember the dreams completely when he woke, did he?

What had made the real Alex return? Did it have anything to do with the vision her dad said he'd shown him? Elizabeth sped through the house, tripping over toys and newspapers and shoes and coats before she reached the front door.

She couldn't send him away yet. Assuming he hadn't called Child Protective Services on her and the stranger with him wasn't a social worker. She'd already had enough grief from CPS since her mom had gone to the hospital.

Were they going to threaten to separate the kids yet again? Really, she knew the house and everything was a horrible mess, but she was getting a system down. She could take care of the kids. Elizabeth pulled open the front door. She still didn't know what to do. She couldn't send him away yet, but it might become the best choice, so she couldn't wrap her arms around him and refuse to let him go either.

Alex and another man knelt at the gate, a toolbox on the sidewalk next to them. Alex looked up at her and smiled, then stood and walked up the sidewalk, his stride confident.

Elizabeth looked from him to the big blond man and beyond, to her SUV parked in front of her house, healthy, whole, and apparently functional. She opened her mouth, then closed it, words deserting her. She appreciated it. God, how she appreciated it. And now, as the blond man demonstrated, her gate latched for the first time in months.

Did Alex think she could afford the equipment to fix up the house and car? Well, she couldn't. Not anymore. Her money was gone and paid time off was dwindling fast. Sadness welled inside her as she realized how much she could have used this help, and could have paid for the time and materials, just a few short months ago. But now . . .

"Good morning, Beth Ann. How are you?" Alex smiled, his eyes sparkling. She smiled back automatically.

"Good morning, Alex. What are you up to?" His eyes ran over her and she knew she must look like crap. A shower could only do so much. It wouldn't take away swollen eyes. She brushed hair from her cheek; it was probably frizzing all over her head.

"We brought back your Durango and noticed the gate needed a little help." Alex grinned, charming as ever. But his eyes were cautious, treading carefully.

"I appreciate you doing that, Alex, but really . . ." She shook her head, trying to keep her tone light and ignore the sinking of her stomach. There was no way she could get through this without sounding either ungrateful or pathetic. "How much do I owe you for the tires?"

He stilled. His gaze narrowed and his grin froze in place. "Don't worry about it. I'm happy to do what I can for an old friend."

She frowned, crossing her arms to hold in her discomfort. She was grateful, but she couldn't let him keep doing stuff she couldn't pay him back for. It went against her nature. "Alex, really, I appreciate—"

"I don't want your gratitude, Beth Ann."

She swallowed the lump in her throat and spoke firmly. "What, exactly, do you want?"

"I just want to help." He looked entirely too innocent.

Her chin lifted. "I am quite capable of taking care of my family on my own."

"I know that. But I thought a little help couldn't hurt."

She stared straight at him. "You're wrong, then. A little help can hurt. A lot."

His eyes narrowed. "I don't expect anything in return."

"Good. Because I don't have anything to give in return."

He took a deep breath and blew it out slowly. She copied him. She really didn't want to fight with him.

"Look." He glanced up at her, his charming grin back in place. "I have five months vacation. I need something to do, have pity."

"So we're your vacation charity project? No, thanks."

"No! That's not what I meant." He bounced up the steps and reached for her arm.

She jerked back. Prophecy or no, she would not become a spineless jellyfish with no pride or sense of self, content to "let a man handle it". "Thank you for what you've done, but I don't think we need your services anymore."

"Elizabeth!"

She ignored him and turned to the door.

"Elizabeth, it's not pity. It's not charity. I want to do this. I want to be here."

She snorted and said bitterly, "*No one* wants to be here."

Nine little gasps sounded behind the partially open front window. She winced and looked at her shoes. She hadn't meant it that way. No matter how she'd meant it, though, her pride was not worth hurting them. Elizabeth pursed her lips, waited a beat, then turned back to him. "I don't have the money to pay you back."

His face was solemn, earnest. "Of course not. Your job is in Seattle, not here. How can you earn a paycheck?"

She had vacation time and emergency funds, though they were long gone. She had also just wrapped up a long-distance project, but her time, and therefore her pay, were reduced. Elizabeth shrugged.

Alex glanced behind him at the other man. "I might be able to help you out with that paycheck. I'd like to introduce you to my friend, Geoffrey. He needs a specially designed research search engine for his personal library."

Elizabeth glanced at Geoffrey and raised her brow skeptically. "You need a library catalog?"

Geoffrey's focused gaze met hers, emanating a calm sense of tranquility. "My needs are a bit more demanding than that. Perhaps we could discuss it inside?"

Elizabeth paused, considering, but dream visions aside, she did need money. She also liked her first impression of Geoffrey. He didn't push for action, just waited patiently. Only after she nodded and opened the door for them did Elizabeth remember one of the graves in her vision had belonged to Geoffrey.

Which meant Geoffrey's life hinged on a choice she would make. He was now her responsibility, too.

• AS SOON AS they walked through the door, the kids swarmed around the two men, dragging them inside. She followed, cringing at the toys and books and clutter that made the house look filthy no matter what she did to clean it up.

"Do you want to see my room?" Tommy asked without his typical cynicism.

"Why would they want to see that pigsty?" Shelly scoffed.

"No, they need to see my dollhouse," Sarah insisted.

The children chattered nonstop at both of the men and swept them upstairs on the grandest tour the house would ever see. Elizabeth watched the men go, glad they'd taken everything in stride. They'd be able to talk in peace once the kids had time to bask in their attention.

Elizabeth headed back to the laundry room to get a load started. Afterward she'd start the coffee and get the dining room ready for an impromptu business meeting. A library catalog? She shook her head. It was a flimsy excuse for giving her a job. Why would anyone need to organize their Stephen King collection that bad? In the end, though, a job was a job.

"You changed your mind." Shelly leaned against the laundry room door, watching her.

Elizabeth finished stuffing the machine full. "You were right. I made the right decision for me, but not necessarily for anyone else."

"And now you're sure?"

Was she sure? Elizabeth answered honestly. "No. Not really."

But she knew her misplaced pride could be dangerous. The gutter could fall at any moment. The rotting, sagging fence would most likely fall over with the next stiff wind, exposing even more rusty nails. And the swing set looked more threatening than fun as it listed to one side. And that was just outside. There was so much more inside that needed to be done.

She'd watched the kids' faces over the last few months as they'd faced their grandmother's illness: hopeless, angry. They struggled so hard to develop a layer of protective armor nothing could pierce. What was the most important thing for her to teach them? Pull yourself up by your bootstraps or don't cut off your nose to spite your face? Be strong and independent or know when to accept help?

Or was the real lesson to show them there was an adult who wouldn't run from responsibility? One who wasn't selfish and self-centered? Who didn't put their addictions above their children? One who would step up to the fucking plate and get the job done?

"No one can afford for me to be too proud. At the very least, I know that part is right." Elizabeth grabbed a handful of clothes and separated them into piles.

"I thought it was pride, but it wasn't. It was self-respect or something, right?"

Elizabeth sighed. "You're giving me whiplash." Like she needed to second-guess her motivations.

Shelly looked away and shrugged, tilting her feet until she balanced on the sides, stretching her ankles in a way that looked painful. "It's just . . . I just . . . didn't get it at first."

"No, you were right. It was pride more than self-respect."

"No. It's because you're just not a whore."

Elizabeth choked and spluttered. "*What*?"

Shelly crossed her arms defensively. "Girls are one

of three types. Sluts 'cause they like it, victims 'cause they didn't want it, or whores 'cause they want something from it. Money, marriage, things."

Elizabeth's brows drew together. Shelly's view of the world was . . . interesting. half-steeped in wisdom and half in a child's black and white view. But she'd have to make sure it didn't hurt more than it helped. "And if she says no, what is she?"

Shelly met Elizabeth's gaze for a few seconds, her eyes sparkling. "Smart."

Elizabeth laughed then cleared her throat. "Okay, so now you're saying I shouldn't accept Alex's offer of help because then I'd be a whore?"

Shelly squirmed. "Well, sorta. I mean, he'll want sex and you'll give it to him or he might not help."

"What if there's no sex involved?"

Shelly frowned, then she scoffed. "Like that could happen."

Elizabeth shook her head, biting back a smile. "I think we need his help too much to turn it down. I won't whore for it, though. Promise."

• ALEX ENTERED THE kitchen just as Elizabeth hung up the phone and grabbed a bottle of aspirin. She scowled, as if the news from her conversation hadn't pleased her. Or maybe the headache came from having to face him again. She really hadn't wanted him here. Not his presence, not even his help, though it was clear how much she needed it.

Judging from the reaction of the kids, they'd played a big part in her decision. Not that *they* exactly wanted him here. The littlest ones might want him, but he could clearly see the wariness in the eyes of the older kids. They liked him, but they knew the drill.

Despite that sad fact, though, he still wanted to be here, to earn their trust and friendship. It was strange, but from the moment he'd walked through the gate that morning he'd felt an all-encompassing sense of belonging. This was his home. He just needed to convince them of that.

No sooner had Elizabeth swallowed the pills and lowered the glass of water, than the phone rang and she snatched it up again. She yanked open a drawer and pulled out a pen and small pad of paper. Scribbling furiously, she said, "Yes, sir. Now is a great time."

Alex grinned. Geoffrey had a job offer, but until they had time to explain it and she had time to consider it and agree, she had a career she couldn't ignore. Besides, Geoffrey had disappeared, checking out the work Alex had done on the bathrooms last night, no doubt. Elizabeth tore off the paper, handed it to Shelly, and sent Alex an apologetic grin on her way out of the kitchen.

Alex watched Elizabeth "yes, sir" her way into the dining room then glanced at the note in Shelly's hand. "What does it say?"

Shelly sighed. "It says, 'Grandma cancelled again' and 'My boss is on the phone'. 'Keep the kids quiet and occupied for a while, please.'"

"Cancelled again?"

Shelly wadded up the paper and tossed it into the trash a few feet away. "She's scared. She knows she's failed us in a lot of ways over the years. She's terrified of seeing us, of possibly scarring us for life. Seeing her hooked up to tubes, pale, bald, and shrunk to bitty bits won't be easy for the younger kids."

"You're not afraid of that?" Alex examined her, knowing the answer before she spoke it. This wasn't a teen who'd hide from life.

Shelly shook her head. "She needs to see us. She needs to know we forgive her."

"She probably knows, Shelly."

"No. She doesn't." She looked at him, her eyes flat, serious. "Because some of us haven't."

Alex followed her gaze into the dining room where Elizabeth talked on the phone with her boss. Her laptop sat on the dining table, a laser mouse to the right and a portable printer to her left. Her hands were steady, her eyes focused as she stared at the screen and typed. "She will, Shelly. She's not a person to leave things unfinished."

"If you say so."

Alex grinned at her and rubbed his hands together. Now was the time to prove how much Elizabeth needed his help. "Can you help me get everyone outside?"

"Sorry." Shelly shook her head and headed for a chipped white door that apparently led to the basement. "Gotta wake Veronica first. I'll be back soon as I can."

Alex nodded to her departing back. He'd just have to recruit some of the others to meet him and Geoffrey outside.

"Give that back! No one said you could play." The angry voice reached easily into the kitchen.

Alex headed to the living room, a grin stretching across his face. Clearly they were ready to be riled up, but it needed to be done outside so Elizabeth could have the peace needed for her call. What was the most effective way to rid them of their excess energy? Run them ragged? That he could do. It would postpone the talk with Geoffrey, but they weren't in a hurry. In fact, they were both right where they needed to be.

Alex looked around and shook his head. How did she do it? How was the house even in as good a shape as it was? The kids were clothed, fed, and except for minor arguments, happy. They weren't even her kids. Beth Ann amazed him with her generosity and compassion. There were too many people that would flat-out refuse the responsibility that had been thrust on her. They would simply hold up their hands and say, "Not my problem."

"Why can't I? You two always play." Tommy struggled for a PS2 controller against one of the twins. On second glance, it was David. The boy who had fallen from the balcony.

Alex looked at the open doorway to the dining room and winced. Elizabeth wouldn't be able to hear anything with them fighting.

"It's only a two-player game. You can't play." David sided with his sister.

"So give it back!" Danielle made a grab for the controller in Tommy's hand and Tommy looked ready to rumble. He'd be a great grappler, considering how he set his shoulders.

"Where are all the others?" Alex looked at them, his voice purposefully pitched low and even.

Danielle glanced briefly at him. "Upstairs or outside."

The question answered, she faced down Tommy. "Now, give it."

Alex moved in between them. "Let's calm down. Think we can get everyone outside in two minutes?"

The three kids gave him identical yeah-right looks.

"Nope. Don't like it outside. We like it in here fine," Tommy said. All three turned to the TV and wouldn't even look at him.

"There's something I wanted to show you, but we have to be outside so we don't disturb your aunt while she's on the phone." Alex purposefully injected a mysterious note in his voice.

They didn't look away from the TV. It was time to make his stand as an adult or they'd walk all over him forever. Alex bit back a grin, bent over, and pulled the plug from the TV and PS2, leaving the TV screen blank and grey. Turning it off, Alex wound up the cord and spotted the perfect high spot to store it in.

"What are you doing?" one twin shrieked.

"You just killed our guys!" said the other.

Tommy started laughing in a way guaranteed to bug the hell out of both of them.

Stashing the cord on top of a bookcase, Alex grinned at them and spoke in a you-can't-fool-me tone. "You weren't that far past the last save point. I've played this game before."

The twins crossed their arms stubbornly. "Why do you want us outside?"

"You'll see." He waited. When no more explanation came, they actually looked at him. He gave them an even, patient expression. The staredown lasted a few moments. They looked at each other, then back to him.

David rolled up his controller and put it in the cabinet

under the TV. "Fine. But I'm coming back for that cord if whatever you want is lame."

They ran through the house, feet pounding against the oak floors, yelling names at the top of their voices. He just prayed Elizabeth would last on the phone until he finally got them outside.

They'd overwhelmed him with names when he first arrived yesterday, then hadn't repeated them since, instead swarming around him, then disappearing as if challenging him. Or maybe Alex only imagined the challenge. If he were their age and men kept coming and leaving, he'd start playing games with them just to piss 'em off too.

Shelly was the oldest and Veronica the youngest. They were easy to remember. So was Tommy, the blond boy with an unholy gleam in his eye. Teddy, with his glasses, was a young, blond Harry Potter. David and Danielle were the twins. That left four to get to know better.

Years of memorizing new faces and names from his classes came to his aid. The little girls were Jessie, Abby, and Sarah, though he didn't know which was which. Then there was the boy with the spider, Kevin.

Alex headed to the back door, glancing around for Geoffrey. When he reached the back without any sign of the man, Alex grunted. The kids were already running toward him, so he just continued outside. By the time eight kids and a baby in a walker assembled, Alex felt like he'd accomplished world peace.

"Kevin's in bed since he's feeling sick," Shelly said, lining up toys on the baby's tray.

Alex nodded his thanks, then looked at the nine kids in front of him, and nearly fell back a step. *En mass*, the vivid blue eyes he'd always admired in Elizabeth were a shocking, unsettling family trait.

Chapter 8

• "OKAY, WHAT DO you want?" The older twins struck identical poses. They knew the power of being twins and were prepared to use it.

Alex couldn't help but wonder what they would do if they realized the power they wielded as a family, despite the hair and attitude differences. Like a football team wearing the same uniform, this family was awe-inspiring to behold.

Alex raised a brow at the expressions facing him now. None of these kids looked ready to cut him any slack, but that was okay. He didn't mind having to earn respect. "Okay, let's line up, three rows of three."

The three toddlers spread out, laughing and seeing who could stand with their legs the farthest apart. The baby banged a toy on her tray with a toothless grin.

"Oh, yuck, he just wants us to exercise," David whispered.

David and Danielle started to walk away, but Shelly

grabbed their shoulders and turned them back around. "You two demons probably need it."

It surprised him that the oft-sullen teen was supporting him, but he knew she wanted something. Whatever it was, he'd clearly have to wait until she was good and ready to tell him.

Alex quickly scrambled for something to hold them all in thrall. "Not exercise. Karate. Judo. Wanna learn?"

Teddy gave Alex the most searching glance he had ever received. No doubt the boy could sniff out BS from fifty paces.

Alex took a deep breath and looked around for Geoffrey again, but the man had disappeared. Alex would kill him for his defection later.

There were several exchanged looks and whispered comments toward the back of the group. He barely caught some of the words, though he couldn't tell who spoke them.

"This is lame."

"At least he's trying."

"Yeah, but what's he trying?"

"He wants us tired so we'll be good."

"And to show Aunt Liz he can help. Impress her."

No doubt they'd all developed their own screening procedures for strangers who suddenly appeared in their lives. Alex winked at the giggling toddlers. Whatever the older kids decided, he'd abide by. From what Elizabeth said, they'd earned their right to be distrustful.

Apparently they finally decided to give him a chance because they lined up in rows and copied Alex and the toddlers. Alex raised his arms and began a few simple stretches.

Teddy pushed back his glasses. "So, which kind of martial arts do you teach?"

"Actually, quite a few of them."

Teddy snorted.

Alex grinned. "When I was little, I wanted to do Karate. So, my dad signed me up. I bought the gee and worked my way through a few levels over a couple of years."

Alex could practically sense every single word being carefully examined. But their bodies were moving with his.

"When I got a little older, I started noticing other styles I'd like to try. I wanted to see which one fit me best. I mean, Steven Seagal had a good style that could kick butt. Van Damme was more aggressive, but just as deadly."

They stared blankly at the actors' names, so Alex hurriedly continued.

"Places sprang up all over, teaching Judo here and Kenpo there and Tae Kwon Do across the street. I wanted to learn them all enough to know the one that really fit me the most."

"But you didn't settle on one?" Tommy asked, his interest truly caught.

Alex shook his head. "I loved them all. I convinced my dad to let me try every one I wanted."

From the back, Shelly warned softly, "Don't even think about it, you guys. No way Aunt Beth could afford that."

Alex winced and forcibly held in promises he may not be allowed to keep. Would they believe them even if he did offer? "Eventually it was six months to a year of classes at one place, then I'd move on. So when my friend Kalyss and I decided to go into business, we purposefully chose to keep it generalized."

"People like that?" David asked.

"Well, yeah. Mom can do Pilates and self-defense. Kalyss teaches most of those classes. At the same time, Dad can do weight lifting or take one of the martial arts classes, and the kids can learn the basics to most of the styles."

"But how can you be good enough to teach all of them? You're too young to have that kind of experience."

"Which is why I don't teach them all." Alex raised his arms, palms together over his head and watched as they copied him. "Each month we focus on one style—the history, spirituality, and basic moves. We have an expert teach a class for more advanced moves in that style, on top of our usual classes for self-defense and aerobics."

"Like some kind of martial arts mall." Definitely Teddy again.

"It sounds pretty cool. We could all go to just one place even if we all wanted to learn something different," Tommy added.

Teddy adjusted his glasses and looked down. "I didn't think of it that way."

Alex smiled at him. These were the things Kalyss and he had discussed before opening the business. "Well, it's good for us that mixed martial arts has turned into such a sought-after business. With competitions like the Ultimate Fighting Championships our dojo has really been able to take off."

Teddy saved him with another question. "Why do you call it a *dojo*? Why not just a gym?"

"You can call it that. I guess Kalyss and I stuck with *dojo* since we were *Highlander* fans."

"What's that?" Danielle asked.

"Okay, now I *know* you're kidding. You have to know Duncan MacLeod."

Shelly chuckled with genuine pity. "We were all still little when it went off the air. And some of us weren't even born yet."

"But there are reruns," Alex tried.

"Not on the Disney channel."

Alex grumbled good-naturedly. "I'm not that freakin' old."

"I only remember it because of the Duncan posters in Aunt Beth's room. She went wild for the long-haired, kick-butt type in high school." Shelly raked her eyes over him, one brow raised.

Alex waggled his brows. "Really?"

Danielle gave him a sassy smile. "Give it up, dude. The Highlander, you ain't."

Alex fake pouted, not one whit deflated. It took a bit of work to keep up with them, but for an hour, Alex led them in move after move, teaching them beginning block patterns and how to keep their knees bent and hold their hands.

A bit of movement in the kitchen window caught Alex's eye. He barely saw a glimpse of Elizabeth before she moved away, but he could have sworn she'd been smiling.

• ELIZABETH SET A stack of plastic cups on the back-yard picnic table, next to the plate of PB&J sandwiches and the bowl of seedless grapes. Gatorade and ice filled a small cooler with a spigot so the kids could serve themselves. They loved eating outside and today that fit her purposes perfectly. To bribe them a bit more, she added a basket full of individually bagged chips.

After talking with Chuck, it was important that she carefully consider Geoffrey's catalog project. The company didn't have anything more for her to work on off-site. Her medical coverage was secure for a few more months, but it was time to seriously consider her options.

Returning to the kitchen, she made some coffee and carried it to the dining room. Paper and pens were stacked in front of her chair and her laptop sat off to the side. It wasn't exactly a desk in a professional office, but it would do.

Geoffrey and Alex stood at one end of the room, examining her grandmother's china hutch. The cherry hutch, table, and sideboard were all a matching set created by her grandfather's tough hands. Scarred from thirty years of hard use and thoughtless neglect, it still stood strong, willing to hold together for decades to come.

"Your grandfather was an amazing craftsman," Alex commented.

Elizabeth eyed the furniture, a smile tugging at her lips. "He had a wood shop out back when I was little. I loved watching him. He could make anything beautiful."

Alex sat in one of the chairs to her right. "My dad was the same. I miss helping him with his projects."

"I'm sorry. Did he pass away?"

His gaze jerked up, his eyes wide and surprised. "Oh,

no. He just closed the shop and went on the road. Now he likes to carve driftwood."

She grinned and settled into her chair. "Sounds like a wonderful retirement."

"Nah, they aren't retired. They just refuse to come home until I give 'em grandkids to spoil."

She laughed. They sounded so *normal*. It was endearing.

Geoffrey settled into the seat closest to her and placed a hard drive the size of a truck key on the table. Sliding the hard drive into the USB slot, Elizabeth clicked open the program.

With a few clicks of her mouse, a window opened showing rows of folders labeled with different religions. Inside each were more folders, labeled with ever more specific categories until they opened to individual books with files separated by chapter. This was not your average home library. In fact, she doubted the Library of Congress was this well sorted.

"Wow. There must be hundreds of books on this drive."

"This represents a fraction of my library."

Elizabeth stared at Geoffrey. "They must have taken decades to acquire."

"You could say it's been a family project, developed over many generations. The Internet and modern storage devices have allowed for major growth over the last two decades, though."

Elizabeth sat back in her chair. This wasn't the simple, quick project she'd been picturing. The sheer amount of information he was talking about would require a major undertaking. "There's a vast amount of information here, but this seems as organized as possible. What do you want me to do?"

Geoffrey sat back in his chair, looking at her thoughtfully. "I'm old-fashioned, Elizabeth."

Knowing the technical skill he must have to acquire and organize a library like this, Elizabeth couldn't imagine Geoffrey being old-fashioned. Her skepticism must have shown because Alex snorted.

"He's so old, he helped Duke William invade England."

She smiled helplessly. "Yeah, okay."

"No, seriously. He's so old, he hand-wrote the first Bible."

This time she laughed outright. Until she met Geoffrey's analytical gaze. In a dry tone, he said, "Alex can do this all night."

She looked at Alex.

He nodded. "It's one of my greatest joys in life."

Elizabeth shook her head. "Okay, so you're old-fashioned. How can I help?"

Geoffrey pointed at the screen. "This is all black-and-white, nice even columns of similarly sized files. I grew up with a different type of library. Manuscripts and books of different sizes and shapes and textures. Covers with different colors. Scrolls with specialized casings, some in silver, some in gold, and some in a simple, soft leather. The paper had different thicknesses and the writing was in different styles.

"I could wander through entire rooms filled with writing from floor to ceiling. I wouldn't have to read a spine to know which book it was. The thickness and height would tell me. And sometimes, if I was asked a question, I only needed to run my eye over the shelves to see a book that held the answer. Our library was a beautiful, peaceful place."

"Like a monastery," Alex interjected.

She grinned and shook her head at him, then returned her gaze to Geoffrey. "But you still need to search through more texts at a faster pace."

Geoffrey nodded. "Correct. However, the more technology advances, the more uniform information becomes. There's not enough color. No texture. Humanity was created in such a way that we can use sense memory for information. Touch, smell, sound, taste. But modern searches only allow for sight."

Elizabeth tilted her head, looking at the rows of information and listening to Geoffrey's words. Thoughts and ideas poured through her mind. How would she create the ideal digital library?

"There is no time limit. I want this done right, not necessarily quickly. Most of all, be creative."

Elizabeth met Geoffrey's gaze again, surprised.

Geoffrey nodded. "I require a specialized service and I understand the price tag that goes with it. I am prepared to pay what we agree to. I will also provide any equipment and supplies necessary. Your schedule is your choice, as is the location you choose to work from. All my files will be made available when you are ready for them."

Elizabeth blinked at the rows of folders on her monitor. Free rein. He was giving her the freedom to create the ultimate searchable library using more than just sight or the occasional sound. Her heart pumped faster and her fingers tingled. Excitement burst inside her chest. Not the typical beginning-project jitters, but all-out mind-swirling fantasy.

Google, eat your heart out. Elizabeth Ann Raines was ready to conquer the search-engine world. Granted, hers wouldn't be for millions of users. But it was the most ambitious project she'd ever headed.

"You really think I can do this?" She looked at Geoffrey.

"I did my research before approaching you about this. I've seen your work. I wouldn't have offered if I didn't think you could."

She looked to Alex, still uncertain, needing confirmation. He grinned, his eyes sparkling with pride. He believed in her.

• ALEX WATCHED ELIZABETH move her mouse, clicking at the speed of light. "I think I'm jealous."

"Just focus on the big picture."

"Right now the big picture is the size of a laptop monitor. You might have to zoom it in for me."

Geoffrey pulled him away from the doorway. "Don't disturb her."

Alex turned back to the dinner he'd started throwing together when Elizabeth and Geoffrey's haggling had reached the one-hour point. They'd nailed down specifics for *everything*. Even worse, he suspected they'd enjoyed the whole process.

"She can't turn this down. She'll be paid well, the kids will be taken care of, and the house can be fixed. She needs you to make it happen."

During the negotiation, Alex had been designated her assistant. He would babysit, help navigate the endless amount of information Geoffrey had gathered over his thousand-plus years on earth—which Alex had already spent the last five months trying to do—and he would be the general contractor overseeing repairs to the house while she worked. It was the perfect position for him. He'd be here to guard them all, to grow closer to the children, and to develop a relationship with their lovely aunt.

If she ever looked up from the monitor.

"Thank you."

Geoffrey shrugged. "I'm getting fair market value. It's not charity."

"I think knowing that is responsible for half her glow." Alex smiled. It was a brilliant plan.

• IT LIVED. THAT was the only way Elizabeth could describe the pile of laundry that had grown despite her best efforts. But for the first time since returning home, the huge piles didn't depress her. She switched out the washer and dryer, thinking of the parameters Geoffrey had given her.

He'd been more than generous, offering a salary and bonus structure for each major stage of the project. And in the end, it had been her choice to refuse. But she'd chosen not to. Even though it meant working with Alex. Even though it meant she'd face him every day, knowing what he wanted from her. But there was more to this than just a steady job.

They were studying angels and demons. As she'd

pored through Geoffrey's files, noting which ones were the most recently accessed, their area of study had been obvious. They wanted to understand the paranormal world that operated in and around the real one.

She didn't have a lot of answers. In truth, she'd hidden from as many as she could over the years. For a long time, she'd even forgotten who and what her father was and why he was trapped in her mind. She'd submerged her gift, terrified of committing the same atrocity that had killed her father's physical form—drawing him into a dream and refusing to let go.

She'd paid for her mistake every night when he showed her his horrific visions of the future. She'd been unable to stop them. To warn anyone. To change anything. Her dream world had become a nightmare land, shrouded in shadow and buried under rock, with a door to lock her father away. A door that never held him unless he allowed it.

She'd hidden the truth, buried it for years. But now Charles Astor Raines had shown Alex a vision of her family, a branch that ended abruptly. He'd then given her dire warnings about her that could sicken the family tree. And he'd used Alex as a guide. A ghost Alex who'd never touched her. One who'd sunk into his grave with a warning on his lips. *The danger is coming. Choose well.* And it didn't seem like her mother's impending death had been the big worry.

Alex and Geoffrey were studying angels and demons. They wanted her to build a program to help them. Something bad was coming. Whatever it was had the ability to destroy her entire family. It was possible her family could be saved, but their path could blacken and twist down roads they shouldn't travel if she didn't think carefully.

Compared to her future self, the maelstrom of her thoughts only highlighted her self-doubt. If only she could be as calm and confident about her choices as she'd been in the vision. She could have that confidence but she'd also be stuck with the rest. Only viewing her future from the outside had highlighted the loneliness and sadness of a Christmas tree with one generic present.

Elizabeth shut the dryer and turned the knob. She'd just have to make the time to think. A few seconds later, the swish of the washer joined in. As she bent to separate and organize piles of clothes, white noise filled her ears and the only sounds she could hear were her own thoughts.

• ELIZABETH LEFT THE laundry room and headed upstairs, noticing the position of the kids as she went. She had a project for them and if she ever wanted to get a jump on the endless piles of laundry, she needed to take what time she had to put it into effect.

Danger was coming, but it wasn't here yet. And she needed to have as much of the chaos around her under control as she could. Pulling a plastic chest of drawers full of plastic hangers, washable paints, and other art supplies from the closet, she picked up the stack and headed back down the hallway. It was bulky and she had to peer around the side to watch her step.

"Elizabeth?" Geoffrey's voice sounded from her right and she jumped. The stack wobbled in her arms. He helped her set it on the ground and she met his gaze.

"Sorry to almost run you over."

He nodded and walked toward the bathroom. "I think this is working now."

Elizabeth frowned as she entered the small room. That was fast. But as she looked around, she noticed even more. A new seat on the toilet. New faucets for the sink and shower. There was no way he'd had time to shop and install all of this in the time she'd been doing laundry.

"Pretty sure of yourselves, weren't you?" She met Geoffrey's enigmatic gaze.

"Alex knew what to get, so we picked it up this morning."

"And you knew you'd be staying." And here she thought she'd had a choice.

Geoffrey shrugged. "Of course. I don't make deals I know will fail. That would waste time."

Of course. That wouldn't be logical, and Geoffrey was nothing if not logical. Elizabeth shook her head and smiled reluctantly. He and her boss, Chuck, would get along so well. Besides, he was right. Time shouldn't be wasted. She had too little in which to accomplish too much.

"Try them out. Make sure they work."

A quick turn of the knob and water rushed from the faucet, filling the bottom of the sink and draining through the new strainer that blocked the drain. The toilet flushed quickly and quietly with no hesitation and the shower worked perfectly. These things had to have been expensive, but they were so necessary.

"Were you a plumber in a past life or something?"

"Why do you ask?"

Elizabeth smiled at him over her shoulder. "They're perfect."

He nodded. "They deserve it."

He meant the kids and he was right. The house had four bathrooms. One in the basement. One on the main floor. One for everyone upstairs, and the master bath off her mom's room. The master bath and the basement had been the only steadily working bathrooms for the last two weeks. Two bathrooms for nine children and Elizabeth. It had been a nightmare.

She smiled. The sink wouldn't spit at her. The toilet wouldn't clog. The shower wouldn't drip. He was right. They needed it. The new job had included a contract bonus with immediate payment. She could afford repairs and tools, but Geoffrey and Alex had offered to do much of the work themselves so the check could stretch further. It was too good to pass up.

Elizabeth infused her voice with all the appreciation she genuinely felt. "Thank you, Geoffrey."

Geoffrey's eyes brightened and his shoulders relaxed the tiniest degree. She hadn't noticed they were tense. "I was thinking I would do the downstairs bathroom next."

She shook her head. How did he do it? Plumbing kicked her butt. "Oh, that one hasn't worked for a month. I don't know if it's fixable at this point."

"I'll fix it." His voice was determined. "Where do you need this?" Geoffrey glanced at the storage chest on the floor.

She waved him away. "I can carry that."

He raised an eyebrow.

Elizabeth's mouth snapped shut. Obeying his unspoken order, she pointed. "In the kitchen."

She followed him as he moved easily through the clutter to the much cleaner kitchen. He set the things on the table and left for the main bathroom. Elizabeth watched him disappear, frowning slightly. She'd never met anyone like Geoffrey before. He decided how a situation should be, set the parameters to make it so, then zoomed toward his target like a heat-seeking missile. He was unstoppable. And luckily, for the time being, his goals coincided with hers.

Elizabeth prayed their goals were never at odds.

Chapter 9

• SHAKING HER HEAD in bemusement, Elizabeth turned around and met Alex's amused gaze. "Is he always in command?"

He grinned. "Pretty much."

Elizabeth watched him deftly chop vegetables with a speed that would have cost her some fingers. Alex moved quickly, his hands lean and capable, strong and in control, handling the sharp blade carefully but without fear of any kind.

Watching him shouldn't have mesmerized her so

completely, but it did. This was Alex, the real Alex in real life, and there were more reasons to let him stay than to push him away. For the first time in twelve years, she could enjoy the way his jeans hugged his ass. The way his shirt stretched across his long back. The way his hair fell into his face. It was long, soft, and touchable, but not girlishly so.

Everything he felt for her was in his eyes. Attraction. Flirtation. Need. Elizabeth licked her lips. A split second before he looked up, she looked away and refused to meet his gaze. It was time for work. Playing wasn't an option.

Elizabeth draped a drop cloth on the table and opened packs of red, white, blue, green, and black hangers. She set squirt bottles of paint in the middle of the table and strung a line for the hangers to dry after being painted. She was ready for the kids.

Glancing out the window, she decided to let them play just a little longer while she set up tubs for the kids' socks. A tower of eight small drawers would hold their underwear, and she taped index cards to the front for their names. The baby wouldn't need a drawer for a while and Shelly kept her clothes separate, so eight drawers would work. Hopefully, having the clothes set up in the laundry room would enable her to put stuff away and find it much easier.

Alex opened cans of stewed tomatoes and olives, dumping them into a pot along with a pinch of this and a dash of that. She couldn't see exactly what he used, but the smells filled the kitchen pretty quickly, making her stomach rumble. It looked like spaghetti, but without red sauce. Instead, he used teriyaki sauce with noodles and vegetables and sausage. It made her mouth water just looking at it.

By the time the kids came in from outside, the laundry was beginning to look under control. Elizabeth directed them to chairs around the table and helped them into little painting smocks made of plastic garbage bags with holes for their heads and arms.

The basement door banged open and a frustrated looking Shelly stomped through the doorway. "She's crying again."

Shelly dropped Veronica into Elizabeth's arms, her eyes full of fatigue. "I already changed and fed her. I don't know what else to do."

When Elizabeth had first arrived, Shelly wouldn't trust her baby sister with anyone, least of all someone she thought would be leaving soon. That she did so now wasn't exactly a sign of confidence. It was more like desperation.

Shelly carried an unrelenting burden as the oldest. One her mother, Dallas, should be shouldering. But until she came home, Elizabeth was all Shelly had to fall back on. Shelly was strong, independent, and capable. Incredibly so for a fourteen-year-old. It was only her sarcastic mouth that made her difficult sometimes.

Elizabeth took the baby and watched Shelly stomp to the door to the basement where her room was. "I bought black hangers for you. Do you want to—"

"It doesn't matter. Just keep them plain. I like plain black."

Then she was gone and Elizabeth was distracted by eight children full of too much energy. She explained the project to them and hurried around the table, juggling the baby until Veronica quit fussing.

Tommy had other ideas, though. Grabbing a stack of white hangers, he piled them up, squirted blue paint over them in a zigzag mess, and yelled, "Done!"

Elizabeth had barely taken them from his hand when he streaked from the room. "Wait! Where are you going?"

He slid to a stop. "To watch Geoffrey."

"But . . ." Elizabeth juggled wet hangers and a struggling baby until they were hung and Veronica was safely in the high chair. It didn't matter, however. Tommy was already gone. Elizabeth looked at the door and sighed.

Alex turned from the stove. "He'll be fine. Don't worry."

"I just don't want him in the way." How could she describe the destruction that followed Tommy like a shadow?

"He won't be. Relax." Alex handed the baby a carrot and returned to the cutting board.

Spotting movement from the corner of her eye, Elizabeth turned in time to see Sarah squirt pink paint in Jessie's hair. The older twins laughed and held their paintbrushes like swords, ready to fence across the kitchen. Elizabeth snatched them up before the red and yellow paint splattered everywhere. The baby banged her carrot on her tray, squealing with joy as Elizabeth rushed around. At least it was washable paint.

After a half-hour that seemed like forever, the twins were back to the PS2. The toddlers laid themselves on the couch, hugging their favorite dolls. The baby banged happily in her high chair and Kevin had disappeared.

Only Teddy remained as he finished carefully painting his name in block letters on the last hanger.

Elizabeth spread the hangers evenly on the line, trying to ignore the cramping in her stomach. Dinner smelled so good, she could almost taste it. When Teddy finished the last hanger, she untaped the drop cloth, balled it up, and threw it and the empty bottles of paint away. The table was clean again and she could take a breath.

"That's a really good idea, for them to each have their own hangers."

Her stomach rumbled again. When had she eaten today? Had she eaten today? "I read about it in a magazine. Next, I hang them with full outfits, pants and shirts or dresses and tights. Then they grab one hanger in the morning and put on the clothes instead of digging through the laundry baskets. I just have to get it all washed and organized now."

She rushed into the laundry room to change the laundry, coming back with a basket of towels to fold. She gave in to her curiosity. "That smells delicious. What is it?"

"Teriyaki spaghetti. My mom taught me how to make it. You just throw ground sausage, noodles, teriyaki sauce, and veggies into a pot and have a salad on the side. I can handle simple cooking."

She laughed. Simple? Not smelling like that. "What do you normally eat?"

"Takeout. Fast food."

"Not exactly healthy."

"I know. And you'd think for someone who runs a martial arts studio, I'd pay more attention to eating healthy, but I guess it's a fatal flaw."

Alex shrugged his shoulders, stretching his T-shirt against his chest. It was firm, hard. Not in a vain, I-want-people-to-notice-my-perfect-body way, but in a sleek, gracefully powerful way. Alex turned back to the stove and her wayward eyes fell lower again. Damn, jeans looked good on him.

"The downstairs bathroom is functional now."

Elizabeth jumped guiltily and spun toward Geoffrey's noncommittal grey eyes. Her face was so hot it hurt.

"The downstairs bathroom is functional now," a gruff voice reiterated.

Elizabeth blinked and looked down. Nine-year-old Tommy stood with his feet braced, his hands at his sides, and a serious look on his face. She tried not to laugh. Really, it would hurt his feelings. She bit the inside of her cheek and stared at Geoffrey until the desire faded.

"Very good, men. Excellent job." She tried, but the humor in her tone couldn't be missed.

Geoffrey nodded and turned toward the living room. Tommy nodded and followed, his head barely higher than Geoffrey's waist. Elizabeth watched them walk off with the same arm-swinging style as a smile tugged at her lips. They looked so cute.

A glob of something wet and warm landed on her nose. She blinked and turned wide eyes to Alex, who was suddenly standing right next to her.

"Don't make me jealous." His eyes were sparkling as he bent and licked off the drip of sauce, then kissed the tip of her nose. "I like it better when you ogle *me*."

Surprise, shock, and embarrassment froze her in place. Speechless and wide-eyed, she stared as he walked over and stirred the pot, mumbling about salt.

Elizabeth looked down at the warm, fluffy towel in her hand. Her mind remained blank for an embarrassingly long moment before she slowly started folding it.

"I'm sorry."

Elizabeth raised her eyes to Alex's sincere gaze. He was sorry? For kissing her? *Don't be sorry*, she wanted to beg. "For what?"

Alex examined her face and came to lean against the table next to her. "For crowding you. Making you feel uncomfortable."

She raised a brow and eyed the nearly nonexistent distance between them. "But you don't stop doing it."

He smiled that infectious smile of his. "I'm not *that* sorry."

She smiled up at him. She was flirting back; she knew it and couldn't seem to stop. It was a bad idea, but things were changing so fast she couldn't even tell where she was, and flirting with him felt good.

"Perhaps I should explain." Elizabeth stepped back a pace and gestured in a circle around her. "*This* is personal space."

Alex reached out, hooked a finger through one of her belt loops and pulled her up against his chest. "I like *this* space better."

That quickly, she lost her breath. Elizabeth pressed her hands to his chest and arched back. "I think you're missing the point."

"Nah." Alex brushed her ponytail back and stared at her neck a moment. He looked for the bite mark, but didn't see it and was disappointed. "I just know what I want, whether it's close to the point or not."

Her gaze fell to his lips as they came closer, slowly,

steadily until Alex rubbed his lips against hers, lightly, then firmer. This wasn't logical. She didn't have the time for this. But his mouth fit hers. His taste. His scent. He appealed to her on a basic level where logic didn't belong.

Alex slid his arm around her waist and braced her neck with his other hand as his mouth opened and the kiss deepened. Elizabeth stretched along him, arching her back and pressing her breasts into his chest. She'd desired him in her dreams, mind to mind, but her body had never flared to life like this.

A door slammed shut behind her, jarring them out of the moment. Elizabeth jumped away from Alex, fighting his hold. When she looked around, Shelly glared back at her. "That sure didn't take long."

"Shelly—" Shelly spun around and went back down the stairs. Elizabeth closed her eyes and took a deep breath. One stinking day. That's all it had taken. One day and she was all over a guy. Like Dallas would have been. Like her mom would have been.

"Elizabeth—"

Shaking her head, she met his gaze and backed away. "I can't."

"Hey, we just kissed. The world may have rocked," he smiled, all charm, "but it didn't end. It's okay."

"I'd love for that to be true."

His eyes took on a hopeful glow. She didn't want to be the one to destroy that hope a second time. If she was braver, she'd circle the table between them, demand another kiss. Try to make all her dreams come true. His, too, if the light in his eyes meant anything.

She wanted to see if there was anything to this physical

chemistry between them. The thought tempted her more than having functional bathrooms. But there were too many other things to consider.

Elizabeth looked at her empty hands. "I'm not looking for a relationship, Alex."

"Sometimes, when we're not looking . . ." he trailed off, his eyes gentle, coaxing.

She shook her head. "Alex—"

"I know." He gave her a lopsided grin. *"It'll never happen."*

Elizabeth winced, the words haunting her. If she could be free to love, she'd want it to be with him, but not even Elizabeth could be cruel enough to tell him that.

Sadness moved like a poison through her system, burning her eyes, making her hands feel weak and heavy. She whispered, "I'm sorry."

Alex smiled and raised a brow. "Don't worry about it. I won't give up that easily."

• ADAD'S ROOM WAS made of black stone, but instead of the darkness that pervaded the tunnels his chamber was lit by hundreds of beeswax candles, each a light in the darkness as he once was, though the spines of his wings were now only smoldering, blackened horns. The fallen Seraph stood before a tall wooden easel with thick pieces of parchment secured in the center.

With a stroke of his charcoal-smeared finger, he finished a sketch of Elizabeth. More of his drawings were scattered around the room and over a broad desk. Some held twisted trees with portraits hung from blackened, dead branches. Every member of Adad's family was depicted.

"She sleeps lightly tonight, afraid to dream. I should be surprised you made it." His deep voice vibrated around Silas, raising every hair, every feather.

"Yet, you aren't." Silas moved from the spot where he and Draven had appeared, closer to the sketches on the desk. "You were expecting us."

Adad ignored the obvious statement and turned to Draven, eyeing the black cloak. "Hiding, Draven?"

"I could ask the same of you." Draven's rich voice answered clearly, unmuffled despite the enveloping cowl.

The fearsome black face softened and a terrifying smile stretched his lips. "I guess we have both chosen our prison."

Silas focused on the drawings, memorizing every nuance. Information was necessary if they hoped to win.

Draven laughed. "It is hard to imagine you choosing a prison, Adad."

"Isn't it, though?" Adad laid his most recent sketch on top of the pile.

Silas tilted it toward himself. It depicted Elizabeth asleep, her head upon her mother's hospital bed. Both women looked at peace, as though it were a final goodbye. It spoke of tenderness and love, and a forgiveness Elizabeth might not be capable of for a long while.

"My daughter has gilded it so well. It feels like home here." Strangely, his tone held no sarcasm.

"Will you tell us how this happened? Or are we

supposed to guess?" Draven moved from the shadows, the pretense of patience long gone. "You've known of our visit for a long time now. Are we really to waste time with secrets?"

"Will explaining help you aid my children?"

Silas raised his head and spoke. "We won't know what knowledge we need until it comes time to use it. I'm sure you understand that."

The fallen Seraph nodded, a small smile still twisting his lips. He lowered into a chair and lounged back. It should have made him less intimidating. It didn't. "I was following the plan. I met Mary Beth while I was a soldier on leave from Vietnam."

The plan? Silas looked toward Draven, who made a dismissive gesture. He'd have to wait for his answer.

"We married and Dallas was conceived. On another leave, Elizabeth. After I returned, before I came here—" He gestured to the chamber around him. "We conceived the twins. But, even from the womb, Elizabeth was different."

"How so?" Draven glided to a wall of pictures and examined them.

"She reached out to me, even in the midst of battle. No matter my location, she always found me. She taught me the unconditional love of a child—a kind of love I hadn't known since my fall. We bonded. She's always known my true form."

No matter how hard he looked, Silas couldn't read Adad's face, but his blue eyes glowed with both sadness and pride. He loved his daughter.

The Seraph rose to stand beside Draven. Silas joined them. Laid out in sequential order on the wall was a sketch of each major moment in his family's life. Nothing was spared. It created a stark portrait of the Raineses' slow disintegration.

"When I returned, I was a husband and father for a few years. Then the new visions came. Visions never gave me a reprieve, but these were different." He made a sweeping gesture that indicated all of the charcoal drawings. "Each portrait was finished weeks, if not years, before the actual events took place."

Adad glided to the desk. He tossed all the drawings Silas had studied into the air and, as if hung from an invisible clothesline, they hovered in place.

"My family is cursed. My wife, my children, my children's children." Adad closed his eyes and turned away, the images no doubt fixed in his mind. "There is only one way it can end. I see that now, though when the visions first came, I thought leaving would alter the tragedies, allowing me the chance to return and fix what was broken."

Silas began at the sketch on the wall that showed Adad leaving and Mary Beth's pain as both Dallas and Elizabeth watched. The next depicted Elizabeth sleeping while a small area at the top right showed Adad in a chamber that looked the same as this one.

"The first few I burned after I drew, in the living room fireplace. I didn't want to leave my family, but that's what the visions were telling me would happen. When I came here, the pictures were on the walls. Elizabeth had seen them and, even at five years old, she'd remembered them."

Five years old. The third sketch was Elizabeth, her tiny arms around her father's charcoal legs. Her eyes were wide, sad, and scared, tears beginning to spill over her lashes. A bubble above them both said, "Daddy, please don't go."

"She found me, captured me, and wouldn't let me go." Adad's vibrant blue eyes met Silas's. "Even an angel can die in a mortal way if his soul is separated from his body long enough."

"You could have fought free," Draven reminded him.

"Love is powerful, Draven. As you will someday learn." Adad returned to his chair. "My daughter's love for me was complete. I could not destroy her, as a fight for freedom would have done."

"Because you loved her in return?" Draven's words cut across the chamber, disbelief obvious in the dark voice.

Adad raised his eyes to the cowled cloak. "Even evil can love, Draven. I was created with the best example of parental love possible. That's not something easily forgotten. The love of a child, in this fallen world, is the closest I'll ever come again to that perfect feeling."

Draven turned away from him.

"Is there no hope for redemption, then?" Silas asked.

Adad turned to Silas. "Repent. Beg forgiveness. Live the rest of your days according to the conscience we've all been given, though some ignore it. And pray that when your day is done, you will be redeemed. That is your hope, Silas."

"And what hope does your family have, Adad?" Draven asked. "How can they break the curse? How did it even begin? Not all demonically begat dynasties suffer this."

Adad laughed, booming and loud. *"Demonically begat?"*

Draven emitted an irritated sigh. "You know what I mean."

Silas grinned and turned away from them both.

Adad sobered. "How did your curse begin?"

"Maeve." Draven whispered the name. "But why curse you? She didn't know—"

"She didn't trust. Anyone. It's not beyond her to place a curse on me that wouldn't take effect unless I betrayed her."

"A thousand years later?"

"A blink of an eye."

"You waited that long to begin your plan?"

"I follow my visions." Adad pointed and both Silas and Draven turned to see a fireplace with a wedding portrait of a tall, auburn-haired soldier with vibrant blue eyes and his blonde and delicate teenaged bride. A golden plaque at the bottom read:

CHARLES ASTOR RAINES • MARY ELIZABETH RAINES

OCTOBER 16, 1972

MAY GOD BLESS THEIR LOVE FOREVER.

Silas folded his arms across his chest and leaned against the desk, facing them. "So what is this plan?"

Adad looked to Draven, amusement shining in his eyes. "He's your partner, Draven. He deserves to know."

Draven's arms crossed, leather gloves fisted tight. "Think, Silas. First, Maeve chose a human husband and bore a child. Now you see *him*," a gloved hand indicated Adad. "With four children and ten grandchildren. But why marry? Fallen angels have borne children without marriage many times over. That's what created most of our race. Many married in the beginning, out of love, guilt, or hope of absolution, but why now? Because of love? I think not."

A low growl vibrated the chamber. "Do not judge my heart, Draven. That is not for you."

Draven nodded to Adad. "My apologies."

Silas raised both brows. Draven knew how to apologize? Respectfully?

Draven continued. "Many of my kind believe that it is only marriage that will create a completely human-looking child. Maeve wanted her son, Kai, to rule both Europe and eventually the rest of our world. Others, though, have different things in mind."

Adad nodded at Draven's words. "Once, humans flocked to anyone with the least bit of power. They worshipped the fallen ones as gods and goddesses. We were able to rule our own kingdoms, either singly, or as part of a pantheon, like the Greeks and Romans."

Silas nodded. "I know this."

Adad acknowledged his words, but continued. "The entire world changed when Jesus came. New gods were not created after him. Only newer names linked with very old ones were given any credence. Who would believe in them? Fallen ones could not rule an ever-shrinking globe with ever-expanding means of communication. But humans could. Our children could."

Silas straightened, frowning.

Adad raised one brow. "Think about it. One human can change the entire world, the most notable example being Hitler. Now, imagine an *entire family* raised by a fallen one. What damage could they inflict?"

"My God," Silas whispered.

"Precisely." Adad nodded.

Silas scowled. "Draven, what have you gotten me into?"

Draven shrugged. "I love how *I* get blamed for this."

Silas glared at Adad. "Just what were you planning to do with this power?"

"Despite what Maeve desired, I merely wished to balance the scales."

"How?"

"By sending Draven to you." Adad's eyes glowed a fiercer shade of blue. "The rest of the future is for me to know and you to find out."

Silas grimaced. "What do Draven and I have to do with your plans for your children?"

Adad ignored his question, turning instead to Draven. "You will not stay hidden forever."

"But long enough," was the husky reply.

Adad shook his head. "You must leave now. Elizabeth is tired."

Chapter 10

• ELIZABETH PRESSED HER cheek to the door, tears of exhaustion and fear sliding down her face. She didn't have the strength left. Not after such a long day. She'd barely dozed and she was so tired. Alex was her addiction, her fantasy, and without him she couldn't sleep.

Maybe tomorrow she could start earlier. Build another room. Create another fantasy. Maybe tomorrow she could give Alex up.

Maybe tomorrow she could remember all the reasons they couldn't be together. Just not tonight. Not right now. Elizabeth rose from the stone floor and eased silently into their room. Into their bed. Alex rolled over. His strong arms surrounded her bare, chilled skin and pulled her closer to his heat.

"Hey, you made it," he rumbled against her ear.

"Hey," Elizabeth whispered back, burrowing into his toasty heat. "I couldn't think of any place I'd rather be than cuddled up next to you."

"Sounds good to me." His voice held a smile as he pulled her closer, his hard naked body burning into her from head to toe.

Elizabeth slid one bare leg along his as he nuzzled her neck. When his hand stroked down her side and over her back, she laughed huskily. What was sleep compared to this?

Alex tightened his hold, crushing her against his chest. Lowering his mouth to her neck, he trapped some of the sensitive skin between his teeth and licked. She exhaled a shaky breath and arched back to give him better access.

His hot, rough hand wrapped around an ankle and slid up her calf, widening over her thigh. Elizabeth moaned, wet and aching and ready.

Alex pushed her thighs wide and she arched even more, pressing her breasts to his chest. His right hand slid under her head as he settled his hips in her embrace. How could she possibly give him up?

Elizabeth brushed his hair back, using both hands to hold it away from his eyes so she could stare into them as he entered her. He was hard and thick where she needed him so intensely, sliding and filling every gap in her body and heart. She nearly cried out. His lips smiled ever so slightly.

He loved when she responded to him like this. And she wanted to give him anything that kept him looking at her with such devotion and pleasure. He thrust with just enough force to curl her toes and steal her breath. Elizabeth opened further to him, stretching her thighs wide to entice him closer.

Was giving him up even an option anymore?

She was beginning to think not.

• HER MOTHER'S BEDROOM window showed it was still dark outside when Elizabeth woke. Stretching and running a hand over the cool sheets, she was surprised when nothing impeded her reach. Blinking her eyes open, she forced herself to be honest. She was disappointed to awaken and not find Alex beside her.

With her body aching like it was, craving a real touch instead of imagined ones, she'd never return to her dreams. She'd suffered this enough to know what it would take to alleviate her tension, but she'd left all those toys in Seattle.

Elizabeth crawled from between the sheets, made the bed, and dressed. She peeked in the other bedrooms and counted eight sleeping kids before tiptoeing down the stairs with a smile on her face.

For the first time in a month, she made a pot of coffee to enjoy the morning with. Even starting on the endless laundry didn't have the same overwhelming, depressing feel in the dark coolness of early morning. Pulling bacon out of the freezer, she set it to defrost as she made a triple batch of pancake batter. She wouldn't cook them for another two hours or so, but now she was prepared.

Still tingling all over, she poured herself a cup of coffee and carried it to the front porch. The breeze was a bit chilly, but she was warm enough to love the way it caressed her skin. Sitting on the top step, Elizabeth stared into the darkness.

The moon barely shone through the tall pine and chestnut trees that filled the neighborhood, leaving everything shadowed and mysterious. In the moonlight, the imperfections in the house and yard weren't so glaringly apparent. With a bit of love and care, the beauty of her childhood home would be unmistakable.

This building had housed four generations of her

family, through good times and bad. Her grandfather had actually helped build it. Her grandparents were the first to move in when the house was brand new. It was a big home, with room for lots of children, but they'd only had Mary Beth. Not that they'd been disappointed.

Eventually, Mary Beth had given them grandchildren. Until the day each grandparent had died, they'd slathered love and attention on Dallas, Elizabeth, and the twins, Bobby and Felicia. Elizabeth looked around and allowed the atmosphere to seep inside her. This house, her grandparents, they both deserved this family to become whole again. And for once, she felt hopeful that it could be done.

She had a project that would pay well and not end anytime soon. The children were together and happy. Her siblings still had problems though. Bobby was locked up, Felicia gone, and Dallas in the midst of a passionate new relationship. Her mom wouldn't be around much longer. There were still many things to pain them, to pain her, but the children would be fine. She'd make sure of that. They were her first priority.

Elizabeth sipped her coffee and nearly spit it through her nose as she watched a familiar truck pull to a stop in front of the house. Alex and Geoffrey stepped out of the cab and walked up to her. Elizabeth rose to her feet and stared helplessly at Alex. She hadn't expected to see him so soon, certainly not after a dream like hers. She could already feel heat climbing into her cheeks. What the hell time was it, anyway?

Geoffrey stopped at her side, and raised a brow in query. "Coffee?"

"Kitchen," she said, barely sparing him a glance.

Geoffrey kept moving and closed the door after him. Alex, however, stopped two steps below her so they were eye to eye. The last time they'd been in this position, he'd sweet-talked his way into her home and into her life. What would she be giving him this time?

"Hi," he said. His eyes were dark and glittering, and deep enough to fall into. Elizabeth forced herself not to sway into him.

"I didn't expect you."

"I said I would be here." They were whispering, though they were outside, as if louder words would wake the world. They both wanted this moment when it was only the two of them. The darkness lent a sense of privacy, of sweet possibility.

"It's Sunday. I shouldn't have expectations." She was staring at his mouth as she spoke. His lips looked soft and tempting enough to nibble on. In her dreams, that mouth did the most incredible things to her. Would reality be just as good? Elizabeth swallowed and raised her eyes back to meet his disturbingly direct gaze.

"Go ahead. Have expectations." His husky words were a promise she was afraid to believe in. Did he mean with the house, with the kids, or with her?

Elizabeth tilted her head, wondering where the conversation had gone. A day ago, she couldn't push him out the door fast enough. Just a few hours ago, she'd dreamed he'd wrapped his arms around her and used his mouth to create entirely different needs than the ones they now discussed. She was well on her way to making the mistake both she and Shelly feared. How could she avoid that? Did she want to? "Like what?"

"Make me a list." Alex smiled.

Her heart thudded in a tight rhythm against her chest. She smiled, knowing it was slightly flirtatious but unable to help it. Her arms prickled with gooseflesh that rose over her chest and up to the base of her neck. "My to-do lists are usually pretty long."

"I do a better job with a little direction." His grin was pure charm as he moved closer to her. "I wouldn't want to bulldoze through when a little sensitivity is required."

The broad wood of the porch post suddenly pressed into her back and Alex loomed over her. She swallowed, her mouth suddenly thick and dry. "That's very wise of you to admit."

He grinned, his mouth closer so they nearly breathed in each other's words. "I like to please. Where would you like me to start?"

Many places came to mind. And just thinking about them made her burn for his touch. Her voice low and breathy, she whispered, "With the fence."

He smiled and she felt it against her cheek. "Sounds like a fine place to start. I'm pretty good with fences."

"You'll have to be. Mine have been in place for a very long time." When was the last time she'd played with a man? Had she ever done so? If she had, it hadn't been this fun. This exciting.

"I know. But when they've aged a while, they're usually ready to fall down." His eyes shone a challenge, though his smile said he knew they were playing.

"That or they've settled in and are next to impossible to remove." She raised a saucy brow, challenging him in return.

"Trust me, they're coming down," he said, then grazed his lips against her jaw.

At his touch, she shuddered. She couldn't let this happen. Couldn't give in. The kids would see her as just another selfish adult. And the danger to Alex . . . well, that was a whole different level of terror. What if he tried to leave her? *What if she didn't let him?*

Alex closed his eyes, as if realizing their game had gone a bit too far. His voice held actual regret when he whispered, "Sorry. Did I ruin the moment?"

Elizabeth froze. In a second, he'd pull away, thinking she'd rejected him for a third time. How could she allow him to keep thinking that what was between them was completely one-sided? He began to pull back and her heart screamed at his withdrawal even as her mind demanded she allow it. In another second the moment would be gone and the chasm between them wider than ever.

Refusing to think about it and risk changing her mind, she tilted her head toward him. Taking his bottom lip between hers, she ran her tongue over it. He shuddered against her, his lip plump enough to nibble on. She trapped him, rubbing her tongue back and forth over his flesh. He tasted as she'd always imagined. Warm and welcoming, like home. Maybe the only home she would ever want.

When want turned to need, Elizabeth pulled back and watched Alex's eyes slowly open. Her voice husky with sadness, she whispered, "There, now we can both be sorry."

The lines around his eyes deepened. "Are you sorry?"

She'd braved her desire for the first time ever and it terrified her to no end. She had responsibilities, and if she allowed him to be a part of her life and he changed his mind about being there, she could hurt him. It was too dangerous. But did she regret kissing him? Pain cramped her heart and the smile she gave him was small and wistful.

"Don't ask, Alex."

• TWO HOURS LATER, Elizabeth put down her to-do list, ready to start breakfast. Alex may have been joking, but she *was* a natural list maker, always had been, though she hadn't made one lately. Instead of overwhelming her, the twelve-page, room-by-room list covered everything, breaking it into manageable steps. Next, she'd make as thorough a list for the computer project. The more she and Alex synced, the more they'd accomplish.

Shelly wandered in as Elizabeth laid bacon in the skillet, filling the room with the mouthwatering smell of a big breakfast on Sunday morning. Glancing through the stack of neat pages on the table, Shelly shook her head. "You're such a freak."

Elizabeth gave her a fatalistic shrug and sighed. "I know."

They shared a grin as Shelly strapped the baby into the high chair, snapping the tray in place. "Is everyone outside, then?"

Elizabeth glanced through the window over the sink. The toddlers were playing in one of the weedy gardens, ripping out the plants and digging with spoons, three little bloomer-clad bottoms stuck in the air. Her mother had always grown pansies and strawberries there. The girls would love planting those and watching them grow.

Teddy and Tommy moved old boards out of the way

while the twins stacked newer ones from the truck bed in a pile closer to Alex and Geoffrey, who supervised them while ripping off the old fencing.

"I think so. Only Kevin is out of sight." Elizabeth pulled out the electric griddle, wiped it down, and sprayed Pam on it.

"I saw him going outside when I came up." She handed a teething biscuit to Veronica, who held it tight in her chubby fist and immediately popped it in her mouth.

"Did you need them for something?"

"Nope. I just need to get some homework done."

"I didn't think you'd have any over Spring Break."

Shelly snorted. "High school's changed, Aunt Beth."

"Thanks." Elizabeth smiled and shook her head as she turned the bacon and laid the cooked pieces on a towel-covered plate to soak up extra grease.

Shelly chuckled, then the room fell into a quiet rhythm of sizzling and page turning. The chimes outside the back door swayed, and clinked in the breeze. Pulling the pancake batter out of the fridge, Elizabeth stopped and looked around.

The house quietly creaked, like the swing hanging from the tall pine in the backyard. It was relaxing, comforting. She heard the high-pitched laughter of the toddlers and the gurgling laughter of Veronica as she enjoyed her treat.

The spring breeze drifted through the open back door, bringing in snatches of conversations between the guys and the kids. The smell of fried bacon, the brightness of the sun, the soft sound of Shelly opening books and spreading papers over the table. Realization swept over her like a warm tide. This was a perfect morning.

Elizabeth blinked, almost surprised she could recognize a good moment as it happened. Grabbing a spoon to stir the batter, she was amazed at the bubble of happy peace that filled her lungs until she could barely breathe.

"Time to wake up, Aunt Beth."

Elizabeth frowned quizzically at her niece. She wasn't asleep.

"You're daydreaming, Aunt Beth." Shelly smiled. "I can always tell because I start hearing your thoughts."

• THE HEAT FROM the morning sun would be a killer if the breeze hadn't come, swaying the trees around them and brushing away the worst of it. Alex sipped from his bottle of water and watched Geoffrey and Tommy struggle with one of the more stubborn boards.

Tommy liked helping, especially if it was Geoffrey that he helped, and the big guy seemed to enjoy it. He was a natural at leading, offering advice then stepping back and letting them learn. The way he worked with Tommy and the twins was damn near inspirational.

The toddlers were lined up along the back garden row, digging up the dead vegetation and turning the soil, as much as toddlers could anyway. They were bent over, little pink bloomers peeking from beneath matching dresses. Their red, blonde, and brunette hair was pulled up in pigtails with pink bows hanging on each side of their heads.

Three baby dolls were carefully placed on the bottom beam of the fence in front of them, overseeing their progress. They were smiling and laughing, talking and throwing the dirt all around them, but never near their babies. Alex chuckled and shook his head. It must be a girl thing.

"Like this, Abby." Jessie demonstrated her instructions, accidentally spraying dirt all over Abby's arm.

"Ew!" Abby shrieked.

Jessie glared. "Big baby!"

Abby pouted and Sarah tried to soothe her cousin with a little hug and a frown at her sister. "Be nice, Jessie."

Alex strolled over and brushed the dirt from Abby's little arm and patted both her and Jessie on the back. "You're doing great, girls. We'll be able to plant new flowers in no time."

He watched them happily resume their work before he turned away. It was then he saw Teddy at the water hose, spraying his hand and frowning. Striding closer, Alex leaned over and noticed blood welling from a cut on his palm. "What happened?"

"I think I snagged a nail." Teddy turned the water off and held his hand out for Alex's inspection.

Alex pulled the hand closer to him, manipulating the flesh to see how deep it was.

"I had a tetanus shot a couple years ago. I shouldn't need another one, but I don't know if I need stitches or not."

Alex frowned. It was deep enough to require one or two. Looking into Teddy's eyes, he swallowed. His secret was going to come out sooner or later. He should probably tell Elizabeth about it first, but Teddy looked like a kid who could handle a few secrets. Besides, he couldn't leave him in pain. Gently, Alex covered the boy's hand with his own. "It'll be fine."

A blue glow flared over their hands briefly. When it receded, Alex pulled his palm back and the gash was gone. Teddy's eyes widened at the sight of his completely healed skin. He held his hand up, bending his fingers and making a fist. "How did you do that?"

Alex smiled, glad he hadn't terrified the kid. Trust Teddy to immediately think of the practical. "It's a little gift I have."

Teddy stared at Alex. "It's not really a *little* gift."

Alex shrugged, trying not to look away from the too perceptive boy. "I know."

"How long have you been able to do it?" Teddy tilted his head, his eyes examining him much the way Elizabeth had just that morning.

"Since I was six. My dad was cutting wood for new kitchen cabinets. His hand slipped, and he nearly severed three fingers." Alex cleared his throat. It had been the scariest moment of his young life.

"Sounds bloody." Teddy clearly wanted more of the story.

"It bled too fast. He needed me to help wrap a towel around his hand. I was scared and upset. I didn't want my dad hurt. He was a construction worker and needed both hands."

"So you healed him?"

Alex nodded. "Until then, I hadn't known I could."

"How did he react?"

Alex raised an eyebrow. There was something in Teddy's tone that made it clear the answer to this question was important to him. "At first, he was really quiet. He cleaned all the blood up, washed the blade, and rinsed out the towel. Then he sat down with me."

"Were you scared? Did you think he'd stop loving you and call you a freak?"

Alex focused his gaze on Teddy, examining the blue, blue eyes behind the glasses as a bad suspicion began creeping over him. "I didn't know how I'd done it and he was so quiet that I didn't know if I'd upset him. So, yeah, I was scared. But he was my dad. I knew he'd love me no matter what."

The sadness in Teddy's eyes nearly broke Alex's heart. "In the end, my dad hugged me and told me to be careful. I had a very special gift and not everyone would understand it."

Teddy nodded. "Does Aunt Liz know?"

Alex stilled. "I don't have a clue how to tell her."

Teddy turned the water back on and washed away the blood on his hand. "She'd probably have to watch you do it to believe it."

"Yeah, probably."

"My grandma's in the hospital." Teddy's tone was far too casual.

"What's wrong with her?"

"Cancer and a bad liver."

Alex looked at his hands and sighed. "I can't heal natural diseases."

Teddy nodded, watching the water stream from the hose, then turned his head and watched Tommy and the twins. "Nothing will help her live, I know that. But maybe if she could feel good enough to say good-bye . . ."

Alex watched Teddy shrug, his shoulders held stiff, like he wouldn't allow himself to believe in anyone enough for them to disappoint him.

"I can try." It was the closest thing to a promise Alex could make.

Teddy nodded, then looked at Alex with a small smile. Alex tilted his head and watched him, puzzled.

Teddy glanced down at the hose, then looked over at the faucet. Slowly, the flower-shaped handle turned by itself until the water stopped.

Alex lost his breath. Not so much because of the telekinesis, but at Teddy's trust.

Teddy looked at him, hesitant now, waiting for his reaction.

Alex glanced at Geoffrey, helping Tommy battle the stubborn fence, then back at Teddy. "People are full of surprises."

Chapter 11

• MARY BETH RAINES'S hospital room was shadowed and almost silent, emphasizing the solitary woman that lay in the center of the hospital bed. A small red light lit the tip of one of her fingers, measuring her oxygen intake. A Hickman port protruded from the base of her neck, directing fluids from the bag hanging above her. A monitor quietly beeped with the beat of her heart.

She didn't stir as her door opened. Pain medication

kept her sleeping. Alex stepped into the room and sat in the chair by her bedside as Silas and Draven entered silently, unseen behind him. For a long moment, Alex simply listened. Breathing slowly and taking in the near silence. When his heart was as calm as the beeping machine, he leaned forward, carefully taking her hand in his.

"Hi, Mrs. Raines. I'm Alex Foster. I went to school with Elizabeth years ago. She doesn't know I'm here, but I came to try to help." He waited for a response from her, but Mary Beth continued her deep and even breathing.

"I can heal wounds. I know you have many inside you. I hope I can work on them without messing with your medicines." Alex swallowed and leaned his head against the rail of her bed. "I just know I have to help. If you were to pass away before Elizabeth and the kids could say good-bye, it would leave a piece of them damaged forever. Please, Mary Beth, your family needs you."

Closing both hands around hers, they began to glow with a low, blue light that spread outward until it encompassed her entire form. His eyes glowed white with power. In order to heal, Alex took the injuries of the other person into himself. Their cuts would appear on his body, then he would rapidly metabolize them, healing lightning fast.

Alex began to gasp as he drew Mary Beth's lung damage into himself. He couldn't do that with cancer as it was simply an abnormal growth of cells. They weren't alien or foreign to her body, though they were destructive. But the damaged sections from decades of smoking—those he could heal.

Silas and Draven took in the scene from their invisible vantage point.

"You made the nail cut Teddy," Silas suddenly accused.

"You nudged Teddy to trust Alex with his secrets," Draven accused right back.

"I didn't know the secret he was hiding. You didn't warn me."

"I didn't know either." Draven took a deep breath, refusing to rise to the bait.

"There's a lot about this family you didn't pay attention to when you chose Elizabeth for Alex. Like the fact her father is a fallen angel who plans to rule the world through his children. Or that they suffer under a curse, on top of facing a future battle with the same bitch who cast the curse."

Draven sighed. "Why am I expected to know everything? Adad and the curse surprised me, too. I'm just not freaking out over them like you are. Besides, they're just kids—they need love and stability to grow up well. Where's the bad in that?"

"Does it never occur to you to examine all the angles before you involve me in one of your plans? No. You just pop in and say, 'Silas, let's stop this curse on Dreux and Kai before it happens' and I say, 'Okay, sounds good'."

"Your dialogue needs work."

"Nowhere was it mentioned that the curse was cast by one of the most powerful of the original fallen angels— *and* that she'd vow deadly vengeance on us both."

"So saying, 'She's one of the evil ones' left it a little too vague for you?"

Silas grunted. "That was warning enough in your

mind, of course." He glared at Draven. "Then I hear, 'Let's help people fall in love. Our destiny is to become a couple of Nephilim matchmakers'."

"Again with the dialogue. I never said that."

He ignored that. "Only, I thought the word Nephilim applied to *us*. Then I come to find out it applies to every human-born descendent of a fallen angel!"

"We've discussed how they can use their powers to help others." Draven shrugged, glad they were on the other side of the realm barrier so Alex wouldn't hear Silas's rapidly rising voice. "I have lied to you about nothing."

"But you haven't been completely honest either. You forgot to mention that demons had a little plan to wipe out free will and that we'd be *helping* them. They want to play with human destiny like the original Watchers did. Are you forgetting that's why *we* were cursed and nearly wiped from the face of the earth?"

"No, I haven't forgotten. I don't intend for them to use their abilities to rule. I just want them to use their gifts for good. To build a solid alliance around Dreux and Kalyss so when Maeve comes, they aren't completely defenseless. *That's* what I intend."

"Well, thanks for finally telling me part of your plan."

Draven sighed tiredly. "I only try to help."

"Yeah, but help do what?" Silas paced the hospital floor. "In trying to help, harm is often the result. I should have stuck to my original instincts and thrown you out the night we met."

"Quit pouting, Silas. I did not force you to do anything. You've been a willing partner. Just because there's more to this family than we first realized—"

"More to them? I thought they were supposed to be human!"

"They are!" Draven exclaimed, then more quietly, "Mostly."

"They were supposed to be our good deed. Instead, we're breaking the rules and helping the race of Nephilim grow. It was one thing when they were just unknowing descendents with a few gifts, but they not only know they have powers, their demon is still with them!"

"They have a chance to be happy and live as humans. For now, they are a broken family that desperately needs to be put back together. How can that be evil in His eyes?"

"Did you ever think that maybe there is a reason for their family to self-destruct? That it's meant to be for more reasons than just Maeve cursing them? Or that by trying to fix them, we may be incurring the hatred of yet another powerful enemy?"

Draven paused. In all honesty, that had never been a thought. "Why would you even think that?"

"Because that's the way it always goes for us."

"Fine," Draven snapped. "The situation is what it is. Adad is trapped for fear of destroying his daughter. Not only does he want the best for his family, but it speaks to his own preservation. His plans are moot. Elizabeth is too much her own person to be his puppet, so there is no battle for supremacy. No bid for world domination. He is an ally."

Silas took a deep breath, then nodded. "I guess I can agree with that."

"The Raineses have gifts that can best be channeled for good. As it stands now, they are at risk for heading in the other direction. Until the curse is broken."

They were at risk, along with anyone else they came into contact with. Helping them break the curse would work to the good. Silas could support that. The other choice would be to kill them, and, Nephilim or not, that just wasn't an option. Not children.

"Our original goal still stands. It just means the allies for Dreux and Kalyss will be even more powerful than we'd imagined. Which is good, because it will take all of us to defeat her."

"What?" Silas's head snapped up. "Defeat Maeve? Are you insane? What makes you imagine we could do that?"

"She should have found us by now."

"At full strength, she would have found us."

"Exactly. She is weak and this may be the only chance we have. Maeve was in the tunnels for nearly a millennium, Silas. She was carried out, a bundle of skin and bones. How long could you last without sustenance?" Draven turned away from him, tucking one hand deep into the sleeve of the robe. "It would have killed me."

"It likely would have killed me, too, but she's different. More so than either of us. When she finds us, she won't be weak. And we haven't been able to find her while she is."

Suddenly a glow lit the other side of the hospital bed, interrupting their debate.

Pink, purple, green, and blue tendrils swirled in loops and curves until a form materialized across from Alex. Downy white wings surrounded the form, stretching until they nearly filled the room. Colors from the deepest depths of a mother-of-pearl shell twisted and shimmered beneath a familiar face of clear-cut crystal.

The Pearl Angel laid a color-filled hand above Mary Beth's head and Alex's aura burned brighter as streaks of blue lightning zapped through the glow. Jagged bolts slashed across the white expanse of his eyes. The Angel was a healer, a compassionate source of strength for those in need. The bright aura traveled around Mary Beth and back to Alex. Almost at once, he began to breathe easier.

Blazing eyes of fire focused on them and Draven couldn't help but eye the swords the Angel carried. One was at the Angel's side, the other across the Angel's back and suddenly, the healing skills of the Angel paled in comparison to the other skills of God's messengers.

The Pearl Angel raised a hand and caught Silas and Draven, holding them immobile. A voice sounded in their heads, soft and flowing like the wind through small chimes. The Angel's eyes scorched straight through Draven. *This is a place to *heal*.*

That quickly, both Draven and Silas were shoved through the walls and onto a small patch of grassy lawn outside. They landed flat on their backs. Draven laid back, gasping for breath, then began to chuckle.

Silas sighed and sat up, brushing twigs and leaves from his robes. "What on earth is so funny?"

"A cursed Nephilim was right there and the Pearl Angel helped him aid someone else. For the second time. Alex wasn't destroyed or cast from this earth for being a descendent or for using his skills. And he was helping Mary Beth. This can only mean one thing."

"What's that?" Silas scowled, already knowing what Draven would say.

"That I was right. We're doing a good thing by trying

to heal this family." Draven looked at Silas, whose irritation was displayed clearly. "Go ahead. Say it. I was right."

Silas raised his eyes to the moon above them. "You must be a woman."

That fast, Draven's laughter fell away and the cloak began to move in odd places, almost like snakes rubbing in a formless pile beneath the cloak. Silas stared, his face going a bit pale.

"Face it, Silas. You don't know *what* I am."

• "I THINK WE need to take it apart, Tommy."

Elizabeth paused and looked outside before starting the washer. After two long days of work, the fence was replaced. With that task complete, there could only be one thing they were talking about.

"Is it really dangerous, sir?" Tommy croaked, still trying to imitate Geoffrey's deep voice. They stood, in identical poses and eyed the swing set. It had been pulled from the front yard to the side of the house where they could examine it. Tommy loved that swing set. He'd probably rather cut off his arm than take it down.

Geoffrey put a hand on one end of the structure and shook the thing all too easily. "Would you risk one of the little ones on it?"

Tommy closed his eyes, his chin wavering a bit. But, his duty as man of the house was clear. Tommy took a deep breath, opened his eyes, and straightened his shoulders. Puffing out his boyish chest, he firmed his chin and shook his head. "Nope. Gotta protect the little ones."

Geoffrey lifted his screwdriver. "Ready to bring it down?"

Tommy raised a matching screwdriver from the new tool belt at his waist, a weapon no one had ever dared place in his hands before. Unholy glee brightened the light of destruction in his eyes. "Oh, yeah."

Elizabeth chuckled, started the wash, and headed back to the living room. Her laundry system was working well. She'd even gotten the kids to bring down the rest of their clothes and clean their rooms. Hopefully soon they could do some repainting upstairs. She wanted to do something to brighten the place up. The kids deserved to grow up in surroundings that weren't more depressing than their circumstances.

She'd developed a system over the last few days, working on the computer early in the morning and after the kids went to bed. She worked best with complete peace and quiet, and that only happened when the kids were comatose.

In just the last two days she'd fixed at least one thing in her mind—how Geoffrey's electronic library would look. Normally, visualizing something so extensive would have taken her forever, but after what had happened on Sunday with Shelly, she'd decided to test her new daydreaming ability.

No one else had ever mentioned hearing her thoughts and feelings while she was daydreaming. So how did Shelly hear them?

Elizabeth scrubbed the fireplace and decided right then, it didn't matter how Shelly had known. Daydreaming about her project was far preferable to living in the moment as she scrubbed away years of dirt.

Elizabeth built the dream, picturing the tunnel—which was all too easy—and stepping away from her body. In her mind, she stood before a steel door with familiar dents. When she entered the cavern beyond, the light was soft, meant to illuminate without blinding. In the center stood a small podium with a simple control panel with a search bar, directional pad, and options for bookmarking, highlighting, compiling, and more.

Shelves rose from floor to ceiling, circling around so there were no corners, only alcoves filled with distinctive classical statuary and stained-glass windows to mark the division of the subjects. A person could stand in the midst of the room, and view from every angle modern paperbacks, classic hardbacks, ancient manuscripts covered in leather and precious stones, and tubes of scrolls made from various precious metals.

It was designed so that each set of shelves held a different subject. Each book was distinctive in both style and color. A person could remember where they'd found the information they sought, even if they didn't have the words for a detailed search.

At the top of the podium was a green book, its script distinctive and flowing. The spine marked it as a version of the Bible. Opening the book revealed a file and displayed the table of contents with links to subjects within each chapter. Flipping to one page at random, she highlighted text, pushed a button to copy it, and placed it in the empty notebook on the podium. More empty notebooks were stacked inside the podium, each awaiting a subject label on the spine.

This would be the basics of the program, with more

fine-tuning to come later. Geoffrey would be comfortable with the layout. Color, placement, and direction would put thousands of titles at his fingertips. The control panel on the podium would search for and locate any topic, and he'd have savable and searchable notebooks to follow his train of thought. She could add sounds easily, and texture could perhaps become a visual pattern that lent the impression of actual parchment or leather. That only left taste and smell.

Perhaps symbols of well-known foods and natural scents. But how could she get more specific without placing an aromatherapy set beside his computer? *Here, Geoffrey, dab a bit of this on and you're well on your way to researching Angels.*

Elizabeth laughed, shaking her head. Generally, anything too complicated was a bad idea. It wouldn't be user-friendly, and that was the first rule of creating software. Make sure people can use it. Well, that, and make sure the computer operating it could handle such a large program.

"Don't worry about the space."

Elizabeth jumped back a step as Geoffrey moved up beside her and examined the controls. She wasn't asleep. *He* wasn't asleep. Like Shelly, she'd drawn him into her daydream. Elizabeth swallowed and stared at him with wide eyes, her heart in her throat.

"I'll make sure I have enough memory to handle this." Geoffrey looked around them, examining the artwork and texts. "This is exactly what I want."

Part of her was happy, relieved. Selling a project was often the difficult part.

His blue-grey gaze landed on her face with a weight she could almost feel. "You certainly have a unique sales approach."

Elizabeth licked her lips nervously. How was he taking this so calmly? "I didn't mean to bring you here like this."

He nodded. "Sudden boosts in skills can be disorienting until we learn to control them."

"We?"

Geoffrey didn't answer. Instead, he walked to the door and put his hand on the knob. When he looked back, she nodded in answer to his silent question. Geoffrey opened the door and the dream library dissolved. With one last glance at her, he said, "Talk to Alex."

His tone held no censure, no anger, but she could recognize a command when she heard one. Talk to Alex, *or he would.* The front door clicked shut behind him and Elizabeth stood still, struggling to understand what had just happened.

• "THE BATHROOMS ARE clean." Shelly collapsed onto the large cushiony chair, flopping her arms over the sides.

Arranging the last clutter-filled box so it didn't overflow, Elizabeth paused to grin at her. "Thank you. Four working, clean bathrooms. It's better than chocolate."

Shelly snorted. "Speak for yourself. I'd rather have chocolate."

Elizabeth hauled the box to the kitchen and set it by the door to the basement, then grabbed a dust rag and polish. Her mother had loved everything ever given to her. So she'd kept it on every available flat space in the living room. Thirty years of childhood art and knick-knacks. It had been past time for them to go, even if they only moved to the basement.

Giving Elizabeth busywork while considering how to spill her secrets to Alex was only a side benefit. Nerves cramped her stomach anyway. The men were gone at the moment, but she would have to tell Alex when he returned. Elizabeth sprayed polish over the coffee table and wiped at it with brisk strokes.

"You know there's no more room down there, right?"

"Don't worry, I won't let the boxes spill over into your room."

"They already have. Between all the junk from your old room and the stuff from here, the storage half of the basement filled up a while ago."

Elizabeth frowned and scrubbed at a stubborn stain on the cherrywood coffee table. "I'll go through it and get rid of a bunch soon, honey. I promise. I just wanted to get the main areas of the house liveable first."

"I know. It's okay." Shelly swung sideways so her head rested on one arm of the chair and her legs bounced on the other side. "It really looks great in here."

The spot finally gone, Elizabeth stood and surveyed her handiwork. The overstuffed couch was against the large window overlooking the porch. A matching loveseat sat adjacent on the right, a thin walkway from the front door to the kitchen behind it. And the chair holding Shelly faced the couch.

The tables at each end of the couch were bare of all but lamps and shiny clean. The mantle over the fireplace was bare of decades-worth of dust and clutter, holding only the most precious of her mother's treasures. Even the fireplace was clean of ash and soot.

Behind Shelly's chair, on the wall shared with the kitchen, was a large TV in an entertainment center/bookcase. Two beanbags were placed directly in front of it for the kids to play games. When everyone was ready to watch movies, only the chair would need to be moved to the side.

It was a good arrangement for visiting, game playing, or a combination of the two. With various pillow accents and the clean curtains opened to let in the sunshine, the living room was cozy, warm, and somehow spaciously inviting. Pride swelled in Elizabeth's chest and she had to agree with Shelly. It did look good.

"I could never have done it without the guys keeping all the kids outside and at the dojo."

"Or without me in here to haul boxes and clean bathrooms," the teen pointed out with an arched brow.

"Yes! Yes. I know." Elizabeth sighed in exaggerated appreciation. "You are all that is wonderful and gracious. Such a gift to everyone in this house. We give thanks to the beauty that is you."

Shelly buffed her nails on her shirt and sniffed. "I know."

Elizabeth laughed and did her own collapsing on the couch.

But it was the quietest moment she'd have for a long while. She had to take her chance. "I want to give my old room to the toddlers. Let them spread out and have room to play with their toys."

Shelly nodded. "Danielle will like sharing with David again."

"Yeah, we could do that. But I was thinking she could share with you, instead. Keep girls with girls. She'll need that in a few years."

Shelly let out a snort. In an irritated voice she snapped, "Where would she go? There's no more room in the basement."

"Well, if the baby was moved upstairs—"

"Forget it." Shelly sat up and crossed her arms, glaring mutinously. "I take care of Veronica just fine. She doesn't need to be moved."

"You need to have a good night's sleep for school—"

"We have a schedule. We go to bed, she sleeps most of the night, and wakes me up in plenty of time to get ready for school."

"I won't neglect her, Shelly. You know that."

"And when you're gone? Can you guarantee the next adult to take care of us won't get irritated with her and start shaking her in the middle of the night?" Shelly's voice was hard, deepening in genuine anger. "Because I've already caught one of Grandma's old boyfriends doing that, Aunt Beth."

Nausea raised the flesh on her arms and Elizabeth stared at the table in front of her. "I didn't know."

"That's why Veronica stays with me."

Elizabeth nodded, then leaned forward and stared straight into Shelly's eyes. "I understand your concerns. You have a right to be worried, I know that. But I'd like you to think about it, Shelly. I think I've earned your trust."

Shelly stared at her shoes.

"Let me give you this break. And if I ever leave, you can take her back downstairs with you." Elizabeth shook her head. "Or hell, Shelly, take Grandma's room and make the next adult sleep in the basement. You probably deserve it."

Shelly smiled, her eyes sparkling as she looked through her lashes at Elizabeth. "Actually, I *do,* you know."

Elizabeth gave her a bland look. "I said if I ever leave. You still got awhile to wait, kid."

Chapter 12

• "Do you think it's made any difference?" Alex shifted the truck into third.

"She's had a few days to see the material we're studying. If she's disturbed by it, she's given no indication. I find that interesting." Geoffrey twisted to check on the boxes in the back of the truck, then turned to face front.

"Why?"

"Teddy is telekinetic. Tommy collapses things with the skill of a demolition expert, which I hope he expands to building someday. There may be another entire layer to this situation than we'd first thought."

Alex frowned, though it fit with a niggling suspicion he had.

"Since when have you had visions of the future, Alex? You're a healer. Dreux turns to stone. Kalyss sees the past. I resurrect. Teddy moves things with his mind. But," Geoffrey shook his head. "None of that is precognition. Whose gift is that?"

"You think it's Elizabeth's gift?"

Geoffrey looked at him. "Do you?"

"No." Alex shook his head with certainty and checked his mirrors. "I think knowing the future and not being able to stop it would defeat her. She needs hope to keep going, to face all she does. Those kinds of visions would discourage her, demoralize her."

"Yet, if two of the Raineses are gifted, it seems a safe bet that they all are."

"Then someone needs to take the first step. Open up and tell the truth before it's too late. I bet you think that someone should be me."

Geoffrey's lips twitched. "Definitely."

Alex shook his head and said dryly, "Keep pushing and it's your gift I'll expose first, old man."

• THE SHRIEKS OF eight excited children brought Elizabeth and Shelly running to the porch. The kids were jumping up and down as Geoffrey and Alex unloaded several large boxes from the back of Alex's truck.

Elizabeth's brows drew together. It was an extremely fancy swing set. How much had that cost? She didn't have cash in her account right now. She'd paid for the materials to replace the fence and bathrooms, but anything else would need to wait for the next phase of the project.

Catching her look, Alex set his box in the center of a large patch of grass. Stepping through the crowd, he approached her, his expression cautious. "It's a gift, Elizabeth."

She raised her brows. Some gift.

"It's from Geoffrey and me, to all the kids. It doesn't belong on that tally I know you're keeping in your head." Though they talked quietly, the kids had hushed, as if knowing there was a possibility they couldn't keep their surprise.

Already she could sense eight little hearts ready to shatter. Elizabeth tried to whisper too low for them to hear. "It's an entire play system, Alex."

Alex raised both brows. "I don't know if you've realized this, Elizabeth, but you've got enough kids here to start your own school."

Elizabeth pressed her lips together, blocking the smile pushing its way out. It sounded funny, but it was oh, so true. "I realize that, but—"

Alex leaned toward her. Their faces were barely inches apart, as they had been the last time they'd shared the porch. "They deserve a playground, Beth Ann. Let them have it."

Elizabeth looked into the hopeful, pleading eyes of the children. How could she say no? She turned a wide, helpless gaze to Alex only to see a pleading pair of eyes from him as well. He really wanted to give them this gift.

The swing set was for them and would have no impact on his relationship with her. There were never strings when it came to the kids. Which was a good thing. Geoffrey had been right. It was time to tell Alex the truth about her dreams. Whether Alex even wanted to speak to her after that, who knew? But as hard as she'd tried to stay away, nothing had worked. And keeping up a secret life on top of an overwhelming one was too much.

Alex leaned closer, his eyes a bit anxious. "Pretty please?"

She raised a teasing brow. "With chocolate syrup on top?"

He glanced down her body and back up. "With chocolate syrup wherever you want it."

Elizabeth's eyes widened and her breath caught.

"Oh, wow." Shelly stepped past them to the stairs. "A man covered in chocolate. Just how strong do you expect a woman from this family to be?"

Heat flared across Elizabeth's face and she looked at her niece in horror. "Shelly!"

Shelly grinned and looked at Alex. "For the record, I don't have a boyfriend. I like my chocolate with caramel."

Alex winked at her. "Good to know."

"Oh, good lord." Elizabeth closed her eyes, holding a hand to her brow. Until Alex kissed her and her eyes flew open.

"See, even Shelly likes the swing set." He smiled hopefully, his eyes sparkling.

"Alex . . . thank you." What else could she say? Especially when she was melting inside.

He kissed her again, wrapping his arms around her and pulling her against his chest in a full body hug. Would he still feel this way after she told him the truth?

Afraid of the answer, Elizabeth resolved to wait until tonight before she told him. Surely that short of a delay wouldn't hurt?

Elizabeth wanted nothing more than to stand there and kiss him again. Instead, she straightened her shoulders and pushed away. "I think I'd better help with the directions before pieces are lost."

• CANDLELIGHT FLICKERED OVER the tapestry-covered walls until it appeared the scenes on them were continuously moving. On one, a woman lay with her head tossed back in wanton pleasure, long wavy dark hair billowing beneath her. Her arms encircled her lover, her fingernails digging long grooves into his muscled back as he licked and nibbled her throat.

Only when the light flickered over the tapestry, exposing burgundy under-threads, did it show that small streams of blood trickled down her neck and the woman's eyes were wide open in death.

Moans filled the room with ancient chants to the Goddess of Lust. Upon sheets of satin and velvet, desperate forms twisted in a tense tangle of limbs and torsos, rubbing and stroking.

Mouths kissed and suckled. Hands grasped, demanding and needy. Hips thrust, front to back, male and female, filling and being filled. They curved around each other, linked together, flesh sweaty and flushed and straining. Nothing was taboo. All that mattered was the rhythm, the pleasure.

Their sexual heat and energy fed the woman at the center of the mass. Dugan paused beside the bed and watched his Goddess writhe beneath the pile. Only her green eyes could be seen as she pleased and was pleasured. Her beautiful eyes glowed, more vibrant than the deepest of the many gems filling her chamber. One slim hand, soft and unlined, extended from the mass of bodies and reached for him.

Dugan bowed low and kissed her fingers, briefly drawing one into his mouth and tasting the juices on it. Pulling back, he smiled into her eyes. "I have a gift for you, my Goddess. Someone with the information you seek."

Her eyes narrowed in speculation. Slowly, Maeve rose from the sea of flesh, her lithe form undulating against the bodies pressed to her, her vibrant red curls and creamy shoulders becoming more visible until only one hand with long red nails curved around Maeve's breast and blocked his view.

Maeve stroked the hand, then pushed it behind her. "Do not tease me, pet. The punishment would be worse than you could bear."

Her smoky voice was pure temptation but they both knew the threat was not a light one. She was near fully restored to her power. She did not depend on him as she had even up to a few days ago. Her appetites had grown with each feeding until he could no longer sustain her. So he'd scoured the earth, finding young, lithesome fodder no one would ever miss to feed her unrelenting desires.

Now only her thirst for vengeance waited to be quenched. As her impatience to destroy her enemies grew, so did her fury. As her strength and power expanded, Dugan became less a caregiver and more a whipping boy, willingly offering his pain to ease her disappointment. Not that his willingness reduced the pain she inflicted. What would be the point of that?

"My words are solid, Beautiful One. I have found someone who has the information."

Maeve's plump red lips curved in pleasure. "Bring my gift to me, pet."

Dugan took a few steps from the cavern then returned pushing a small, stout man before him. Maeve sat on the edge of the bed, her legs curled to the side. The bodies writhed behind her, grinding and moaning and occasionally reaching for her, attempting to draw her back. Maeve absently stroked a delicate hand that curved around her waist, parting her legs for its exploration. Pleasure spasmed across her face before she narrowed her gaze at the man.

"He's a scribe, my lady, one of Abacus's own. If any would know the answers to your questions, it would be him." Dugan shoved the scribe to his knees. His Goddess deserved respect from lesser beings. "I questioned him, but he refused to say anything."

Maeve smiled wickedly and ran her tongue over her lips. "That's because he is magically muted, my pet. Only Abacus can free his tongue. It's a safeguard against the spilling of his secrets."

Dugan froze, staring at her. He'd really thought this would be the perfect answer, that he wouldn't disappoint her once again. But studying her expression, Dugan realized she didn't appear angry with him. Instead, her eyes sparkled and her lush mouth curved in a secretive half-smile.

"All is well." Maeve pulled a velvet robe around her

and belted it loosely so that when she stepped from the bed she was exposed from one slim, shapely ankle to her glistening thigh. Trailing a manicured nail across the scribe's shoulders as she circled behind him, Maeve leaned over his back and spoke softly against his ear. "There's more than one way to learn your secrets, isn't there?"

The scribe suddenly paled, as if her knowledge surprised and terrified him. Standing in front of him again, Maeve trailed the sharp edge of her nail from his cheek to his chin, leaving a long welt in the wake of her touch, using her fingernail to prod his chin up until the scribe's eyes met hers.

"Yes, I know more than you thought." Maeve smiled, her eyes darkening with power. "Now, how do you want to share this information? Shall we try the easy way and have you give it willingly? Or would you rather die for it?"

Her green eyes sparkled with the hard edge of diamonds and her dark red hair seemed a mass of living strands. Her skin glowed with power. She was his Goddess. Dugan smiled, pride filling him at the sight of what his devotion had wrought.

For a long moment, the scribe did not respond. Dugan watched the little man's face, forcibly holding in his irritation at the man's stubborn silence.

When Maeve's brows rose, the scribe met her gaze with a small, goading smirk on his lips. Dugan grasped the hilt of his battle-axe, but Maeve held up a hand to stay him.

Maeve snarled. "Then you will die, little fool."

Dugan would have thought the man would tremble

and beg, but his smirk never slipped. Not as Maeve bent to one knee before him. Not even when she opened her mouth and allowed her incisors to lengthen. Her green eyes tilted, the pupils becoming vertical slits, like a cat's.

Dugan smiled. Maeve turned, angled the scribe's head and bit into his jugular like the first bite of a ripe, red apple. Unlike vampires, Maeve didn't need blood to survive. She just liked it.

Even with the pain, the scribe's eyes didn't fill with terror. Instead, his face settled into an expression of utter peace and contentment. Dugan relaxed infinitesimally. It was as it should be. Maeve was a Goddess worthy of reverence and worship.

But when the scribe's eyes filled with a blazing orange fire brighter than the flames of hell, Dugan knew something was wrong.

• THE MOMENT SHE'D felt his skin break against her fangs, even before the thick blood heated them from the inside, Maeve knew bliss. The salty copper was sharp and vivid on her tongue. A rush of pure joy she'd nearly forgotten.

Maeve cradled the scribe in her arms, stroking the hair at the back of his head in loving gratitude for his choice of death before dishonor. His gift granted her this pleasure, one she hadn't felt in centuries.

The scribe could have chosen to record his knowledge on special scrolls for her to read. It was a scribe's prerogative should he ever learn a secret he decided should be known. A secret too dangerous to be kept. The catch was, no scribe could be *forced* to write anything. They had to be willing.

Which left only one way to gain the answers she sought. One secret key to unlock the door to a scribe's mind. Only the oldest of those fallen knew how to find this key.

It was held safe in the very last drop of the scribe's blood.

Maeve drank long and deep, certain each draw would be the last, until finally, it was. The key was in her mind and she used it to unlock the door to his. In an overwhelming, orgasmic tide, information rushed at her, filling all the starved corners of her brain.

Formulas and sciences, art and histories, they filled her until she was full, bloated, ready to burst, though she knew she'd once held inside her more knowledge than even this.

Humans were said to use only 10 percent of their powerful minds. Such a waste. The half-breeds of Angels and humans could use up to 50 percent.

But now she felt it keenly. At the moment when her knowledge was the greatest it had been in eons, she finally realized how diminished she'd become.

Once, she had reached for the pinnacle of knowledge. Then she'd fallen. And now her brain could not hold all that she was as well as all the scribe knew. His vast knowledge could break her completely.

Desperate to gain the information she needed, Maeve entered the room behind the newly unlocked door of the scribe's mind. Like a palace with a million rooms, the scribe's mind was daunting. How did she find the one golden chest she needed? Room by room, she rummaged, throwing boxes out of her way, looking for that elusive one.

Maeve's heart strained, working inadequately despite all the blood she was consuming. The realization was slow and all the more horrible for it. She'd remembered how to free a scribe's secrets, but she'd forgotten that to do so could kill her.

It was a scribe's nature to need nothing more than knowledge. That was his sustenance. They wasted no room on desires and wants, leaving even those parts of their minds free, like the pages of a diary waiting to be filled.

Maeve's mind was nearly full, but the flow of information didn't slow. The devastating force continued until she was ready to explode. Telling her so much, but nothing she needed to know. Her fury exploded the pointless boxes around her and she shrieked.

"No! I will have my answers." With fierce determination, Maeve threw her question like a command. "Who trapped me in the tunnels?"

Like a fact-seeking missile, the command arrowed through the rooms and hallways, blasting aside boxes of irrelevant data until only one remained.

Rushed for time, knowing she only had seconds before the roar of information scrambled her brain, Maeve tossed open the lid and beheld her answer.

As though it were in slow motion, the recorded memory blossomed before her. A tree-shrouded clearing at the edge of dawn. Her barrier trapping three fallen bodies: two men and a woman. One of the men was her only son, Kai, and the other was the bastard son of Maeve's worthless human husband.

The woman wasn't important, except the bastard crawled to her and pulled her convulsing body lovingly into his arms. She would die for that alone. The image blinked and the light barrier fell. Someone's heart had stopped, and only one body lay still. No. He wasn't meant to die.

Maeve watched as the energies of her curse against the bastard disbursed into the air, awakening and freeing her from the tunnels. But Kai continued to lie still as death while the bastard and his woman moved. With the barrier down, a third man entered the picture. He turned his back on Kai and laid healing hands on the woman.

Maeve's hands clenched tight enough for her nails to draw blood from her palms. She shook, panted. They would die. Every single one of them would die.

The bastard leaned over Kai and broke the chain of Maeve's most powerful emerald, removing it from Kai's neck. Rage blurred her vision and Maeve looked to the side, and saw her enemies in clear relief.

Silas, with his long white wings and powerful heritage. And beside him, a mysterious cloaked figure whose demeanor bespoke a different heritage altogether.

It was an alliance doomed to be destroyed. Maeve vowed it.

She blinked, and the vision ended as a trap was sprung. In her fury, she almost didn't realize it. At dizzying speeds, the information overwhelming her reversed directions, moving like a tornado out of her mind, sucking parts of her with it. As swiftly as she'd gained knowledge, she was losing it. At this rate, she'd lose all of herself before she could mount a single defense.

Holding tight to the answer she'd come for before it was swept out on the receding tide of information, Maeve struggled to break the connection, but the trap deep in the scribe's mind held her. Escape was impossible. Maeve couldn't even retract her fangs.

Losing more of herself every moment, Maeve fought frantically, finally able to at least open her eyes in panic. Just in time to watch Dugan's battle-axe sing toward her.

Throwing the scribe's head from her, Maeve fell back, panting. Blood dripped from Dugan's axe, so dark a red it was almost black in the candlelight. It mocked every drop that now tasted like acid in her mouth.

The moans behind her rose, screeching in her ears, jarring her nerves. Fury rose in her breast as she stared at the beheaded scribe. His memories were vile. Disgusting.

Silas and his accomplice had *taken* from her. Centuries of her life, gone, never to be regained. They'd left her helpless and weak. She, a Goddess, reduced to nothing more than a witless pawn while her enemies had destroyed her most precious possession. Her son.

They'd killed her child, yet saved his bastard brother. Even now she could see Kai, handsome as the day she'd left him, his body limp and lifeless. She shouldn't have been gone so long. That had never been her plan. She would never have purposely left him to suffer on his own. But they'd interfered. And the one who'd vowed to guard her, had betrayed her.

Adad might be beyond her at the moment, and was

surely too powerful to confront just yet. But Silas and whoever lay beneath the cloak were going to pay for all they'd stolen from her, just as the scribe had paid for his trap. No one would violate her and escape her vengeance.

Snarling, Maeve struck at the headless body before her, her nails becoming claws as she ripped into him like a lioness on the hunt, rending and tearing, breaking and shredding. The scent of blood and raw meat filled her lungs and added to her fury.

When there was nothing left of the scribe but a head, Maeve turned her ferocity onto the lovers, shredding them all until the chamber dripped blood like wine. Then there was nothing left but Dugan.

Swiftly, he wrestled her to the sharp, rocky ground, barely able to hold her long enough to alter her passion from violence to sex.

Chapter 13

• SWEET AND CREAMY, each sip was worthy of closed eyes and a moment of reverent silence. After living alone for twelve years, Elizabeth had all the experience she needed to make the perfect cup of coffee. Yet, Alex did it better.

Within just a few days, he knew her likes and dislikes almost as well as she did. It seemed he'd studied her as hard as she'd focused on her program codes. He made her coffee and late-night snacks, and kept all the materials she needed organized and at her fingertips.

From dinner on, she worked. She could accomplish a good five or six hours before her body demanded sleep. During that time, Alex readied the kids for bed, sent them to her for hugs and kisses, then tucked them in with stories.

He was the perfect secretary, the best of babysitters. If only he didn't want more than that from her. If only she was free to give more.

Elizabeth glanced to her right, where Alex worked on his own laptop, gathering images of stained-glass, sculptures, and paintings for the library design. Once they were chosen, she could incorporate them into the alcoves marking the different sections of the library.

Alex glanced up at her.

Elizabeth looked back to her screen, but could tell he was grinning. Without thinking, she blurted, "I'm surprised we work so well together."

"Why is that?"

She couldn't resist a smile. "I figured you'd be a distraction."

She peeked at his reaction in time to see his silent chuckle. The dining room felt like the only space that existed in the world, and it grew smaller with each word spoken between the two of them.

"I can keep my hormones in check when necessary," he said in a dry tone.

Elizabeth's face heated and she turned her wide-eyed

gaze on him. "I didn't mean . . . Of course you can control yourself."

Alex leaned back in his chair and faced her. "I've been honest about what I want from you. Pushing you every time we're alone together would be counterproductive to achieving that goal."

Elizabeth looked away. After seeing how seamlessly Alex fit into their lives, her reluctance probably made no sense to him.

"I'm not saying that to make you feel bad, Elizabeth. But you've rejected me twice. I'm not in a rush to reach strike three."

"I have solid reasons for not getting involved, Alex." Could that sound any lamer?

"Solid fears, maybe."

Elizabeth stiffened in her chair, her brows lowering.

"A good reason would be if you objected to something about me, but you don't. Do you?"

She shook her head.

"There's no one else, is there?"

Again, she shook her head. But she also bit her lip and focused on the screen in front of her. If he took that as interest in someone else, maybe that would be a good thing.

At this point, she only had to tell him about dreamweaving. That's all Geoffrey had seen. She wasn't obligated to mention her father or his visions. Though Daddy had said he'd already shown one to Alex. Did Alex know what he'd seen? Or did he just think he'd had a weird night of strange dreams?

"Why are you and Geoffrey studying angels and demons, Alex?"

Alex froze. "Does it bother you?"

She looked him in the eye. "Not really. I'm just curious."

For once, he was the one at a loss for words and she found that infinitely interesting. He seemed to be searching for what to say. Elizabeth waited, breath held. She would be as open with him as he was with her. So the question was: how much did Alex trust her?

"I believe in angels, Elizabeth."

She raised her brows again. "Many people do, Alex."

He shook his head. "No, I mean 'angels walking among us'. Interventions, messages, and supernatural gifts."

Elizabeth sat back in her chair. He was serious. She kept her tone calm—cautious, controlled—and hinting at a subtext she couldn't explain just yet. "So do I. The Bible, the Koran, the Torah, they all mention angels and their work in the world. What I wonder is, what about it particularly interests *you*?"

Alex nodded at the discs, sketches of the program design, and hard drives Geoffrey had brought for her to draw images from. "As you can tell, Geoffrey's been working at this for a very long time."

"So he sparked your interest?"

Alex looked away for a moment. "More like, meeting him sparked a need for answers to questions I'd tried to forget."

"Like a crisis of faith?"

"I needed to know more about what I believed."

"You've found that in the study of angels?"

"I may never have all the answers, but I have more than I would if I did nothing."

Perhaps there was a game being played, with neither offering full disclosure, but then maybe it really was that simple for him.

Alex cocked his head and looked at her quizzically, the beginnings of a smile tugging at his lips. "What?"

"This is the side of you people rarely see. The one that competed with me for the highest grades. The one that opened a successful business. Serious Alex." She shook her head. "Who knew?"

He chuckled briefly, then sobered and sat forward, leaning toward her. "Seriously, does the subject bother you?"

"No. Why would it?"

"Some people don't like delving into religion like this."

"That isn't logical."

"Does everything have to be logical?"

"It is easier to think things through if you have the facts before you form an opinion. It's irresponsible to ignore the research."

"Do you believe faith is an opinion?"

"Faith is one of the few *feelings* I think I can trust." Elizabeth sighed.

"What about love?'

"I've never trusted love."

Her statement clicked home the last puzzle piece in his mind. A satisfied smile crossed Alex's face. "That's the real reason you refuse to have a relationship with me."

Elizabeth looked away.

"You don't trust me with your heart," he said.

"I don't distrust you. There's no reason to."

"Yet." He voiced the word dangling silently at the end of her statement. "Is it men in general then?"

Elizabeth shook her head, fighting the temptation to squirm. "No. Not really."

"Then, what? Who?"

Elizabeth took a deep breath that was shakier than she'd intended. "Me."

Alex collapsed back in his chair, appearing thoroughly confused. "Why?"

Elizabeth shook her head. The answer should be obvious. "Alex, look around you."

He frowned. "I told you. This is just a situation, not a statement about your entire future."

"I don't mean that." Elizabeth waved his words away. "But consider the situation. Ten children. No responsible parents. Alex, there hasn't been a single healthy relationship in my family since my grandparents were alive."

"And you think that's your fault?"

"No. But it is the fault of my family." When he frowned his confusion, she leaned forward to impress him with her seriousness. "Specifically the women. My father may have left, but most women eventually get over that. My mom never did. My sisters never did."

"But you have?"

Elizabeth paused. She had to tread carefully. "You could say he never really left me. I don't mourn him as much as the effect *losing* him has had on my family. And *that* effect has scarred me."

Alex scooted his chair closer to her, and leaned forward. Taking her hand in his, he met her eyes.

"Let's talk about that."

She looked at him skeptically. "Since when do guys want to talk?"

He smiled slightly and shrugged. "With the proper motivation, any guy will talk."

"And yours is?"

"You." His tone was flat, but he said so much with one word. Nothing had changed for him. She looked away and tried to stand, but his hands tightened on hers, keeping her in place. "Talk."

Looking down, Elizabeth closed her eyes and sighed. Alex leaned forward, his forehead against hers, and the band around her chest loosened. That connection made talking to him a little easier.

"What if . . ." She fell silent and had to take another deep breath. Alex held quiet and waited. "What if it's never enough?"

"It?"

"Love." The only way to get through it was to rush the words out, so she inhaled and rushed. "What if you love me; you stay with me; I love you back; we build a life together; but I'm still always scared? Scared you'll leave; you'll lose interest; you'll meet someone else, someone better?"

He shook his head, but she covered his mouth before he could speak. Looking into his eyes, Elizabeth said, "Exactly. You would assure me. You would battle all my insecurities, all my jealousies. You would be steadfast. Until the day came when you grew tired of proving yourself. Sick of trying to fill this bottomless pit with all your love, knowing it will never be enough."

His hand cupped her cheek as he vowed, "My love *will* be enough."

Oh, how she wanted to believe him. She wanted to have faith, take that leap. The effort to stand tough nearly brought her to tears. "What if . . ."

He shook his head. "No more what ifs."

She brushed her fingers over his soft lips, tempted to kiss him again. "What if you left me—"

He growled and the sound vibrated from her fingertips, up her arm, and down to the tips of her breasts. She shivered.

"What if you left me—but I didn't let you go?"

"Sounds good to me." Alex smiled.

Her lips quirked before she could pull them straight. "Right now it does, but what if you wanted to leave and I didn't let you?"

"Do you mean some kind of *Fatal Attraction* thing?" He raised an amused brow.

Elizabeth did not smile. "Yeah, sorta."

"But no rabbits?"

"No rabbits."

"Well, then." Alex brushed hair from her eyes, stared straight into them—and kissed her. There was nothing tentative, nothing gentle, and he didn't need to coax.

Elizabeth threw her arms around his shoulders and straddled Alex, squeezing her thighs around his waist, locking her ankles behind the chair. Warm hands slid up the back of her shirt, teasing the cool skin of her lower back. Elizabeth moaned and Alex thrust his tongue deep, tasting it.

His hands slid down to her thighs, and he rubbed against the denim. A frustrated groan erupted from deep in his chest and he pulled away long enough to say,

"What happened to the good ol' days when women wore skirts?"

"Self-preservation," she gasped. Elizabeth arched her back and pushed against him.

One hand curved over her ass, pressing them closer, while his other hand slid under her shirt to cup one breast.

Elizabeth buried both hands in his thick hair and began to rock against him, hard and steady. Her toes curled inside her shoes. Her thighs bunched, tight as bricks. To her shock, she heard herself gasp and moan, high-pitched and needy.

Instead of muting her, Alex moved down her throat, licking and sucking and nipping at the skin of her neck. Apparently the fact that she sounded like a porn star didn't bother him a bit. If anything, when he thrust up, the ridge of his cock was harder than before.

Breath stuttered out of her and she moaned again, soft and guaranteed to rev his engine even more. "Alex?"

"No," he growled in a low voice against her throat. "We can't just be friends."

She laughed and pushed against his chest. "Neither are we christening the table my grandfather built."

"Oh, come on." He smiled up at her. "Every 'ship needs a proper inauguration before its maiden voyage."

"Ugh." She laughed and slapped his arm at his relationship analogy. "As long as the, 'ship doesn't go back to the boat yard, I'm happy."

He sounded happy. And she felt happy. But losing him would hurt worse later. Elizabeth's smile died and she buried her nose against his neck, inhaling his scent for a lifetime of memories. "It's time for you to leave, Alex. Go home, go to bed, and get some sleep."

"I like holding you in real life much more than in my dreams."

"Yeah." She stared at the wall behind him. "This *is* better.'

He sighed. "But dreams are all I have for tonight, huh? At least I'll see you in them."

"Yes. You will see me." She sounded almost sad as she said it. Elizabeth pulled back and kissed him gently. "Sweet dreams."

He arched a brow. "With you in them, they'd have to be."

Her smile wobbled. "Unfortunately, Alex, that's not always a guarantee."

• ELIZABETH SHUT THE steel door and looked around the empty stone cavern. It wasn't always so bare. It actually housed some of her most powerful memories, but tonight she needed to make everything as easy on Alex as possible and that meant waiting until he was in the room before pressing play.

He wouldn't understand at first. There was no way to explain it in words, it had to be shown. Alex would think he was dreaming, then something would click and he would *know.* How long it took for that to happen, she had no clue.

There were three steel doors in this cavern. The one she'd entered through, the one connected to the next memory she would show him, and one smaller door she prayed he'd never notice. The third door rested in a small, curved alcove. The steel was old, scratched, and worn.

He may hate her after tonight, but then, that could be a good thing. She couldn't seem to make the break by herself. If he hated her, maybe it would be easier. Just what did she wish for? To end it or to begin it? Her heart and mind had battled over that question for years.

She summoned Alex and he appeared, standing in the center of the empty room and glancing around. "Where are we?"

Elizabeth held out her hands to indicate the room around them. "The boatyard."

"Damn it, Elizabeth." He scowled and stalked toward her. "When will we get past this?"

"Tonight," she said definitively.

He stopped and studied her expression.

"We're about to test how seaworthy our 'ship really is." Elizabeth bit her lip.

Alex tilted his head, noting her apprehension. "And how do you propose we do that?"

"It's time to spill secrets."

His eyes narrowed.

Elizabeth took a deep breath. "My secrets, specifically."

He raised a brow. "Then mine next?"

Elizabeth smiled. "You've lived in Spokane all your life. You aren't married, or otherwise attached. Your parents are traveling the United States, one carving wood and one selling it online. You have one best friend and have been by her side forever, come what may. You are the most honorable, *normal* man I can imagine. I think we'll survive any secrets you have."

He looked away, shaking his head. "One can only hope."

It was Elizabeth's turn to look away. No one thought their life was boringly normal. Every story was unique, in and of itself. It was part of the beauty of life—when it wasn't potentially devastating like Elizabeth's.

"I'll start at the beginning. That's really the best place."

Alex joined her and they watched as rock disappeared and became old walls lined with lockers and occasional doors. Straight ahead, a high school–aged Beth Ann struggled to arrange her books in her locker before everything fell out.

"I remember your rejection for prom, Elizabeth. There's nothing secret here." Alex sighed.

"Just watch, Alex. You might see something you don't expect."

From their left, eighteen-year-old Alex appeared. Tall, dark haired, and wearing a black leather jacket, with gold, black, and orange LC letters and patches for basketball and track, he was the guy every girl wanted.

"Not *every* girl," Alex grumbled.

Elizabeth rolled her eyes. "Just keep watching."

High school Alex walked up behind Beth Ann, who was studiously pretending she hadn't seen him. They were friends in class, but contact between them always tied her stomach in knots. The day had been hard enough, listening as other girls talked about their dates and their dresses and their appointments with the hairdresser. It was only a *dance*. Why did they have to act like it was the most important thing ever? Graduation was important. This was just a party.

Or so she'd worked all day to convince herself. She didn't have a date. She didn't have a dress. But none of it would matter because soon she would be gone and the entire prom would be a distant memory.

"Beth Ann?"

She froze a moment, then shut her locker door and lifted her backpack over one shoulder. "Hi, Alex."

He grinned that lopsided grin that always made her melt inside.

"It does?"

"Shut up, Alex. This is the closest thing to a date we've ever had."

"Then I should at least get to hold your hand."

Elizabeth shook her head. She should have known better than to trust him to be serious. Sighing, she held her hand out and let him take it. But once his grip surrounded her fingers, she realized he was anxious.

"Is that surprising?" He raised a brow.

Elizabeth watched his face in the dim light, wondering how long it would take for him to understand what was happening.

He frowned and followed her gaze back to the memory.

"Did you finish that CWA assignment?"

Beth Ann grinned. "Of course. Can't graduate without passing Current World Affairs."

He laughed. "It's probably going to piss some people off when we blow the curve."

She shrugged. "Not my problem. I researched that paper for months."

Alex leaned against the lockers and his smile softened. "Yeah, that's what I've always liked about you. More prepared than a Girl Scout."

"Exactly what I always hoped you'd notice about me," Beth Ann said with a dry tone. Then she blushed because it came out more flirtatious than she'd intended.

Alex smiled, looked down to the floor, then back at her. "Actually, I noticed a lot more than that."

She raised a brow, trying and failing to control her grin. "I'm afraid to ask."

He laughed, then sobered again. "So what are your plans for the night? I think you're the only one I haven't heard talk about dresses and makeup."

"My plans include a hot bath, funny movies, and eating chips." Beth Ann's smile died. "I'm not going to the prom."

"Well." Alex awkwardly pulled two tickets from his pocket and held them up between them. "Would you go to prom with me, Beth Ann?"

Her expression froze a bit. "Did your date dump you?"

His eyes widened. "No. I, uh, didn't have one."

"I figured you were going with Kalyss."

"Oh, no. She's going with Sam. They've been dating for a while now."

"Oh." She looked at her shoes, more tempted than she'd ever been in her life. Prom with Alex Foster. Getting dressed up, feeling girly. Dancing in his arms, her cheek against his. Feeling warm and cared for.

She wanted a night with him. A date. A dance. If she had to trade all her future dreams to have one date with

Prince Charming as everyone called him, it would be worth it.

"Did you say 'oh' or 'no'?" Alex leaned closer, his expression confused and anxious.

Beth Ann looked into his eyes and shook her head. "No."

Alex turned pale. "What?"

Beth Ann shook her head again. "It'll never happen."

Before Alex could respond or try to change her mind, Beth Ann briskly walked away, her head held up, but her eyes blinded with tears. Behind her, Alex leaned against the lockers, his shoulders slumping. As the outside door closed behind Beth Ann, he slammed his head against the lockers.

"Great." Alex leaned his head against the wall behind them. "I so needed to see that again."

"I'm sorry, Alex." Elizabeth sighed. The scene changed, Alex was gone and Beth Ann had returned. Only the area where she stood was lit with a small glow. On the floor in front of her locker was a clear plastic corsage box with a pale pink orchid.

"I had it tucked in my jacket." Alex watched Beth Ann, his eyes full of memories. "I bought it for you, so I wanted you to have it."

Beth Ann knelt beside the box and carefully lifted it in both hands. Tears filled her eyes as she opened the lid and sniffed, inhaling the sweet scent of the flower. Pulling back, she stroked each petal with a tender finger and whispered to it.

"I wanted to say yes, Alex. Today. Tonight. Tomorrow." Beth Ann inhaled raggedly and her voice became strained and shaky. *"Always."*

Always to hold him, kiss him, love him. She wanted that. No, she yearned to have that with him.

Alex squeezed Elizabeth's hand. "Hey, I was game."

Elizabeth stroked her thumb against his skin. He was game now, but that could very well change in the next five minutes. He didn't know the whole story yet.

"Still right here, lady."

"Trust me, Alex. I always know where to find you."

Beth Ann slowly closed the box. "I had to say no. It can't be." Closing her eyes, Beth Ann leaned her head back and continued. "I'm leaving. I can't stay. I've made so many plans—college, jobs, scholarships. This may be the only opportunity I'll ever have to leave. I have to do this, for me. I need to be someone. If I stay, it may never happen.

"Just like Mom. I'll stay here, marry too young, have too many kids, and never recover when it all falls apart. I can't just give up on everything I've worked for. I have to do this by myself. I'm sorry." Beth Ann hugged the box to her chest and a few tears escaped to drip down her face.

Alex squeezed Elizabeth's hand again. "Never say never."

"You understand now?"

He frowned, his brows drawn together. "Yeah, I do."

He wasn't ready to fully get it, she could tell. But he would, very soon.

Chapter 14

◈

• THE SCENE IN front of them changed, and they stood inside Mary Beth's bedroom. Elizabeth looked around at the simple blue bedspread and the knickknacks scattered across the vanity.

Slowly, hesitantly, she faced the door of the bedroom, waiting for the approaching footsteps to reveal the person they belonged to. Nerves cramped her stomach and bile rose to the back of her throat. Elizabeth had known this would be tough, but she'd had no idea it would be this hard.

Alex frowned and looked around. This room held no meaning for him, no memory other than a quick peek as he walked down the upstairs hall. Judging by Elizabeth's tight grip on his hand, though, there was more here than he'd ever suspected. His focus sharpened, taking in everything he saw and heard.

Elizabeth sucked in a breath as she saw her mother enter the room. A slim, beautiful woman in the prime of her life, Mary Beth's makeup was done to perfection, her hair big and full of ringlets, as if declaring the eighties weren't over no matter what the calendar said. But tight blue jeans and a bosom-hugging shirt fit any era, and she filled them well.

"Beth Ann Raines, come on. Quit moping. I have a

surprise for you." Mary Beth posed at the end of the bed, close to the closet.

"Mom." Beth Ann entered the room, glasses firmly on her face, her hair pulled back, and her jeans and T-shirt showing her complete lack of interest in anything fashionable. "It's been a long day. I'm tired and just want to go lie down."

"You can't do that, Beth Ann. Even I know what day this is."

Elizabeth's eyes met Alex's, unable to hide her fear. She'd never been so vulnerable, her heart laid open before someone in this way. Gently pulling her hand free, Elizabeth crossed her arms and backed away. She needed distance to watch how he handled the rest of what she was showing him.

"Okay. I'll let you go, but only for now," he whispered.

"It doesn't matter, Mama." Beth Ann leaned against the door frame, her fingers hooked in her belt. "I'm not going to prom."

Mary Beth's head tilted. "Didn't the right boy ask you to go?"

The shadow of a smile briefly graced Beth Ann's lips. "Actually, the perfect guy asked me. But I said no."

"Why the hell would you do that?" Mary Beth's hands landed on her hips, then she shook her head. "Never mind. You'll get ready to go and surprise him."

Beth Ann wandered over to the vanity. A large, round mirror reflected her sad face back to her. "There's no point, Mama. I'm heading off to the University of Washington as soon as graduation is over."

"But maybe if you really like this guy, you can stay,

go somewhere closer. Like Eastern. Then you could live at home and not have to work so hard. I can help you out." Mary Beth looked so earnest, but Beth Ann had known then that the kind offer would have soured very quickly.

Beth Ann smiled sweetly and stuck to her decision. "I've gotta leave sometime, Mama."

Mary Beth pursed her lips, then nodded. "Fine. But you're going to prom. It's the last thing I'll ask you to do for me. Promise."

Beth Ann refrained from rolling her eyes, but Elizabeth didn't hold back.

Alex chuckled.

Beth Ann looked at her mother's grinning face and sighed. "I don't have a dress."

Mary Beth smiled wickedly. "Take a look." Vibrating with excitement, Mary Beth ripped open the closet door and removed a dress from the hook. Swirling around and holding the dress against her, she danced with all the grace of a fairy princess. "Well, what do you think?"

Beth Ann grinned and leaned against the vanity. "Ginger Rogers had nothing on you."

Mary Beth smiled at the compliment. "I *meant* about the dress."

Beth Ann looked at the heart-shaped satin bodice, the thin spaghetti straps, and the slightly fuller, calf-length satin skirt. A layer of ice-pink chiffon split over the skirt, adding a touch of delicacy. It floated, swishing like the dresses Beth Ann had dreamed of when she was little. "It's *pink.*"

Her mother gave her a look. Beth Ann grinned, relenting. "It's a pretty pink. How did you get it?"

Mary Beth raised a mysterious brow. "I have my ways. Now, sit. Let me do your hair and nails. We only have a few hours and you still have to track down your date."

"I'm not sure I should bother him, Mama. He probably has another date by now. I'll just go alone." Beth Ann tried not to wince as her mother dragged a brush through her hair. The tears prickling her eyes were more from the wounded expression in Alex's eyes. Her reasons for her rejection still stood, but she'd hated causing that crushed look.

"If he waited until this late to ask you, chances are he won't." Mary Beth met Beth Ann's eyes in the mirror, her own serious and a little sad. "It's not better to be alone, Beth Ann, despite what you may think. It's lonely and painful. I would never wish that for you."

Beth Ann lowered her eyes and meekly submitted as her mom twisted her hair up in a French knot, leaving the ends to curl into ringlets. She left two tendrils to hang in curls on either side of Beth Ann's face. By the time Beth Ann's makeup and nails were done, it was getting late.

She rushed from the room and grabbed the corsage Alex had left by her locker after her rejection. Hurrying into the dress, she let her mother pin the delicate orchid into place. Beth Ann Raines was ready for the prom.

The heels gave her height and the classic hairstyle matched the delicate beauty of the dress, making her look more elegant than she'd ever thought possible. After looking in her mom's full-length mirror, Beth Ann felt like dancing around the room and letting the dress swirl around her calves. So she did.

Alex reached out and yanked Elizabeth into his arms

and squeezed her around the waist. He breathed against her ear and she shivered. "You were so beautiful."

"Now for some pictures." Mary Beth rushed to the vanity drawer and pulled out her camera.

"Mom!" Beth Ann complained. "You hid that on purpose!"

"Of course I did. Or you would've run a long time ago." Mary Beth smirked, her eyes sparkling.

"Fine." Beth Ann smiled, pretending to feel put out. "But you have to hurry or I'll be late."

At her mom's insistence, Beth Ann twirled for the camera, trying not to be blinded by the flash. Finally, she paused, her eyes sparkling and her mouth in the widest smile she'd ever had. Quickly, her mother snapped one final picture before the camera ran out of film.

"Oh, baby, Alex is going to think you're a princess."

Looking over her shoulder at him now, Elizabeth could only think her mother had been right. Judging by his furrowed brow, he was still a little confused, but then, he didn't know how the night had ended. He only knew she'd never shown up for prom.

"Why didn't I see you?" he whispered against her ear.

"You'll see." Much more than he could imagine.

"You'd be surprised at what I can imagine, Elizabeth. I know your secret."

"Only one of them, Alex."

Beth Ann stood straight and stared at her mom, her mouth dropping open in surprise. "How do you know his name is Alex?"

Her mom laughed. "What, you think I've never saw his pictures under the *Highlander* posters? Please, that's an old trick."

Beth Ann didn't know if she should be outraged at the invasion of her privacy, or horrified at her transparency. Elizabeth knew to be unsurprised at either, but embarrassed by both. Alex chuckled against her ear as a shocked Beth Ann asked, "How long have you known?"

Mary Beth arched her brows in a superior expression. "Dallas trained me well to pay close attention, honey. I knew your freshman year."

Alex's arms tensed and when she looked at him, his gaze was wistful, as if aching for all the time they'd missed. Tears blurred her vision, knowing exactly how that ache felt. But she'd made the best choice for them, then. Even the distance time brought couldn't convince her otherwise.

"Mary Beth!" A loud male voice boomed from the hallway, heavy steps approaching the bedroom.

Elizabeth flinched, but didn't turn. Her fingers wrapped around Alex's arms and her nails dug into his skin. She already knew what was coming. Instead, her eyes stayed focused on Alex, watching closely to see every thought that crossed his face. As much as she dreaded the memory, she was here to give Alex answers.

• ALEX FELT HER gaze slam into him, hard and focused. So far, the memory had been sweet. Poignant. But the last time Kalyss had produced a vision as vivid as this dream, it hadn't been a sweet one. And judging by Elizabeth's tense inspection of his face, this could be just as devastating.

But didn't she understand? He'd share every nightmare if she'd let him. Alex held his gaze steady, though his heart beat faster with each step coming from the hallway. When the man appeared, anyone expecting someone bigger would have been disappointed. He wasn't ugly, but his eyes held enough anger and pure meanness that Alex knew not to dismiss him.

"Grady!" Mary Beth faced the man with a smile on her face, though the openness she'd shared with her daughter only moments before was now slammed closed. Her light blue gaze darkened and fine lines appeared at the corners of her eyes and mouth. "I wondered when you'd get home."

Beth Ann froze in the middle of the room, looking like she wanted to just disappear.

Grady's eyes lit on Beth Ann with a gaze that still had the power to make Elizabeth shiver. Alex hugged her tighter, leaning down to rub his cheek against hers in comfort.

"Wow, Beth Ann." Grady licked his already wet lips. "I didn't know you owned anything so pretty."

Mary Beth stepped in front of her daughter, putting her hands on her waist so her chest pushed out. "I bought it for her prom."

Grady's eyes narrowed and the anger was back as he glanced at Mary Beth for a split second before focusing on Beth Ann's legs. "So, that's why there's a couple hundred missing from my wallet."

Beth Ann flinched, her worried gaze flying between her mother and Grady. She'd never felt comfortable with him. He hadn't done anything overt, however, so she'd just ignored him. But she knew the look in his eyes. She'd seen it before, directed at her mother, but now, with it focused on her, she was scared.

Alex heard her thoughts and *felt* her feelings, the bile at the back of her throat, the cramp of her empty stomach. But at the same time, he felt his *own* feelings, the tenseness in his muscles, the preparation to attack and defend the women.

But he knew nothing could change the past. The moment was lived, then gone, never to be regained. This was about the woman he held in his arms. Her pain. Not his anger. She'd said her father's absence had left scars. This, he realized, was one of them. He just needed to understand how to heal it.

Mary Beth lost her smile at Grady's accusation. She raised a cool brow. "Missing? I don't think so. Consider it rent."

"Since when do I pay rent?" He laughed, short and nasty, then grabbed his crotch. "Besides with this."

"Since you started fucking Leslie, you gross son of a bitch." Mary Beth took her daughter's hand and began easing her closer to the door. Unfortunately, Grady still blocked it.

Grady shifted, keeping Mary Beth in front of him. "You heard about that, huh?"

Mary Beth rolled her eyes. "Who didn't hear?"

"Gotta love a woman who moans like that." Grady grinned, mean and nasty. Then he raised his voice to a high-pitched whine. "*Quiet, Grady. We'll wake the kids, Grady.* At least Leslie isn't afraid of passion. Who wouldn't be all over that?"

Mary Beth raised her chin. "Fine, then. Get the hell out and go climb all over *that*."

Her emphasis on *that,* unlike his, was full of disgust. Grady recognized it and snarled. At that moment, the women had almost reached the door. Grady finally realized what they were doing. "I'd rather be all over *this*."

Quick as an adder, he reached around Mary Beth, grabbed Beth Ann's wrist, and pulled her out from behind her mother. Unsteady in her heels, Beth Ann stumbled toward him and he flipped her around, his free fist going into her hair. He released her wrist to slide an arm around her waist. With the extra inches from her heels, she and Grady were nearly matched in height. Grady backed away, his eyes bright with unholy glee at the fury on Mary Beth's face.

Beth Ann whimpered and Alex barely restrained himself from barreling into images that couldn't be hurt by him, all in the name of saving a woman who'd obviously saved herself long ago. Alex focused on Elizabeth, unable to erase the grimness from his face, but trying his best to express a calm acceptance. But she wasn't looking at him anymore. Her gaze had been helplessly drawn back to the memory playing before them.

Alex returned his gaze to the terrified girl in the ice-pink dress. Elizabeth had been afraid of him seeing this. Afraid of him knowing the depths her family had sunk to. But her mother had protected her. Had loved and cared for her. Did she consider that when she was embarrassed?

Mary Beth clenched her fists in preparation to attack. "You let her go. Now," she snarled.

Beth Ann tried to escape, but Grady tugged her hair, forcing her to be still. He pushed his nose into it, sniffing. His eyes, small and evil, stayed on Mary Beth. Beth Ann's eyes were wide, her chest heaving as she struggled for breath. Her hands scratched at the arm around her waist, trying to make him release her.

"Well, you think Leslie is a little too *used*. But—" He ran a hand down the front of Beth Ann's dress, stopping over one breast and giving it a squeeze. Beth gave a high-pitched cry of distress. "I bet this little thing is the freshest piece around."

Alex held in a low growl, but there was no way he could hide his anger from Elizabeth. Beth Ann quit straining against Grady's arm, and planted the sharp heel of her shoe against his foot. The spike broke against the steel toe of his boot, but Grady's surprise loosened his hold. Beth Ann's elbow to his side gained her even more freedom.

Alex grinned. "Good girl."

Unfortunately, she stumbled on her broken heel as she brought it down. Grady grabbed for her, but Mary Beth launched herself at him, her nails shredding his face, her knee ramming hard into his crotch.

Elizabeth jumped, huddling into Alex.

Beth Ann fell, her ankle twisting as she went down. She screamed. The tide of the battle had turned. Grady had hit back and knocked her mom into the vanity. Gasping, Beth Ann looked around her mom's bed, to the phone on the nightstand. They needed help, fast. Carefully, she slid around the edge of the bed, toward the phone, her hand stretching for it.

At her movement, Grady glanced over. Seeing her reach for the phone, he knocked Mary Beth to the side and ran toward Beth Ann. Her mom grabbed him, pulled one arm back, but he swung with the other and Mary Beth's eyes rolled back in her head.

Elizabeth gasped as her mother slowly fell. Tight as he held her, Alex felt every tremor.

Grady slammed his fist into her mom's face again and twisted back to Beth Ann. She turned to face him, the phone in her hand. Grady circled the end of the bed and stared down at her. His fists were clenched tight, scraped and bloodied, though she knew the blood wasn't all his.

"911, what's your emergency?"

"Help—"

Grady rushed her and she turned away, shielding the phone. He pulled her by the hair, flipped her over, and stretched out over her body. Releasing her hair, one hand wrapped around her neck, squeezing, and the other hand clicked the phone off. "Not so fast, precious. We'll have our fun long before they get here."

His free hand roughly dug under her skirts, grabbing the waistband of her pantyhose and underwear and pulling, his fingernails leaving welts on her thighs. Beth Ann struggled, gasping for air as he squeezed harder. She dug her fingernails into his wrist and grabbed blindly behind her, searching for the statue that had fallen when she grabbed the phone.

Just before she passed out, Beth Ann swung. The arch of the stone angel's wings slammed into the back of Grady's head and he slumped over, unconscious. His weight crushed the air out of her lungs and sent Beth Ann reeling into blackness right after him.

The entire room turned black for a moment, then brightened again as Beth Ann's eyes struggled open. Grady still lay over her, unmoving and barely breathing. She shoved him off her, struggling free from the small space between the bed and the wall. Tears had soaked her face by the time she was free.

"Mom?" Beth Ann sobbed, crawling closer until she could lean over Mary Beth. Her mom's eyes were swollen shut and cuts from Grady's ring marked her face. Her lip was split and her nose was broken. Beth Ann brushed hair away from Mary Beth's injuries, her hands shaking but gentle. "Mommy?"

Mary Beth coughed, slowly coming round. Beth Ann helped her sit up so she wouldn't choke. Using the hem of her dress to help staunch the flow of blood from her mom's broken nose, Beth Ann shook her head. All this over sex and money. Hurt pride and a prom dress. Still crying, she said, "I think you were wrong, Mom. It really is better to be alone."

Her mom blinked, trying to open her eyes. When she couldn't, she turned her head to the side and lay limp.

Alex sighed. "I'm so sorry, sweetheart. I wish I'd been there for you that night."

"Don't worry, Alex. You were. Later."

He frowned, confused, before turning to watch mother and daughter. "She fought hard for you."

Elizabeth sighed and wiped at her cheeks. "I never doubted that she loved me."

"Then what did you doubt?" Because there *was* something. It was in her tone, her expression, every time she thought of her mother. And he was beginning to believe it colored her actions in more areas of her life than even Elizabeth realized.

Elizabeth shook her head. "This isn't about my mother, Alex. Pay attention."

"Trust me, honey. Nothing escapes me here. Where were your brother and sisters?"

"Bobby and Felicia were at a friend's. Dallas was with Shelly's dad, trying to get him to spend time with his baby."

"He didn't want to?"

"By then, Shelly was three and the novelty had worn off." Elizabeth shook her head. "Dallas got home as the paramedics were taking Mom out. She's really squeamish about blood and hospitals, so she let me go with Mom while she stayed here.

"I followed the ambulance in Mom's car, filled out the forms, gave a statement to the police, and sat in the ER for several hours before driving her home."

The room changed to show Beth Ann tucking her mother into bed, leaving a glass of water and her pain pills within easy reach. Beth Ann glanced at the clock. Prom was almost over. Not that she could have gone. Her dress was ruined.

As she stepped away from the bed, Mary Beth reached out and caught her wrist. For a second, her mother stiffened in pain, but she fought through it and peeled open one of her eyes. "I remember what you said, Bethy. It's not better to be alone. You just have to choose better than I have."

Beth Ann frowned. "How can you still believe that? Mom, Grady almost raped me. Almost killed us."

"I know it was bad, Beth." Mary Beth's eyes closed and her head relaxed against the pillow. "But you'll see. When it's right, all the bad stuff just fades away."

Beth Ann choked back the words she wanted to

scream. Her mom was drugged, ready to sleep off the events of the night. She was in pain and deserved a few hours to dream. The problem was, when she woke up, nothing would have changed.

"I'll show you." Mary Beth patted her hand, her eyes closed. "Next time, I'll show you."

Beth Ann's eyes filled with tears as she backed away, quietly shutting her mom's door. Shaking her head in refusal of her mom's plans, she tiptoed to her room and stared into her mirror. Blood soaked the pink dress, staining it beyond repair. Her mom wouldn't be able to return it. Shedding the blood-smeared dress, Beth Ann pulled out a duffel bag and filled it only with absolute necessities.

No way in hell would she stick around for her mother to show her "next time". Within minutes, Beth Ann was packed. She stole into the twins' room and kissed each of them on the cheek, then silently made her way downstairs. Dallas was there, walking a fussy Shelly. The little girl had laid her head on Dallas's shoulder and, her sleepy eyes blinking, cried in a weak, miserable voice.

"Going somewhere?"

Beth Ann looked at her solitary bag, knowing it didn't look like much. By the time they knew she was gone for good, she'd be too far away for them to drag her back. "Yeah."

Dallas shrugged. "Have fun."

Beth Ann paused, her hand on the doorknob, and smiled slightly. "Thanks."

Chapter 15

◆

• THE IMAGES DISSIPATED, and like a theater when the credits have rolled, the room brightened. Alex's hold loosened and Elizabeth forced herself to pull away completely so she could face him. Bile still sat at the back of her throat and nausea twisted her stomach. Elizabeth pushed hair from her eyes with shaking hands.

Why had she done this? To show him her dreams, yes, but why start with the worst, most brutally disturbing of all her memories? She should have started at a different time altogether. Then she wouldn't have had to face this again. It could have remained a memory locked away on an endless loop deep in her subconscious, but easily ignored.

"You were coming to me." Alex leaned against the wall and slid his hands into his front pockets. "I'm sorry you didn't make it."

Elizabeth took a deep breath and hugged herself, already missing the caring support he'd given her. "Me, too."

Tension eased from his shoulders. "You told me it wasn't my fault, but this explains so much. Why you left. Why you stayed away. Why you said no."

Elizabeth frowned. He didn't seem to see the deeper meaning. He was talking as if they were still standing in her dining room, not here, surrounded by stone walls. "What do you think it explains, Alex?"

"That you're afraid I'm just like Grady or any number of other guys your mom and sister have dated. Okay at first, but suddenly a monster."

Elizabeth swallowed, but returned his gaze steadily. "Actually, as many fears as I have, that's never been one of them."

"But you don't trust yourself enough to *know*, beyond a doubt, either."

She blinked and looked away, her lips twisting ruefully at his insight. "I'm sorry. I wish I could be different."

"I don't. I like you as you are."

Elizabeth returned her gaze to him. "Don't you notice anything strange here?"

He shrugged. "You showed me a very vivid, painful memory."

"While we're sleeping." Elizabeth narrowed her gaze. Why wasn't he reacting? Why wasn't he freaking out? Didn't he understand what she'd done?

Alex's lips quirked. Withdrawing his hands from his pockets, he took hold of hers and pulled her closer. "Of course I understand. You have a gift similar to the one Kalyss has. She can see someone's memories and show them to others, very similar to what you just did. Only you do it in dreams."

Elizabeth blinked. "Kalyss sees memories?"

He smiled. "Yeah. And—"

Elizabeth shook her head. "This isn't all of it, Alex. I have more to show you, because I still think you're missing the bigger picture."

He shook his head. "Elizabeth—"

She turned and headed for the second door, ready to move him to the next memory. As she reached for the latch, his hand on her shoulder stopped her. "Elizabeth, what's behind the other door?"

The third door. The one she had desperately needed him to miss. Closing her eyes and bowing her head, she said, "Nothing anymore."

"Then why is it there?"

"It was once used."

"Who tried to escape?"

Opening her eyes, Elizabeth turned and leaned back against the door. He was too relentless to simply let it go. She'd have to tell him. Have to explain. "Someone I let go."

Alex tilted his head, and stared straight to the heart of her soul. Then his eyes widened and he looked at the door. "Grady."

"He woke up in the hospital the next day."

Alex strode to the third door, touched the frantic grooves of a man digging to escape. He swallowed and looked back and Elizabeth had never felt sicker in her life. There was fear in the back of his eyes. A dawning realization. "But until then, he was here."

"I let him go, Alex. As soon as I realized what I'd done."

Alex opened the door and looked at the solitary cot with dingy blankets. The room was bare of all but the scrapes Grady had made. "There were no satin sheets to make *him* want to stay."

Elizabeth swallowed and squeezed her eyes shut. "I tried to warn you."

Alex swung back, staring at her with betrayed, furious

eyes. "And from that one high school memory, I was supposed to understand *this*? How the *hell* could I do that?"

She watched him, hurting. She had no defense, no words to say to make it better. She'd endangered him. Nearly killed Grady. And he still didn't know—

Elizabeth's eyes flew wide as Alex moved toward her. "What, Elizabeth? What do I still not know?"

He angled her chin up so she couldn't look away. Then he looked behind her, at the door she leaned against.

"No." She couldn't show him now. Not like this.

Alex met her gaze again, his eyes hard and cold. "Open the door. Show me the rest. Show me everything."

She laughed bitterly. "That's what you wanted, right? Everything."

"Be careful what I wish for, right?"

Elizabeth swallowed. "Exactly."

Alex relaxed, releasing her chin. "Open the door."

Elizabeth looked down as she grabbed the latch. How ironic to have relived the last conversation she'd had with Mary Beth that night. About whether or not it was better to be alone. She'd finally begun to agree with her mom, far too late.

"Why would you agree *now*?" Alex all but growled in her ear.

"Because I finally realized how much those conversations affected my actions for the last twelve years."

"Yeah." Alex prodded her through the doorway. "Talks with our parents can do that."

"I really should have thought about that before letting it control me."

He sighed. "Sometimes, remembering a conversation with your parent is the best thing you can do."

Elizabeth looked back, but he prodded her further.

"No more secrets, Elizabeth. It's time to spill them all."

Then that's what she'd give him. No more secrets, no lies, no cover-ups. No delays and no hesitations. It was time to just jump in.

• BETH ANN RAINES couldn't lie to herself, though she'd tried to all day. Now, sitting in front of Spokane Falls Community College watching prom-goers emerge into the dark night, she knew she'd barely escaped. Everything she needed was in the duffel bag in the backseat, her clothes, the money she'd been saving, and a few personal items she hadn't wanted to leave. Not much, but it was all she'd need for a while.

A new wave of partygoers passed through the doors, the light from above them bathing their faces. Beth Ann tightened her grip on the steering wheel, dried blood caked in each crack of her knuckles. No matter how much she'd scrubbed, it would stain her skin and under her fingernails until she could soak in a tub.

She searched the faces of each tuxedo-clad guy as he exited the double doors. It was a strange compulsion, one she'd tried to ignore. She wouldn't talk to him again, but in her own way, this was good-bye for both of them.

Alexander Michael Foster. She'd sat in front of or beside him in most of their classes for the past four years. They'd talked and laughed, been paired together for projects, yet she'd never told him how she felt. Not even when she'd caught a few glances from him that said he might feel the same.

But when he'd asked her to the prom, though she'd

been tempted, though she'd tried to convince herself it would be okay, that nothing would change if she gave in just this once, she'd pulled herself from the brink and told him no. She'd told him it would *never* happen.

It had probably seemed like the harshest of rejections, but she hadn't meant it that way. It didn't matter now, though. He'd never know the regret she felt.

The door opened again and in the midst of another rush of exiting seniors, there was Alex. Beside him stood Kalyss and Sam, her midnight-blue dress vivid against the black of their suits. With a wide smile and a happy laugh, Kalyss threw her arms around Alex and gave him a swift hug. Sam smiled and pulled her away, waving good-bye to Alex and tugging Kalyss after him.

Alex grinned until he turned away. As he walked toward the parked cars, shadows chased away his smile. Every few steps someone would call out his name and he'd wave his hand without turning around, acknowledging them, but remaining alone. She'd done that to him. She'd put those shadows there. And there was nothing she could do to take them away.

• BETH ANN HUGGED her knees to her chest and watched her mother's blood sluice down the hotel shower drain. She wanted to cry and let the steaming water wash the tears from her face, but her eyes were so dry they burned. She wanted to scream, but Beth Ann was far too controlled for that.

Less than twenty-four hours ago, her most heart-wrenching problem had been telling Alex she wouldn't go to the prom with him.

Just ten hours ago, her mother had fixed her hair and makeup for a prom date she'd already turned down, but something about those magical moments in her mother's room had made it seem possible that Alex would still accept her.

Now hatred and violence colored what should have been the best memory of her life. Instead of spending hours dancing in the arms of the boy she'd crushed on throughout her high school career, she'd sat next to her mother's bed in the emergency room.

Fifteen minutes could change a person's life forever. But it wasn't always a man that brought destruction.

Next time it will be better. You'll see, Bethy. How could her mother say the words with such honest sincerity? How could she have that kind of faith?

No. Beth Ann would not see. She refused to stick around long enough to see. She had escaped. She'd run all the way across Washington, away from her mother's delusions that the perfect love was just waiting around the corner to fix all of life's little disappointments. And she wouldn't go back. She would never return to *that*.

The last of the blood trickled away and Beth Ann soaped up one more time, just to make sure it was gone, wishing she could feel clean again. She eventually left the shower and dressed, leaning against the sink counter as she dragged a brush through her wet hair. Alex would have loved the chiffon-and-silk prom dress with its sexy spaghetti straps. Or, at least, she imagined he would have.

How would he have reacted if he'd seen her covered in her mother's blood? Angry. Ready to defend her. Protective. Nurturing. He was just that kind of guy.

"Damn straight," Alex muttered.

But then, he was young. In a few more years how would he be? Like Grady? She hoped not, of course. But so did her mother and older sister, every time they entered a new relationship. *This one will be different. This one will be everything I'm looking for. This one will fulfill all my dreams.*

"I knew you thought that."

"Twelve years ago, I guess. But I've learned better over time."

Beth Ann set down the brush and limped to the double bed she'd spend the weekend in.

Noises from outside penetrated the thin walls. There was so little protection. The room felt like a tent with tin locks and a rubber dead bolt, when what she wanted most was a fortress complete with a spiked gate and deadly moat to keep away the predators.

Much as she'd hated living surrounded by other people, she'd felt safer than she did here, alone. Crawling under her thin sheet and equally spare blanket, Beth Ann pulled one pillow behind her head and lay on her side, hugging the second pillow to her chest.

If she closed her eyes, she could almost imagine she wasn't alone. But she didn't want to close her eyes. She wanted to stay awake, needed to be prepared. Fear cramped her stomach and tears burned her eyes. She'd gotten what she'd wanted. She was alone and dependent on herself. She just hadn't expected it to scare her.

A yearning built inside her again, the part of her that wished she had someone to hold during rough moments like this. She wanted Alex next to her on the eve of her new life. Alex to hug, to help her feel safe.

So there, in the dead of night, in a hotel hundreds of miles from home, she allowed herself to imagine. To dream. Just for one night. Just because she needed him. She closed her eyes and let herself believe it wasn't a pillow she hugged, but Alex as he sat with his back against the headboard.

Alex's fingers threaded through her hair, soothing against her scalp. An inch at a time, she relaxed against him, her vision going fuzzy and soft. The clock blinked in front of her, but she could no longer see the numbers. He slid lower, drawing her against him, surrounding her with his embrace. Alex's heart beat against her ear, his chest warm and strong against the side of her face.

"Did you know you'd made it real?" Alex watched the two teenagers sleeping on the bed, holding each other tight enough to keep the world at bay.

"Not yet." Elizabeth looked around the darkened hotel room with its small TV and not much else. If she'd known what she could do that night, she wouldn't have kept the room they slept in similar to the hotel room. They would have had their chamber from the beginning.

Alex looked at her with eyes devoid of anger. He was calm, accepting.

She was afraid to trust he really felt that way.

"You were scared. You needed me." Alex brushed his fingertips against her jaw. "I'm glad you had the gifts necessary to reach for me."

"Why aren't you mad anymore?"

He smiled sadly. "I always promised myself that if a child ever showed me a gift they couldn't help but have, that I would remain calm and prove to them that I loved them no matter what."

"It's not so easy with an adult you are afraid will hurt you."

"Or with someone you think plays with your dreams to take what they need from you and never give in return."

She flinched. "I did take and not give."

He brushed hair behind her ear. "But there was nothing cold about it. You weren't arrogantly arranging life to suit you. Tell me, was there ever a time you reached for me just because you could?"

Elizabeth shook her head. "I was tempted. I could have a relationship that went only as far as I allowed it to. There were times I almost reached for you just because I wanted to. But I couldn't abuse what we had."

Alex leaned closer, his lips a breath from hers. "Then you protected me, cared for me. Needed me."

Elizabeth bit her lip. His forgiveness washed over her, brought tears to her eyes. She only had one more thing to explain. "I didn't know, at first, the danger I was putting you in. The danger I'd put Grady in."

Alex looked over her shoulder, at the innocent faces in the bed.

"It wasn't until later that night that he came to me."

Alex switched his gaze to the window, his heart nearly stopping in his chest.

"At first, just a face in the window. My monster."

A black face made of molten lava as it cooled. Thick, lumpy ridges over blue, blue eyes. The face of a monster. The face of a being who knew the future. Alex flinched because that face in the window wasn't from the past. He wasn't staring at the teenagers on the bed. Elizabeth's father was looking straight at Alex. Now twelve years later.

"My father."

Alex flinched.

"He told me about Grady. He reminded me . . ."

Alex finished what she couldn't say. "What you did to him when he tried to leave you."

• IN DARKNESS, MAEVE cloaked herself, moving silently through two worlds. Dugan had hidden her well. He'd cared for her just as efficiently. And now her body thrummed with a satisfying hum of pleasure. With her hands shoved deep in the pockets of her black and burgundy dress, Maeve manipulated several small emeralds between her fingers and allowed a satisfied smile to stretch her lips. She fairly vibrated, not just from Dugan's skill in riding her the way she liked, but also from the aftermath of violence. A temporary release of tension. An orgasm of destruction.

Which was just as well. If she'd released that fury on the ones who deserved it, they would have died too quickly and she would have been stuck with this ball of cold rage still lodged inside her. But now she had the serenity to do this the way she liked. Their pain would be all the greater for her patience.

Find her son. Find her emerald. Repay her enemies. They were simple things, in theory. But her emerald was hidden from her. She'd called to it, but it was silent, as if it had never existed. Her power, her strength. It couldn't have been destroyed. Without it, her search for Kai was more difficult.

Silas and his accomplice had done much in the time she'd healed. But they'd only slowed, not halted her.

Silas led her to the ones he now watched over. Did he believe the bastard was safe? Was he working to ensure it? Either way, he brought her to another that deserved her special attention. The healer—Alex.

With an innate stealth, Maeve gracefully slid through that which was solid in the human realm and insubstantial in hers, and halted where she wished—the healer's bedroom. At the side of his bed as he lay sleeping, bare to the waist. The show stopped at the dark green cotton pants he wore.

Alex stretched across his bed, his muscled arms to either side of him. Maeve leaned close, inhaling the scent at his neck, thrilling at the pheromones. A scent that called to who she was, at the core. He smelled clean, with just a hint of natural musk. Her fangs itched to taste him, but she was still full. Too bad.

Maeve licked her lips and held her hand just over his skin, feeling curls of hair mixed with his aura of power. Considering whether she'd feel more.

Sinuously, she drifted her hand down his chest, stroking him in a way that wouldn't wake him, but that his spirit would feel. Down she moved, to the spot she valued most. Her hand hovered, her heart pounding with the thrill. He wasn't hard, not yet, but there was plenty to the package waiting to be unwrapped. She could do so much with a relaxed, slumbering cock. Maeve smiled, her tongue moistening her bottom lip.

Her fangs itched for more than just one type of taste. She imagined sliding her fangs down his hard shaft, allowing just a small nick from one of them. Not deep enough for blood, just shallow enough to hurt. Then she could take his sac into her mouth. With the right angle, she could bite deep, could suck him so dry, Alex would never have children.

So clever, so diabolical. That was vengeance with finesse.

Maeve opened her eyes, imagining the satisfaction. The pleasure. From what she'd seen so far tonight, that would pain him tremendously. No man, even a half-angel, could resist the need to build his own dynasty.

So sweetly, humanly vulnerable. So many ways to destroy him. She didn't need vicious violence. Now it was time to use her mind, to cause pain that lasted longer than hours. But perhaps Alex was not the right candidate for that. She couldn't find her emerald, or her son, until Silas was pulled away from his current mission.

With the healer gone, Silas would return to the bastard, raise the drawbridge and flood the moat with poisons. Everything Maeve wanted would be in that metaphorical castle, her ally, her tool, and her enemies, and if there was anything she'd learned from Kai's Norman father, it was how to crumble castle walls.

She would kill the healer, but—Maeve pressed her hand to the hardened flesh beneath the cotton—she didn't have to do it quickly. Leaning forward, she kissed his chest, inhaling his scent and allowing it to power her own desire.

Suddenly, an arc of strangely familiar power surged from her lips, through Alex's body, up through her hand and inside her. Completing its circuit too quickly for her to defend herself, Maeve fell.

Chapter 16

◈

• THE FACE DISAPPEARED from the window a split second before the hotel door burst open. Elizabeth jumped, spinning around. Alex tried to pull her back from the furious giant with the demonic horns, but she resisted.

"Daddy!"

All ironic quips fled from Alex's mind when the demon's blue eyes rested squarely on him. "The battle has begun. She is loose."

Alex's heart stopped for one endless beat, terror sliding over his flesh like swamp water, hot, sticky, and completely unpleasant.

Elizabeth frowned. "What battle? Who?"

Alex grabbed her arm and pulled her back to him. A glance to the left of the demon answered every question he had. Maeve's green eyes narrowed on him, hate slithering around inside them like venomous snakes.

Holding Elizabeth tight to him, Alex said, "Time to go."

Her father raised his hand and the night went black around the sight of Maeve attacking the giant's back.

• ADAD SENT THEM away, not to their own bodies, but to their chamber until it was safe for Elizabeth. Maeve's presence, here of all places, was the worst sort of danger to his daughter. He spun, the hotel room disappearing behind him. The walls of Elizabeth's rock tunnels disappeared, becoming a wide expanse of sand and rock, peppered in the distance with willow and sorgum. Perhaps not perfectly Babylonian in design, but there was no place he'd ever been that he wanted to ruin with the presence of Maeve.

"Adad?" she snarled, furious, disbelieving. She rushed for him, her nails extended like claws. "You will die for your treachery."

Adad grabbed her wrists, struggling with her. His flesh appeared impenetrable stone, but Maeve knew best how to damage him. Still, she did not terrify him. He crushed her against him and laughed mockingly. "Surely you can appreciate a Judas kiss? It comes so naturally to you."

She froze against him, then softened. Her eyes dampened. Her whisper was tragic, her pain fathomless. "I trusted you."

His lips twisted into a sardonic smile. Adad refused to be weakened by sympathy in remembered closeness. "I seriously doubt that."

The wounded look disappeared as if it had never been. In its place was the hardened whore he knew so well. "As much as I trusted anyone. But you abandoned me. You betrayed me. Do you realize how I have suffered?"

"You were imprisoned as you should have been long ago. As you would yet have been, if you weren't so clever about the letter of the law."

"For a thousand years, Adad! Since when do you care

so much for the law?" she demanded. "I know what you've done. You've stolen my plan for yourself."

"I may have fallen, beautiful witch." Adad met her gaze with an unflinching stare. "But I have never promoted destruction."

"Ruling is not destruction," she snarled. "It is the very opposite. You agreed at one time."

"Yes, I considered your truth. It seemed a possibility, until I saw where your decisions would lead you." His lips curved mockingly again. "Would you like to know, sweet Maeve? I could show you."

She thought about accepting his offer. But then she stiffened with caution as her alluring green gaze considered him. "Bribing me, Adad?"

"Why would I do that?" he purred, a breath from her lips.

"Why, indeed." Her green eyes narrowed on his blue ones, her thick lashes swooping down, as if preparing for his kiss. When he made no move to do so, her lashes flew up and her gaze focused on him. "Your daughter has your eyes."

His gaze narrowed. "She is protected. You can't touch her with me here."

Maeve grinned slowly. "Perhaps not. But what about the others, Adad? Can you protect them all?"

He shoved her from him. "You will leave them alone. You've cursed them enough."

"Nothing is enough, not after what you did. If you want to save them, try to stop me." Maeve laughed wickedly and held her arms open in invitation, her body wavering, ready to disappear. When Adad didn't move, her eyes widened. She looked at him from the tips of his horns to his feet. With a flick of her lashes, her green eyes met his. "You are trapped."

Maeve threw back her head and laughed to the starless sky. When she finally straightened, she said, "Protect them as best you can, but I have an enormous debt to repay."

Adad stared at the space she'd occupied long after she left. He knew the risks, the options, the paths that lay before them all. He knew the future, the failures, and the triumphs. But he'd forgotten one simple fact. Maeve terrified him.

• ELIZABETH STEPPED FROM behind a tower of rocks, watching her father. He hadn't been able to maintain his human form since she was little. Illusions were lies here. Neither the brimstone that formed him, nor the sharp horns protruding from his body scared her.

No. What terrified her had always and ever been his visions. His glimpses of the future, her family's future, destroyed from the inside out. Her inability to stop them had turned her nightmares into hours of helpless torment. But never, in all that time, had she considered the cause of their annihilation to be her father's fault. After all, he'd only left. It was *she* who'd ensured he never returned.

Rigid with fury, she faced her father. *Adad,* his lover had called him. "So you need to protect us from what, exactly?"

"Elizabeth!" He actually seemed surprised to see her.

She waved his response away. "This is my mind. As powerful as you are, you *do* have limits. You can't simply dismiss me."

His eyes narrowed and the black stone of his face settled into harsh, forbidding lines. "No, it seems I can't."

"What can she do to us?"

"Anything she pleases," Adad stated bluntly.

"Aren't there rules?"

"Of course, and she knows every one of them. She's capable of inventing loopholes where none should exist."

"So she's the goddess of lawyers. Great." Elizabeth looked to the side as Alex approached. His eyes were calm and focused, his stance self-assured.

Halting at her side, Alex took Elizabeth's hand before facing her dad. "How did she get here?"

"I brought her through Elizabeth's connection to you, before she could harm your physical form."

"And now she's back there again?"

Adad nodded. "I couldn't prevent her return, so now I must hasten yours."

Alex swallowed, nodding. He had so many urgent questions. Quickly he tried to think, to sift and sort through them before time ran out. "How did she find us?"

Adad shrugged. "It doesn't matter. It was destined that she would."

"Like it's destined for her to threaten all of us."

Elizabeth frowned at his matter-of-fact tone. Was he speaking of the vision her father had shown him? The branch of the tree that was abruptly cut? The one her father had shown her had moved beyond that, to a time when they'd all survived but taken a broken road. So the threat was preordained, but either result was still a possibility.

Adad inclined his head to both of them. "Exactly."

"How do we survive her attack?" she asked.

His blue eyes closed briefly. "Through all of your choices. All of your sacrifices."

"What was the plan she mentioned? The one she accused you of stealing?" Alex asked.

"Her son—" Adad turned his head, as if listening to an unheard voice. His eyes flashed with sudden fire, flames moving within their depths so not a hint of blue was seen. A second later, Adad's eyes cleared and he looked straight at Alex. "Go."

Elizabeth's eyes widened and her breath stilled in her chest. Quickly, she sent Alex away, but, much as she desired to follow, she couldn't leave yet. The answers she needed were too crucial. Gritting her teeth against the anxiety tightly coiling inside her stomach, Elizabeth faced her father.

All these years she'd blamed her mother's poor decisions, her mother's weakness, her mother's *failures* for the destruction of their family. But it was his fault. Her father's poor choices a thousand and more years ago doomed their family now.

"My intentions were good, Elizabeth. I was not power-hungry. Instead, I was convinced I knew a better way to give the best to mankind. I had ideas, plans to bring help and aid and happiness. Ultimately, I was corrupted with visions of glory, believing I knew best and that the dynasty I founded would lead this world into the next golden age."

Good for him. That made the danger to Shelly, Teddy, Tommy, and the others *so* much more bearable. "And how is that different from what *she* wants?"

"She wants to deliver humanity into slavery." At her

raised brows, he became more specific. "After wreaking vengeance for what she considers a terrible injustice."

"Was it unjust?"

"Imprisoning Maeve for the deeds she has done is justice. Imprisoning her for the deeds I *know* she will do, is mankind's only hope for survival."

"Nice woman you chose." Elizabeth shook her head and squeezed her eyes shut. "I hated having her in my head. I hated her thoughts, her feelings. Especially the *images*. How can I stop someone like that?"

"Whatever you gleaned was only the surface, Elizabeth. Never forget the surface is deceiving. It's the depths which—"

Elizabeth exhaled in a short, frustrated burst. "I get it. I just don't know how to fight her."

"You don't. Until the battle comes to you, the rest is just damage control."

Elizabeth frowned. "What?"

"She fights beneath the surface, Elizabeth. It is how she bends the rules."

• ALEX LAY FLAT on his back, arms outstretched. Maeve sat next to him, her feet on the floor, but her cheek rested on his chest. Her full red lips were pursed, her deep red curls fanned over his chest. Her hands were the worst. A thumb and forefinger pinched his left nipple while her right hand thoroughly cupped his groin.

No. Silas froze in place, staring with wide, horrified eyes. This couldn't happen. Maeve was a destroyer, a villain. He moved forward, but Draven, who'd stood motionless in the corner far too long, stopped him.

"We can't touch them, Silas. They are linked, mind to mind, by Elizabeth's dreams and Adad's power. If we touch them, we'll fall into them, too."

"How do you know?"

"Because it's how Maeve fell."

"You mean you just stood here and watched?" Silas scowled.

"I know how to cloak my presence. She didn't know I was here."

"So you sacrificed Alex for your own protection?"

"That's it, Silas. Think the worst." Draven sighed impatiently. "My protection was only a side benefit. While she is like this, her body is weak. Vulnerable."

Silas sighed and relaxed his shoulders. "But untouchable."

"Yes. But when she awakens it will be our moment to catch her off guard. Fight her or follow the tracking spell I have in place to capture her."

"So we bind her, take her away from Alex, and then what's your plan?"

Draven shrunk further into the shadows of the corner. "That part I'm not so sure of, Silas."

Silas crossed his arms. "I am."

"What?"

"I know who we can take her to. They'll never let her go free."

"Can they hold one of her power? I thought only the Tunnels of the Forgotten Ones were strong enough for that."

"For long enough to figure out how to destroy her, they will hold. I never suggested it before because I didn't think we would have this chance."

No sooner had Silas spoken, then Maeve opened her eyes. Seeing Draven and Silas, she flashed from lying prone to face them both. "You think you have a chance?"

Neither said a word. Moving as one, they clasped hands and channeled their gifts into a whirlwind of light that wrapped around Maeve, constricting like golden boas, attempting to bind her. Maeve shook them off, freeing herself easily. Looking at Silas and Draven, Maeve laughed.

Blackened barbed wire snapped around Maeve, cutting her skin into bloodied strips. Maeve tried to shake them off as she had the boas, but the barbed wire only tightened, coiling around her. Extending her claws, she cut at them, striking desperately, frowning at the difficulty of their silent battle. Hope renewed, Silas raised his snakes again, transforming them into golden wires that entwined with the barbed wire, strengthening its hold.

It was working. No matter how she struggled, Maeve could not break free. No matter that he strained to keep the power in place, Silas knew at that moment they really could win. He smiled and began preparing the portal to take them to safety, maneuvered one hand in ancient symbols to match the words in his mind. The portal began to form, opening as a pinpoint in space and slowly expanding.

A presence formed behind them, solidifying into a dark danger. Something pushed him, throwing Silas to his right. Draven flew to the left, their hands breaking contact. The tall, cloaked form strode briskly past them both and wrapped dark appendages around Maeve. A blink later, they were gone.

"What the hell?" Silas burst out. The entire maneuver

had lasted only a split second, leaving him sprawled ig-nominiously on the floor.

Draven sat up, huffing, gloved hands braced against the floor. "Dugan."

• ELIZABETH OPENED HER eyes to high-pitched wails of fury. She stumbled out of bed, nearly falling over as the sheets twisted around her ankles. Putting one arm on the bed for balance, she freed one foot and tugged the other loose, kicking it into the leg of the bed. "Son of a—"

"Aunt Beth! Can you come help me?" Shelly's voice sounded strangely distant, as if she were yelling from downstairs. But then why were there screams coming from just down the hall?

Elizabeth hobbled to the hall stairs. "Just a sec, Shelly."

Jerking open the door to the toddlers' room, Abby and Jessie froze in mid tug, a shirt twisted between them. Elizabeth snapped, "*What* is going on?"

"Wanna wear it! I want the shirt!" Jessie whined an-grily.

"It's mine." Abby stomped her foot.

"I asked for it," Jessie accused.

"You stole it!" Abby yelled back.

"I'm trying to sleep!" Elizabeth looked up to the top bunk in time to see Sarah tug her blankets over her head. But neither Abby nor Jessie paid a bit of attention, continuing to twist and tug on the shirt.

"Give it to me." Elizabeth held out her hand. Both girls looked at her, one chewing her lip, the other with tears pooling in her eyes. Reluctantly, they both held out their end of the shirt. Elizabeth nodded. "Thank you. I will keep the shirt. Find something else to wear."

"Aunt Beth!"

"Coming!" Elizabeth watched the toddlers pull out more clothes from a dresser that should have been empty now that she was using the hanger system. They pouted, mutinously glaring at each other, but otherwise were calm. Elizabeth left them to it and marched down the stairs in a thigh-high T-shirt and bare feet. "What's wrong, Shel?"

Shelly perched on the edge of the couch, Veronica's ankles in one hand, dirty wipes in the other. "The bag fell over and I can't reach the diapers and wipes."

Veronica giggled and stuffed the head of her little bear in her mouth. Elizabeth grabbed what had fallen out of the diaper bag and brought the whole pack over. Pulling out another diaper and the box of wipes, she asked, "Where are the others?"

"Tommy and the twins were ready to kill each other when I came up, so I sent them back to bed. I don't think that's where they went, though. They probably took it outside. Then I heard Abby and Jessie start in. I don't know about the rest." Shelly wiped up the baby and re-diapered her with skilled efficiency.

Elizabeth headed to the kitchen. She would need to take something before the pounding behind her eyes got worse. Grabbing a bottle of ibuprofen and a glass of water, she looked out the back window to see Tommy and the twins practicing the punches and kicks that Alex had taught them. No one was bleeding, crying, or unconscious, so they must have worked out whatever it was they'd fought over. Elizabeth shook her head, popped two pills in her mouth, and guzzled the water like she hadn't had a drink in decades.

Teddy left the laundry room, clicking the light off behind him as he shut the door. The sounds of the washer and dryer running emerged from behind him. She wanted to kiss him. "Thank you for getting that started, honey."

He nodded. "I was looking for something for Abby and Jessie, but I heard you through the vent."

Elizabeth winced. She sighed and rinsed out the glass. She could go get dressed now, no one was dying yet. Alex and Geoffrey weren't here and she had a chance to dash upstairs before they showed. Somehow, she didn't think her father's words about damage control applied to clothing tug-of-wars or diaper emergencies. She sighed.

Before she could leave the kitchen and head back upstairs the phone rang.

• MAEVE PACED IN the Raineses' dank basement, her high heels clicking against the cement floor with each sharp step. Small emeralds and silver wires tangled in her hands. She twisted and turned the silver, wrapping it around the emeralds in short, delicate patterns.

Dugan glanced up from where he sat next to the little boy, playing with the spiders that crossed the floor in front of them. Dugan was having fun, in love with spiders as he was. He enjoyed sharing his fascination with someone as equally enthralled by the leggy little buggers.

There had been a time when Maeve would have

found joy watching the harmful and potentially deadly arachnids scrambling over the child's arms, but at the moment she was too angry to be indulgent. She was almost too angry to make her beautiful jewelry, but she had plans for this piece.

Through walls that seemed paper thin, she heard Elizabeth respond to the hospital nurse. Adad's wife had been an easy, helpless target. Fun as that was, it hadn't even begun to lessen Maeve's fury over his betrayal. She'd come for Alex, seeking justice, but she'd found so much more. Adad sought protection for his family, therefore it was obvious how to hurt him most. That she would also repay Alex for turning his back on Kai was a bonus. He would endure the same pain she had, watching someone he loved suffer with no aid.

She paced before Dugan and the child yet again, then paused, watching a hobo spider crawl onto the palm of the child's hand, furry legs scrambling along his skin. A bite wouldn't hurt, but in half an hour a blister would form, slowly growing larger and deeper and more painful. The scars it left weren't pretty either. But it was the potentially deadly staph infection that came after the bite he'd have to worry about most.

Maeve stared at the flood of *Tegenaria agrestise* working their way toward the boy, drawn by Dugan's whispers. They weren't the only types available. Dugan had also enticed a black jumping spider from the basement windowsill; unfortunately it wasn't dangerous but merely pretty for the boy to look at. Add a dash of wolf spiders and several that looked threateningly like poisonous brown recluses and it resulted in a virtual witch's brew of both potential and definite danger.

Maeve smiled and set the emerald-and-silver earrings upon the most visible box in the area. She wasn't going to slowly unravel this family, she was going to build a bomb. The explosion would obliterate every descendant of Adad ever born. But every fuse had to be lit—and Kevin looked like a lovely little match.

• "SHELLY!" ELIZABETH RIPPED away the paper from the notepad and headed toward the living room. "I need to go to the hospital and see Mom. I need you to watch the kids until the guys arrive if they don't get here before I leave, okay?"

"Uh, sure. Aunt Beth?"

Elizabeth skidded to a stop, her mouth open and her eyes wide, staring past Shelly straight into the surprised faces of the crowd.

Elizabeth gaped at the crowd of people in the doorway. Geoffrey glanced at her, then turned away. Kalyss looked like she wanted to die of embarrassment. The man behind her, most likely her husband, looked amused as he gave her a curious glance before following Geoffrey into the dining room. At least his look hadn't been lecherous. No, that was saved for Alex as he eyed her bare legs and obviously unfettered breasts.

Elizabeth tugged at the hem of the shirt, praying it at least covered her underwear. There was no hiding her lack of a bra, though.

Shelly choked on her laughter. Elizabeth glared at her niece. "Laugh now, because later . . ."

Shelly smiled. "I'd be scared if you weren't wearing your 'I love fluffy bunnies' T-shirt."

Elizabeth growled. Shelly laughed harder and went to the kitchen.

"I'm so sorry, Elizabeth. We'll just go occupy ourselves." Kalyss blushed and followed her husband into the dining room, leaving Elizabeth alone with Alex.

He held up his hands peacefully. "I invited them along because I think there's a lot we need to talk about."

Elizabeth shook her head and headed toward the stairs. "There probably is, but I really need to leave for a bit."

"What's happened with your mom?" Alex followed her up the stairs and to her room. For a second, he paused and looked around, recognizing all the furniture.

Elizabeth turned to order him out, then shook her head and sighed. There just didn't seem to be much to hide from him anymore. Instead, she grabbed a pair of jeans from the dresser and started tugging them on. "I was just asked to come up and talk to the doctor. That might not seem too important—"

"Of course it is. She's dying."

"—but she's getting worse and there's not much more that can be done for her. They're probably going to give me a time frame." Elizabeth zipped and buttoned her jeans, looking around for the rest of the clothes she needed to hurry into.

Alex stepped in front of her, his hands rubbing her shoulders and biceps. "It's very important, Elizabeth. She'll still be gone later and these moments are all you have left."

Elizabeth looked up, into his eyes, and couldn't control the burning and blurring in her own. "I've been so damn angry with her. I don't deserve comfort, Alex."

"Everyone deserves comfort, honey." He pulled her

closer to his chest and tightened his arms around her. "Just try to stop me."

She was so tempted to melt into him and soak in his heat. If she had more time, she would. Quickly, she squeezed him and pushed him away. "I need to get dressed."

He nodded and backed away. "We'll take care of everything here. Don't worry about it. We'll talk when you get back."

Alex left and Elizabeth hurried. Ten minutes later, she was dressed and headed down the stairs. Kalyss sat on the couch, Abby on her lap, and Jessie and Sarah pressed up to her sides. Tommy perched on the arm of the chair across from her, his blue eyes sparkling and the small cowlick at the back of his head sticking up despite his shower. "So whatcha naming your baby?"

Kalyss's lips twitched. Tommy was always a force to behold. "I'm not sure. There are so many options."

Tommy put an arm across the back of the chair and swung his leg with restless energy. "You could always do what my mom did. She wasn't sure who my dad was, so she named me after both of them. Tommy Jack."

Elizabeth abruptly halted at the bottom of the stairs, trying not to choke. *Good God, Dallas.* She rifled through her purse, partially to check she had everything and partially to hide her burning face. At least Tommy didn't see anything wrong with how his name came about.

After a long pause, Kalyss spoke, good humor filling her voice. "I know my baby's dad. So that only gives me one name, though I can see the benefit of having two names to choose from."

Tommy shrugged. "Aw, that's okay. Maybe you could do what she did for Teddy."

Teddy looked up from his book and growled, "Shut up, Tommy."

Tommy's face lit with mischief. "Mom loved his dad so much, she named him Thee-Adore Michael. But his nickname is from what she wore when—"

"Tommy!" Elizabeth gasped, horribly afraid of the many embarrassing things that could come out of his mouth next.

"I'm going to kill you!" Teddy threw his book aside, not even marking his spot first, and chased a giggling Tommy upstairs.

"Boys!" But they were gone, slamming doors, giggling, and issuing threats. Elizabeth closed her eyes a second, then turned a red face to Kalyss, who luckily seemed to be amused.

Shelly finished snapping a pink dress on Veronica and unfolded a pair of tiny socks. "Teddy's hated his name since he found out what it stood for. But Mom thought it was cute."

Kalyss nodded. "I can see that. Where did your name come from?"

Shelly finished the socks and slid on little slippers. "My mom's best friends. Shelly and Kate."

"What about the baby?" Kalyss asked and Elizabeth held her breath, waiting for the answer. It could be anything.

Shelly froze a moment, pursed her lips, then stood Veronica up to straighten her tights. "Veronica Mars."

Elizabeth asked, "From the TV show?"

"No." Shelly shook her head briefly, then shrugged

and stood up, the baby on her hip. "It seemed fitting. Veronica was a friend who was good at listening. And men are from Mars."

Shelly handed the baby over to Kalyss and left. Elizabeth watched her leave, wondering at the strange look on Shelly's face. When she looked back at the baby, Veronica was happy and content in Kalyss's arms and Alex's best friend was busy falling in love.

Chapter 17

• THE CURTAINS AROUND her mother's bed were pulled closed and the room was silent. The air was cool and still, empty. It was a room for someone to die in. Just the thought gave Elizabeth chills. For a second, she couldn't breathe and she was ready to cry again, but a touch of anger warmed her.

Her mother needed to see the kids tomorrow. Mary Beth could pull herself together for a few hours. The children could handle seeing her sick. It was her sudden disappearance and complete absence from their lives they had so much trouble with. Why couldn't she understand that?

Elizabeth stared at the foot of the bed. Her mom was a lump, unmoving in the center. The blankets were pulled around her head so only the side of her face peeked out.

The whole atmosphere was somber and hushed, practically shouting, "Someone is dying here."

The door burst open behind her and a man with a clipboard in one hand walked in. Dr. Mason smiled gently at her. "Good to see you again, Ms. Raines."

"Hi." Elizabeth smiled. She gestured vaguely toward the bed in front of her. Her mother still hadn't moved. "One of the nurses called."

He nodded. "Your mom asked me to fill you in on her condition."

Elizabeth nodded, even more puzzled. Mary Beth had shown plenty of energy all week when she'd argued with Elizabeth over the kids' visits. Now she suddenly didn't have enough strength to explain her own health? "She's not getting better, right?"

"Right. The cancer has metastasized further."

Elizabeth stared blankly.

"It means it has spread further into her lungs and into her bloodstream." He explained with a kind tone and expression.

"I see." Elizabeth's brows drew together. Her mom was dying. Cancer was eating her body. But none of that was new, Mary Beth had been fighting the cancer for months and had sounded fine just yesterday, so why the emergency phone call?

"It means, if there's anyone who hasn't said their good-byes yet, they need to do so now or they won't have a chance," he clarified for her.

Elizabeth frowned, her brows drawing together as she glanced at the bed. Had her mom known she was getting worse? Had she thought all her delays and cancellations over the last few weeks would help her squeeze out of saying good-bye? *Not going to happen, Mother.* "That's what I've been trying to do, but she's resistant. She doesn't want the kids to see her sick. But they need to say good-bye."

He nodded in understanding. "Many patients feel this way. It's sad for those who haven't had that chance for a last visit, but it happens. Maybe she'll change her mind."

It was a weak hope he offered, but it was all he could give. Elizabeth gave a small smile and nodded. "I thought this kind of thing took longer than just a few months."

"On the contrary. It usually happens quite fast. It was likely her age that helped her battle this long, but in the end . . ." He shrugged, his brown eyes sympathetic.

Elizabeth looked into the doctor's kind eyes, then away. He had a horrible job and didn't need her bad attitude making it worse. "Thank you, doctor."

He paused, meeting her eyes for a moment. "Let me know if there's anything I can do, Ms. Raines."

"The kids—"

"If she agrees, they can come. Perhaps one or two at a time?"

She nodded gratefully and he left the room.

Elizabeth looked at her mother again. She would have to explain it to the children, plan a visit for tomorrow, call Dallas again. And find Felicia. Elizabeth had been preparing for this for weeks, but now that the time had come, she still wasn't ready. There was so much to do, so much to say. And that was without her father's revelations.

Well, soon it wouldn't matter. Elizabeth turned to

leave when her mother called in a thin, weak voice, "Beth Ann? Did you finally come?"

Elizabeth circled the bed to stare into her mother's yellow face. Her blue eyes were nearly transparent, the whites an unnatural creamy color. "Finally? You've been fighting me all week."

"Not fighting you. Only the idea of seeing them. Can you sit with me? Just for a little while?" The hope lighting Mary Beth's face was almost pitiable.

The plea tugged at Elizabeth more than she wanted it to, though she had to wonder if her mother was really that weak. It just didn't seem possible. Any minute now, Mary Beth would toss back the covers, put on her makeup, and be ready to party. "Just a little while. The kids need me home soon."

"Yeah. How are they?" Mary Beth loved her grandchildren. There was never a doubt about that.

"They're good. I'm bringing them tomorrow," Elizabeth said firmly.

"Beth—" Mary Beth drew her head back in a negative tilt.

"There won't be another chance, Mom. Give them one more hug." Elizabeth spoke firmly, inflexibly. "See the little ones. Tell the older ones you love them."

"You know I don't want them to see me like this." Mary Beth pursed her lips in that irritated way she had.

Elizabeth narrowed her eyes. "Why not? They watched you get like this."

Mary Beth huffed against the pillow, no longer seeming quite so weak and wasted. They'd had this argument many times over. The last one just two weeks ago.

She'd always known it would happen sooner or later.

After all, she'd brought home the pamphlets in the third grade, reading them out aloud cover to cover in a vain hope of convincing her mom to stop smoking. Such a wasted effort.

She'd been so angry, said hateful horrible things in anger. Who can be perfect all the time? Mary Beth wasn't faking and she wouldn't recover. Suddenly the time was so short, and Elizabeth felt so tired. So unprepared. Very soon she wouldn't have her mother. She'd be orphaned. The last twelve years suddenly didn't seem like an oasis of peace. They seemed full of wasted opportunities. Maybe if she'd stayed, they could have grown to understand each other.

Elizabeth had lived with her anger for so long, but there'd also been a strange hope that one day it would be better. Her mother would realize the damage she'd done, apologize, and change. Elizabeth could let go of her anger and bitterness. They could become the kind of mother and daughter she'd always dreamed of. But soon, that hope would be gone.

Mary Beth opened her eyes and looked into Elizabeth's. "Just one more hug. Okay?"

Elizabeth smiled briefly, and reached out to squeeze her mom's hand. This was more than she could've hoped for five minutes ago. "Okay."

Mary Beth stroked her thumb over the back of Elizabeth's hand and closed her eyes. Elizabeth stayed, letting the touch connect them, for as long as she could.

• "WHAT DO YOU mean you can't come home right now?" Elizabeth gripped the edge of the sink and stared through the window to the dusky backyard. She hadn't planned to stay at the hospital nearly so long. But as she'd sat with her mom, hospice had come to talk to her about the specifics of dying. Would her mom be buried or cremated? Did she have an obituary planned? Did she know who would perform the funeral service?

Elizabeth knew none of it. She'd been given the paperwork to think these things over weeks ago, but it had fallen through the cracks. Partially because she was busy, but equally because she hadn't wanted to believe it was happening. It would be wasted effort when Mary Beth miraculously recovered and walked out of there. But today she'd had to take the time to see to all of it. Alex had been amazing, stepping in at home and freeing her to do what had to be done.

The four adults she'd been embarrassed to see that morning had pulled together to keep the kids busy painting the hallway upstairs, allowing them the freedom to make it theirs. It was something she'd discussed with Alex a few nights ago, but today they'd made it happen. As a side benefit, they'd all been well supervised and kept safely inside, though Maeve seemed a distant, vague worry at the moment. Right now she had to convince her selfish bitch of a sister that no was not an option.

"Dallas," she said. But her sister started talking to someone in the background. A door shut and it was quiet on the phone line again. "Dallas, you don't understand. This is it. She's going to die."

"She's been dying for months now, Beth Ann. Come on . . ." Her sister's voice reached that annoying whine that scraped Elizabeth's last nerve. "I'm so close to building something here. Just a few more days and," her voice hushed, filled with unadulterated glee, "I think he's going to propose."

Their mom had begun having tests months ago but there was such a lag between appointments and results. Mary Beth's battle had lasted longer than three months but Dallas was talking like it was years.

Elizabeth forced herself to silently, slowly exhale before speaking. "Dallas, I doubt Mom has a few more days."

There. Her voice was even. Calm. She was doing good.

"Damn it, Beth. I just can't. I know she's dying, I'm sorry about that. I really am. But I can't throw this away." Dallas sighed. "She'd want this for me, Beth. You know she would. I'll be able to come get the kids and bring them back here. John has family surrounding him, a huge house, and all the money he needs. This is for their future."

"Just come home for a day or two, say good-bye to Mom, hug the kids, attend the funeral." Why should she have to bargain for this? Dallas knew this was important. She should have come here when Elizabeth had first called.

"Yeah. Just a few days. How long have you been there now? I can't get trapped there. I'll lose him. Things are at a critical stage."

Trapped? Half of these kids were hers! She belonged here with them, helping them cope with the death of their beloved grandmother. Elizabeth gripped the sink rim even tighter. "Then bring him, Dallas. If he'd let your mother die without letting you say good-bye, he's not worth it anyway."

"Of course he's not that way. It's not Mom." Dallas lowered her voice. "I haven't told him about the kids. Not all of them, anyway. Just that my kids are staying with their grandma while I get a home set up for them. Besides, he thinks they'll be happier there until we know where this is headed."

"Of *course* he does." She sighed.

"Don't be such a bitch, Beth. Just 'cause you don't want men, doesn't mean the rest of us shouldn't have them."

It was time to end the call before it disintegrated completely. "Bring him, don't bring him, dump him in a river, whatever. Just get your ass here before Mom dies, Dallas."

Elizabeth hung up the phone and gripped the sink with both hands. Why was it so hard to convince her older sister to do the right thing? It should be common sense, but heaven forbid a member of her family have *that*. The sad truth was Dallas was the easiest call she had to make. Bobby would take awhile, demanding comfort for not being able to make it. And then there was Felicia.

Footsteps halted behind her and she raised her gaze to meet Alex's. He leaned a hip against the counter and stared back solemnly. "The kids are just about ready for you to see."

She looked into his somber hazel eyes and smiled. "Thank you."

He crossed his arms as he watched her, his stance more relaxed than his gaze. "Bad news?"

She shrugged. "Typical BS. Dallas doesn't want to come home, even though her kids are here and Mom only has a few days left."

Elizabeth looked away. This was a side of her that she'd always wanted to keep secret from him, but it seemed pointless anymore. Maybe it was vain to worry about how her family's dysfunction reflected on her, but she also feared that somehow, no matter how much she tried to avoid it, she was just as screwed up. And, no matter how she tried to eliminate or bury them, Alex would see her flaws.

"This is another reason why I said no to prom, Alex. Why I left. I wanted away from all their drama. I didn't want to be like them and I was afraid . . ." She inhaled, her words wobbling a bit. "Afraid that if I went with you, I'd never want to leave. I'd stay and I'd become exactly what I hated most."

Raising her burning eyes to him, she spoke with a hoarse voice. "But I don't think I have a choice anymore. No matter what kind of person I become, no matter how I screw up, I have to stay. Because I'm all they have left."

She'd never had a relationship or kids of her own, knowing she'd probably ruin them. But now, she'd have to take on the biggest responsibility of her life. She couldn't count on Dallas and Bobby and Felicia. It was her or foster care. Anxiety made her sick to her stomach. What the hell did she know about doing this long term?

Alex reached for her, but Elizabeth flinched away

from the compassion she read in his expression. She had to ask him for more. Use him again. As if he hadn't done enough. But she'd already learned that rejecting his help would be a more horrible mistake than accepting it.

Whatever was between them needed to be on hold for a bit. She was just so damn tired.

"I need to ask you . . ." She looked down and away, wrapping her arms around herself. She could go by herself, but the last time she'd blithely gone to find Felicia, she'd found herself in a few perilous situations. She was damn lucky she hadn't been hurt. Considering the responsibility she had now, it was crucial nothing happened to her. She looked back up at him.

Alex's eyes searched her face, watching her. Finally, he pulled her into his embrace, and gruffly said, "Just ask."

"Will you go with me to find Felicia?" She had to ask before just pulling him along with her.

He tilted his head a fraction, his face oddly sad and vulnerable. "I'd go with you anywhere."

Elizabeth sighed and bit her lip. They still hadn't had their talk yet. There hadn't been a chance. And now the uncertainty over that tied her in knots. She shook her head. "Never mind. Where she'll likely be is—"

His hand on her arm silenced her and made her open her eyes. His look was grim and resolute. "I'm not stupid. I can guess what kind of place she's at. And if you think I'd let you go alone, you're dead wrong."

Her back went straight like a rod suddenly fused her spine. Her objection was instinctive. "It's not for you to *let* me."

"No." For once, he didn't even smile. He was completely serious and his hazel eyes were dark with it. "I can't stop you from going, but I can and will be right by your side."

It was that serious and determined side of him again, the one she wasn't quite used to. The one, most likely, who kicked serious butt in martial arts. Finally, she nodded. "I'd rather wait until the kids are in bed before we go. Do you think Geoffrey will mind babysitting?"

"Not at all." Alex grinned, a mischievous glint lighting his eyes.

Elizabeth narrowed her gaze in question, but he didn't elaborate. She just shook her head and laid her cheek against his chest.

• ELIZABETH HUNG UP the phone. Call to Bobby— check. She set down the pencil and went to the next number on the list she and her mom had prepared. There weren't many more family members to call, but the list of her friends was huge. She'd only called half before Bobby had called her, as per the nightly ritual they'd established in the last few weeks, but that half had been devastated to hear the news. No doubt the rest would be equally sad. As many problems as she'd had with her mom over the years, Mary Beth had been a great friend. Kind, caring, generous.

Shelly clattered into the room, a frown on her face. Plopping a paint can, tray, and roller before her door, she gave Elizabeth a look. Elizabeth sighed. "What's wrong?"

"Alex said I had to paint my door."

Elizabeth gave the door a once-over. It was cracked and peeling and in such bad shape, it needed the work. "So?"

"Whatever." Shelly rolled her eyes and turned to her paint can, muttering loud enough to make sure Elizabeth overheard. "Not my house, I guess."

"I take it you don't like the hallway?" Elizabeth asked. She hadn't seen it yet. With her long absence earlier and the phone calls she was making tonight, they'd chosen to surprise her when they were done. "At least the kids seem happy. I can hear them laughing and carrying on from here. Besides, the hallway's being repainted and they get to be a part of it. What's wrong with that?"

"Kevin's painting big, furry black spiders in his mural and the toddlers scream and run every time they pass it." Irritation made Shelly's tone dry.

Elizabeth grinned. "Which means they pass by every chance they get. I think they're having fun with it. You should have fun, too."

Shelly shook her head and her dangling silver earrings swung side to side.

"Those are pretty."

Shelly glared, defensive and ready to attack at the same time. "They were in a box. I figured they'd get more use if I wore them."

"Aunt Lizzie, we're ready!" sang a chorus of voices from upstairs.

Elizabeth shrugged, pushed her chair back from the table, and stood up, not really caring about the earrings. "They look good on you. I say enjoy them."

Shelly ducked her head to the paint pan and Elizabeth strode past her. She reached out to squeeze Shelly's shoulder as she passed, but the teen shrugged away her touch. Elizabeth frowned, but tried not to let it bother her.

Chapter 18

• THE UPSTAIRS HALLWAY was divided in half, with old wallpaper covering the top and providing a clear border to separate it from the bottom half. They'd remove it and paint it a creamy off-white color when the kids were done. The bottom half had been stripped of its old scratched paneling and was now divided into seven clear sections. It used to be eight, but the twins had combined theirs.

The kids had worked hard, allowed to draw whatever pictures they wanted. Small containers of vivid paints and various-sized brushes were scattered all over the dropcloth covering the floor. At one end of the hallway, Alex held Jessie's green-painted hands to the bottom of her picture of multicolored spring flowers.

"Dere's me!" Jessie grinned and clapped her hands, spraying small specks of green everywhere.

"There's you," Alex agreed. He tickled her by running

a small paintbrush over her palms. "Now let's write your name and age so we'll always know who painted it."

Geoffrey knelt by Abby's drawing, painting her hands bright blue. The twins were staring at her painting. David looked confused and Danielle was trying to look at it sideways, her neck bent almost in half.

"I still say it's a blob," he said, his hands on his hips.

"Not if you look at it like this," Danielle insisted. "Then it's a snowman on skis."

Elizabeth tilted her head and examined Abby's painting. "I can see it. Good job, sweetie."

Abby grinned at her, then slapped her hands against the wall. Geoffrey labeled it and moved to help Sarah sign her house. In a circle around the house, from top to bottom, were stick figures of the whole family holding hands. Alex winked at Elizabeth as he passed her, taking Jessie and Abby to wash up. Elizabeth smiled and moved around the hall, checking out the paintings.

David and Danielle's were dark and vivid anime-style cartoons. Good guys battled monsters to save the captured woman in the background. The twins were actually very talented, which she'd known, but to see something they'd *created* with that talent was a near spiritual experience.

Listening to Sarah explain to Geoffrey who each stick figure was and what she'd done to make it resemble the real person, Elizabeth strode over to Tommy's picture. He'd drawn a very realistic nighttime vision of a campfire surrounded by old-style army tents and towering pine trees. Ten sets of bare feet, complete with tiny toes, peeked out from under the tent flaps.

In the background, under the canopy of trees, were

three adult shadows. Two were clearly a man and a woman holding hands. The third, though, a tall man, was more distant. Blue-gray eyes reflected the moonlight as he stood back, watching them all.

"That's you, Geoffrey." Elizabeth looked around, noticing the twins had left already, and watched Sarah point to a blond man in the twelve o'clock position over the house, appearing to straddle the apex of the roof.

Geoffrey stared silently at the painting, his eyes darkening to liquid mercury. "You did a great job, Sarah."

Sarah beamed at him, then threw her arms around his neck and kissed his cheek. "Thank you, Geoffrey."

Geoffrey painted her hands red, helped her mark her picture, then she held her hands in front of her as she headed toward the bathroom where Alex still helped the other two. Elizabeth smiled at Geoffrey, who still stood staring at the picture.

"Looks like you've been adopted," she teased.

For a long moment, he didn't move or say anything. Then he nodded and stood. Reaching up, he began taking down the wallpaper above the picture before the paint could dry and rip as the paper came off. Grinning, Elizabeth walked past Kevin's spiders. Black furry ones, red bodied ones, green fanged ones, and some even had stripes. She had no idea what kind they were or how poisonous they might be, but that was okay. They were scary enough to make her shiver just with their detail. No wonder the toddlers screamed when they passed it.

But it didn't matter how scary they were. This was all about creating memories and making the home theirs. She had friends who'd have a heart attack at the mere thought of kids painting their walls, but she didn't regret her decision. The pictures were beautiful, each in varying stages of skill, saying so much about the artists who'd drawn them. She wouldn't trade it for any professionally decorated hallway in the world.

Last, but definitely not least, Teddy knelt before his, carefully painting a frame in a dark brown color that did a really good job of matching the wood floor. "I love that frame, Teddy. Lots better than the simple rectangles I was planning."

"Thank you, Aunt Lizzie," he said quietly, concentrating on each interlocking stroke.

Elizabeth eyed the other murals and the plain straight line revealed as Geoffrey peeled off the wallpaper. "Would you be interested in making that border around all of them? Then it would show how they all belong together. After we paint the cream on top, you could even do the border there. Would you like that?"

Teddy leaned back and eyed the pictures around the hall, then looked straight at Elizabeth, his eyes shining with excitement. "Really? You'd let me frame them all?"

"Yeah. I love the job you're doing."

He grinned. "Okay."

He'd been about to do the frame at the top of his picture, but chose to move to the next mural and start the bottom and sides of the frame, saving the top for later. Elizabeth briefly touched his head, running her fingers over his silky hair. He stilled for a moment, then continued what he was doing. His acceptance of her affection warmed her heart, especially after Shelly's rejection.

Elizabeth stared at his mural, taking in the almost

medieval simplicity of it. The background was a cream slightly darker than what she'd chosen for the top, and a yellowed scroll with black calligraphy took center stage. The first letter was elaborately drawn, like in old manuscripts, but the rest was simple black calligraphy. She lowered to her haunches, trying not to weep as she read the verse Teddy had chosen.

> "And that these days should be remembered and kept throughout every generation, every family, every province, and every city . . ."
>
> —ESTHER 9:28

He wanted to remember. Knowing that at least one of them wanted to remember it that way melted her heart. She had only hoped that someday they would look back and say, for that time, my whole family was together.

It was a big moment for them all and she'd made it possible. By staying when her mother was sick and dying and their parents were gone, she'd held them together so they could have this feeling of family. Despite the accomplishments she'd been praised and rewarded for in the past, this was the best thing Elizabeth had ever done.

Alex's hand settled on her shoulder. "I bought a clear sealant to protect these from fading. Might help some with scratches, too."

Her throat so full she could barely swallow, Elizabeth touched his hand. "Thank you."

Geoffrey had strips of the old wallpaper down, though parts still clung to the wall and would need to be scraped off later. Alex and Elizabeth each took an end of the wall and started peeling, trying not to drop the scraps all over Teddy.

"I'll finish this when you guys are done." Taking his paint and brushes, Teddy went to clean up, then headed downstairs with the others.

Elizabeth nodded. With the older kids downstairs with them, the younger ones would be okay for a while.

"How was your mom?" Geoffrey asked.

Elizabeth shook her head slowly and focused on what she was doing. "Not well at all. I've called half her list of people and they should be visiting over the next few days. It's going to wear her out more, but this will be their last chance."

"I'm sorry to hear that," he offered.

"Thanks." Elizabeth nodded. "There's so much left to do, though. Not just with her but with my sisters and the kids." Elizabeth looked at Alex and raised her eyebrow while talking to Geoffrey. "I assume Alex filled you in about last night?"

"He did." Geoffrey nodded. "There's a lot for you two to work out personally, I understand that. But I hope you realize the biggest worry is Maeve."

Alex looked at Elizabeth's scowl and shook his head. "There's too much you don't know."

"Like what?"

"Remember I told you about Kalyss's gift with memories?"

Elizabeth nodded.

Alex began to speak, to tell her a story that should have been pure fantasy, yet, strangely, wasn't. Kalyss had lived ten lifetimes, died in nine of them during efforts to free Dreux, the husband Elizabeth had met just that morning. He'd been trapped as a statue due to the hatred of his half-brother and his stepmother—Maeve.

Elizabeth peeled more of the paper as Geoffrey left. He already knew the story. It was Alex's turn to tell it. So she plucked at the paper, trying to understand and process each thing Alex told her. "So, they were cursed? By Maeve?"

"Yes."

"So, Dreux and Kai, who are half-brothers," she re-capped slowly, "were cursed by a fallen angel. Kalyss and Geoffrey got stuck in the middle of their battle, with Kalyss trying to save Dreux and getting killed by Kai. Nine times. And Geoffrey lived for a thousand years trying to reunite them. But when he did almost die, he was saved by an angel and the grim reaper?"

"Pretty much." Alex smiled innocently. "And you are the daughter of a fallen angel. When your father, who sees the future, tried to leave his family, you trapped him in your mind. Where you sometimes see him in the dreams you weave. The same dreams you've pulled one man into for vengeance and another for . . ."

Alex let the sentence trail off and she watched him, trying to think of the word to fill in the blank. Love sprang most immediately to mind, but did she love him? She shied away from that explanation. But it hadn't been just about sex. That sounded so crude and wrong on a bone-deep level.

Elizabeth bit her lip and stared at him helplessly. Alex raised a brow and stared back, his gaze firm. He wasn't going to let her off the hook. He wanted an answer, one he deserved to have. She'd shown him truths about her, about them, and he'd listened, watched, forgiven. But now he wanted not just a statement of her intentions all these years, but a statement about their future. This was the point they would branch from, for good or ill. Where did she want their relationship to go?

"For possibility. For dreams. For comfort and closeness and . . ." She took a deep breath. Alex smiled gently and moved closer, brushing hair from her face. Licking her lips, she finished, "For hope."

Lightly, Alex traced a finger from her temple to her jaw. He backed her to an unpainted section of wall between two doors, his eyes soft. His lips curved, darkly flushed and full and lickable. Slowly, Alex lowered his head. "Hope is good. I like hope."

When they touched hers, his lips were warm and tender. Coaxing her to open and fulfilling every promise with a nudge of his tongue against hers. Hot tingles flashed from the tips of her breasts, up to her shoulders and down to the hands she slid over his shoulders. Arching her back and standing on her toes she pressed into him, tight, aching.

Alex caressed one hand up the back of her neck to clench in her hair and small explosions cascaded through her system, rocking every nerve. Elizabeth widened her stance, hooking one ankle behind his calf, and stroked his tongue, swallowed his heat, wordlessly begged for more.

This was better than dreams. Better than fantasy. She could hardly breathe with the tingling in her stomach, the sensitivity of her nerves, but she wanted more. Elizabeth wanted Alex. Just thinking the words was a sort of freedom. An admission of so much she tried to deny. But also terrifying, because the words weren't enough.

This kiss wasn't enough. She wanted—needed—more. So much more.

Tightening her hold, Elizabeth pulled herself up, nearly crawling up his lean form. Alex raised her, pressed her back against the wall and the kiss became devouring. Deep and needy and desperate. Rough. Their abstinence was a painful starvation and her body wasn't willing to be good anymore. She hungered.

Alex pulled back far enough to gaze into her eyes. Elizabeth gasped for air and met his serious look. "We can't do this here."

She frowned, scowled, wanted to argue, but as she looked around the hallway of her mother's home, the door to the only room where she could find privacy— her mother's bedroom—she wanted to cry. Sometimes dreams were better. Returning her gaze to Alex's, she imagined . . . and the walls became black stone against her back. A bed formed behind Alex. Their bed with the sheet pulled back and the pillows plumped invitingly.

Alex looked around briefly. Elizabeth melted the clothes between them, thrilling to the slide of her thighs around his hips. Alex grinned, then pinched her bottom. "Wake up."

Elizabeth blinked and they were in the hallway, fully clothed, her legs regrettably *not* clutching him close. She pouted. "Why?"

Alex kissed her and smiled gently. "Because I want the real thing, not more dreams."

Elizabeth sighed. "But what if we never get the real thing?"

"Shh." He brushed her lips with his thumb. "That's what hope is for."

"That and stopping Maeve," she reminded him.

"Yeah. Did your dad have any ideas for how we should do that?"

"Not really. He just said that until she brings the battle to me, the rest is damage control."

He hugged her close. "You'd think a fallen angel would have more ideas."

"No. He won't tell me anything. He says teaching humans things they were supposed to learn on their own was part of the reason he fell. That giving us facts ruins the purpose of faith." She grimaced. Time to calm the hormones. "Ready for dinner? I should go start it."

Alex shook his head. "Geoffrey's cooking. He wanted to make his special chili."

She gave him a worried look. "It won't be too spicy, will it?"

Alex grinned. "Trust us."

Elizabeth shook her head, smiling. "Mama always said, don't trust a boy who *asks* you to trust him."

Alex winked at her. "I'm not a boy, though."

Turning from her, he bent and scooped a bunch of the stripped wallpaper. Elizabeth eyed his butt again. Nope. Definitely not a boy.

• AN HOUR LATER, Geoffrey's chili was making her stomach growl like it had been a year since lunch. Scraping the last of the wallpaper into the garbage bag, she looked up at Alex. "We're pretty much finished. After dinner, you and I can get ready to go find Felicia. You sure Geoffrey won't mind babysitting?"

"Not at all. We've already discussed it. Besides, the kids will be safer with him here."

She nodded. "I know they will. Otherwise I'd be too afraid to leave them."

"Don't worry. We can only do what we can do. In the meantime . . ." Alex raised a brow in challenge. "Race you to the kitchen."

She gave him a considering look and when he turned to set the bag to the side, Elizabeth laughed and ran past him.

"Cheater." Alex growled playfully from behind her.

Elizabeth headed down the stairs and to the kitchen, a bounce to her step. It was fun playing with him like this. No angst. No self-doubt. Just the freedom to laugh without feeling like it was a betrayal to someone.

Reaching the doorway, she froze and stared blankly at Shelly's door. Alex stopped abruptly behind her, his hands on her waist to keep from knocking her over. Shelly stepped back from her door and looked at them.

"What?" she demanded sullenly.

"It's black." Very black. Every rough chip, dent, and crack showed perfectly. Elizabeth stared from the door to her niece in confusion.

"So?" Shelly crossed her arms, her stance mutinous.

"Why didn't you paint a picture?" Or use a different color or anything except a flat black that sucks the life out of a person when they stare at it?

"I didn't want to. Alex said paint it. You said have fun. So I did." Her eyes said she'd known the door would upset Elizabeth, which had made doing it even more "fun".

"An all-black door is very depressing." Elizabeth tried

to say it tactfully, not wanting to explode the balance the family had accomplished. Lord knew, Shelly had enough attitude without fighting over a door, though this defiance was worse than usual.

"You didn't tell Kevin his spiders were too scary," Shelly reminded her.

Elizabeth raised a brow. Shelly had a point. The kids had been allowed to draw anything. If this was what Shelly wanted, why should the rules be different? But black? "Kevin's spiders were a picture. Art. With color."

"You want art? Fine." Shelly skimmed a finger over a white pan of paint and pressed it to the center of the door. "There you go."

Before Elizabeth could blink, Shelly threw open the door and stomped down the stairs.

"Dinner's almost ready, Shelly," Elizabeth called after her.

"I'm not hungry."

The door swung closed and Elizabeth sighed. Now the door was all black with a grayish white fingerprint in the center of it. "How is that art?"

Alex squeezed her shoulders sympathetically. "It's not too bad."

Geoffrey left the stove, grabbed something from the top of Shelly's backpack, and handed it to Elizabeth. "It's probably inspired by this."

Elizabeth flipped over the old paperback and read the back. The fingerprint represented the light at the end of the tunnel. Apparently, Shelly was stuck pretty deep for her light to be as small as a fingerprint on a tall, black door. A chill rose over Elizabeth's flesh, making every

goose pimple stand up. She shivered. "Why is she reading about teen suicide?"

"She said her teacher assigned it to give kids an idea of
how dark days are misguiding. That there are more people who love you and will grieve for you than you think."
Geoffrey went back to the stove and stirred the chili.

Elizabeth looked from the book's title to the door.

It was a good thing the teacher was trying to teach.
Still . . . to have a teenager dwell on suicide was scary.
Elizabeth frowned and tapped the book against her hand.
"Is that chili ready, Geoffrey? I should take her a bowl."

• "SHELLY?" ELIZABETH FOUND the bottom step in
the pitch dark and gingerly lowered her foot to the basement floor. She held one hand out to guide her way, feeling around the boxes and piles. There really was too
much stuff down here. It needed to be weeded out, because the last thing she wanted Shelly to feel was like
just another piece of worthless junk. "Shelly?"

Something rustled a few feet ahead of her, then a
small lamp snapped on. Shelly leaned back in her bed
and scowled at Elizabeth. "I said I wasn't hungry."

"I know." Elizabeth eased through the narrow walkway to the bed, thankful for the small glow of light, and
handed Shelly the bowl. "But after smelling it all this
time, I thought you'd be curious how it tasted. Besides,
you wouldn't want to hurt Geoffrey's feelings."

Shelly snorted. "I've seen enough to doubt he has any."

"Everyone has feelings. Even if they're locked up
tight." The living space in this room was miniscule. Between Shelly's bed, Veronica's crib, and the small

computer desk, complete with ancient computer, there really wasn't much room down here.

Shelly dipped a spoonful into her mouth and eyed Elizabeth speculatively. "He showed you the book, huh?"

"Yeah." Elizabeth eased back on one hand, leaning toward the foot of the bed so she could watch Shelly better. "Have you thought about committing suicide?"

"What self-respecting teenager hasn't?" Elizabeth gave her a look and she grinned. "You know it's true."

Elizabeth shook her head. "But you're angry. And not in the typical teenager way."

"Well, yeah." Shelly's voice had a "duh" tone. "Look at how much you're changing everything. You're re-arranging everyone."

"I'm cleaning up the house to make it better for all of you to grow up in." Where was the harm in that? Or did Shelly fear change?

"But we're not going to grow up here. And the more you change everything to make us feel at home, the more it's going to hurt when we leave here." Shelly spoke in a practical, matter-of-fact tone.

Elizabeth frowned. "Why won't you grow up here?"

"Because even though you haven't faced the truth, I have. We're all about to be split up. The baby and toddlers will be adopted out first. Kevin next. The twins will be separated." Shelly shrugged like it was a foregone conclusion.

Elizabeth shook her head, ready to deny Shelly's words.

"And I'll end up in foster home after foster home until I graduate, get out, and rescue Teddy and Tommy from the system." Shelly scooped more chili into her mouth and shook her head, not meeting Elizabeth's gaze.

"You won't be separated. This is the house all of you belong in. Together." She wasn't just wasting time on the place for appearances. She really wanted to make a home for all of them.

"Get real, Aunt Beth. You're leaving as soon as you can."

Elizabeth frowned, puzzled. "I haven't completely decided anything, but my life is set up in Seattle. But do you really think I'd do it at the sacrifice of your welfare?"

"If even you don't know what you'll do, how can I?" Shelly glared at her, the bowl forgotten in her lap. "All I know is, when you leave, no one is going to be here. Not Uncle Bobby or Aunt Felicia. There's *no one* else."

Elizabeth's eyes widened, at last understanding Shelly's fear. "Your mom will come back, Shelly. Dallas loves you. You were her first, her baby. She used to sit in her room and sing you to sleep. Being a mother is the one thing she's always been good at."

Shelly rolled her eyes and shook her head, like Elizabeth still didn't understand. "Times change, Aunt Beth. She won't come back. Not to stay."

Shelly seemed so sure, there was nothing Elizabeth could say to change her opinion. She could only make promises and hope she could keep them. "I will make sure you're fine first, Shelly. I won't just drop all of you."

"Sure, Aunt Beth." The phone rang on Shelly's nightstand and she grabbed it. "Hello?"

Elizabeth sighed. There always seemed to be an interruption in the middle of important conversations.

Shelly listened for a second, then scowled. Handing the phone over, she snapped, "It's Uncle Bobby."

Frowning, Elizabeth pulled the phone to her ear. They'd already talked once that night. "What's wrong?"

"You remember I wasn't feelin' too good?" Her brother sounded cautious.

"Yeah?" She tried to smile reassuringly at Shelly.

"I think it's Felicia, Beth. I think something's wrong."

"Like what?" They'd always been linked pretty close, but his warning was vague.

"Look, I know it's weird," Bobby said, his tone tense. "Just call it a twin thing."

"I don't doubt you, Bobby. But can you give me any more to go on? I'm planning to head out anyway, but is it urgent?"

A loud sigh blew over the receiver. "There's nothin' more. It's not urgent, but it's strong and it keeps building."

Elizabeth stared at the wall, waiting and trying to think. "Last time I spent all night searching for her, Bobby."

"I don't think she has all night, Beth."

She swallowed. "Then where do I go? Has she called you? Talked about anyone? Any place?"

"She won't say. She's still mad about last time."

"Then last time is all I have to go on." A few addresses, a bar, and the name of one drug dealer. That's what her brother had been able to give her last time she'd looked for her sister. It wasn't enough if time was an issue.

"Just . . ." He paused and spoke to someone with him. "Just one minute, please." Then his voice came back. "I have to go."

"I'll find her," Elizabeth promised.

"Yeah, okay."

She couldn't tell if he believed her or not. Clearly it was a task he was reluctant to delegate. But Elizabeth was the only option. Looking at Shelly, she sighed. She was the only option for all of them, it seemed.

Chapter 19

• ELIZABETH APPLIED ONE more coat of lipstick, darkening the coral hue just a bit more. She'd learned her lesson last time. If she wanted to find her sister, she'd get more help if she fit in. Not that she was willing to wear some of the slutty outfits she'd seen, but baby spit wouldn't get her far, either. And dressing up had the added benefit of giving her confidence.

She unbuttoned the top of her mother's silky maroon top, exposing just a hint of cleavage, and eyed the line of her very tight jeans. This was about as far as she was willing to go. In a few economical moves, she checked the laces of her black half-boots, flipped back the fringe of hair brushing her forehead, and flicked her emerald earrings. The simple, clipped-back hairstyle, along with the darker makeup, emphasized her eyes and mouth. This was as good as she got.

"You're just gonna find Aunt Felicia and come home, right?" Shelly eyed her doubtfully.

"Right," Elizabeth confirmed. "Hopefully it won't be so hard this time."

"You look more like you're going on a date."

"Well, I'm not. But I won't get answers from the people I'll need to talk to tonight if they won't give me the time of day." Elizabeth squirted lotion on her hand, flipped off the bathroom light, and entered the bedroom, rubbing her hands together.

Shelly's eyes narrowed, then she nodded. "Just try to hurry. It's one thing to leave us during the day with strange men, but nighttime is different."

Elizabeth eyed her seriously, seeing the worry in Shelly's eyes. "I realize it's only been a week since we met him, honey, but I wouldn't leave you with him if I didn't think we could trust Geoffrey."

"It's the people you trust that do the most damage." The teen's eyes darkened.

Elizabeth stared at the strain around her eyes, the pinched look to her mouth. God, when Shelly was like this, it broke her heart. How could she look at that face and tell her that fears about men were the least of their problems?

Finally, she shook her head. Finding Felicia was one of the things she had to do. And Geoffrey was dependable. "I promise I'll hurry."

Shelly nodded reluctantly before leaving the room.

Elizabeth followed her, sliding her check card and ID into her back pocket. No sense in carrying a purse and risking it being stolen. She grabbed a small bag of clean clothes and toiletries for Felicia and flipped off the bedroom light. Stopping at the toddler's soon-to-be old room, she pushed the door open.

Two bunk beds occupied opposite walls, with two tall dressers in between. Toys were boxed up neatly, waiting to be set up in the other room once the paint dried.

Jessie and Sarah were asleep, their little bottoms sticking up in the air, thumbs in their mouths. She freed the digits and tucked the covers around their little shoulders. On the other side of the room lay Abby, asleep on the bottom bunk. Danielle lay on the top, wide awake and probably missing her twin.

When she moved to tuck Danielle in, the girl turned her head, her gaze meeting Elizabeth's. "You're going out tonight?"

"Yeah. Just for a few hours." She wouldn't mention searching for Felicia. The girl had been hurt enough and Elizabeth would hate to face her disappointment if she failed to bring Danielle's mother home.

"You'll be okay? No drinking?" Her face was pale, pinched.

"No. I won't drink," she promised.

"Have fun." Danielle smiled a wobbly smile.

Elizabeth smiled back, a little wobbly herself, and pulled up the blankets. Her mother and sisters had done quite a job on these kids if they found it so hard to see her leave for a few hours at night. "I won't be gone long."

She kissed the girl on the forehead and quietly left the room, keeping the door cracked open for the hall light to shine in. The weight of her promises made over the last several weeks settled around her, nearly crippling her. What did she know about being a good mother? They had so many needs, how could she meet them all? But who would be there if not her?

According to Shelly, no one.

The boys slept on bunk beds, also. Toys poured from their closet and under the beds. She covered each of them, hating the worry in their eyes as they noticed her outfit. Honestly, it wasn't her first choice either. Plush jammies with comfy slippers sounded so much better at the moment.

"You won't be gone all night, will you?"

"No, Teddy. Just a few hours." Elizabeth straightened his already perfect covers and kissed him on the cheek.

"Have fun, Aunt Lizzie," a small voice called from the lower bunk.

"Thanks, Kevin. You get some sleep, okay?" The baby of the boys, Kevin was only six and had remained remarkably innocent through all of the family drama. But even he was tense at the thought of Elizabeth going out.

"Just don't sleep with him," Tommy advised. "They always leave after you sleep with them."

Tommy was only nine, but always knew how to throw Elizabeth into a tailspin. "I have no plans to sleep with him."

She pulled the covers up to his chin, but Tommy reached out and held her hand. "It's okay when they do go. I'm learning all I can for when they're gone."

Elizabeth met his blue eyes, so like her own. "Is that why you follow Geoffrey?"

"Don't worry. I won't get too attached."

Elizabeth swallowed against the lump in her throat and nodded. Alex wanted more than the one week they'd had, but there was no guarantee what the future held. Even the visions her father had shared were maddeningly unclear.

When she came to David, he was staring at her with an unnerving thoughtfulness. His video games were loud. When playing and mischief making, he was loud. But now he was uncharacteristically solemn. Elizabeth tucked him in and met his gaze steadily until he was ready to say what was on his mind.

Finally, "Do you think you'll see my mom?"

Elizabeth bit her lip, then answered him honestly. "I hope so."

He closed his eyes and faced the wall.

Elizabeth closed her eyes and sighed.

In a tiny voice, he said, "Tell her we said hi."

Hastily blinking back tears, she patted his shoulder, blew them all a kiss, and backed through the door. Downstairs, Geoffrey waited with Shelly. She sat patting Veronica's bottom as the baby patted her shoulder. The baby's little round face was relaxed, eyes blinking lazily and fighting sleep as her chubby hand moved up and down. Elizabeth rubbed the little back and kissed her cheek. Then she reached out and ran Shelly's ponytail through her fingers. Shelly jerked away.

"Did you leave Alex's cell number?" she demanded.

"On the fridge." Elizabeth studied the puffy redness around the silver earrings in Shelly's ears.

"You gonna be gone all night?" Shelly raised a brow.

"I promised I'd hurry." Elizabeth frowned and indicated the jewelry. She, her mom, and her sisters were all allergic to fake jewelry. It looked like Shelly was, too. "You might want to take those off soon."

Shelly angled her chin. "They're fine."

Elizabeth sighed, wanting to argue, but knew it wouldn't make a difference what she said. Shelly was a stubborn person and Elizabeth needed to pick her battles very carefully. "At least get some rest."

"Sure," Shelly snapped with heavy sarcasm.

Elizabeth gave her a warning glare. Her patience did have a limit and it was rapidly approaching.

Alex entered the living room. "Ready?"

Elizabeth stared at Shelly's closed face and took a deep breath. Geoffrey sat in a chair, his long legs stretched before him. He looked calm, as if Shelly's obvious distrust were a challenge he'd deal with.

Elizabeth's stomach twisted with tension. Would saying good-bye even matter to Felicia? She knew Mom was sick. Was this rapid dash to find her worth leaving the kids for? If Elizabeth were hurt, she could handle that. But she couldn't face the children being hurt by one of her decisions.

"All will be well." Geoffrey's calm voice and confident words brought her gaze to him. His attitude eased her tension.

Elizabeth rolled her shoulders and nodded. "Thank you."

He inclined his head.

"See you later." She smiled at Shelly, who hid her face in the curve of the baby's neck. Elizabeth swallowed her disappointment and turned toward Alex.

His hazel eyes glowed warmth and compassion. She took a step toward him, suddenly afraid the night would hold so much more than she'd planned. Nothing was ever easy.

• ELIZABETH SHIVERED AND rubbed her arms. It was a chilly night and the wind cut right through her jacket. Other than the quaking trees, the dark street was completely silent. Nothing moved in the inky black shadows, or at least, nothing she'd like to meet.

The party house where she'd found Felicia last time was closed for business. Or so the dark windows and empty yard seemed to suggest. She knocked, just in case, but the empty rooms beyond the bare windows told her only that the house had been abandoned.

"Nothing around back, either."

The sudden sound of Alex's voice jangled up her spine and she gasped, barely keeping in a screech. When she saw him rounding the corner of the house, she held a hand over her heart, struggling for breath.

He grinned. "Sorry."

"Sure you are." She shook her head. "There are still a few more places to check."

Elizabeth and Alex revisited three other places she'd searched two and a half months ago. The first was in the middle of a party. She walked quietly past staring, critical eyes. But here was where dressing up to fit in came in handy.

After a glance or two, people took her for someone who belonged and left her alone to search for Felicia's friend. Not that finding Tonya got her anywhere. She was otherwise occupied behind a locked bedroom door. Alex eyed her hand on the knob, his eyebrows raised.

Elizabeth shrugged. She had to find Felicia and she didn't care what she interrupted to do it.

Pulling out her most recent picture of Felicia, Elizabeth quit trying to be subtle. A few people recognized her picture, but they hadn't seen her that night. By eleven thirty, the other two places were also a lost cause. Elizabeth rubbed her temples as they exited the last house. The bar was all they had left. And the name of someone she didn't want to speak to again.

Alex put a hand on her back, supporting her as they walked down the ragged concrete stairs. A brunette in a micro-mini and halter top stumbled and fell against the porch post to their left. Her eyes were glassy and she laughed in a way that said the beer in her hand wasn't the first.

"You the one lookin' for Felicia?"

Elizabeth eyed her hopefully. "Yeah. She's my sister."

The woman nodded and almost tripped down the front steps. Elizabeth reached out to help her, but she caught herself at the last moment. "She mentioned going to the bar. You might want to try Litz's Tavern over on . . . um . . ."

"I know where it is." Felicia had mentioned the bar a few times. "Thank you." Elizabeth beat a hasty retreat, thankful she'd gotten something.

After climbing into Alex's truck, she turned to him. "It's getting pretty late. You don't have to—"

Resting one forearm on the steering wheel, he shook his head and interrupted, "I'm not done until you are, Elizabeth. We'll go to the bar. If she's not there, we continue to wherever else we can think of."

His eyes glittered mere inches away from hers and

she couldn't help but feel happy he was with her. Just his presence made her feel safer. "Thank you."

Alex grinned and leaned forward. "Thank me later."

Elizabeth laughed as his lips settled on hers for a quick peck. He was definitely going above and beyond in a search that took him places he should never have to go. Two words didn't seem enough appreciation for that.

• IT WAS KARAOKE night at Litz's Tavern and a slim woman in hip-huggers and a midriff-baring tank top belted out an off-key version of "My Immortal" by Evanescence. A few friends danced and sang along while other people played pool toward the back. It was a weeknight, but you couldn't tell that from the crowd.

Elizabeth searched the people around her for a familiar face. She had to find her sister, but she couldn't continue the search forever. For one thing, she didn't know where else to look. For another, there was no way in the world she would leave the kids to barhop every night. Then there was Bobby's "bad feeling".

Alex followed close behind her, his hand on her waist. Part of her wanted to assure him she was just fine and had done this before—by herself—but she tamped down the impulse. His touch was protective and guiding, and considering how out of her element she was, Elizabeth kept her mouth shut.

At the back of the bar, nearer the pool tables, she finally recognized someone. Sean? John? His black eyes sparkled when he saw her and a grin tugged at the corner of his mouth.

"Hey, sister." At least he wasn't calling her babe this time. She could handle sister. Plus, that's who she was. Felicia's sister.

Alex settled solid and warm against her back. "Hi, Ron."

Elizabeth blinked as Ron nodded over her head. They knew each other? Did Alex have a habit she should worry about? Elizabeth smiled weakly into the dealer's eyes.

"You out lookin' for her again, or is this my lucky night?" Ron wagged his brows suggestively. He had to know he'd get nowhere with her, but he was so playful with his flirting it was almost charming. And he was probably trying to annoy Alex, judging by the quick nod and grin he gave him.

"Do you know where she is?" Elizabeth tamped down a spurt of hope before it could build too high.

Ron's grin melted away and his eyes got serious. He leaned in. Alex stiffened against her back, but other than a slight smile, the drug dealer didn't react. Thank God. She did *not* need a pissing contest.

"Honey, why are you doing this? You tried taking her away, but she's made her choice. You can keep trying to change her, but it's only going to hurt you. She won't change until she's ready."

"I'm learning." She nodded. "But this time it's different."

He raised his eyebrows doubtfully, like he'd already heard every reason before.

"Mom only has a few days left. It's Felicia's last chance to say good-bye."

He narrowed his eyes, judging her honesty.

Ron looked around the bar, then back at them. "She'll be pissed if I just turn her over again."

"I just want to talk to her. No pushing her anywhere."

He gave her a skeptical look.

Returning his cynicism, Elizabeth spoke with a low, dry tone. "I can't force her to change, right?"

"Right," he said slowly. Then he shrugged. "I could always take her to the hospital myself."

Elizabeth raised a doubtful brow. "You want to go to a hospital to visit a dying woman?"

He grinned. "No, not really."

Elizabeth smiled in spite of herself. At least he knew himself well enough to be honest.

"Okay." Ron nodded decisively. "Give me a number to call when I find her."

"You don't know where she is?" Elizabeth frowned.

Ron shrugged. "She was going out with friends tonight."

Alex passed a card over her shoulder and she could see AK MARTIAL ARTS in big, bold letters. "My cell is on the back."

The guy met Alex's gaze for a long moment, then nodded as he pocketed the card. "I don't know how long it'll take. Give me about an hour or so."

Elizabeth nodded. "Thank you."

Alex put a hand at the small of her back and guided her out. The breeze was very nice after the clouds of smoky air inside the bar. "Was giving him your business card a good choice?"

Alex shrugged as he held the truck door open for her. "I know him. He's the son of one of my parents' neighbors. We haven't spoken in years, though. Honestly, if he wants to hurt me, he's got a more direct line. My parents haven't moved in thirty-five years."

As he shut the door and circled the truck, Elizabeth shook her head. For all its growth, Spokane was still a very small world. Alex climbed in beside her and started the engine.

"Where do we wait, then?" Elizabeth warmed her hands under her thighs.

Alex looked down, playing with his keys. "In the bar?"

She shook her head. Too loud, too smoky.

"Or go home?"

Only to leave again? Just the thought of waking any of the kids and saying another tense good-bye nixed that idea.

"We can go to Perkins and have a drink." He raised a brow and glanced at her.

Crowds of strangers just didn't appeal right then. She wrinkled her nose.

He grinned. "My apartment isn't far from here."

She snorted.

"I can show you my etchings and maybe it'll be my lucky night." He waggled his brows as she laughed.

Suddenly loud, angry voices cut through the night. Elizabeth turned and looked through the back window. Several dark shadows were grouped together in an empty lot across the street. The sudden click of the truck door had Elizabeth swinging toward Alex's empty seat. He swiftly approached the group, running the last few steps. Fumbling with the door latch, Elizabeth hurried after him.

"Dude, this is none of your damn business." One younger guy blocked Alex, warning him off. A wife-beater showed off his well-defined arms.

"If it was one-on-one, it would be none of my busi-ness," Alex stated calmly. "However, four against a nearly unconscious one is a different story." Alex walked around the guy, entering the mix.

"You don't even know the story, man. Just stay back." Another guy tried to push Alex, but Alex easily avoided his hands and stepped around the guy while he was off balance.

"Stories are good. Tell me one." Alex placed himself to the side of a man kneeling on the ground. He kept the group in clear view, but Elizabeth's breath caught. This could go so wrong.

"This asshole kept grabbing my girlfriend's ass, so I'm gonna kick his." The speaker had a crew cut and blood trailing from his nose. He nodded at one of the women standing in the circle around them.

"No I didn't!"

Elizabeth pushed her way to the front, but stayed quiet. Distracting Alex wouldn't be a good thing right now. She followed the boyfriend's glance to a woman with long, permed brown hair, tight hip-huggers, a belly-baring tube top, and an excited gleam in her eye. Apparently, the girlfriend enjoyed being fought over, no matter how much someone else got hurt.

Dallas used to say the best way to see if a man was losing interest was to see if he fought for his girl. This woman seemed to follow the same tenet. Elizabeth pressed her lips and wrapped her arms around herself, struggling to hold in her irritation. The couple would probably go home and have the hottest sex two drunk people could manage and this whole fight would become just another ego-boosting story for them both.

But the man on the ground had the real damage. Both eyes were nearly swollen shut, blood ran steadily from a cut on his forehead, and his arm was wrapped around his torso. He probably had a few bruised or broken ribs. Getting beat down by four guys because of one immature, insecure female meant taking a lot of damage for nothing.

"Well, his ass looks pretty kicked. Your job here is done." Alex held his hands up peaceably, trying his hardest to diffuse the situation.

"Hell, no. I'm gonna make sure he keeps his hands to himself from now on." The boyfriend stepped forward, attempting to shoulder Alex out of the way.

Alex stood his ground. It forced the guy to back up. "No. I don't think that's necessary."

"Look man, I got the point. You want to stop the fight, but unless you want your ass kicked, move." The boyfriend squared off in front of Alex, nose to nose, his fists clenched, doing his damnedest to appear intimidating.

Alex didn't move. Elizabeth growled low in her throat. What was he trying to prove? But then she glanced to the man struggling to rise from the ground and knew Alex wasn't proving anything. He was trying to keep someone from getting hurt any further. She could support that, as long as he didn't end up getting himself hurt.

The boyfriend puffed up his chest and shoved. "I said *move*!"

Alex twisted so the shove glanced ineffectually off his chest. Straightening, he shook his head and quietly said, "Not gonna happen."

Chapter 20

◈

• ELIZABETH COULD ONLY stare in horrified fascination as the boyfriend threw a punch at Alex while his friends went for the guy still on the ground, but Alex grabbed his wrist and sent the boyfriend flying into his buddies. The four of them crashed together and hit the dirt.

They rose, angrier than ever, and rushed him as a group. Elizabeth could see Alex's foot shoot out low while his hands reached into the midst of them, pulling arms and angling wrists and a few other things too quick for her eyes to fully catch. Whatever it was he did, Alex still stood while the others ended up on the ground again.

Elizabeth couldn't help but be wowed. He wasn't hitting or fighting at all. The only bruises the guys would go home with were the ones they acquired from falling. Which made Alex even more impressive. Protective and strong, brave enough to face down a group of drunken guys and win, with no one getting hurt.

Until the boyfriend stood, wiped more blood from his nose, and said, "Fuck this."

Alex's eyes narrowed as the guy pulled a gun. Elizabeth barely had time to blink before a loud boom sounded in the barely lit field. Alex flinched. The crowd ran. By the time Elizabeth reached Alex's side, they were nearly alone. He wrapped an arm over her shoulders and pulled her tight to his side.

"Looks like you know your business." Ron's voice came from their left and Elizabeth angled her head, the rest of her unable to move with Alex's grip so tight.

"Well enough," Alex said, an odd, rough pitch to his voice.

Elizabeth studied his face, pale in the glow of the passing headlights. She frowned, puzzled until she felt a warm wetness spreading between them. He'd been shot? She gasped and Alex pressed his lips to hers, hard. His eyes were glittering, his message unmistakable. But why?

"Maybe I should check your dojo out."

Alex met Ron's gaze, his expression implacable. "As long as it's understood there's only one business on the premises."

Ron nodded. "That's a reasonable request."

Alex raised a brow. "It's not a request."

Ron laughed. "Agreed."

The man with the broken ribs was being helped to his feet by two other guys. He nodded to Alex. "Thanks, man. For the record, I never touched the stupid bitch."

"No problem." Alex grinned as if his weight weren't resting on Elizabeth more and more as the seconds passed. She had her arms wrapped tight around him, hugging him as though she was scared and needed reassurance.

Elizabeth started tugging against Alex. "We need to go."

Ron nodded. "Yeah. The cops will be here soon. You did nothing wrong, but you'll be stuck here explaining that all night and probably get arrested anyway. It would suck to be the only man arrested for this."

"Yeah, it would." Alex started walking, Elizabeth matching him step for step. He was still mostly under his own steam, but from her bra-line to her hip, they were fused by soaked material. At the truck, he pulled open the driver's door. "Get in and slide over."

Elizabeth scowled. "You can't—"

He exhaled an impatient breath. "I'll be fine. Just slide in—"

"No."

"The kids aren't at risk here, Elizabeth. So please, at least for now, trust me and get in the damn truck."

He looked impatient and irritated with her, an air of danger surrounding him in the darkness. Whiskers darkened his jaw and his eyes glittered with a hard edge. She wasn't used to seeing him like this. It was unnerving. But the longer she delayed, the more likely they'd still be here when the cops arrived. Which meant the longer he would have to wait to get patched up since he seemed unwilling to admit to anyone that he was hurt. Gritting her teeth, Elizabeth climbed in, lifted the armrest, and slid over to the passenger's side.

* * *

• GREY LIGHT FILTERED through dingy windows, dimly lighting the bed and the naked man lying there. Ron had said to keep Dave happy, and Felicia had done her job well. Pulling on her silky thong and his long T-shirt, she padded over to the end of the bed and slid down to sit beside the room's only other piece of furniture—a small wooden end table that held all she would need for the rest of the night.

Grabbing the bottle of water off of it, she took a drink, then leaned her head back against the wall and closed her eyes. She had a little time left before Dave would be ready for another go 'round. She exhaled a shaky breath and opened her eyes, willing away the hot sting of tears.

It's not supposed to be this way.

Felicia held her breath against another hot rush of tears. If she woke Dave, he'd want more and he wouldn't care if she was crying while he fucked her.

You were never meant to be alone.

Chills broke along her arms as hot tears rolled down her cheeks. She wasn't supposed to be alone. She wasn't supposed to need drugs in order to stomach sex. She wasn't supposed to hurt every time she thought of her children.

And yet, she did.

He promised he'd be here to help you, but he's not. No one is.

Felicia had never been designed for solitude. From the moment of conception, Bobby had been with her. Her twin, her other half. Felicia raised her hand and wiggled her fingers at the ceiling, drawing the light from the window and casting a rainbow of colors against the plaster. Watching with a smile as the rainbow split apart, showering sparks of light like fireworks.

She wasn't hallucinating. She'd already come down from the last hit. Besides, ice didn't cause these hallucinations. This had been her gift since she and Bobby were little. Only he knew about it.

They'd used to make the most incredible light shows back when only a few feet had separated their beds. She'd called herself Mistress of Light and he'd been Master of Shadows, able to draw shadows into any shape, with any density. He'd always made the ceiling darker as she'd drawn light from an outside lamppost, making her colorful sparks show up even brighter.

It's not as pretty without him. It's like only half the show.

Raw grief crushed her chest and she clamped her lips shut, holding in her moans. Her shoulders shook from the strength of her sobs and she tried again to force it away. Dave stirred in the bed, the covers rustling against his legs. Felicia shivered, hugging the shirt around her as she held her breath. Please, not yet. She wasn't ready.

He stilled, his snores returning. She eyed the glass pipe on the table beside two little baggies of clear crystals and a tiny scoop. Dave had emptied his pockets and shared a few hits with her hours earlier. Felicia picked up a bag of meth and struggled with the Ziploc at the top. She wouldn't have much longer, and if he touched her while she wasn't stoned . . . she shuddered.

Bobby had been trying to help her the first time he'd brought a joint home. He hadn't realized what he was beginning for them both, or that he'd cause a greater pain than the one already killing her.

Stupid boy. He should have known what bringing home drugs would do.

Maybe. But until they were fifteen, they'd shared everything. Then she'd been raped. He couldn't share that.

He didn't wanted to share your suffering. He'd only wanted to shut you up.

No! Everything in her balked at that thought. She *knew.* She remembered.

Dave's snores slowed, then stopped. He'd wake up soon.

How sad that you still have to get stoned before you can bear another man's touch.

Felicia grabbed the baggie off the table, spilling meth onto the table where she could use the scoop to put some at the bubble-shaped end of her pipe. Flicking her lighter on, she gently rolled the glass bowl over the flame, side to side so it wouldn't burn and taste horrible. She hiccupped and more tears poured from her eyes, blurring the melting crystals until they looked like a snowy blanket.

Yes, it really was sad. She hated it, but the alternative was unbearable. She'd already endured enough pain, she couldn't stand withdrawals on top of it. Dave stirred again and she hurriedly lowered her lips to the pipe, inhaling and quickly blowing out.

Another puff or two and she'd be okay.

But you're still alone and that's never okay for you. Bobby left you to suffer by yourself yet again.

Felicia relaxed back her head against the wall, her hands fallen to the floor. She stared straight ahead, her gaze glassy and unfocused.

Maeve stepped back and smiled. That had been too easy. Still enjoyable, but easy. The man stirred on the bed just as the pipe fell from Felicia's hand.

Tossing back the covers, he strode into the bathroom, not bothering with a light. Maeve's lips curled contemptuously at his rude noises. After a few minutes, he returned to the room and stared at Felicia's eyes. He sighed.

"I want my shirt back." Turning his back, Dave pulled his pants on. When he turned back, Felicia was convulsing. Swearing, he checked the empty bags on the table, and cussed more. Pocketing what was left, he rushed to the door. Felicia had fallen still. Dave shook his head and pulled the door shut.

"Stupid bitch."

• ALEX SHUT HIS door, started the truck, and was already pulling away as Elizabeth buckled her seat belt. She almost reminded him to buckle his until she realized the seat belt would press against his wound. But wouldn't pressure be good? Something about his grim silence kept her from trying. They were around the corner and down the block before she even heard sirens. Alex calmly continued on, his face forbidding, but his hands relaxed on the wheel.

When they were a few blocks away, she'd had enough of the silence. "Why won't you go to a hospital?"

"Because I don't need one. Elizabeth—"

"What kind of macho bullshit is that?" At least he was driving straight, seemingly in control. Would he pass out? Elizabeth eyed the driver's side of the cab, planning each move she would have to make to take control if he did.

Alex took a deep breath and whistled it through clenched teeth. "Apparently the kind I have to show you."

"What?" Was the blood loss making him delusional now? She reached over and felt his forehead for a fever.

He shrugged her away, batting her hand in irritation. "Believe me, this was not my preferred way of doing this. A quiet atmosphere, a soundproofed room . . ."

"Alex!"

"A gag . . ."

She growled loudly. He pulled into the parking lot of some apartments and she reined her temper in. She prayed she wouldn't lose him because she'd had to go looking for her drug-addicted sister. Her breath whooshed out like she'd been punched. In her vision she'd watched him slowly disappear into a grave.

God, she hated her father's visions. She always failed to prevent them. Always. Rushing out of the truck and around to his side, Elizabeth helped him climb the stairs to the apartment Alex pointed out, unlocked the door for him, and kicked it shut behind them. She barely kept him from falling over until they reached his bed.

Alex pulled off his shirt and scrunched it under him as Elizabeth turned on the overhead light. When she returned to his side, his head was on a pillow and his eyes were closed. His skin was so pale, almost translucent. Bile burned at the back of her throat.

"You need a doctor." Alex ignored her, his body tense, his eyes squeezed shut. No doubt trying to control the pain as much as a macho, brain-dead male could without hospitals and anesthesia and painkillers. Gasping for breath, Elizabeth rushed to his bathroom and scrambled around for anything that seemed like it would help. A clean towel, bandages. "I don't understand your hesitation, Alex. You could die."

Elizabeth blinked away the prick of tears, washed her hands, and hurried back to him. Alex's eyes were open as she knelt by the bed.

"I'm sorry you had to find out this way," he gasped.

"What?" Elizabeth shook her head and scowled, wiping away some of the blood so she could see the bullet wound. It was dark and red, jagged around the edges. Blood gushed from it in a thick trickle. She nearly gagged.

Alex wrapped a hand around her wrist, stopping her from applying pressure. "Wait."

She scowled at him. "Why?"

He didn't say anything, but when she looked at his side, she saw. Alex lay perfectly still, but the wound *moved*. A small bump quivered beneath his raw flesh, coming closer and closer to the surface. What was it? Nausea churned her stomach and her hands started shaking. Was she going to pass out before she could help him? Alex's hand slid from her wrist.

"Oh my God." And it was a prayer, probably the most eloquent one she could produce at the moment, considering how the nausea triggered the gag reflex at the back of her throat. Elizabeth looked to Alex, trying to focus through the tears gathering in her eyes, but his eyes were closed again.

Whatever it was in the wound appeared at the edges, small and black. Elizabeth wiped more blood away to see it better. Hard. Metallic. It was the bullet. Every episode of *CSI* she'd ever watched told her so, but nothing had prepared her for the sight of it emerging, without aid, from inside someone she cared for. Right as she watched. How the hell?

"Take it," Alex gasped.

Elizabeth glanced at his face, then back to the bullet. She spread the wound with one hand and tried to grasp the slippery bullet with her fingernails. She hadn't run across tweezers in her hurried examination of his bathroom. Blood ran hot over her hands and tears fell from her eyes. "I'm not trained for this, Alex."

"You're doing good, honey. Just hang in there. It'll be okay."

He was the one shot, yet he could console her? The bullet slipped from her grasp again, and she choked on her tears. It was sticking out by millimeters now.

"It's almost out, Alex. Almost." She tried to grab the bullet, using the edges of the towel as a grip against the slippery metal, refusing to worry about threads being in the wound. The whole towel would be pressed to it soon anyway. And then she'd have to worry about stitching him up. Did bachelors have sewing kits? How could she give him stitches without one? Hysteria welled faster than her tears.

"Its okay, Elizabeth," Alex said as the bullet came free.

Her hands were so sticky she could barely maneuver them. She hurriedly wiped them on an end of the towel, but froze as a soft blue light emerged from within Alex's wound. Her jaw dropped and she could only stare, inhaling raggedly. The blood slowed to a lazy stream, then barely a trickle and she could tell the flesh was knitting together behind it. Clearly, she didn't need to give him stitches. He didn't need a hospital.

Her terror was for naught. Her fear, her anxiety. All because Alex had a secret he hadn't managed to share. Gritting her teeth, she unscrewed the rubbing alcohol and dumped it over his wound just before it closed completely.

Alex bowed his back off the bed. "Holy shit, Elizabeth!"

Sniffing, she capped the bottle and rose to her feet. His wound was only a pink scar now. "At least it won't get infected."

"Infected?"

She angled her chin stubbornly.

"You did that for pure freakin' meanness!"

"Like it would have been so hard just to say, 'Don't worry about my bullet, Elizabeth. As soon as it's out, I'll be fine.'" She gestured toward herself. "I have been freaking out over here, worried sick."

"I'm sorry I scared you."

Elizabeth wrapped her shaky arms around her torso and strode toward the bathroom, holding in her tears, anger, and relief. It was all she could do not to explode. "If I had a gun, I'd shoot you again."

"Elizabeth—"

She slammed the door and locked herself in, then leaned against the wall and stared at her blood-covered self in the mirror.

• "THEY LOOK COZY."

Draven's sudden appearance on Alex's shadowed

balcony forced Silas back into the wrought-iron railing. "There's a reason airplanes have control towers."

"I am not as big as an airplane."

"No, but if you push me off this, you're going to fly," Silas threatened.

Draven snorted, obviously unimpressed. "Mary Beth is stable. One visit from the bitch goddess and all Alex's work was undone."

Silas sighed. "She's getting busy, then, attacking from multiple fronts. Alex was shot tonight."

"She was there?"

"I don't know for sure. I was with the children and arrived as he healed."

"Elizabeth must have freaked."

"She did." Silas gestured through the window to Alex's bedroom. Alex stood by the door Elizabeth had just slammed between them.

"How are the children?"

"They're fine. Shelly is sleeping. I've tried to convince her to remove the earrings all day, but she's good at ignoring me."

"She trusts Geoffrey enough to fall asleep?" Draven queried doubtfully, not surprised someone could ignore Silas. In fact, it was one of Draven's favorite things to do.

"Geoffrey would accept no less."

"If Maeve has already visited Mary Beth and Alex, then that leaves the kids, Dreux, and Kalyss, right?"

"And Felicia. But Dreux and Kalyss are safe. The shields for the emerald obscure both the dojo and the apartment above it."

Draven nodded. "You find Felicia. Whisper in her ear

to come home. I'll go to the kids, convince Shelly to remove the earrings. Maeve can't have that link to the children."

Silas grabbed Draven's arm. "Check in before morning. Sooner if you see Maeve."

The cowled head bent to look at Silas's hand and said sarcastically, "Yes, Daddy."

Silas shuddered and released his grip.

Draven disappeared, leaving only a husky chuckle drifting in the wind.

• As THE CLEAR stream rushed over her arms, turned rusty, and circled down the drain, Elizabeth knew Alex's blood was actually there. It was soaked into her skin, under her fingernails, and had definitely ruined her silk shirt.

Shrugging off the blouse, she dropped it into the sink, plugged it, and let it fill with cold water. Last thing they needed was for a bloody shirt to be found in the garbage. Searching under the sink, she found some tile cleaner with bleach and scrubbed it into the shirt. The silk bled and bleached white in spots, but the blood came out for the most part. Whatever was left on it would be ruined by the bleach.

Elizabeth stared at her reflection. Almost two in the morning and she stood in nice, normal, boy-next-door's bathroom wearing jeans, a black lace bra, and blood on her face. So much for knowing him. She officially knew nothing about Alexander Foster, except that he could heal himself, even from a bullet.

And that he'd selflessly stepped into the middle of a

potentially deadly drunken brawl to save a stranger. Just as he'd selflessly come to her house every day for the past week. He was patient and gentle with the kids. And he'd accepted her strange gifts. Not only that, but he'd forgiven her for the way she'd endangered him with their dreams.

Elizabeth closed her eyes and leaned her head against the wall. Forgiving him for having secrets was a non-issue. She couldn't blame him for not exposing his gifts before she had. She'd been searching for reasons to push him away. He would have seen his ability as a definite reason for her to shove.

She sighed. There was too much information for a single day to hold. No, she wasn't angry. But she still shook, deep past her muscles and into her bones. Fear was loosening its grip, but it had clamped so tight she shivered as it left. She could barely breathe between the cramps in her chest as she tried to hold herself together. The vision of his headstone wouldn't leave her. *He was love.*

She blinked back more tears. "Two in the freaking morning is too late for this."

A soft rap sounded on the door. Too exhausted to care about modesty, she flipped the lock and waited. The handle turned and the door swung slowly open. Alex's jeans clung stiff and damp from thigh to hip to a trim waist and defined stomach, his chest was lightly sprinkled with hair and marked with streaks of dried blood as if he'd tried to wipe it off. His long hair had come untied and now framed his face, neck, and collarbone—the perfect dark backdrop to his glittering hazel eyes.

She took in Alex's cautious expression and the grim set of his clenched jaw. "Still mad?"

She bit her lip as her eyes filled with yet more tears. She shook her head. No. Anger was not the emotion she battled.

Alex released a sigh and the stiffness flowed out of his posture. In one fluid motion, his arms snaked around her and pulled her against his warmth. Sliding one palm under her hair to her nape, he whispered, "I'm sorry I scared you."

Elizabeth rubbed her cheek against his chest, the hairs rough against her skin. Embracing him in return, she held him tight, pressed together from cheek to thighs, but it still wasn't enough. She wanted to crawl inside him, feel him on every inch of her. For so long she'd held them separate, first by distance, then by sheer willpower. But that was gone now, drained away by the sure knowledge that Alex might still earn that grave her father had shown her. This might be their last chance to experience everything she'd denied them.

Sliding one hand up Alex's torso, to curve behind his neck and tangle in his hair, Elizabeth locked her gaze with his. Clearly, succinctly, she demanded, "Closer."

• ALEX SWALLOWED AGAINST the lump in his throat, not daring to speak. He'd held his body under such tight control, he was afraid to relax. Alex met her gaze, praying he understood what she meant. Then the button below his navel unsnapped as she loosened his jeans—until he jerked and swelled against her hand, his reaction automatic and uncontrollable.

"Elizabeth?" Her eyes were dark and determined. Her front teeth trapped the full center of her bottom lip for a second, then she licked it, softening and wetting the plump flesh. If he was dreaming again, he just didn't care. To hell with questions. Alex dipped his head and captured her mouth with his as he unclasped her bra. Even in dreams, they weren't going to make love covered in his blood.

Elizabeth sneaked her hands beneath the sides of his jeans and pushed them down his hips and thighs. He returned the favor. Alex knelt as he lowered her jeans, kissing her breasts, then her soft stomach. It was a dream, a fantasy he'd lived a million times or more, but it still felt new. There was extra electricity zapping over his skin as he smoothed his hands down her thighs and over her calves.

Making short work of her boots and socks, then his, Alex rose before her. Hugging her to his chest, he picked her up and backed her to the shower, pressing her into the cold tile. Elizabeth gasped and arched into him. Reaching back, he fumbled with the knob and turned the water on. Freezing cold, the spray pelted him. He jerked. Elizabeth shrieked and shrank before Alex, letting him block her.

Alex laughed, loud and triumphant. "Thank you, thank you, thank you!"

Elizabeth glared at him, peeking up as the water warmed. "Are you insane?"

"Nope." He grinned charmingly and kissed her cheek. "I'm not dreaming, either."

"Oh." She smiled and looked away, reaching for the body wash. Squirting some in her hand, she closed her eyes, inhaled deep, and smiled. When her eyes opened again, they shone that amazing blue that had stolen his heart twelve years ago. "No wonder you always smell so good."

Alex grinned and reached for the bottle. Squirting a bunch on one hand, he dipped a finger in and brushed at the blood on her cheek, keeping his touch gentle, still amazed this was real. Elizabeth didn't share his hesitance, though. Rubbing the soap on both her hands, she caressed his chest and side. Alex shivered, loving the way her delicate hands brushed through his chest hair, her fingers gliding in appreciation of the body he'd managed to sculpt.

Bodybuilding wasn't his thing, but he was vain enough to want to look good. Elizabeth seemed to agree he'd made a good choice. The air warmed, and a clean, rain-fresh scent filled the shower.

Finishing her face, Alex soaped both hands and reached for her. But he moved slowly, caressing her delicate neck, relaxing the tension that had built in her shoulders from the moment she'd realized he'd been shot. Stroking, caressing, knowing the warm flesh beneath his grasp was real. His dream, his fantasy, standing in his shower, her head tilting back against the wall, her eyes closing as he soaped and molded her taut breasts. She arched her back as he moved down, soaping her stomach and her hips.

Alex leaned forward and kissed her stomach, nuzzling the soft skin as he soaped down her thighs, to her calves and feet. He reached between her legs and dipped his fingers into every fold, crack, and crevice, feeling her arch and swell around him.

Alex nuzzled against her torso, giving his hands free rein as she widened her stance, then braced one foot on the side of the tub, allowing him more and more access.

Alex opened his eyes to the most perfectly formed breast. He couldn't wait to taste it.

He tested the texture with his tongue, around and around, then sucked the sensitive peak into his mouth. Sliding Elizabeth up the wall until her legs wrapped around his waist, he took the tip of her breast into his mouth again and groaned. She shuddered and rocked against his stomach, shimmying and moaning.

"Alex."

Her hair. He didn't want to forget her hair. Releasing her breast, Alex grabbed the bottle and squirted a small puddle of shampoo into his palm. As he massaged it into her scalp, Elizabeth leaned forward, her head on his shoulder and her thighs squeezing his waist. Tilting her head, Alex took her lips again, massaged her scalp and ground against her, meeting each thrust until they were both moaning.

Conditioner. He grabbed for the bottle, struggling to give her the same sensual enjoyment she'd given him. It was likely abbreviated in comparison, though. By the time he'd wrapped a couple of towels around them both and left the bathroom, he was hard, straining and impatient.

Shoving the bloody blankets to the floor, Alex pulled a pillow to the middle of the bed and laid her down with her hips propped up and angled toward him. He wanted in, he wanted deep, and he was through waiting. Sliding his fingers over her moist labia, Alex leaned forward and kissed her. "I've waited forever for this."

Elizabeth tangled both hands in his wet hair and corrected him. "We've *both* been waiting. I promise it was mutual."

"Everything?" Alex paused, but when she held her legs open, his pause didn't last long.

He thrust, gliding through silken hot tissue. He growled, forcing himself deeper. Elizabeth panted encouragement in his ear, her fingers digging into his scalp, her heels pressing his flanks until he bottomed out inside her.

Alex held her, keeping them tightly fused and straining for more as he struggled for breath. "Elizabeth?"

Elizabeth rippled around him and cried out, strain in her voice. "You are so much better than plastic!"

Alex's eyes nearly crossed. He'd have to pull out, despite every cell in his body screaming a protest. "I forgot a condom."

She squeezed her legs around him. "That's fine. I really doubt you have any diseases."

Alex buried his face against her neck and gasped, "Pregnancy."

Elizabeth giggled and her body tightened around him.

Alex moaned helplessly.

"Implants. Checked like clockwork. Damned things better work the first time I put them to use." She laughed again and it was the best, most freeing feeling ever.

Alex pushed up for leverage, stared straight into her eyes and pulled out. Disappointment passed over her features milliseconds before he thrust back in, hard and deep. "Elizabeth, I love when you laugh."

She smiled and he kissed her, his hips moving, finding a rhythm to please them both. "I love to see you smile."

Her sighs brushed his ear, sending small shocks down his spine. He rocked into her, slow and thorough, deep and fast. Then faster, until his blood thundered through his system and his muscles tightened, coiling like a spring. His fingers tensed. His arms and shoulders. His toes and calves. His back and thighs. Ever spiraling until all sensation focused on his tight balls and shaft.

The harder he grew, the more Elizabeth melted beneath him, opening and giving, accepting everything he had. Alex thrust hard, almost jerking against her. She was his. Elizabeth screamed, her body arching, her hips rising, her inner muscles tightening and pulsing, milking him. Alex rode her through her orgasm, kept it going, until shivers scraped the edge of his skin and he couldn't hold back.

Sweating, almost aching from the release of tension, Alex rolled, bringing her with him. After that, neither could move. They could only lie, sprawled side by side, legs entwined, as nerves sizzled and danced from the tips of their fingers to the tips of their toes.

"Definitely better than plastic," Elizabeth panted.

"Don't like condoms, huh?"

"Not condoms. Toys."

Alex groaned. "In about twenty minutes, that will get me really hot."

"Oh no, there's no way I can survive that again," she choked.

"What? Never gone twice in a night?"

"Once is usually sufficient."

"Lazy lovers, lady," he admonished, a note of humor underlying his voice.

"Not lovers. Toys."

"Lazy toys?" He frowned, his brain still on meltdown.

She giggled.

"Do that in twenty-one minutes." Right after he recovered and slid inside her body again.

Elizabeth laughed, then her smile slowly died. She took a deep breath and let it out. "I'm a control freak, Alex. I haven't trusted anyone else to fulfill my needs."

Alex turned his head on his pillow to see her face.

Elizabeth faced him, her expression serious and more than a little vulnerable. "I've heard the stories. A girl finds someone she's attracted to, gets his attention, and sleeps with him. Then she finds out he sucks in bed. Selfish, vain, or just plain inept. There's not enough chemistry, or nothing but chemistry. The girl gets pregnant, he gets possessive, or she otherwise becomes stuck with that choice. There's no way I was ever going to sleep around while I looked for a decent lover. Or give some random attraction that much influence over my future. Much better all around to take care of myself, meet my own needs."

But she'd had sex with him. Meaning she had trusted him to take care of her. Alex smiled gently, sincerely. "I'm honored."

Elizabeth didn't smile back. Actually, she shook her head and looked away a second, before meeting his gaze again. "With you, I'm more worried that I'll become the stalker. I just wanted you, inside me, a part of me, for however long we could manage."

That was even better. Twenty minutes, hell. Alex tugged her hand to his mouth. "I love you."

"Well, just so you know. . . ." The smile she gave him was a perfect mix of shyly sweet and challengingly wicked. "I have much higher expectations now."

• FELICIA WAS COMATOSE when Silas found her. She'd fallen over, her back to the wall, tears still wet on her face. With an exclamation, he rushed to her side and knelt, automatically reaching for her. But just before that first touch, he froze, his hands hovering in the air. Was she meant to die? In this time, in this place? How would Elizabeth feel when she saw her sister's body abandoned on the worn floor of a sleazy motel? Would she be able to move forward, past the destruction in Adad's vision?

Felicia's thoughts still streamed through her mind, the only sign besides her shallow breathing that she still lived. He'd never been close to such pain, such intense loneliness and despair. Humans felt so deeply, every cut and bruise visible on their heart and mind. He'd passed by them, through them, for centuries, forcing an emotional barrier between himself and the outer world so he barely noticed their inner torment. But like Kalyss, Felicia was different. Alex would care, Elizabeth would care, and the children would be hurt beyond repair. His attachment to them expanded, making Felicia's suffering more personal, more acute.

Despite the gifts that marked her Nephilim, it was Felicia's humanity that ruled her. And everything that was human in her called to the human in him, crying her utter hopelessness straight to his heart. How could he do nothing?

But still, he hesitated. Watching her face, listening to her thoughts. So many nightmares flying close to the surface. So many destroyed dreams. Sympathy such as he'd never known enveloped Silas until he held his hands out to Felicia again, ready to do anything, but again, he froze before touching her.

Do not interfere. The greatest law he'd been taught. The one he fought so hard to follow. God had a plan and humans needed to trust it, even when it meant loss and pain. But Felicia's sadness reached for him. Her mental cries grabbed his heart and wouldn't let go. Silas hadn't expected this when he'd come for her. He wanted, needed, to do something, anything. But when would he stop? Had he passed that point already? Who was in charge of his direction? Because he certainly did not believe it was him.

He had a choice to make, and not just the immediate one. But Felicia came first and his honest answer for her was that he couldn't just lay there and watch her suffer.

Silas palmed her face, directing it toward his until they were nose to nose. He would hold her. Give her a chance for Alex to arrive and save her. It wasn't everything he could do, but it wasn't *nothing*. Silas's innate glow spread, covering them both in a blanket of light. Smoothing his hand over hair and cheek, he took in her hopelessness, absorbing it so she could absorb some of his hope.

Entering her mind with his, Silas searched for the small spark of light that was her soul. As she'd once huddled in the blackest depths of her mother's basement, the spark that was Felicia now hid in the darkest corners of her mind. It surrounded her with concrete walls and a cold stone floor. All around him were shadowed images of her memories, good and bad, reenacted in excruciating detail, side by side, with no walls to separate them, to mute the noise or even to hide the worst of her memories. Rape, not once, not twice, but countless times as she traded her body for a drugged illusion of pain-free living. Fights, brutality, tissue-thin semblances of affection exposed for the shams they were because she knew what it was to truly love. And to lose that love.

Felicia had no protection. No way to lock away her nightmares. One fact rang out above all others. Felicia had led a life of crippling pain and torment. He'd entered her mind without any protective barriers, nothing to block his focus, and now the intense visuals he walked past cut into his heart like a million slicing blades.

It was so overwhelmingly loud in her mind. When he found her at last, she was naked and trembling, wrapped around herself, making herself as small as possible. If she couldn't hide her memories, then she had to hide herself.

Silas looked down at her bruised and scarred soul. "I know it hurts, but they are coming for you. Your sister loves you."

Felicia shivered, all warmth slowly leaching away from her soul. Death waited, ready to take her as soon as that light diminished. "Dallas won't look for me, she doesn't care."

Silas drew closer, slowly banishing every shadow that surrounded her with his glowing heat and creating an insulating barrier around them both to dull the noise. "Not Dallas. Elizabeth. Elizabeth is coming for you."

Felicia shook her head, hiding her eyes from him. "Beth Ann hates me. She hates everything I've become. She won't waste her time on me again."

Silas shook his head. "She loves you. You'll see."

"It's too late."

"It's never too late."

Felicia raised her head and stared at Silas's long, brown hair and cream-colored robes. Then her gaze traveled to the tall arc of downy white feathers that rose above his head and fell gracefully to his ankles. Silas held his hand out to her. She squinted against the glow around them, but offered her hand in return.

"Are you Jesus?"

He smiled sadly. "No one near so grand. I'm too far from perfection."

Felicia smiled a little through her tears. "I'm far from perfect, too."

His brown eyes softened so gently. "Then come, Mistress of the Light. Let us pray for redemption together."

Slowly, she reached for him, allowing his hand to close around hers. As she stood, her nudity was fully exposed. She huddled, hiding behind her hair. "I *must* be stoned."

Silas grinned wryly and pulled her close, helping her stand on trembling legs that threatened to buckle and offering comfort. "No, you don't need that false strength anymore, you'll see."

Lying in the dark hotel room, stretched out on the floor alongside Felicia, Silas continued to pet her hair while holding the image of him helping her in his mind. He allowed her to continue to absorb his light, his strength. He only prayed Elizabeth and Alex arrived before it was gone. Because Silas now knew one thing bone deep. He'd let himself drain completely and perish before he allowed this woman, who'd already suffered so much, to be abandoned again. Interference be damned. He'd made his choice and he would not deviate.

• SHELLY APPEARED TO be sleeping, her feet dangling over the side of the love seat, the baby balanced on her chest with one hand to hold her secure. She looked the picture of peace, until Draven drew closer. Asleep, it would be easier to whisper in her ear and hope she heard. There would be a likelier chance even that she would listen. Those earrings were the worst sort of gift. Any gift from Maeve was the same.

Draven drew closer to the teenager and could hear her dreams like a movie played in a distant room. The music for suspense. The whispered prayers of a frightened child. A dark room with the camera focused on a black doorway. Bright whitish light pierced the edge of the door, a thin line along the sides, thicker at the bottom. The camera zoomed in on the slow turn of a handle.

Shit. No. Draven knelt at Shelly's side, one hand covering Shelly's forehead and pressing at the temples. Able to see and touch Shelly, but not be seen by Geoffrey, though he sat straight and alert, his eyes piercing the softly lit living room as if Draven's invisible advantage wouldn't last long.

It didn't matter, though. Geoffrey could do his best, but Shelly could not be left alone. Her memories, combined with Maeve's earrings, spelled destruction on an epic scale. There had to be a way to break the link. Draven cast about the teen's mind, looking for a way to break the endless loop of memory. No matter what the attempt, though, Draven repeatedly hit a wall of failure.

Pulling back, Draven slowly rose, black cloak billowing to the floor with smoky tendrils flaring out like a low, dark fog. Other checks must be made before returning to this task, hopefully with a better plan. One that would work. Drifting room to room, Draven breathed in, until the air from every silent corner spilled its secrets. From the dining room to the kitchen, down to the cluttered basement and up the stairs to where the rest of the children slept. Geoffrey followed him, sensing the danger that emanated from Draven, but not knowing what to do, how to protect them.

Draven ignored him and examined everything, needing to know if only Shelly was affected by Maeve's machinations. There was only one plan that came to mind. No doubt it would break Silas's rules, but Draven was hard-pressed to really care. Yes, the rules were important. Yes, they were in place to be obeyed for the greater good, but there had to be a time when it was okay to break rules.

Like Robin Hood, stealing from the rich to aid the poor. Like Jesus harvesting grain on the Sabbath to feed the hungry. Sometimes, one wrong act held more weight than a million days of following the rules.

Satisfied at last, Draven returned to the girl, knelt by

her side. The baby turned her head, bright blue eyes looking straight into the depths of Draven's cowl. With one leather-clad finger, slightly longer than the average human's, Draven traced Veronica's gently rounded cheek. The baby twitched, blinked, then her eyes slowly drifted closed. Geoffrey returned to his chair, his posture straight, his vigilance absolute.

He was the protector, the guardian. The kindest thing would be to give him a cause to champion. Draven held one palm up, fingers pointed at Geoffrey. Leaning close, Draven blew and black smoke drifted across the distance until Geoffrey breathed it in. He blinked, relaxed, sinking into the cushioned depths of the chair. Then his eyes closed and his breathing deepened, slowed.

Draven turned to Shelly and the same smoke drifted over her face. She fell deeper into her dreams, but this time she wasn't alone. She would have Geoffrey. Looking at the silver earrings turning the girl's ears red, Draven reached for them. It was time to remove them, crush them. They could be replaced with fakes and Shelly would never know.

The moment Draven touched them, electricity burst from Shelly's ears, knocking Draven several feet back. Then the silver bolt arced through the air, through the smoky cloak, obliterating every hint of fabric until Draven laid still and bare upon the floor.

• SHELLY HUDDLED UNDER the covers, though the thick blankets did nothing to warm her. The cold that filled her went clear to the bone. "No. Not tonight. Please."

She whispered the prayer over and over, but it didn't halt the turning of the handle. It didn't calm the beating of her heart or the shaking of her limbs. Tears streamed down her cheeks in a steady flood. She was thirteen again, but still too old to cry like this, but it didn't seem to make an impact. The sobs breaking her chest never lessened.

The door cracked, opening in a silent, slow sweep. The man filling the doorway was built of shadow, seeming all the bigger for the darkness inside him. His boots struck the floor, bringing him closer one step at a time. Behind him, her door shut, taking the light with it until all she could hear was excited breaths and the steady thud of boots closing the distance between them. Until the boots stopped, poised, waiting. Then the sounds doubled. Two large men breathing, struggling, panting until . . . stillness.

Shelly shrieked, burying her head against the pillows and repeating her prayers, speaking faster and faster. Shelly lay still, afraid to look, afraid to know.

But then a calm voice demanded, "Turn on the light, Shelly."

She flinched, holding the covers around her even tighter.

Patiently, he called to her again. "It's okay now, Shelly. Turn on the light."

"Geoffrey?" Shelly tugged the blanket to her nose and peeked into the blackness of her bedroom.

"Yes."

Fumbling an arm free, she reached to the lamp beside her bed and touched the base. A low glow filled the room, illuminating two men at the end of her bed.

Geoffrey held her nightmare man, one hand on his chin, the other hand at the back of his head. With one twist, she heard bones break. Like black oil, the shadow pooled at Geoffrey's feet, then disappeared through the floor.

His gaze steady, Geoffrey stood alone, his strong hands at his sides. "We'll do this as many times as you need."

Shelly trembled, her hands fisted on the blankets. She heard the promise in his tone, saw it in his stance, but she still needed the reassurance. "You'll stop him?"

"Every time," he vowed.

Shelly thought for a moment, then nodded. Lying back, she pulled the covers to her chin. Quickly, she snaked one arm free to turn off the light, then tucked it back and faced her nightmare. Already she felt better, stronger, just knowing Geoffrey was there with her.

• "WHAT DO YOU mean she's dying?" Elizabeth sat straighter in the bed, Geoffrey's voice sounding clearly through Alex's cell phone.

"That's what he said when he called a minute ago. Felicia is dying and it's a twin thing. That you'd understand."

"I do." The twin-sense between Bobby and Felicia was near-legendary. Even when frustratingly vague, it was *always* accurate. "Did he say anything else?"

"Not exactly. He mumbled something about her being with the angels."

Elizabeth gathered her clothes from the bathroom

floor and tossed them on the rumpled bed. "But nothing about what's hurting her?"

"No."

She sighed as she sat on the edge of the bed. "Thank you, Geoffrey."

Closing the phone, she closed her eyes, trying to breathe. A warm body settled next to her and a familiar hand rested on the bare skin of her back. "We'll find her. Don't worry. Just pull your clothes on and I'll get ahold of Ron again."

Opening her eyes to Alex's concerned, hazel gaze, Elizabeth smiled. "Thank you."

"Anytime." He took the phone and strode from the room, leaving her to dress in privacy.

And worry. Bobby had to be going crazy, stuck behind bars while his other half was "with the angels". Elizabeth might not approve of all the choices he'd made, but he was still her brother. Just as she cared about her sister, despite how she'd landed in whatever situation she faced tonight. Pulling on her jeans, Elizabeth donned the shirt Alex had laid out for her and did her best to hide the blood-stiffened side of her jeans. She could wash them later. At least they were black denim.

Chapter 21

◆

• MAEVE WATCHED GEOFFREY through narrowed eyes. He hung up the phone and turned to face her, leaning one hip against the counter. A small, mocking grin stretched his lips. Why didn't she recognize the being behind that look? She scowled. "You're not Geoffrey."

Faux-Geoffrey grinned wider. "Brilliant of you to deduce. Especially after seeing his sleeping body in the next room."

Maeve snarled, curling her hands so her fingernails formed claws. "Show your true self."

Faux-Geoffrey paused, as if considering the wisdom of challenging her demand, before straightening from the edge of the counter. Short for a half-breed, he was a giant of a man. He angled his blond head and his blue-grey eyes hardened. Only the unnatural smirk that twisted his lips gave any hint of the person behind the mask.

Black smoke built behind him, framing his shoulders and his face with dark wisps that slowly condensed, becoming solid before swallowing him, absorbing him into the cloaked and cowled form of Silas's ally. The figure faced Maeve, the black hole where a face should be hinting at terrifying shadows and painful secrets. "Happy now?"

Of course not, but at least this was closer to the truth.

Maeve curled her lip and barely refrained from attacking. "Scared to show your true form? That surprises me from one such as you."

Gloved hands crossed one over the other, and the figure taunted. "I sincerely doubt it surprises you, since you know nothing of me. I hope you go insane with curiosity."

"Do you really believe insanity would make me less of an enemy?"

"No, but you'd be more challenging. Less likely to create clichéd traps like the earrings."

"Clichéd?" Maeve's hands fisted. "*You* fell for it."

"Yes, pitiful me. I should have suspected such antiquated tactics from a relic like you. I'm surprised I recovered so quickly."

Despite the anonymity of the cowl, Maeve could sense the smirk on whatever passed for the figure's mouth. Whatever inhabited that cloak now understood the level to which she'd been weakened, first by the tunnels and then by the scribe. Sharp claws of fear dug into her stomach. Screeching her rage, Maeve raised her fists and charged forward.

Prepared for her attack, the figure raised linked hands, palms out, and a barrier formed. One a weakened Maeve could not penetrate. "You are not welcome here, hell bitch. In His name, *be gone.*"

Draven smiled beneath the cloak, watching as Maeve bounced off Draven's personal barrier and was yanked back, like an invisible lasso had tightened around her waist. Before she could stop it, Maeve was sucked away. Even if the price of invoking His name sent Draven straight to hell itself, watching Maeve's face was worth it.

Draven chuckled, the husky voice drifting throughout

the sleeping house just moments before the physical form followed. Those housed within the walls would now be protected from Maeve's presence.

• ELIZABETH TRIED TO hold back her fear during the twenty-minute drive to the faded, run-down motel Ron had directed them to. It had been so long since she and Felicia had lived as sisters. Time during which she'd struggled to maintain an emotional distance from her family, if only out of a desperate search for self-preservation. But when they arrived, what would they find? It wouldn't be good. Felicia was hurt somehow. Either by the drugs or by whatever man had taken her to the motel.

It wasn't her pain that mattered, though, but the kids'. Abby was too young to remember her mother. But David and Danielle knew their mother, loved her beyond all logic as children were wont to do, and despite their overt cynicism their young hearts would shatter if they lost her.

Elizabeth would do anything to keep that pain away from them. That was why, when she'd come home three months ago, she'd spent weeks tracking down Felicia and coaxing her home. She'd talked to her sister, gave her time with her children, and watched the slow deterioration of an addict forced to do without. It hadn't taken long for Elizabeth realize ten kids, a dying mother, and an addict in the midst of withdrawals was too much. So she'd taken her sister to rehab and checked her in.

Maybe that isolation had been too much for Felicia.

How could someone fight the lure of an addiction when the reasons for her fight were kept away from her?

Alex pulled to a stop in front of the room Ron had mentioned and they were out of the truck in moments. Just when she would have veered off to find a manager and get the key, Elizabeth saw the door was open a few inches. She rushed in, not caring about any danger to herself, then skidded to a stop in the center of the room, frozen in the middle of a moment she'd feared would come.

Felicia lay alongside the wall. A white foam covered her mouth and her entire body was limp. Alex brushed past Elizabeth and settled beside Felicia, listening for breath. Finding what he needed, he laid his palms over her heart and abdomen.

Elizabeth stared in horrified fascination, hoping Felicia lived, and thankful Alex knew what to do. Elizabeth hugged her arms tightly around herself and watched as Alex's eyes rolled back, showing only white, and a blue glow spread from his hands, reaching out to cover Felicia's bare limbs in color.

Elizabeth backed up until the door clicked shut behind her. She stared around the room, then back at her sister. Whoever had been here with Felicia had taken their fun and split when it began turning ugly. Leaving her baby sister to die. Fury welled inside her even as her mind pointed out that this was where Felicia's choices had been leading her. But logic didn't calm the fury.

The helplessness of watching someone she loved self-destruct while she couldn't stop them was all too terribly familiar. Alex's breathing became heavier, deeper. The meager light from the windows struck his arms, high-lighting the sweat running down his arms and emphasizing his struggle.

Elizabeth flipped the light switch and the room lit up, bathing them all in a dingy glow. Elizabeth moved toward them, halting to kneel by Felicia's head. Reaching out, her hand hovered hesitantly over the long brown hair. Could she touch her or would it interfere with Alex's healing? The blue light emanating from his hands gave off a comforting warmth, but Elizabeth pulled back, afraid of hurting the process. Could he really heal someone this close to death? And what would it do to him?

Elizabeth looked up in time to see a bruise forming around Alex's left eye, dark and purple, as if someone had hit him. Had someone from the bar gotten in a lucky punch after all? But no, another bruise was blooming under his right eye and a split began separating the fullness of his lip even as the first bruise faded away. Elizabeth looked down at Felicia. Her pale skin was now free of the bruises that had marked it.

Somewhere, a clock ticked with a steady, thin sound. Elizabeth leaned back against the wall, her legs curled to the side as she stared at Alex. His body was rigid, his concentration total.

No one had ever focused so hard on saving her family the way he did. And not just for her. Despite all their scars and traumas, Alex cared for each member of her family. He opened up to each one of them, as if he didn't comprehend the meaning of self-preservation. Of protecting his heart from the pain loving someone could bring.

Elizabeth reached toward the light again, wanting to

touch her sister, but kept her hand just above the blue surface.

"It's okay. You can touch her."

Elizabeth jumped.

Alex's voice betrayed none of the strain the sweat on his arms bespoke of. "She needs your love."

Cautiously, Elizabeth lowered her hand and ran her fingers through her sister's hair, the strands greasy but soft. When she was cleaned up, Felicia was so beautiful. Her features fine and delicate, like a porcelain doll. As a little girl, she'd often climbed into Elizabeth's lap with a tattered copy of *Highlights*.

They'd spent hours going through those magazines, much to Bobby's disgust. It had been the one pastime the twins had never shared. He'd preferred G.I. Joe. So Elizabeth and Felicia would cuddle and search for the hidden pictures together.

Alex smiled and the blue glow deepened, darkening to a pure cobalt, strong and shining. Elizabeth brushed the hair from Felicia's face, her hand surrounded by the light. What had happened to change her from the beautiful, hopeful little girl to the broken, destructive, and hopeless woman she was now?

Alex would heal her and Elizabeth would bring her home. Make her say good-bye to Mom, hug the kids, and then what? Felicia would leave again because Elizabeth couldn't force good decisions on someone determined not to make them.

"No, Elizabeth. Only love."

Elizabeth closed her eyes and her hand shook. It was so much easier to be angry. It didn't hurt as much if you were angry. But Alex was right. She could actually feel it. The healing light grew warmer, stronger, when she thought of the love she felt for Felicia.

No matter what she'd done to be here, no matter the justice or logic of it, Felicia was her sister. She'd changed her diaper, taken baths with her, fed her. It was Elizabeth who'd dressed her for her first day at school, pulling her long hair into a curly ponytail tied with a turquoise ribbon that matched her dress. It was Elizabeth who'd read to Felicia.

And now that little girl was dying. Elizabeth's eyes traced the soft contours of Felicia's face. Then she watched Alex, her eyes filling with tears of amazement. Such a beautiful gift. He healed with love. Love powered his gift. Elizabeth narrowed her eyes on him, watching him inhale slowly and exhale even more slowly. Liquid dripped steadily down Alex's muscled forearms, too thick to be sweat. Was he drawing the drugs into himself, then pushing them out like he had the bullet? He accepted the damage in Felicia, making it his. Because he cared enough to save her.

He was love. One big blue light of love. For a man to hold that much love inside himself for others, whether he knew them or not, was such an inspiring sight. A humbling example. Had she ever loved someone enough to do something so extraordinary? The kids, obviously, but they were easy to love.

Elizabeth looked back to her sister and ran her fingers through her hair again. Suddenly, it was there. All the love and hope she'd ever felt for her mother, Felicia, Bobby, and even Dallas. So strong and overwhelming, fear tried to close her off again, but Elizabeth pushed it away, concentrating on the positive feelings.

The light deepened again, running in tight swirls over Felicia's body, Elizabeth's hands, and up Alex's arms until they were all linked together. Elizabeth looked at Alex, her heart the most open to him it had ever been.

He looked into her eyes and smiled. Sitting back on his heels, the blue light absorbed inside him and she didn't need to hear Felicia's steady breaths to know he'd saved her sister.

"You are the most amazing man I've ever met." She stared at Alex, more sure than ever that out of all the men in the world, he was the one she could love the most. Hell, who was she kidding? She *did* love him the most.

"Don't sell yourself short, sweetheart. I couldn't have done it without you."

Elizabeth shook her head, not believing him for a second.

Felicia opened her eyes, struggling to rise more from instinct than need. Elizabeth helped her sit up, her back against the wall. At first, Felicia blinked dazedly, but when the confusion cleared and she noticed who was with her, she started tugging at the hem of the shirt. Alex withdrew to the other side of the room, affording them a semblance of privacy.

Felicia leaned her head against the wall, her brows drawing together. "Where's Dave?"

Elizabeth shook her head. "I don't know. There was no one here when we arrived."

Felicia snorted, shaking her head. "Figures. How did you find me?"

"Ron told me where you were. He said you weren't doing well." Elizabeth studied her sister's eyes. They were the clearest they'd been in many years. Did she know she'd almost died?

"He shouldn't have called you. I just took a longer trip than I meant to. I would have been fine."

Where had Elizabeth heard that kind of brash assurance before? "No, honey. You almost died."

Felicia rolled her eyes. Bitterness laced her tone. "Like that would have been so bad."

Oh, how familiar those words were, as well as the attention-seeking ploy behind them. Elizabeth so did not have the time or patience for those tricks, not after a night like they'd had. "You have three kids who hope to see you again real soon."

"Come on, Beth Ann. Excuse me, *Elizabeth*," Felicia stressed mockingly. "Rehab wasn't working. Besides, they're better off without a mom like me."

Elizabeth gritted her teeth. "This isn't the time for self-pity, Felicia. You need to come home. Mom—"

"It's not self-pity," she said defensively. "They have you, the perfect sister. They don't need a fuck-up like me."

Elizabeth took a deep breath, refusing to rise to the bait. She was far from perfect, she knew that well. "Fuck-up or not, they need you. And Mom is dying. You need to see her before she goes, Felicia."

Her little sister flinched, then covered it up by laughing. "Poor Elizabeth. Stuck in a family full of imperfect people. None of us can make you happy, no matter what we do."

"You don't have to be perfect or try to make me happy. That's not your responsibility, it's mine. But you do need to quit hurting yourself and making life harder than it has to be."

Felicia rolled her eyes, shook her head, and climbed to her feet. "Quit preaching to me, Elizabeth. It might have helped when I was thirteen, but then you graduated and took off. It's too late to come back and pretend you care about us. That we're a *family.*"

Elizabeth scowled. "This isn't a pretense, Felicia. You know that. I love you and we *are* a family."

"Whatever." Felicia tried to push past her, but the anger Elizabeth had been holding back erupted. The women in her family were so damn pigheaded.

"Fine," Elizabeth snapped. "If you're so determined to kill yourself, go ahead. I won't keep beating my head against a brick wall. But first, you will damn well give me twenty-four hours. You will see Mom before she dies and you will see your kids before *you* die. Now get in the shower. I won't take you home in this shape."

Felicia looked downright murderous as she stomped to the bathroom. Moments later the shower was running. Elizabeth fisted her hands in her hair and pulled. "So much for being full of love, huh?"

Alex rose from his quiet spot on the corner of the bed and strode over to her. Kissing her lightly on the forehead, he said, "I heard nothing but love. I'll get her stuff."

Elizabeth frowned at his slightly unsteady gait as he left the room. No doubt he needed the cooler, fresher air outside. They needed to get out of here soon. Quickly looking around, she tried to gather anything that might be important to her sister, but there wasn't much. Finally, Elizabeth sat on the edge of the bed and waited.

* * *

• IT WAS EARLY morning by the time Alex stopped his truck in front of Elizabeth's house. The kind of deep night where all lights were out and nothing moved. Elizabeth climbed out of the truck, moving her seat forward so Felicia could extricate herself from the back of the extended cab. Without a word to either of them, Felicia stomped through the gate, up the stairs, and through the front door.

Elizabeth sighed, exhausted to her core. Alex waited for her, leaning against the truck. She rounded the front of his truck and stopped uncertainly before him, sliding her hands into her back pockets and staring up into his bright eyes.

"What do we do now?" She'd never had a lover before. She'd also never been threatened by a fallen angel bent on revenge. "I'm not so sure it's wise for you to leave."

"You're probably right. I can sleep on the couch," he offered.

Elizabeth smiled, grateful. He understood that sleeping in her room would send a bad message to the kids. They'd seen enough men come and go. They didn't need to believe he would do the same.

Elizabeth braced her hands on his chest, stood on her tiptoes, and gently brushed her lips over his. His arms surrounded her, warming her against the cool breeze. His hair was silky against her fingers, his jaw warm and scratchy.

When Elizabeth finally leaned back, she stared at the lips she'd just kissed and wished she could simply lay her head against his chest and stay in the circle of his embrace for the rest of the night. "Thank you."

"Anytime, sweetheart." He pressed his lips to the center of her forehead and reluctantly released her. "Could you send Geoffrey out for a minute? I'll catch him up on events without little ears around. I don't want to scare anyone."

Elizabeth chuckled. She was worried the kids were too jaded and he worried they were too innocent. "Sure."

Alex's warm eyes crinkled at the corners. "You better watch out, a smile like that can make a guy weak in the knees."

Elizabeth smiled wider.

"Oh, gag me." Shelly's voice cut through the darkness.

Alex laughed at Elizabeth's blush, enjoying the sight of her perfectly formed derriere as it swayed away from him. A silly grin spread across his face. He stared until all he could see were the buttons of Geoffrey's shirt.

Alex slumped back, letting his controlled façade slip. "Hey, buddy."

Geoffrey raised a brow, his knowing gaze narrowed on Alex.

"Felicia almost died," Alex said defensively. "What's a healer to do?"

"Nearly kill himself to impress his girlfriend?"

"Exactly." Alex nodded. The truck decided not to hold him up anymore and he began a slow slide to the ground. Geoffrey's shoulder in his gut halted the slide and Alex grunted. Patting the shoulder, he frowned and said, "Thanks, buddy. But, maybe next time, not so hard."

Geoffrey grunted and rose to his full height, leaving

Alex to dangle over his shoulder and stare at the moving ground as Geoffrey walked back up the sidewalk.

"I was hoping you'd be discreet about my little problem here. Maybe help me hide it." Alex's stomach started to heave and he squeezed his eyes shut.

"Puke on me and I'll castrate you."

Okay, so no discretion. Elizabeth would have to see him weak as a baby. And whoever else happened to be nearby.

Alex tried to still his stomach. Geoffrey's shoulder was doing more damage to him than an entire night of torture at Kai's hands.

Geoffrey stomped up the stairs to the front door, then stood him on his feet.

Alex fell back against the frame, blood rushing painfully out of his head. "Now that's just plain mean. I wouldn't threaten you while you suffered the aftereffects of . . . you know . . . dying."

"Yes, you would," Geoffrey stated flatly.

"Well, yeah." Alex thought for a moment, fumbling with his keys and dropping them. "But I'd shut up when you could hear again."

Geoffrey leaned down and snatched the key ring off the porch and slapped them into his hand. "The drugs should be out of your system by now."

Alex closed his eyes and leaned back. "At least I got the bullet out okay."

Geoffrey growled. "I'm never letting you go out alone again."

"I wasn't alone." Alex grinned. "Elizabeth was there. She got mad and used rubbing alcohol at the last minute."

"Good." Geoffrey grunted and opened the door.

Alex stumbled in before him, pausing to lean on the banister until he could make it to the couch.

• "NICE SHIRT."

Elizabeth sighed and pulled the door shut. "I got something all over my blouse and had to change."

"Right." Shelly rolled her eyes and shook her head. "Whatever. I don't know why people feel they have to lie to me, then insult me with lame cover stories."

She swung around and headed for the baby. Gathering Veronica gently in her arms, Shelly stood and tugged a blanket around her.

Elizabeth held up her hands. "Fine, you caught me. Alex and I shirked our duty to find Felicia, had hot, un-inhibited sex, and the shirt got ruined in the process."

Shelly froze and stared at Elizabeth with wide blue eyes for a few stunned moments. "Alright already. I believe you spilled something on it."

Elizabeth's mouth fell open and she couldn't tell if she should laugh or feel insulted.

Shelly laid the baby on the love seat, her ponytail bouncing behind her as she shook her head. "I swear, you have to be the only person in this family who sucks at lying."

Elizabeth raised her eyes to the ceiling, actually thankful when the phone rang.

• ALEX BARELY HAD time to catch his breath before he saw Elizabeth run toward him.

"I need to go to the hospital. Mom's really bad." Her eyes were wide, her features pale.

Alex pulled his keys from his pocket. "Okay, let's go."

Elizabeth shook her head. "I'd rather you were here with the kids. Besides, you look really tired. You were shot, and with Felicia—"

"I can go," Geoffrey offered.

Elizabeth refused. "I'll be okay alone. Just please watch over everyone."

He nodded and walked to the chair.

Alex reached out a hand to touch her hair. "I might be able to help."

Elizabeth grimaced. "She's in a coma already."

Alex quit trying to convince her. He was more than willing to try to help, but he knew he wasn't ready yet. He needed some sleep first, at the very least. "Be safe. And take the truck since it's already warmed up."

She nodded and pecked his lips. "Thank you again."

He grinned until she left, then wobbled over to the couch and collapsed. Shelly finished the baby's diaper and wrapped her tight in her blanket. Alex watched the glances she threw Geoffrey. Afraid to believe in the goodness of men, just like her aunt.

Alex had no doubt that Geoffrey wouldn't let her down. He lived for damsels in distress as much as he died for them. With a grin, he closed his eyes and sank deeper into the couch.

Chapter 22

❖

• MAEVE'S CHAMBER SHOWED no trace of her brutality other than the scribe's head, which now graced a long, thin table against one wall. On either side sat a branch of tapered candles, the flickering flames illuminating the tapestry above.

Maeve sat at her vanity table, Dugan behind her slowly stroking a brush through curls still not quite as red and thick as before. "She was dead, or nearly dead when I left. So I went for the rest of them and that damned ally of Silas's was there."

"Do you recognize his ally, yet?"

"No." She scowled into the mirror. The voice had tugged at her viscerally, but it was lowered, disguised. Maeve shrugged away Dugan's suddenly irritating touch. He placed the brush on the table and stood behind her, silent. Maeve tilted her head and watched herself in the mirror. She really hated those lines around her lips. "But he had enough power to force me out."

"Then where did you go?"

"To whisper in ears and wreak havoc, of course." She shook her head and rose. "By the end of the night, the sickly, pitiful wife, two of Adad's children, and all of his grandchildren will die. The two remaining brats will be easy to find. And in the midst of that will be the delicious agony of one misguided healer."

"Will this help you find Kai? Or your emerald?"

Maeve frowned at his reminder and her eyes narrowed, expressing her displeasure clearly. Dugan *questioned* her? "My vengeance is small compared to what that seditious half-breed deserves. Kai would understand his mother avenging him as he tried so hard to do for me."

Dugan bowed his head. "Yes of course, Goddess. Please forgive my rudeness."

Maeve turned to the bed, black silk brushing high on her thighs. Gracefully, she pulled back the covers, her every movement a tease, the curves of her bottom playing peek-a-boo with the man behind her.

Before she could slide inside the bed and farther away from him, Dugan pressed into her from behind, his erection nudging her through his robes. Brushing his lips over her shoulders, he brought his hands up to cradle her breasts and gently pluck the nipples.

Her servant definitely knew how to beg forgiveness. Maeve held still and allowed him to continue.

Dugan traced the thin straps of her nightgown with his tongue, his many limbs rubbing the silk against her skin in slow, tantalizing caresses. Maeve arched her neck, allowing him to continue, but withheld her moans of pleasure.

He knew her needs so well. What would make her shiver, what made her wet. As soon as he stroked her inner thigh, she pulled away, sliding onto the bed in a move that had her on her hands and knees before him.

Looking over her shoulder, she snarled. Dugan withdrew and stood straight, his eyes burning with hunger.

She needed him.

He inhaled deeply and licked his lips, but rigidly obeyed her order to not touch.

She needed his hard shaft, but she also needed his lust to build, to fill their air with heat and sweat and desperation. She needed it to soak into her pores and replenish her strength.

Denial would frustrate him, tighten the coil of tension and desire, raising her power exponentially. Dugan's eyes glowed the strange yellow-green of his arousal. Maeve smiled wickedly, a reminder of every passionate, lusty, depraved thing they'd ever done together.

His breathing changed, growing shallow and rapid, expanding and contracting his broad chest.

"Remove your clothes."

Two strong, tanned hands released the clasps at his throat so his cloak fell in folds to the floor, baring the scarred, transformed perfection that was Dugan. She burned, ached for the ride he would give her.

Eight thin limbs extended from his back and bent forward around his arms and sides until they ended in sharp, obsidian points. In the middle of his chest was the spider's face, nearly the size of a human head.

Other than the spider, Dugan was as perfect as a man could be. Sandy brown-blond hair fell to just beneath his shoulders, long and silky. A single braid fell from one temple, entwined with the symbols of his tribe.

Yes, Dugan was exactly what she needed.

She'd forbidden him to move, but the spider obeyed

no such rules. One by one, each limb slipped under her negligee and rubbed against the bare skin of her back, her stomach, coiling around her waist.

She purred as Dugan pressed his fists against his hips, his teeth gritted against the temptation to touch her. Maeve closed her eyes and bowed her forehead to the bed. Heat swamped the air around her, stirring her blood until she was flushed and aching.

His thoughts, his fantasies, flooded into her mind.

She wanted them all, and she would have them. As soon as she destroyed the Raineses and the healer who loved them.

Maeve looked at the cavern wall alongside her bed, willing the rock into smooth grey glass that mirrored her and Dugan so well.

Her nightgown slid to her shoulders and she could see the spider's legs undulating against her skin. She licked her lips, scraping her teeth against the full bottom lip until it pouted more red and tempting than any forbidden fruit.

She smiled at Dugan, releasing him from her command. With a low growl, he mounted the bed, then her. With his hands cupping her breasts, he raised her up, her back pressed to his chest, her gown drifting to her hips again.

Dugan ducked his head to kiss her shoulder, his right hand switching between her breasts, plucking at the nipples until they were engorged and tight. He thrust, rocking into her in a steady rhythm, building the energy between them.

Maeve gasped, tingling with small chills that heralded the climax to come. They rocked and rubbed, friction tightening her skin until she reached the pinnacle and stopped, muscles straining, breathless with a painful need that made her want to beg. Oh, she *loved* when it was good enough to beg.

As one, eight spidery limbs bent, their sharp tips stabbing into her with just enough pressure to send her screaming over the edge. Power soaked into her from the air, from his semen, from his devotion. Her body sucked in every last drop, then exploded with light.

They collapsed against the pillows, spooned together. Maeve was already drifting, a pleased exhaustion weighing her limbs.

"Is your plan to fight her in her dreams, Goddess? Do you desire my presence?" He whispered the questions gently into her ear as he piled the blankets around them both.

"Of course I'll need you, pet. But I've no wish to enter her world. Instead, I plan to bring them all to mine."

• ELIZABETH TOOK A deep breath and slowly pushed open the door to her mother's room. Light from the streetlamps outside the rain-splashed windows glowed in the darkness, the brightest of them coming from the cathedral at the top of the hill. St. John's, hovering over the town, protective and watchful.

Mary Beth lay with her head to the right, next to the monitors and machines. Elizabeth wrapped her arms around herself and stepped tentatively into the room. Tonight was different from any other time she'd been in her mother's presence. When she left this room, she'd never see Mary Beth alive again.

The room felt hushed, expectant. Like she only had these few moments of quiet left. Elizabeth slid her foot against the door, making it swing closed so it latched with only a soft click. Mary Beth didn't move. Seeing her lying so silent and still while the monitor beeped in time with her heart didn't make any kind of sense. Elizabeth's breath hitched in her chest as her mind whispered words she didn't want to acknowledge. She wiped at her nose and forced herself forward. Her shoes squeaked against the laminate, but still Mary Beth didn't move.

Elizabeth rounded the foot of the bed and stared at her mother's peaceful face. Even in sleep, Mary Beth had never before appeared so relaxed. Her face was completely clean and free of makeup and her hair had begun to grow again. Without hair dyes and bleaches to dry it out and change it, it was left looking soft and blond. For once, Mary Beth looked real.

Her body was frail compared to how she'd always looked. Now she was as slim as she'd always wanted to be, but she would die before she could have fun with it.

"Those jeans will probably fit you now. They've been hanging on the closet door all these years, just waiting for you." Elizabeth sighed.

Mary Beth didn't stir. Elizabeth moved to Mary Beth's side and reached for her hand. It was thin and fragile, the veins showing through the pale, yellowish skin. Rain ran in steady rivulets against the windows, causing the colorful city lights to dance over her face. An occasional voice sounded outside the room as people walked by.

Elizabeth hooked the chair with her foot and pulled it closer to the bed. She used her free hand to lower the bed rail then scooted even closer.

Elizabeth trailed one finger gently down her mother's cheek, looking for signs of life. Her throat clogged and she fought the sting in her eyes. "I was so focused on everyone else needing to say good-bye that I didn't realize I would need that, too."

Elizabeth squeezed her hand, hating the lack of response. "Wake up, Mom. I need to talk to you."

When there was no response, Elizabeth's lips trembled. "Please."

There was still so much left to say. So much to ask. Even though she'd known this was coming, it suddenly felt so real.

Elizabeth laid her head beside Mary Beth's, her hand gripping her mother's chilled fingers. Only the red light of the oxygen monitor on Mary Beth's left hand proved that there was still life inside her. Elizabeth settled her head against her mother's shoulder and listened to her soft, shallow breaths. She hadn't felt this scared and uncertain since she was a child. Receiving her mother's comfort had never felt so essential, so imperative.

"I really need you, Mama." She wouldn't get a response, but she had to speak anyway. "Dallas won't come home. Felicia nearly died. I don't know she'll ever kick drugs. There's only me."

Her voice broke. Was this how her mother had felt all these years? Abandoned by the four people who should have loved her most? Always before, Elizabeth had viewed her exodus as an escape. But what if she was just as guilty of abandonment as Dallas? She pictured all those little faces pressed against the window, hoping she'd stay but not daring to ask for fear of rejection.

Suddenly it wasn't just their faces she imagined.

There was Alex, standing on her porch with his arms crossed.

"What do I do?" Elizabeth sniffed and watched her mother's delicate profile. "Oh come on, you've never shied away from pointing out my mistakes and how I should fix them before. Wake up and tell me."

She held her breath and waited. "You gotta tell me, Mama. I actually asked you for advice. Is it snowing in hell?"

Elizabeth choked out a small laugh, knowing her mother would have appreciated the joke. If she'd heard it. But Mary Beth was obviously someplace far away from this dark room.

It was impossible to lie in dreams, but what would Elizabeth discover if she brought her mother into one of hers? Would it be better if she could go to Mary Beth, wherever she was, and talk to her there?

"Mama, please. Let me find you." Elizabeth closed her eyes, her hand tight around her mother's fingers. She took a deep breath, then let her mind drift, searching for a connection between them. Colors, images, and random thoughts from the day whirled past. The newly painted hallway. A place that was theirs. Shelly, already suffering so many teenage emotions, darker than most. Dallas refusing to come home, selfish to the end. Alex as he kissed her hand and said, "I love you."

The spinning stopped and she was left standing outside a familiar dark entrance. Her caves. She didn't want to go there. Not this time. She wanted Mary Beth's dream, not hers. Elizabeth took a deep breath, squared her shoulders, and turned around.

Chapter 23

◈

• SHE DIDN'T SEE her mother at first, just a large field of smooth-cut grass as far as she could see. Along the horizon was one long row of black granite with 58,249 names engraved in light grey letters.

It was a breathtaking, heartrending sight. There was no doubt the Vietnam Veteran's Memorial was her mother's own Room of Sorrows.

Had her mother spent the last twenty-five or so years searching for Charles Astor Raines among the thousands of names?

It wasn't until Elizabeth's hands touched the cool granite and her fingers traced the letters of an overwhelming number of names that she realized she'd crossed the field. It wasn't until the heavy granite towered over her that she understood the true meaning of "overwhelming".

"No one asked the little old lady in the shoe what happened to her husband." Mary Beth spoke quietly behind her.

Elizabeth turned to where she sat on a bench and before she could halt the bitter words, said, "Would you have preferred to be the little old widow so that people would feel sorry for you?"

Mary Beth met her gaze without rancor or disapproval.

It was as if she'd expected nothing different from her second child. Elizabeth winced. "I'm sorry."

Mary Beth raised her perfectly shaped eyebrows, her flawlessly made-up eyes widening. "It *must* be snowing in hell. Asking for advice and apologizing in the same night." Mary Beth shook her head, her shoulder-length hair bouncing around her shoulders. "Wow."

Elizabeth rolled her eyes and sat on the grass at her mother's feet. "Why didn't you tell me you were searching for him?"

"What good would it do? It was bad enough he left us."

"What would you do if you found him? What if he's dead?"

Her mother gestured furiously. "But he's not on the wall, Bethy! Over fifty-eight thousand names and not one is his!"

Elizabeth frowned. Hadn't her father's body been found and identified? Even vets who hadn't died in the war were added later, when they did pass. "Are you sure? Could they have misspelled his name?"

"I know how to use a computer, Beth Ann. I've looked at every single name on this wall. He's not there." Mary Beth's hand fell to her side. "He just decided he couldn't face the responsibility of a wife and four kids and disappeared."

"Was he really like that?" All these years she'd hurt her mom, taking from her the love she was meant to have. There'd been no closure for her mother with his death. Elizabeth could have located missing person records, found his grave, something to relieve her mother's mind.

"He didn't used to be. The man I married never would have abandoned his family." Mary Beth paused and her voice came out low. "But something in him changed. War changes men, Bethy."

"Maybe it didn't change him that much."

Mary Beth grinned and tugged at a lock of Elizabeth's hair. "I named you Elizabeth because of him. He always called me Bethy. Said it was his favorite name. No one else used it."

Elizabeth smiled, hugging her legs to her chest. "Why didn't you ever talk about him, Mom?"

Mary Beth sighed and started finger-combing the tangles out of Elizabeth's hair. Elizabeth scooted closer to make it easier, enjoying the closeness, the bonding they'd never allowed time for when she was younger.

"It hurt unbearably. Especially since I could never stop hoping that he would return." She parted the smooth side of Elizabeth's hair and started working on another section. "I didn't want you four to suffer that same hope and disappointment. Do you remember Earl?"

"Yeah." He was the one her mother had cried over when he'd left.

"He wanted to marry me. He understood for a while that I didn't want to declare your father dead or divorce him. For a couple of years, anyway. But the more time piled up, the less he understood."

"I remember you fighting. He made you cry a lot."

"He burned all your father's pictures. I had our wedding picture because it had been packed away with my mother's things. But the rest . . . Charlie and me . . . Charlie and you kids . . . they were all gone. Then Earl was gone." Mary Beth's voice lowered. "I had no one."

"You had us." Elizabeth briefly felt the flare of old resentment, but it fizzled and died. Now wasn't the time for anger.

"Much as I loved you kids, you couldn't pay the bills and put food on the table." She tugged Elizabeth's face toward hers. "Nor could you hold me in strong arms at night and make me feel safe."

Elizabeth looked into Mary Beth's eyes, seeing an honest acknowledgement of her own needs. The same needs Elizabeth was so torn about. But sometimes complete independence was not the most desirable state of being. Elizabeth nodded.

Mary Beth started combing again and Elizabeth stared at the wall. She and her mother were mirrored in the shiny granite.

"After Earl left, I went a bit wild. Drinking, partying. Men." Mary Beth shook her head. "Do you understand now?"

Elizabeth nodded. "Men always leave."

"I taught you well," Mary Beth admitted sadly. "I should have worked harder. Given you stability. Kept my family together mentally and emotionally, instead of just physically. I could have prevented so much pain."

"I'll take care of the kids, Mom. Don't worry." Elizabeth looked into her eyes. "I'll fix it."

Mary Beth smiled gently and ran a hand over Elizabeth's cheek. "First love is so powerful. It never quite leaves you, even if you move on and find someone new."

"Even if he leaves?"

"I had Dallas, you, and the twins. I was married to the handsomest man to ever grace a uniform." Mary Beth arched a wicked brow. "Trust me, honey, that was worth any sacrifice."

Elizabeth snorted and groaned. "Mooom."

Mary Beth laughed and combed in silence, loosely French braiding Elizabeth's hair. She understood so much more now. Mary Beth was being honest.

She hadn't been the best mother. On many occasions, not even a good one. But for once, Elizabeth could accept that, make peace with it. Her mother tugged on her hair again and Elizabeth looked up at her.

"Bethy, don't bury me in some stupid formalwear. Heaven, hell, or haunting the house, I want to look *hot*." Mary Beth gave a little wiggle.

Elizabeth laughed and eyed the black jeans her mom wore, the same ones she'd been thinking of earlier.

Elizabeth's eyes trailed up to the silky shirt outlining her mother's torso and her smile became uncomfortable and guilty. "Um, I think I'll have to buy you a new shirt, though."

Mary Beth's lips curved into a playful smile. "See some action, did it? Damn, that shirt gets around."

Elizabeth blushed and looked away. "Not anymore. It's pretty much staying where it is."

"Ahh, my Charlie always loved to pop a few buttons. More than a few the night you were conceived."

"Mom!" Elizabeth gave her a pained look.

Mary Beth smiled beatifically.

Elizabeth hid her smile against her mother's lap and Mary Beth began brushing her fingers through the braid until it came out. It was so soothing. She wanted this time, selfish or not, before she told her mom about her dreams. Before she brought her brother and sisters to say good-bye. Elizabeth barely noticed time passing until a few feathery strands tickled her nose.

Mary Beth's hand curved under her chin. She smiled sadly. "It's time to go, Bethy."

Elizabeth frowned in puzzlement, her heart suddenly thumping hard, causing a strange buzzing in her ears. Then her eyes widened with understanding. Her face twisted, trying to hold her tears in. "Not yet. Mom, the others—"

"It's not my choice, honey. They waited as long as they could." Mary Beth looked up. Elizabeth turned to see an obsidian angel standing beside a pearlescent, crystal angel with snow-white wings. She rose to her feet.

"Just a little bit longer—" Tears streamed down her face. Too late. They'd waited too long to fix their relationship. To have the one they were always meant to have.

"We're not supposed to waste time, Bethy. We have too few years to live." Mary Beth rose, glanced at the two waiting for her then back at Elizabeth. "I don't know where I'm going, Bethy. I know how I lived, but I've always hoped . . ."

Elizabeth grabbed her mother's hand as Mary Beth's voice trailed away. "I hope, too."

Mary Beth's smile wobbled. "Tell the kids—"

"I'll tell them your heart is always with them, even if they can't see you." Elizabeth pulled her mother close and hugged her tight.

"Thank you." Mary Beth whispered into her hair. With a shuddering breath, she kissed Elizabeth on top of her head, like she used to when she was a baby.

"It's time to go, honey," a man's voice interjected.

Elizabeth pulled back, staring in disbelief at the familiar, handsome man in dress blues. Mary Beth turned toward him and froze, shock and wonderment on her face.

"Charlie," she breathed.

Her father reached for her mother's hands, his face somber, his eyes the deepest blue Elizabeth had ever seen. "I always promised I'd come back, Bethy. It just took a bit longer than I planned."

His jaw bunched and tightened. "I've been waiting for you."

Mary Beth's eyes filled with regret. "I didn't wait—"

"Yes, you did." He stared into his wife's eyes, starkly sincere. "You waited longer than I could have wished for. You sacrificed more than I ever wanted you to. I know what you've done, and I know why."

Mary Beth shook her head, her lips trembling. "I don't deserve—"

Charles leaned down and kissed her gently, then gazed into her eyes. "We have forever to compare notes."

Mary Beth collapsed against him and his arms surrounded her tightly. Then he met Elizabeth's gaze. Father stared at daughter for long moments.

Mary Beth straightened. "I'll wait for you over there."

One last hug for Elizabeth and Mary Beth walked toward the Angels. Charles watched her walk, love filling his eyes. Then he turned to Elizabeth and spoke. "The mind plays tricks, sweetheart."

She looked at him. How was he even here? This was her mother's mind. Had she brought him with her? Why was he different?

"Sometimes what you think is the outside is really the inside looking out."

Elizabeth looked around a little wildly, then she found it. The steel door was open and black tunnels lay beyond it. Her heart pumped faster and faster. Had her moments with her mother been real? They'd felt real.

"Sometimes a familiar dark cave can look like a field. Sometimes you think you are in one place, but it's been altered to look like another."

Elizabeth gulped. She was in the Room of Sorrows. His hand clamped around her wrist and she waited for the screaming to begin.

"I know you fear me. I am sorry. This prison was my penance. My redemption. I regret none of these years with you. So don't carry guilt for me any longer. If it weren't for my interference in the first place, Mary Beth could have married Earl and lived a normal, happy life. You are my chance to fix the damage I caused."

Elizabeth nodded shakily, trying to understand.

"If it weren't for my genes, you wouldn't have the gift that enabled you to say good-bye."

Elizabeth's eyes widened. "It was real?"

"Oh, yes." He smiled. "A good-bye is always real."

Her heart jumped to her throat. "Daddy? Are you leaving?"

He searched her eyes. "You did it, Elizabeth. You healed the rift between you and your mother. You opened your heart to her, knowing it could get crushed. You took the leap."

Elizabeth could see what was coming and shook her head.

He nodded. "You can do it again. You can heal our entire family."

"I can't do it alone. I need you."

"No, you need someone else. All little girls leave their daddies at some point. It's the way life works."

"But there's so much I still don't know. Maeve is coming, Daddy." Elizabeth grabbed his arm. "I don't know how to stop her. I don't know how to save everyone from her. If you don't help, how can we defeat her?"

"You'll figure it out. You have everything you need. Just remember, you are a *dreamwalker,* one of the strongest ever made. No matter what strengths and skills Maeve has, she can't take away yours."

Elizabeth frowned. Adad kissed her cheek and walked to the steel door. This time, the other side wasn't a dark tunnel. It was the field where her mother and the Angels were waiting. Adad walked through the doorway, switching forms as he passed the threshold. Elizabeth stayed in the Room of Sorrows, watching Charles Raines join his wife. Then they were gone.

Elizabeth looked around the room her father had occupied most of her life. The candles and wooden furniture were sparse but comfortable. His drawings decorated the walls, visions of the future on each poster-size page. They would tell her the truth. He'd left them to guide her, to help her heal their family.

But good or bad, she didn't want to know the future. She wanted to live in the present. Elizabeth backed out of the room, pulling the door closed and sealing it shut. This was one room she wouldn't ever return to. Familiar blackness surrounded her, then she realized something not so familiar was pressed against her throat.

* * *

• ALEX STEPPED FORWARD and soft, thick leaves brushed his face. Forward he continued, never hesitating, to the clearing of his worst nightmares. He'd love nothing more than to avoid it, but the people he loved most in the world were waiting and they needed him to save them.

There hadn't been enough time. With more time, he could have questioned Adad further. Studied Geoffrey's research harder. Gone to the dojo and practiced. He could have done *something* so his journey wouldn't be so full of doubt. Bile coated his throat and tongue because he knew even all that effort wouldn't have helped. Geoffrey. He needed Geoffrey to win. He needed Geoffrey to die.

Alex pushed through the last of the tangling vines and stopped at the edge of the clearing. They were waiting for him as predicted, but this time he *knew* the children so pale with terror. The twins were tied side-by-side beneath a tree. Not far from them, Tommy glared at Maeve, only his bindings held him back. Beside him sat Teddy, clearly focused on the blade Maeve held to Elizabeth's throat.

The toddlers were grouped together. The baby dangled from a branch by a small sling, the straps slowly fraying. Sarah dug her hands into the soil at her sides. Abby pouted, tears filling her eyes as full as the stormy grey clouds overhead. Just as the lightning reflected in Jessie's eyes arced from corner to corner, spinning into circles in the center. Below her was a small puddle of sand, but as still as it lie, Alex knew too much to hope it was only sand. Mewls escaped Veronica's mouth as she waved her hands and feet fussily. Shelly struggled at the base of the tree, forcibly held by thick, twining vines as she reached for Veronica, hoping to catch her when she fell.

Where was Kevin? Where was Geoffrey when he needed him? Alex took a step closer, stopping just short of the line that would trigger the barrier, looking for them both. Maeve tightened her grip on the knife, nicking Elizabeth's skin. One more step and the trap was sprung. Light bent around them like a dome. Like glass, only tougher, more impenetrable. Alex closed his eyes and took a deep breath. It was time to clear his mind and pray.

"Come forward, healer. We have much to discuss."

With no idea of the way free from this mess, Alex did the only thing he could. He stalled for time. Alex raised his hands and walked forward as slowly as he could get away with.

Behind Maeve, Geoffrey and a cloaked figure appeared. The same one Geoffrey had seen last time he died? They approached the barrier, but neither could cross. It figured.

Maeve turned and looked at them both. She laughed. "Did you really think it would be that easy?"

At that moment, Alex felt a presence beside him. Felicia raised wide, fearful eyes to his. Where had she come from? Alex looked behind her. The angel Geoffrey had seen before stood behind them both, his hands on the barrier, unable to pass.

"How did you get through?" Alex asked.

"I am the Mistress of the Light," Felicia answered.

Somehow, it made sense to him. He'd known they all had gifts, though not what kind. Alex faced Maeve, his gaze bouncing from Elizabeth to the children and back. The clearing would run red with all their blood. He couldn't prevent it. He and Geoffrey had already figured that out. Ten people would die before he saved one. "How much do you love them?"

Felicia's hand tightened on his. "More than my own life."

"That may be the price."

She nodded. "I understand. I'm here willingly." She glanced to the angel, then back to Alex. "I trust you."

"I see you've gained a friend." Maeve switched her gaze from Alex to glare at Felicia. "One who should be *dead.*"

Alex scowled at Maeve. "Where is Kevin?"

Maeve smirked. "My Dugan has become quite . . . *attached* to him."

Alex followed her gaze to the man behind her. With both hands he parted his brown cloak, until two black appendages held it open for him, exposing him from his neck to the waistband of his pants. His hands rested on Kevin's shoulders.

Just above the small boy's head was a round, black face with more shining eyes than fur. Fangs glittered, extending to just over the nape of Kevin's neck. Four long black limbs curled around his wrists and ankles, one held him securely around his waist, and the last pressed its tip into the skin over his heart. At their feet, piles of spiders swarmed around them.

Kevin watched the spiders, a frown of confusion on his face. But it wouldn't take much to turn that frown to outright horror. Felicia swallowed back a scream. Elizabeth bit her lip and closed her eyes.

Growling, Alex looked at Maeve. "You fucking bitch."

She grinned. "Why, thank you."

Maeve watched them closely. She didn't move or speak, drawing the tension out. She glared at Alex, her eyes narrowed in a look that could only be personal. Why? What had he done to her?

The baby slipped another inch and Shelly gasped. The strap was unraveling faster now. He didn't have much time, but how could he stop it? How could he heal them? How could he do it all at once? When Kalyss had faced an impossible situation, she said she'd learned if she could imagine it, could visualize it in her mind, her gift would meet her there. How would his meet him?

"You seem to hate me," he stalled.

"I do." Maeve's smile died, twisting with a ferocious bitterness.

Alex waited, seeing in her eyes that she wanted to tell him why. *Needed* to. Her fury demanded that he know what he'd done to cause her suffering.

"I'm only doing what you did to me. Allowing those you care about to dwell in pain."

Alex narrowed his gaze. *Kai.* Who else would she care about? "How the hell do you figure? You're causing their pain, and I did nothing to cause his, even though I wanted to."

She growled, not liking his comment. "You caused his death. You turned your back on him to help the bastard and his whore. I saw what you did."

Alex stilled. She thought Kai was dead. Alex had helped her psycho son, saved him even though it made no logical sense. Alex was a healer and it felt unnatural not to try. Although without love, he wasn't sure it had done much good. Kai was still in a coma, so he doubted telling her Kai lived would aid them in any way.

Maeve waved a hand and invisible blades sliced everyone in the clearing. Thin lines of blood appeared then began to drip down cheeks, down arms, down necks. The toddlers started crying loudly. Tears covered Kevin's face while the older boys just looked pissed off. But the worst was the baby's cry. Shelly started sobbing. In a flash, Alex and Felicia healed. The glow from his wound, and the one he absorbed from Felicia, reached out into the darkness. But fell far short of helping the others.

You can save them if your love is strong enough.

Love powered Alex's gift and his gift came from his mind. If he loved them enough, he could visualize his healing power surrounding the area inside the barrier.

Maeve chuckled and Alex's gaze swung back to her. She was enjoying the tears on everyone's faces, soaking in their anxiety and dread. "Did you honestly believe you could ignore my child without reprisal?"

Alex let her words continue, flowing around him as he tried to imagine stretching his touch, his gift. Felicia was Mistress of the Light and the barrier around them was made of light. Light would reflect his gift, bouncing it around the dome, around all of them. He only needed to love enough, to accept all their pain, bringing it into himself. He could draw on Felicia's love to reach out to her family and . . . Maeve.

His mind nearly froze on the thought.

Maeve and her spider-minion. No matter how he stretched it, no matter how he bent the light and the healing, there was no way he could omit part of the dome. No way he could tell his gift to go here and there, but not in that one spot. Could he risk holding back?

Freaking hell. He'd heard the phrase "love thy enemy" so many times, but this was worse. So much worse. Love Maeve? How could he possibly? Die bitch. Suffer endlessly. Those things he could honestly feel. Love? Not likely. Yet, if he didn't do it, if his enmity canceled out any of his power, he would fail.

Alex examined the faces of the children. They'd opened their hearts to him this week. Elizabeth's eyes were wide and tear-filled, her gaze so dark it almost wasn't blue anymore. She was caught, helpless, and he was the only one who could save her. Her expression spoke of her belief in him. Her acceptance. She knew he was trying and she understood if he failed. Who could possibly win against someone like Maeve? So destructive. Fierce. Evil.

"He was my son!" Maeve screamed the words, almost as if she cared. He just couldn't imagine that to be true.

But Kai had loved her. The son's love for his mother may have been poisoned, but it had been real. Kai had killed to avenge her. He'd suffered for centuries, tormented by the vision of her "death". Alex knew Maeve couldn't die. At least, he had no idea how to kill her. But once, nearly a thousand years ago, she'd lived as a human. She'd married. She'd borne a son. Then she had "died" in Kai's arms, her body broken, falsely accusing his half-brother, Dreux. Her lie had launched centuries of vengeance.

Her son had loved her. Not only did Alex remember Kai's love, but he could understand it. A son's love for his mother. Shelly's love for the precious baby that was slipping one more notch closer to the quicksand beneath her. Even Kevin's for the spiders that crawled up his legs, around his hands and arms. Felicia's for her children. Elizabeth's for her family.

Alex looked into Elizabeth's eyes, wanting to stroke her hair. Wanting to kiss her, to redo their time at his apartment, spend it more wisely, say everything he felt. Say good-bye. He knew what he was about to sacrifice. Kalyss had demanded too much from her gift and she'd nearly died, needing Alex to heal her. But there would be no one to heal him. Alex wanted to say what he felt, that all the love he needed was right in front of him.

Instead, he winked.

Chapter 24

• THE ENTIRE SCENE was all too familiar to Draven, and yet so different. So much more dangerous. Tension vibrated in the air. Last time it had been Kai and two lovers in a barrier of light. The lives of three adults at stake. Now an entire family's future was at risk.

And Alex clearly knew it.

It happened in a blink. Almost too fast to watch.

The strap holding the baby snapped and Veronica plummeted toward the quicksand. Jessie unleashed a bolt of lightning, sending it to strike the vines restraining Shelly. They burst so suddenly that she fell over, catching Veronica as she went down. Sarah worked her fingers deep into the soil, hardening the ground under the quicksand.

The twins clasped hands and created an electrical burst that burned through their bonds, then Teddy and Tommy's.

Tommy brought his hands together, then pushed out toward Dugan, blasting him backward with a forceful concussion of air that blew past Kevin. Kevin turned, directing a flood of spiders to swarm over Dugan, inside his mouth, eyes, ears, and nose. Teddy directed the vines that had bound Shelly to climb Maeve's skirts and entwine around her neck, arms, and hands, attempting to pull her away from Elizabeth.

Each movement was orchestrated perfectly, each Raines moving in unison, quicker than a blink. Draven smiled, proud of their strength, proud of them. They fought well, but as Alex had known, they couldn't win alone. Knowing what was to come, he held his position.

As soon as Maeve felt the vines, she screamed and sliced Elizabeth's throat. Simultaneously, she unleashed invisible blades opening long gashes and deepening wounds on all of them until the clearing ran red with blood.

Knowing his cue, Alex spread his arms wide. Felicia mimicked him, their hands still clasped tight. Blue light surrounded Alex and Felicia directed it out in rays, bouncing them from one end of the dome to the other in continuously rebounding streaks. The light covered everyone, blue electricity crackling in tiny, multiple bursts over them.

Alex threw his head back, roaring as his body absorbed all their wounds. Like a hundred blades striking him at once, his neck opened in a long, straight gash. His shoulder split, the wound thin but deep. Blood spread, ugly and thick, soaking through his shirt. Slashes appeared over his arms, across his forehead. Blood pooled under the skin of his neck and jaw. He'd be one big bruise if he lived till morning.

Light zapped from within his wounds, his body attempting to heal as fast as it absorbed, but the moment Maeve's weaknesses hit him, he staggered to his knees. Still he fought to keep going, making sure he could heal his family.

Felicia stepped behind him, holding him as he fell. She fed her love into him, willing him to heal. But when her attention swerved to him and away from the children, the light in the dome grew dim.

Alex opened his eyes and saw Elizabeth on the ground. He fought to speak. "Don't stop."

The demand was clear. Felicia held him and continued to direct the light. But he grew weaker, choking as Dugan's injuries were absorbed. He knew he couldn't last much longer, so Alex gathered his gift into one swirling mass and exploded. Blue light filled the dome so completely, nothing could be seen within it.

Geoffrey pounded on the barrier, his strength fully behind each punch, the dome bending with the force of each blow. Draven joined Silas and they clasped hands, preparing for the moment the barrier fell.

• ELIZABETH OPENED HER eyes to grass and dirt. She could barely squint through the shining light. Like fog, it slowly dissipated, leaving only a thin blanket of mist hovering over the ground. A few yards away, Alex lay on the ground, braced by her crying sister. The barrier held strong around them, so he was alive, but blood soaked through his clothes, covered his skin, poured from his mouth as he choked.

Elizabeth gasped, stretching her hand out. She had to get to him, touch him. She crawled toward him, scrambling as fast as she could. Laughter filled the air behind her, sounding strong and healthy.

Elizabeth rose to her feet, and turned around slowly. Maeve held her arms wide, her black skirts billowing around her ankles. Her hair was the darkest, richest red Elizabeth had ever seen. Her skin shone with health. She laughed as her devoted servant approached her. This was not good.

Elizabeth looked at Alex, at the kids surrounding him and holding his hands, his feet, touching any part of him they could reach. He didn't move. His wounds had frozen in place, not healing shut. She needed to be there, to join everyone around him. But she was the only person standing between everyone she loved and Maeve.

You are the dreamwalker, one of the strongest ever made. No matter what strengths and skills Maeve has, she can't take away yours. Maeve fights under the surface, he'd said. The dream world was under the surface. Maeve's world or not, this was Elizabeth's playground.

Elizabeth faced the bitch. "You can't have them."

Maeve smiled. "Don't make me laugh."

Elizabeth snarled.

"Really, Elizabeth, you can't truly believe you have the power to stop me? It's time to eradicate all of Adad's poisoned fruit." Maeve raised her hand.

Elizabeth put out a hand to repel whatever Maeve threw at her. "I said *no.*"

"Aunt Beth!" Shelly shouted just as the barrier fell.

Alex. Elizabeth screamed, her voice full of wordless rage. Maeve began to laugh as the ground beneath her feet quaked. Thunderclouds massed over her head and the wind blew her back into a mountainous cave of black granite that trembled ominously. Steel doors slammed closed over the entrance, blocking Maeve from escape. The mountain shuddered and crashed in on itself, sealing her inside.

Elizabeth looked at the monster Maeve had called Dugan. "You aren't needed here."

Dugan disappeared from the landscape.

Elizabeth spun around and ran to Alex's side.

• GEOFFREY PRESSED BOTH hands down on Alex's chest, pumping his heart for him. Felicia's fingers rested on the pulse point in his neck. Elizabeth knelt in the grass at his side. She was afraid to touch him, afraid he was already growing cold. Elizabeth bit her lip and reached for him anyway. Sliding his shirt up, she laid her palm over his stomach.

"Alex, come back," Jessie whispered.

"We'll take care of you," Teddy promised as he watched blood slowly trickle back into the wound at Alex's neck.

"We love you, Alex," Sarah told him.

Each child pressed their hand over a different wound, holding it closed. Shelly leaned toward her, tears streaming down his face. "He needs love to heal, Aunt Beth. He used all of his on us."

Elizabeth's eyes widened. "What?"

"He needs more. He needs *us*."

Elizabeth stared at each of them, her hand rubbing over Alex's stomach. She couldn't let him go. She'd waited so long already. She'd wasted so much damn time. Her throat clogged shut and she coughed, willing away the tears burning behind her eyes. "Don't stop, Geoffrey. Don't you dare stop."

Geoffrey never paused. "I won't."

Shelly leaned toward her. "We can't help him here. You have to send us back."

Elizabeth shook her head. "I can't leave him."

"You stay, but we have to go, Aunt Beth."

Elizabeth looked at her niece. "I can't let you go back alone."

"We have Geoffrey and Aunt Felicia. We'll be fine. We'll help Alex."

Elizabeth looked behind her, toward the mountain. Fine tremors already shook the ground. Elizabeth was all that stood between that demonic bitch and everyone she loved. Dugan was there, awake, and the kids couldn't protect themselves while they were asleep. But the real threat, Maeve, was still here.

"Trust us. We'll be there for you. We won't let you down."

Elizabeth straddled Alex and her hands replaced Geoffrey's over Alex's heart. Once in place, she nodded. In a blink, they were gone and it was only her and Alex, alone in the rain. The ground trembled as Maeve's anger rose. She would fight her way free soon.

Elizabeth pushed three times and leaned forward, placing her lips against his neck. He was so still. She pumped his chest again, as hard as she could. "Please, please, Alex, wake up."

The ground rumbled, louder and more forceful. Time was running out. Time was always running out. She hadn't even told him how she felt, how she'd always felt. "It was you, Alex. Always you. My hero. My haven."

The rain poured down harder around them, soaking the ground. The sky was crying for her. She leaned forward again, testing his lips, his pulse. His heart still didn't beat. But why would it? CPR was for bodies. Not minds. Not hearts.

He needs our love. He used all his on us.

Elizabeth fell forward, pressing her lips over his heart, then her ear. "I bet this poor thing is worn out. Exhausted. You healed all of us, Alex. Even Maeve and Dugan. Just like you meant to. I knew. As soon as you winked at me, I knew."

Rock groaned, shifting and falling, first a few pebbles, then more. Elizabeth put her arms around him, determined to hold on as long as she could. "You sacrificed so much for us. Everything you are. Everything you could be. I know it. You have nothing to prove. Come back to me. Stay with me." Her throat closed enough that she could only whisper, "Please don't leave me."

With one last violent shove, the rocks exploded outward. At the same moment, Alex disappeared. He could have awakened. Or maybe he'd died. Gasping against the pain, Elizabeth held still.

"Did you truly think that would be enough to stop me?"

"No." Elizabeth rose to her feet and faced Maeve.

This time anger didn't feed her, only cold determination. Alex had willingly died for her family. She would *live* for them. "Only I can stop you."

Moving in a burst of speed, Maeve suddenly stood before her, one hand wrapped tight around Elizabeth's throat. "Think so?"

Elizabeth stared at the woman responsible for her family's curse. She'd kidnapped and tortured the children. Used them to force Elizabeth's compliance. Well, there were no more children here for her to threaten. Just one pissed-off adult.

"You're only strong enough to hold me because Alex loved you," Elizabeth stated.

Maeve blinked, the sneer on her lips dying.

"You felt it, didn't you? Genuine love."

Maeve's eyes narrowed. "You think that means anything to me? You think love influences me?"

"No." Elizabeth released a sneer of her own. "But I have to wonder how long it's been since you've felt so cared for. Who was the last to feel that way toward you?"

Maeve's hand trembled. "My son."

Elizabeth raised one cool brow, ignoring the hand that tightened around her throat. She could still breathe. She could still talk. "You will release me. Then you will leave us alone, tonight and every night thereafter. You will not touch me or mine."

Maeve laughed. "Are you insane? Why would I obey any of that?"

"Because I said so."

"Or what?"

Elizabeth wrapped her hand around Maeve's wrist. "Or I'll make the lights go out."

Like a switch had flipped, darkness weighed down on them both, confining and oppressive. Maeve's hand trembled against her neck, then she firmed her grip. "You honestly think that scares me? That I can't change this with a snap of my fingers?"

"Try."

Maeve snapped. Nothing happened. Elizabeth waited as Maeve concentrated and tried again. Smiling at her, though she couldn't see it, Elizabeth pulled Maeve's hand away from her throat. "You're in my brain now, bitch."

Like a slow burn, Maeve spread poison throughout the world around them. Lime-green and deadly, it washed over the ground, wilted the trees, and cast a sickly light.

Elizabeth held strong, fighting away the effects. If she lost here, her family would suffer. Fire roared across her mind, searing, blistering, charring. Another attack from Maeve. Elizabeth pushed back with all her strength, all her endurance, returning the darkness. Maeve trembled—and lost.

Elizabeth felt the moment of weakness. "Every time you close your eyes—night or day."

"Don't threaten me, you little bitch."

"But I win," Elizabeth stated calmly.

"Yes." Reluctance dragged at Maeve's words. "You win. All Raineses past, present—"

"And future."

"—are safe from me."

"Now," Elizabeth said, returning light to the landscape. "Take your hand away from my throat."

One by one, Maeve released her fingers. Backing away, she eyed Elizabeth with all the hatred in her heart. "You think you understand. This isn't your *brain*, Elizabeth. It's a world created the moment it is willed into being. It has breath and a heartbeat, theories and guiding principles set from the first thought. Be careful or you will destroy your family all on your own."

With those words, Maeve was gone, leaving Elizabeth to stare around her with new eyes.

• GEOFFREY AWAKENED AND reached Alex before Draven and Silas arrived. He hovered over Alex, both hands pushing firmly against his chest. Alex was sprawled on the couch, his feet hanging off the overstuffed end. The only blood visible was a faint, thin film over his lips. One by one, the children surrounded the men. The little ones were crying, holding each other. The older ones stared in silence.

David placed a hand on Geoffrey's shoulder. "We'll need you to step back a little. We don't want to hurt you."

Geoffrey looked at the boy and nodded. He stepped back as the twins replaced him. Felicia placed a hand on each of her children's shoulders, guiding them.

This time their hands did not shed sparks. Instead, Felicia guided their electrical light so it burst around their hands. They lowered them to Alex's chest and he arched. They pulled their hands back as Geoffrey checked Alex for a pulse.

Everyone froze, waiting, praying. Then Geoffrey nodded. Immediately, all of them surrounded Alex, reaching out to touch him. As Alex inhaled, a blue glow covered him from head to toe.

"They have this," Draven said. "Let's go to Elizabeth."

"You don't think Maeve will keep her word, do you?"

"And you do?" Draven's tone was scathing.

Silas sighed. "No, not really."

• JUST WHO DID that little bitch think she was? Maeve fumed the entire way to the hospital. To threaten *her* of all people! Did Elizabeth honestly believe she could stand her ground with a Goddess? Not in this universe.

Maeve hadn't lied about the dreamscape. It was a world willed into being. Maeve had created the world with the purpose of destroying her enemies, but greater truths had defeated her.

Elizabeth had clearly practiced building dreamscapes more than Maeve. Which made sense, because Maeve much preferred the physical world to a mental one. Why create a fantasyland she could only visit in dreams when she could live it instead?

The truth had been meant to scare Elizabeth, to prevent her further exercise until Maeve could confront her again on a mental battleground.

But Maeve wasn't patient enough for that. Though she felt strong and healthy now, poison rolled around inside her. The same poison that had weakened her hold on the dreamscape, allowing Elizabeth's strength and skill to wrest control from Maeve. That same poison that still moved through her, causing Maeve's hands to shake and her steps to falter. *Love. Acceptance. Forgiveness.*

Alex had healed her and weakened her at the same time. Maeve refused to feel remorse. Guilt had no place in her unblessed life. She had chosen to live a life for herself, not others.

First, she'd kill Elizabeth. There was no way Alex's heroic self-sacrifice would go unpunished, so she'd destroy his biggest strength—Elizabeth and her love. Then she'd kill him. Nodding, Maeve strode down the hospital hallway toward Mary Beth's room.

Silas and his mysterious companion appeared, blocking her way, but Maeve was out of patience. Telekinetically, she knocked them aside. She walked through the door and prepared to cross the veil into the human realm where she could do the most immediate damage.

Mary Beth lay still as death, sun shining down on her and her daughter. The heart monitor beeped quietly, Mary Beth's body was still alive as her spirit said good-bye.

Maeve focused on Elizabeth, but when she stepped forward, black smoke emerged from every shadow, darkening the room. Even as she struggled to breathe past her panic, Maeve knew this wasn't the darkness Elizabeth had promised. This was much worse.

The shadows thickened and solidified, becoming a nightmare of towering strength. Black muscle gleamed as he stood, his arms crossed over his hulking chest. Obsidian wings stretched from one side of the room to the other, so that Maeve's vision was filled with only him. He was so black she couldn't detect any features other than the eyes of flame that condemned her.

Silas and his cloaked demon appeared behind her, trapping her. She couldn't teleport. Not with the Angel so near. Considering her choices, Maeve did the only thing she could. She ran.

Chapter 25

• ELIZABETH WOKE TO the high-pitched squeal of her mother's heart monitor. She'd flatlined. Elizabeth blinked, her eyes dry but her heart heavy. Bright morning sunshine spilled into the large room from the broad window behind her. Unfortunately, she hadn't been able to provide a room full of family for her mom.

Sunlight splashed over Mary Beth's peaceful face. No pain marred her features. No more bitterness marked lines around her lips. A nurse entered and turned off the machine. Silence fell, abruptly. "I'm sorry for your loss, Miss Raines."

"Me, too." Elizabeth stretched her lips into a small smile and turned her back to the room as the necessary motions of death were carried out.

What would she find when she returned home? All her dreams come true? Or all her nightmares? It could go either way. For now, though, Elizabeth chose to have hope.

• As ELIZABETH CLIMBED the steps of her front porch, the social worker exited the front door.

"Mrs. Hastings," Elizabeth said with surprise.

"Miss Raines," she acknowledged.

How had she forgotten about the visit? She'd been warned it would come, but not when. Could there have been a worse morning for this? Anxiety tightened into a ball inside her and the woman's considering silence just made it worse. "I was at the hospital."

Mrs. Hastings smiled a little. "How is your mother?"

Elizabeth looked away. She'd have to get used to saying it, but this was the first time and tears filled her eyes. Trying to smile through her tears, she said, "She passed away."

Mrs. Hastings's face warmed with sympathy. "I am sorry to hear that. Do you know what your plans will be?"

Leave her drug-addicted sister to be overwhelmed with ten kids? Count on her irresponsible older sister to return? Wait around for her jailbird brother to be free? "I was hoping, in a week or so, to discuss adoption."

Mrs. Hastings's eyes widened and alarm crossed her face.

Elizabeth hastily added, "For *me*. I mean, I want to adopt them. Keep them together."

The older lady sighed, then relaxed. She nodded. "Once the funeral is over, I'll come back by."

Elizabeth smiled her relief. "Thank you."

Mrs. Hastings looked around at the new fence, the new swing set, and the green grass. Amazing how fast a yard could turn around after just a week's worth of attention. "The house looks wonderful, Elizabeth. The basement—"

"Of course. That's next on the list."

The lady smiled and shook her head. "You don't have to be super mom. You've shown that you care. The kids are happy and well taken care of. Their clothes are clean and their environment is well tended. There is food in the kitchen. Even your sister Felicia has shown marked improvement."

Elizabeth grinned. "I'm so glad. Thank you."

Mrs. Hastings walked around her and down the steps. Elizabeth put her hand on the knob and stilled. God, she was so scared to hope.

"Miss Raines?"

Elizabeth looked behind her. "Yes?"

"I like your fiancé. He's a good man."

A smile blossomed over Elizabeth's face and she nearly floated from the porch. "Yes. Yes, he is."

Throwing open the door, she saw the entire family, Geoffrey included, sitting in the living room. Elizabeth pushed the door shut and approached Alex slowly. Elizabeth's gaze roamed over him, noting his clean clothes and damp hair, the grin on his face, the love in his sparkling hazel eyes. But nothing was more noticeable than the strands of dark red and white in his normally chestnut-brown hair.

Elizabeth raised a brow. "Had time to get your hair done, huh?"

Alex laughed and held out his arms.

Elizabeth slid into his lap, hugging him tight, her face in his neck. "How?"

His arms tightened around her. "Turns out you have the most amazing family. They'll help you through anything. Just never try to keep a secret. Or, if you have a secret, don't leave it sitting on the dining room table."

Elizabeth pulled back as she looked at the kids. "My laptop is password protected."

David looked innocently up at the ceiling. Danielle

swung her arms and clapped her hands awkwardly. "So, Shelly, you want to get started on our room? We have a lot of cleaning to do."

Shelly hid her laugh behind Veronica. "Yeah, we can do that. Everyone should help, though. Maybe we can have a yard sale and use the money for a day at the movies?"

Elizabeth met Shelly's hopeful look. "I think we can manage that."

Geoffrey stood, a small grin tugging at his lips. "I'll go supervise."

"I'll make dinner." Felicia nodded and rose, but paused, looking at Elizabeth and Alex. "But, if you two decide to get a little freaky, you might want to take it elsewhere."

Elizabeth and Alex both laughed.

Felicia circled her finger around. "I'm just saying, we've already established the lack of privacy around here."

"Duly noted."

"And I heard what you said about adoption."

Elizabeth's smile died and she shifted. "Felicia—"

Her sister nodded. "There's a lot to discuss."

Elizabeth watched her leave, sinking back into Alex's embrace. She never wanted to get up. Leaning her head on his shoulder, she looked him in the eye. "So, you want to get married?"

"Would you like me to convince you it's a good idea?"

She shook her head. "I don't think that'll be necessary."

Alex stared at her lips. "Damn."

Elizabeth laughed, threaded her fingers through his hair, and finally did what she'd fantasized about all through high school. She sat on the couch and made out with her boyfriend.

• STRAIGHT THROUGH WALLS, up and down floors, Maeve ran. Silas and his sidekick were never far behind. Instinct kicked in. A respite for Alex's poisonous healing called to her, new and yet somehow strangely familiar. Someone expecting something from her, needy but understanding how far short she fell. Somehow, that love stirred both guilt and fear. It was strange that she should feel that way. Illogical.

Maeve paused, her hand on the foot of a patient's bed. She closed her eyes, out of breath and panting. She'd lost them, at least temporarily. She had no idea what floor, what room she was in. Maeve took a deep breath and opened her eyes, searching for a clue as to her whereabouts. Instead, she found the culmination of her journey, the reason for the familiar feelings of love and her damning sense of guilt.

"Kai."

Epilogue

◈

• "I NOW PRONOUNCE you, Alexander Michael and Elizabeth Ann . . ?"

Elizabeth stood close to Alex, meeting his warm gaze, and waited for permission to kiss her husband. No doubt, that's why the dang pastor dragged the words out as long as he could, like each one needed a special hand-engraved invitation. Her hands crept up the front of Alex's black tux and his hands warmed the white satin at her waist. She stood on tiptoe and Alex leaned down, meeting her halfway.

"Raines." Like a benediction, Alex's new last name announced his protection from Maeve.

The pastor chuckled and shook his head. "You may continue your kiss."

Everyone laughed, the hardest being her family. All of whom were in the wedding party, with the special additions of Geoffrey, Dreux, and, of course, Kalyss—who had half-reluctantly worn a dress instead of a tux to balance out the adults on either side of the bride and groom. The guests, long-time acquaintances, friends, and clients of both the bride and groom filled several beribboned, candlelit pews.

"I told you this would work." Draven elbowed Silas in the side.

"You did not." Silas scowled. "You suggested running or hiding, and I really believe you meant both."

"I said it, but I knew you'd never run. You wouldn't back out."

Silas frowned and looked back at the wedding. "You think I'm so predictable?"

"You don't?"

No. Not anymore. Not after the lines he'd crossed. He'd saved a life. Kept Felicia alive long enough to have a chance at a true future. One with love and healing and redemption. Her course had been corrected. That was good. It was all good. But where were his rules? His guiding principles? And how would ignoring them effect the future?

• "So, THAT'S WHAT my son's been up to." Abacus turned away from the scribe's head and paced his chamber, his long, white wings trailing behind him. The wedding still showed in the midst of the head's fiery eyes, recording to memory every detail. Maeve should have known better than to try to destroy a scribe. They were indestructible. It was a careless mistake on her part, but a boon for Abacus.

Returning to the scribe, Abacus leaned down against the table, watching carefully. "Now, show me his enemy."